IN THE
WRONG
HANDS

To Phil Given —
Buckle up and
enjoy!

michael Bearsi

IN THE
WRONG
HANDS

MICHAEL PIERSON

Northwest Publishing Inc.
Salt Lake City, Utah

In The Wrong Hands

This is a work of fiction.
All characters and events portrayed in this book are fictional,
and any resemblance to real people or incidents is purely coincidental.
For information address: Northwest Publishing, Inc.
6906 South 300 West, Salt Lake City, Utah 84047

JAC 2.28.94

PRINTING HISTORY
First Printing 1994

ISBN: 1-56901-322-5

NPI books are published by Northwest Publishing, Incorporated,
6906 South 300 West, Salt Lake City, Utah 84047.
The name "NPI" and the "NPI" logo are trademarks belonging to
Northwest Publishing, Incorporated.

PRINTED IN THE UNITED STATES OF AMERICA.
10 9 8 7 6 5 4 3 2 1

For my brother, Lee, the global strategist.

And thank you, ITO II

ACKNOWLEDGEMENTS

First come my good buddies, the guys I went to for technical expertise: Colonel (Ret.) Tom Spencer; Captain Craig Armstrong (USNR); Lieutenant Mike Gard, USN, and his trusty A-6; and Chief Mike Rudolph, USN. And thanks to Dale Gerschutz for lending his expertise in the fine art of weapons-grade knives.

In addition to the unwavering support received from my mom and dad, there were those who never lost the faith: Shirley Battey, Don and Patsey Cherry, and Mary and Myron Hayse.

For editorial review and logistics, I was fortunate to have a wonderful group at my side: Marian Bumbalek, Gloria Morris, Billie and Ron Reed, Connie Pierson, Serena Rudolph,

Denise Breton & Chris Largent, Judy Kraemer, and the *WordPerfect Corporation.*

There is always that one person on the journey, without whom, all of this would not seem possible. For me, I wish to express my eternal gratitude to Copy Editor Marian Lowing for her sage advice, unquestioned support, and most of all, her love of the craft.

And finally, a cat-thanks to Cosmo and Steven.

In Greek mythology, Pandora was the first woman. Zeus sought revenge against Prometheus for his use of trickery to help mortal man, including stealing fire from heaven. Made on Zeus's orders, Pandora, possessing grace as well as treachery, was sent to Prometheus's brother, Epimetheus. She brought with her a box that she had been forbidden to open. As the gods had anticipated, she opened the box, allowing all the evils of the human race to fly out.

PROLOGUE

Secured to Joe Weber's left wrist was a handcuff, attached to it a locked briefcase. As usual when Joe played courier, switching his watch to his right wrist bothered him in some subliminal way. Like now as he referenced it for the fifth time in as many minutes.

The briefcase made him nervous—and now the traffic. He'd made the pickup this morning at the U.S. Military's Center for Disease Control at Fort Collins, Colorado. Only one man knew his route and schedule, the director of Vector-Borne Viral Diseases himself, the same man who secured the briefcase to his wrist.

Weber leaned forward, listening to the radio from the back seat of the cab, "An update on that chemical spill in Torrance, southbound on the San Diego freeway. All lanes, both directions, are closed. Traffic, we got traffic, southbound backs up into the next state, northbound..." Five minutes ago, when he got the chance, the cabbie exited the knotted ribbon of overheated engines and tempers. Presently, he worked his way east on Century Boulevard where again traffic was heavy, everyone seeking a similar escape. The watch.

One hour: deliver the consignment, then get himself back to Los Angeles International. Joe's mind flashed to Ellen's kissing him good-bye this morning, reminding him of Ryan's birthday party tonight. He had promised his son he'd be there. And if there was anything for which Joe Weber prided himself, it was that he always delivered the goods and always kept his promises, especially to his children.

Joe's thoughts drifted to Ryan, hoping he'd like the bicycle. He'd better, it was the one in that bicycle store two months ago, the one he had flipped over. Somewhat big, Ellen had thought, but he'd grow into it quick enough, Joe had assured. He—

The cab came to an abrupt stop. "Sorry, mister," came the cabbie. "I was going for the yellow, then this idiot steps..." The cabbie's remarks degenerated further into animated gestures directed toward the crosswalk. Crossing the street, a neatly dressed Hispanic kid, heavy gold all over, became aware of the adverse attention. He stepped quickly to the driver's side window.

It all happened so fast, Joe's awareness refused to mesh with reality: The young man pulled from his long leather jacket an assault rifle, complete with folded stock and clip. The weapon leveled. In less than a heartbeat, three deafening rounds slammed into the cabbie's unbelieving face.

Stunned, Joe's eyes followed the black barrel swinging towards his head. Accelerated time began to slow, reaching real time, slowing further still...

Joe watched the kid lean down, looking at him like a hyena eyes a trapped rabbit when it isn't hungry. His eyes were cold, flat, hooded like a snake. Tattooed under the outer corner of the left eye were two black teardrops. It was another world, a world in which this kid had nothing better to do than bring home the hate. Inexplicably, Joe tried to guess the young man's age. An age he'd never see his own kids reach. No more birthday parties, no more promises, no more briefcases.

CHAPTER 1

INVITED GUEST

Three months later, August fourth:

The Japanese are noted for acknowledging and accepting "what is." Even so, there are still things the Japanese highly prize, if not covet. At the top of this list is privacy and space.

Atsuko Kojima had done very well in his career with NASDA, and even better financially, "investing" in the Tokyo stock market. A tip here, a nod there had over the years placed Kojima's financial standing among Japan's top ten percent, a ranking easily reflected in the private elegance of his home. Located in an exclusive residential area north-west of Tsukuba "Science City," and only a fifteen minute drive from his office, Kojima's home possessed that all-important appearance of solitude.

It stood on a corner lot, behind the privacy of a five-foot high stucco wall, a single level contemporary version of a traditional Japanese home. The exterior, cedar and stucco, made a subtle contrast with the pebble gray ceramic tile covering the roof and projecting eaves. An upward flair at the end of each hip gave the visual impression of a seventh century Buddhist temple. All lines, all colors, flowed with the quiet serenity of the surrounding manicure of the wooded grounds.

It was noon hour, as Kojima stepped from his attached garage through the kitchen door. He motioned his American guest to follow. Yes, by Japanese standards, Kojima had everything a man could want. Everything, except an unburdened mind, a mind at peace. Today, finally, the angry voices would stop.

In a way it was sort of nice, John Westin thought, getting away from the intense meetings. The Japanese obviously didn't want him here. It showed in their attitude, in their reluctance to open their records, to divulge an accounting of their secret activities over the last five years. They had agreed, of course; they had been given no choice.

Agreement or not, today, Westin had made a mistake and he knew it. Here he was on special assignment from the White House, and at this moment no one knew where the hell he was. To make matters worse, he barely knew this man called Kojima.

It was to see an ancient sword, a thirteenth century Nyudo. Westin was a sucker for Japanese swords and had jumped at the spontaneous invitation extended not an hour ago. Though, it did seem strange: the Japanese weren't exactly hospitable when it came to invading the privacy of their homes, especially with Westerners. The Japanese, Westin mused; he truly doubted that he'd ever really understand them.

And he was right. For how could he understand what it meant to exist in the ultra-closed world that is Japanese? How could he fathom a lifetime of hate fatefully drawn toward this final moment? How could he know the blight etched upon the soul of his host?

The host: Kojima, ultimately, was the product of centuries of cultural conditioning where social structures revolved around the group. It derived from his society placing a high degree of importance on the household, *uchi*, traditionally a very cohesive unit. This family-like structure was the basis on which Japanese management had organized itself since the Meiji period. Today, Kojima and his fellow employees had in essence become part of the company "house" or its "extended family"—the group.

Kojima's employer was NASDA. He and its employees believed they were bound by fate, a man-to-man relationship often closer than husband and wife. Kojima was no exception, and would do anything for NASDA, a sentiment easily pervading into the private lives of his family. The common Japanese maxim said it all: "The enterprise *is* the people."

With such a total emotional dependence on the group, strongly independent closed worlds inevitably developed, each fostering a polarized consciousness: "us" versus "them." The ultimate group, of course, was to be Japanese. Within the group Kojima's behavior was governed by a very sophisticated set of rules, delicate rules evolved over the centuries. Outside the group, there were no rules, and in extremes like war, anyone not Japanese was considered subhuman.

The term was *gaijin*. It meant foreigner, yet as a social code word it held a much more powerful and complex meaning: foreigner, outsider, barbarian. Westin was *gaijin*. That, and much, much more, would make today's killing an easy matter, a destined matter.

The two men removed their shoes in the inside foot-well. It led into the kitchen, the only Western-style room in the entire house, explained Kojima. Westin wondered how a man of Kojima's means afforded such a spread. Beyond the kitchen, he could see the traditional living room, both rooms comprised the east-wing of the house.

Kojima's home exemplified the traditional elements of Japanese style: simplicity, functionalism, and minimalism. Everywhere were lines, straight lines, and right angles: the dark-brown-edged tan *tatami* mats, the Chinese juniper latticework, windows and sliding *shoji* screens, cypress wood crossbeams and slats of the ceiling. It was this orthogonal background that gave the arranged flowers their beautiful curves, just as the flowers themselves acknowledged the strength and solid character of their indoor environment.

Westin noted the sparse appointments, everything so damn neat and clean. Nice to look at, he thought, but frankly, give me that lived-in look, him and Earl, his dog. From the kitchen, Westin followed Kojima down a small hallway, turning right at its intersection with a larger hallway.

As they turned toward the back of the west-wing, Westin regarded his host. Except for today, he'd only met Kojima once before, a chance encounter. *The invitation.* Maybe it wasn't so unusual after all, his mind rationalized trying to put itself at ease. After all, each man was affiliated with their respective nation's space programs—a professional camaraderie.

Kojima was a project director with Japan's NASDA (National Space Development Agency), Westin an ex-NASA astronaut. For sure, he was no spy, but Westin's special assignment seemed to take him off Japan's "proper" byways and into situations better left unadvertised—not exactly terms for endearment. The thought flashed through his mind, wondering if Kojima had any inkling. Unlikely, his mind reasoned, though his senses instinctively attenuated.

Kojima stopped at the first of two doors on the left, then gestured his guest inward. At fifty-three, Kojima's body still displayed the hard lines of one seriously practiced in the art of *kendo*. He had fine ink-black hair and widely separated eyebrows bridging cold lampblack exteriors. Indeed, his flat-black eyes were Kojima's most prominent feature, eyes displaying a supreme professional confidence, yet to most observers, they failed to mask some deep inner turmoil.

"I am afraid I have acquired some Western habits," said Kojima. Westin looked in, and had to laugh as he walked past Kojima. With paper, magazines, and books, scattered everywhere, it was a study more disorganized and messy than his ever was. First Japanese he ever met that let him see an imperfection—*human after all.*

Westin walked to the bookcase, then picked up a small framed photograph: a boy and an old woman in front of a wooden house. "Is this you?" Westin asked, smiling at the missing tooth.

Why are Americans so meddlesome, prying into private things? "I was seven. I lived with my grandmother in Numazu."

"What brand is this?" Westin asked inspecting the personal computer.

"I believe you call it an IBM clone. It was assembled for me at a small electronic parts store near here."

Kojima was obviously dedicated to his work, all the books and papers seemed to concern themselves with matters aerospace. Westin reflected on his own study and what it said about himself. Unlike Kojima, he was no longer married, one of the few NASA astronauts that wasn't. He had a modest condominium in Houston, it's second "bedroom" served as a study filled with ex-Navy and NASA memorabilia.

Westin smiled to himself. It was a bitter-sweet smile for everything in that Houston study represented flying, his life…a past life. It was a T-38 trainer and a two dollar bolt that caused his ejection seat to pre-fire on a routine hop from Huntsville to Houston's Ellington Field. The result was one broken airplane and one broken shoulder, neither of which would fly again. At the time, if anyone had told him he'd be over here sleuthing, exposing secret weapons programs, briefing the U.S. President himself, John Westin would have laughed. And laughed.

Kojima broke the thought. "Please come, the Tea Ceremony Room." It took a couple of seconds, but *there it was again*, Westin senses seemed to register: it was in Kojima's voice, a hint of anxiety, maybe. Westin followed his host on back and through the doorway of the Tea Ceremony Room.

Westin took in the room: A glass door to the right muted the harsh August sunlight passing through its closed *shoji* screen; a ceremonial knife lay glass-encased on a pedestal to the left, and at the back of the *tatami* room, two enclaves, the left one concealed by a closed *shoji* screen. That was it, otherwise, the room was completely empty.

At the back enclaves, Kojima slid the *shoji* screen slowly

to the right, revealing a mesmerizing stark beauty: on the back wall hung a red Rising Sun; spotlights on its bright silk fabric illuminated the flag's brilliant majestic strength. On the cabinet at the flag's base, sat the graceful bowed lines of polished black wood, the *okidai*, its flat upward arching vault spanned the two *katana* within its keep. Directly under the arch sat the timeless Nyudo *katana* bowed in curved synchronicity just five inches below; and under it, again in unison with the two upward curves lay a shorter ceremonial sword.

Kojima removed the *katana* from its rest and handed it to the American. Westin inspected the sheath, then quickly withdrew twelve centimeters of brightly honed hard tempered steel. Both men sensed the conflict of feeling: power, beauty, awe, terror.

However Kojima sensed more. As the blue hue of the blade captured his eye, Kojima stood transfixed, his head resonating with the jubilant voices of his ancestors, his grandmother's anxious voice among them. His mind soared, *Today I avenge you, and free your dishonored souls!*

Westin slipped the exposed blade back into its sheath, then handed it to Kojima expressing his awe and gratitude. Invariably, at moments like this John felt a slight emptiness, his not having someone special here to share the experience. The thought made him wonder what Beth might be up to at this moment.

Westin stepped over to the left wall to inspect the ceremonial knife. Stooped over the encased glass, his eye glimpsed movement in its refection. Re-focusing, he saw Kojima, both hands grasping the unsheathed Nyudo. Slashing down on his exposed back!

John reacted. The tip of the sword came crashing through the ceremonial case. Splintered glass flew everywhere. John found himself tucked and rolling to his feet, searching. The room, spartan, contained nothing handy to use to protect himself. The door.

Too late. Kojima covered it instinctively after his initial move. Time ceased. Eyes. Kojima's epicanthic slits narrowed further still. Westin's alert, sizing. Finally, they locked on each other, a binding tension of wills: the will to kill, the will to survive.

With the *katana*, Kojima's attack came furious. John used his quickness, dodging the thrust, the swings. But for how long? The assault seemed like a wild flurry, yet John saw technique too: controlled, disciplined. The *katana*'s blade thrust down, slicing fabric. At the completion of the downstroke, John dove to the side, grabbed the metal legs of the broken ceremonial knife case, and deflected the next blow. And the next. How long? He found himself backing up, toward the wall. The onslaught. Backing further still.

The last volley literally sliced the metal frame from his grasp. Yet beyond Kojima's glazed eyes, the flurry increased as if a demon's strength had been summoned. John took his last backward step—the wall. The *katana* swinging. His foot.

The ceremonial knife! John ducked the lateral swing aimed at his head, while simultaneously feeling, grabbing. The knife!

He dove, missing the *katana*'s razor edge by a breath. To his feet. Another lateral swing. Backward. Kojima's swing extended. Like a cat, John bolted inside. Thrusting. He plunged the ceremonial knife to its hilt...an exploding gut; simultaneously, his left hand grabbed Kojima's upper arm—the power arm swinging the deadly blade. Eye matched, strength...beginning to mismatch. John twisted the knife's blade. Finally, he watched Kojima's crazed eyes wince, then widen, realize. The Japanese collapsed.

The two men went down in unison, the knife pressing deeper still. Westin landed almost atop his fallen enemy, his heart pounding as thoughts of defeat began to pass. Finally, with his splayed left foot, he managed to kick at Kojima's loosened grip. The sword bucked awkwardly, its tip wedging into the *tatami* mat's tightly woven reed. Westin watched the ancient blade lean low, its handle wavering as if mocking him. As if it possessed a spirit unimpressed—a malevolent spirit.

He tried to shake the imagery, studying Kojima's still body for what seem an eternity, then he saw the man's lips begin to move. The American hesitated, then leaned in closer.

CHAPTER 2

LONG SHADOWS

If forced to think about it, U.S.N. Commander Stan Tanner figured, the two of them had indeed killed their share. His long-time friendship with John Westin began back in Viet Nam, the two of them teamed as an A-6 flight crew "pounding mud," as they used to say. But this was different: this was murder. Only thirty-two hours ago.

"So you make it look like a suicide," Tanner came back trying to keep emotion out of his voice, "and didn't call the police. Shit, John. I don't get it."

They were at "O-Club" at the Atsugi Naval Air Facility located on the west side of Tokyo Bay. Tanner had them tucked well away from the usual Saturday night crowd; and seeing the shape his friend was in, he'd kept the drinks coming throughout the evening. Tanner thought it was beginning to work, too, numbing the haunting questions that must be roiling in John's mind right now.

John Kreuger Westin fingered back an errant strand of

nickel-brown hair, then made an attempt at a credible response. "Not sure I do either. But you know, Stan, when you think
about it, a Japanese national would of done the same thing."

Stan Tanner returned a puzzled look. At the moment,
Tanner thought, Westin presented anything but the stalwart
image of a NASA astronaut.

Westin stared at his drink, occasionally submerging an ice
cube with a finger. "You've seen how it goes over here," his
reflective logic went. "It has to do with face. The Japanese fall
all over themselves trying to keep from embarrassing you or
themselves in public. If one gets caught or admits to doing
something disgraceful, then he embarrasses himself, loses his
own face. Do that, and his buddies, even the local police, think
he's stupid. An asshole.

"And if that asshole's a foreigner," Westin added, directing
his thumb toward himself, "might as well pack it up. Forget about
getting anything done, much less the President's report."

The report.

"Their rules," Westin summed, his finger back to holding
an ice cube down for the count.

This was the first time Tanner ever heard John defer to
rules; usually there wasn't a rule John Westin wouldn't break,
if it didn't make sense to him. Surveying his friend's lean face,
remarkably showing little stress, Tanner pressed for the story,
"So this guy Kojima invites you to his house to see his sword
collection, then tries to kill you? I still don't get it."

"Don't feel like the lone stranger." Westin took a moment
staring half-distance as if replaying the scene, then responded,
"But here's a kicker: As he was dying, the guy whispers
something about my father. Said my father raped his mother,
destroyed his family, dishonored his ancestors." Westin drained
his glass—whisky.

"Christ. What's that supposed to mean?"

"That's it. Two seconds later, he died."

"But you never knew your father," Stan Tanner protested
as if in his friend's behalf. Normally Tanner's reedy, sandy-
haired, sun-browned face carried an easy smile communicat-

ing his easy coming, easy going, easy everything outlook on life. His current rank, Commander U.S.N. Weapons Expert, was about as high on the Navy's "bullshit" ladder as he ever expected to get.

John reached into his shirt pocket, and tossed a small metal plate across the table's laminate top, breaking the ambient background into an uneasy silence. "Found it next to the *okidai*—sword holder—before I left."

Tanner picked up the American dog tag and read, "Westin, J.K." then asked, "Your dad?"

John nodded, "Looks like it. And, he was here during the U.S. occupation." Two more drinks.

As the jukebox measured out "American Pie," Tanner shifted the subject slightly, "How'd you make it look like suicide?"

Westin leaned forward, lowering his voice, then recounted the story: the invitation, Kojima's luxurious home, the sword, the attack and the bloody outcome. Bet this Kojima character was surprised, Tanner thought; Westin had the reaction of a cat, the quickness of gun fighter. Still the best damn pilot he'd ever seen.

"After he said what he did about my father," John continued, "I just did it. Took the sword, put it in the knife wound, then ran it across his gut and up, *seppuku* style—just like the movies. Cleaned off the knife, and set a low-burning candle on the *tatami* mat next to him. Grabbed my shoes, and left. Just like that, I left."

"Christ…Anybody see you?"

"It was lunch time. Spur of the moment, or so it seemed. Haven't heard a thing since it happened yesterday. No cops, no nothin'."

"It burn?" Tanner knew if the flame got to the woven reed of a *tatami* mat, it'd be a tinder box.

"I think so. Fifteen minutes later from the elevated platform at Tsuchiura station, I saw a trail of black smoke."

Tanner had a lot of respect for John Westin, laid-back on the outside, cool and tempered on the inside, but this, Christ!

"How'd you meet him?"

"Takara, of all people. Tokyo. Chance meeting in a park." Takara was CEO of the powerful Misawa Group, their senior contact while in Japan researching the report.

"Takara makes me nervous. Maybe it wasn't so chance after all. Think about it."

Westin had. One didn't meet Takara and easily forget the man's cold arrogance, his thinly veneered disdain for Americans.

"Anything I can do?" Tanner asked. Westin shook his head, negative. The issues were complex, his roles many. If Tanner only knew the half of it. And now this. *A connection?...Not likely.*

"Well pal, this stays under my hat," Tanner assured. "So when do I see you again?" It was the report that had brought the two of them together again, full circle: John's current special assignment to President Temple and Tanner's intelligent-weapons expertise.

"Two weeks. Got one more trip after that. Coleman's really pushing; he doesn't think eight weeks is enough time for us to get the report out. Can't say as I blame him. Here, eight weeks is nothing, the way these Japanese take their time warming up and all. And now this shit."

"We'll get it done," Tanner affirmed, then let his eyes scan the room, adding, "But in the meantime, ace, if I were you, I'd be watchin' my six."

"Yes, mother." There was more to the moment than John's easy grin. It was communicated in the tone, the fix of the eyes. Of one man awkwardly acknowledging the concern and friendship of another.

But still, Tanner wasn't sure he was getting through the jet-jock self-confidence that was John. "Look, John. How do I say this," Tanner hesitated, a thoughtful glance fell upon a Japanese flag on the far opposite wall. The image stirred his response, "It's been my experience here that the Rising Sun can cast some pretty long shadows."

"Yeah. Like all the way back to 1946."

CHAPTER 3

HORATIO'S LESSON

She stepped out of the shower, using one towel for her rich silky brown hair, patting her body with another mindful of her soft skin. From the full-length mirror, she took a moment to regard her reflection. She was proud of her body, tan lines sharp against aerobically conditioned muscle-tone. Only a scar across her shoulder-blade blemished her smooth, taut, supple skin. Her neck was long and slender, almost aristocratic. Her waist was narrow, her butt not as full as she would have liked. Her legs were long and firm, their muscles taut and shapely. She watched the muscles of her athletic body softly tense as she worked the peach-colored towel, and felt it seeking moisture from her wet and richly glowing skin. Her breasts sloped gently, full and firm, with her nipples cinnamon brown and somewhat large, she sometimes thought. They stood erect at the rough contact and she felt the beginning warmth. She thought about the evening. She thought about tonight.

She came out of the bathroom wearing the two peach-colored towels. He lay on the king-sized waterbed appreciating the way she moved, like a dancer, he thought. At each step, he tried not to stare at the movement of her breasts but had given himself an impossible task. She came to him lowering her head, like a bull.

He stood extending both arms, music in the background. He was mesmerized by her eyes, a cayman blue blaze from the depths of exquisite black opals. She said nothing, stepping closer. He felt the heat of her fingers, the touch of confidence and sharing, electrically tender. Magnets drawn together, his lips covered hers.

"I like the apron. It's really you, you know," Beth Storey cajoled, emerging from her bedroom and a wonderful night's sleep. She sauntered up to the cook, giving him a squeeze and a long languid kiss. John Westin stood holding a drip coffee pot in one hand, cups in the other. With valor, he withstood the amorous onslaught.

"Maybe the Spanish omelet can wait," John quipped with a grin of obvious interest.

She took the cups, holding them while John poured. "Umm, the Texas *señor* make the Spanish omelet? The *señorita* hungry as a Mexican mule," she came back, pouring on the accent.

"The *señor* can't imagine why," John quipped, his natural All-American grin wider still. "Breakfast in three minutes."

Beth kept her white bathrobe wrapped about her warm relaxed body. Westin was mostly dressed. He had an eight o'clock meeting at Paxton International's Sunnyvale Labs. It would be peak traffic across the Bay Bridge which meant he'd leave before seven. Dr. Beth Storey taught mathematics at Berkeley University, just a mile from her house, and needn't be in until nine. Beth also consulted for Paxton on computer viruses. That's how they met six months ago. Project JAM.

Project JAM was a joint Japan-American project chartered to build the world's first practical neural network processor—a computer designed to function like the human brain.

Japan built the hardware, America the software. Early on, someone playing off the name, "Japan-AMerican, coined the term "Project JAM." The name stuck.

NASA's Johnson Space Center was chosen to develop the required software. NASA also provided launch services for Japan's chip manufacturing in microgravity. Six month's ago, John had been NASA's liaison with their Japanese counterparts, NASDA (National Space Development Agency of Japan).

Beth liked the name the Japanese had given their artificial brain chips, calling them, NIQE; the Americans pronounced it *Nike*, like the Greek Goddess of Victory. NIQE meant Neural-net IQ Emulator, its massively parallel optical circuitry ran on laser light, instead of electricity.

NIQE architecture emulated the same nervous systems found in the body. Nervous systems were nothing more than bundles of nerve fibers, or *neurons*—the brain being the most complex. A nervous system learned, or gained intelligence, as its neurons, through repeated experiences, automatically set up internal rules and connected with each other. Once connected into a network, neuron communication delivered an intelligent response when triggered by a stimulus. The more neurons and interconnections, the greater the intelligence of the response.

$NIQE_1$ had the intelligence level of a fly, eighty million interconnections. $NIQE_2$ had the intelligence level of a cockroach—five billion interconnects. $NIQE_3$ emulated a small primate. $NIQE_4$ would attain human intelligence—one hundred trillion interconnects. Japan, to date, had successfully produced a few $NIQE_3$ chips.

Beth remembered her first briefing on Project JAM and her mind flashing to Act 1, Scene 5, line 166 of her favorite play, "There are more things in heaven and earth, Horatio, than are dreamt of in your philosophy." She'd gotten used to it now.

But not to John's living in Houston, and her in Berkeley. In a strange way, the distance was both nice and stressful. Nice in that she could concentrate on her work. Stressful, because she liked being near him. He was fun, even gentle. That, coupled with an inner toughness, made him irresistibly attractive. So when she did see him, like last night, the *homecomings* were incredibly delicious.

She'd even considered a future with him. But—there were always buts. It wasn't even his need to be in control, *like most men*. It was bizarre, really. John Kreuger Westin, somehow, had a disturbing knack. Of stirring of things up. Of creating chaos out of order.

This morning, she studied this man of chaos, lost in thought across the table. Solidly built, he had fairly short brown hair receding slightly at the temples, and a nose almost a half-size too large for his lean, alert face. He had an easy confident grin, almost boyish but for the serious slate blue eyes and faded scar across his chin. Keeping himself fit was important to John Westin and she liked him for that. It kept him looking closer to her age.

"That was some picante sauce," she appraised, reaching for a glass of water.

"Ugh."

"Whatcha thinking?"

"My father," John answered coming back to present space.

"You said he died before you were born?"

"Never laid eyes on the man," John confirmed. Before Beth, Westin had dated a lawyer. A woman who always played it close to the vest. Wouldn't do anything that might later be construed as incriminating emotional evidence, like signing a card with "Love." Naturally, he'd held back too.

For sure, Beth was no lawyer, but she wasn't exactly Miss Trusting either. Nevertheless, usually when she asked the tough questions, he spoke openly—sort of. This morning, somehow, it all came out.

He answered two dozen questions along the way: Yes, he was almost killed. No, he didn't call the police. Why? What purpose would it serve, and besides a publicized incident would have shut down his sources and his ability to get the report out. Yes, the specter of his father's past had him apprehensive, especially in view of this ill-fated legacy. And no, he couldn't really identify the mixed feelings he now experienced. Whatever they were, he seemed not able to shut them down.

When it was over, he knew in some vague way, he had reached out to her. He wondered what she now thought knowing that the man she'd slept with last night had three days ago killed a man.

"What are you going to do?" she asked finally.

"Find out the truth," came the obvious answer. Seeing her body tense surprised him. "Look Beth, you just can't ignore something like this."

"I understand that. It's just that...that you don't know what you're getting yourself into. Whatever it is, it sounds really dangerous."

"Can't argue that. But you see, once you're hit with a question like this, you can't just let it go. Sure as hell, it won't let you go. Trying to ignore it just lets it eat on you...the worst kind of cancer."

Beth looked away.

"Beth, I got to know the truth. For me, whatever it is, it can't be any worse than not knowing at all, always wondering." John hesitated, glancing away into an interior space, then added, "Does that make any sense?"

"Who else knows?" she asked, absently rearranging utensils on her plate.

Out of a thousand responses, John liked that one. "Stan Tanner. Best friend a man could want. Stewart's godfather."

"One of your Navy SEAL buddies?"

John ignored the minimizing tone. "No. Just my old B/N in Nam. By coincidence, our paths crossed again. He's the guy helping me with the report. Back to your question, 'Who else knows about the attack?'" John stood collecting dishes, then answered, "Just you and Stan. Say, how were the eggs?"

Beth glanced away, not knowing what to think. Chaos just turned into trouble.

CHAPTER 4

MORE CHIPS

"So I noticed Paxton's stock sliding off lately," said Marine Lieutenant Colonel Judd Coleman making conversation this early morning. Craig MacIsaac, Paxton's JAM Project Manager, considered the remark as he led the two visitors from the $NIQE_2$-based Battlefield Management System.

John Westin followed, making his way back through the organized clutter, passing massive concentrations of computers, electronics, and industrial robots, about a dozen of the beasts grouped in clusters about the lab. At the moment, Westin's senses barely registered the intense hum of active machines, heightened by an air conditioning system laboring to keep them too cool. Eleven hours of jet lag, and an intense night with Beth had worked to take the edge off his senses. And his father's ghost taking up residence in a dark corner of his mind didn't help either. He now wished he'd jogged this morning before breakfast.

"Yeah, Craig. When you gonna fix that?" Westin baited.

John served two masters: In his recent move to Paxton International, Craig MacIsaac "officially" held his card. However, in his current special assignment to the President, Coleman gave him his direction.

Craig MacIsaac, a man with an easy manner, had a sharp rawboned face, somewhat flat like his wide racquetball lean body, short reddish hair, and tobacco brown eyes. At least once a year his back went out, upon which the doctor always diagnosed the problem as a twenty-year old mind over-stressing a fifty-year old body. He and John were long time friends.

"Paxton stock. Yeah, tell me about it," MacIsaac answered introspectively. "We bet on Yucca Mountain, DOE's permanent nuclear waste dump. That was to be Paxton's revenue bridge from the DOD eighties until NIQE-based systems and products came on line. Losing that contract really hurt us." MacIsaac hesitated, still smelling a rat there.

At the opposite side of the lab, the three men approached a chest-high electro-mechanical monster; MacIsaac likened it to a cross between a diesel engine and a microscope. Nearing the contraption, MacIsaac introduced them to a professorial-looking man wearing a white lab coat, Dr. Slaughter.

To Westin, Slaughter depicted the stereotypical "Dr. Freud," graying hair flanked the sides of a polished head, white patches streaked a matching goatee, and black-rimmed half-glasses edged down on his somewhat small nose; but unlike the other psychologists, Westin appreciated, Slaughter seemed more approachable with the dumb questions.

Coleman asked, "What's a psychologist doing on the project?"

Dr. Slaughter explained when the $NIQE_3$ chips showed up, issues of consciousness began to arise. Just one of many issues, he said. Slaughter motioned them near an adjacent worktable, its surface uncharacteristically clear of electronic debris.

Coleman leaned against the worktable. Marine Lieutenant Colonel Judd T. Coleman was an aide to the President's National Security Advisor. Because of his boss' lingering illness, Coleman of late had become a favorite with President Temple. Temple, like Coleman's now ill boss, recognized and coveted Coleman's talent for managing information: synthesizing, organizing, presenting, and dispatching. A big black man with a fit body, Coleman had a razor-rough face, full mustache and half-inch long hair, slightly receding at the temples. In his presence, one sensed his terse no nonsense eyes, born of experience, not birth.

Coleman jumped. It was a cat, a domestic black and white short hair. From the opposite side of the worktable, it leapt effortlessly from the floor onto the table top. Coleman liked cats, especially cats that liked him. Its back was mostly black sweeping symmetrically forward down its face to include both hazel-green eyes, then retreated across its upper cheeks. It had a solid white under-belly, save a black splotch on its upper left leg. It was indescribably cute, sporting a black "Hitler" mustache.

"Oh! Colonel Coleman, may I introduce you to Ms. Fritz." Coleman judged Fritz just under a year old as she moved up closer allowing herself to be picked up and stroked. She purred.

Dr. Slaughter began his part of the lecture turning back to the electro-mechanical contraption, "This showed up on the back docks last month. It's from JNN Laboratories—Japan. It's called ALPHA—Atomic Level Processing and Hybrid Assembler. This is what made the revolutionary optical transistor possible, a technology breakthrough, in my opinion, akin to harnessing electricity."

MacIsaac took over explaining how ALPHA allowed the assembling of customized molecules and fabrication of extremely small electronic devices, such as the optical transistor. To create a chip, the process was like "knitting" a fabric layer. Successive layers upon atomic layers integrated with each other to form a three-dimensional solid material, in this case a NIQE optical chip. (The term "knitting" was used because a pair of electronic needles "pulled" each atom or molecule to a desired position. Thousands of tiny needle-pairs, angled in a straight line, marched forward advancing from one end of the chip substrate to the other, creating the "next" atomic layer. The effect was like the angled blade of a road grader, except instead of successively building up dirt to form a road, ALPHA assembled atoms, molecules, and micro-devices in successive layers to form a solid integrated chip.) The resultant NIQE chip consisted of optical components such as mirrors, lenses, high-speed programmable spatial light modulators, diffraction gratings, and an astronomical array of optical bistable devices that functioned as optical neurons—a completely integrated optical chip. All formed per instructions from the American software.

MacIsaac reached for one of two boxes laying on the cleared worktable behind them. He hinged it open to reveal a match box-sized taupe-gray chip nestled in its anti-static foil packaging. "We got two of these from the Japanese. I don't know what kind of pressure Washington put on Japan, but I'll tell you, it sure worked."

Westin inspected the second box. "Where's the second chip?"

"Colonel Coleman has it," Dr. Slaughter replied flatly, barely concealing an insider's grin.

Only then, did it hit Coleman. He almost dropped the cat. "Are you serious? Christ! I should of known." Tasked by the President to oversee the JAM Program, he'd read Paxton's proposal. But still… It's so real. Coleman had ceased stroking the black and white fur. Fritz looked up at him in the most secure and trusting way. Coleman looked back. "Jeeesus."

"Too bad you didn't choose a Poodle," John quipped, knowing Coleman hated Poodles.

"Didn't have much choice," Slaughter responded, "Guys down in Robotics created her: chassis, servo motors, sensors, fur, everything. They'd abandoned her because of a problem, two problems, actually. First, it took a high-performance floor-standing computer workstation to receive navigation input and then determine guidance and body control commands based on some desired goal-oriented behavior.

"The second problem was more subtle: the chassis and its servoed parts could move like a cat, that is, six degrees of freedom and all that; but when it walked, it just didn't *look* like a cat. It lacked grace, it lacked…cat personality."

"Control programs," Westin interjected.

"Correct. Not nearly sophisticated enough. When the $NIQE_3$ chips came in, I got an idea and wrote a proposal for funding. It was approved, by you, I think, Colonel." Coleman nodded, still not quite believing this…Fritz; he handed the cat to Westin.

Slaughter continued, "I had the knowledge engineers teach the $NIQE_3$ neural processor chip how to be a nine month old cat, but with near-human intellect. She came to me equipped with several sensors: olfactory, electro-magnetic, infrared, vision, audio—in and out. Her electro-mechanical motors and actuators are designed to muffle their noise emitting a soft purr.

"For the cat part, the knowledge engineers showed Fritz videos of cats walking, preening, laying around, just being cats. That training went quickly. Next, they put Fritz in a room with two other nine month old cats. At first, the two real cats didn't want anything to do with her. After a day or so, they simply ignored her, then she became something to play with. As you can now see, she moves very much like a cat, behaves like a cat, and to a great extent, our knowledge engineers claim, when expressing her cathood even thinks like a cat, instincts et cetera." Slaughter was obviously impressed with himself.

"You mentioned the Poodle earlier, Mr. Westin. Fritz is kind of like a dog, really: we teach her tricks like recognizing human speech, obeying instruction, or mimicking behavior."

"Why nine months," Coleman asked.

"Well, you see, her design function is infiltration, friendly infiltration. The Robotics guys wanted something cute and unassuming, friendly. At three or four months, cats are in their berserk stage. At one year, they've gone off into cat independence, not very lovable. Nine months suited their purposes perfectly. Not fully grown, she's approachable, playful, but still large enough to climb trees, stairs, fences."

"Toys R Us could sell a million of these," Westin joked.

"Batteries not included," chimed MacIsaac.

"What is the battery life?"

"Five hours," Slaughter answered.

"How do you program her?" Coleman asked.

"NIQE processors aren't programmed, their taught. First of all, she understands about ten thousand English words, and can execute a variety of goal-oriented instructions. Let me demonstrate." Slaughter turned to Fritz and said, "Zee-tirf." Fritz responded with a meow. Slaughter then pointed to a mannequin in a corner, dressed to look like an exaggerated burglar, mask and all. "Fritz, terminate."

Fritz meowed again. When Slaughter said, "Go," Fritz jumped from Westin's arms, trotted over to the mannequin, then rubbed against its leg. Ten seconds later, Fritz, now sitting on her haunches, nonchalantly reached her left paw up to the mannequin's leg. Two seconds later, she returned to rub against Coleman's leg.

"Now gentlemen," Slaughter spoke professorially as he moved toward the mannequin, "let's inspect what just happened." With the others gathered around, he called attention to two small puncture holes just above the mannequin's right ankle. "Fritz is equipped with hypodermic-like claws. Had the dose actually been strychnos toxifera, and this a real man, he would have stopped breathing within seconds."

"Christ. I was holding that cat. Hell, it even rubbed up against my leg. Would it kill me too?"

"No Colonel. Fritz is no more and no less lethal than a pistol. You load it, you point it, and you pull the trigger. With Fritz, I loaded her with a code word, 'zee-tirf,' said immediately after her name. By the way, that's Fritz pronounced backward. When Fritz responds with a meow, which means she's ready to be instructed, you describe or point to the target and its location. One target or multiples, doesn't matter. Again, as soon as she's understood, she acknowledges with a meow. Now she's aimed. The trigger pulls when you say,

'Go,' and she then executes your instructions."

"Anybody can say, 'Zee-tirf.'"

"Yes. But Fritz obeys only those voices she's been taught to. I authorize the voices for her."

Westin tested, "Zee-tirf." Nothing.

"Is there anything else?" Slaughter asked sensing Coleman's time short.

"That should do it," Coleman replied looking at his watch. "John, I need to be shoving off, like now." Westin had promised to drive Coleman to the airport. "Thank you, Dr. Slaughter, Craig. I'm very impressed with your progress here. Very impressed."

MacIsaac accompanied the two visitors to the front building door. "Oh John," MacIsaac said remembering something. "Mrs. Thielken called here yesterday, looking for you." MacIsaac once saw how Carrera Thielken came on to John; just a matter of time, he thought.

John knew what Craig was thinking, but to no avail, John tried to convince himself. Number one, Carrera Thielken, being a married women, was definitely off limits. Number two, he was now trying to settle in with Beth—whatever that meant. Number three, "She's a bitch."

"Uh-huh," responded MacIsaac, his tone questioning the nature of the objection.

"Wants a token astronaut—ex-astronaut—to season a party with. Invitation said it's in Vice President Reed's honor. Ignored it."

"Uh-huh."

"And darn." Westin snapped his fingers in mock frustration while staring at his watch. "I'm in Japan that week. Such is the life of government servitude."

"Uh-huh."

John grinned back. "The beverage of your choice," came the bet.

"Scotch will be fine, thank you."

Out of the Paxton lab and onto the Bayshore Freeway,

Westin made good time heading north in the light mid-morning traffic. Coleman had a noon flight back to Washington, plenty of time for each man to say what was on his mind.

"You fly airplanes like you drive cars?" Coleman asked reaching to buckle up his shoulder restraint.

"Only the ones with wings."

Coleman was a bit worried about John Westin. Really about himself, or rather his coming promotion. Full Bird. Keep his nose clean for two months, and it was his. The most visible thing on his plate for now was the NIQE-based Weapons Report due to the National Security Council in less than eight weeks. After that, he'd surely brief the Joint Chiefs, and that would punch his ticket.

It all hinged on that report. It seemed the Japs hadn't been completely above board with their JAM partner, actual NIQE chip yields being higher than reported. Those held back went to a secret advanced weapons development program. Some weapons were well on the way to certification, too. That was, until John Westin followed up on a hunch; snooping around he discovered extra chips being produced but not accounted for.

President John Adam Temple held Project JAM as vital to the nation's future military and economic security. Without it, he was convinced, America's only hope to revitalize was doomed, forever relegating her to second class status. That's why Temple gave the project his personal attention, much to the chagrin of those trying to minimize schedule slippages. Westin's discovery quickly got Temple's attention.

In the ensuing situation meetings, it was agreed that only Westin had the best chance of covertly getting to the bottom of the missing chip mystery. Pursuant to that task, he left NASA joining Paxton International; it was felt that more "rules" could be bent outside the NASA organization, keeping NASA clean and within it's "lofty" charter.

Three months of detective work led Westin to a Naval Self-Defense Force Admiral Kamikura, head of Japan's SDF's Weapons Research, Development, and Evaluation Center. Westin quietly blew the whistle.

Coleman remembered the President going ballistic, having Westin brief him personally on the discovery. Out of that meeting came the order to conduct a survey of Japan's progress in creating intelligent weapons controlled by the NIQE chip technology. The Japanese, caught red-handed and losing "face," reluctantly agreed to cooperate. The survey would culminate in a definitive accounting called the NIQE-based Weapons Report. Westin was to conduct the survey and draft the report, Coleman to coordinate resources. Coleman would present the findings to the National Security Council, Westin to the President.

But to Coleman, Westin had a troubling habit. He tended to get off on tangents. After all, that's how the man discovered the NIQE chip production discrepancy. But still, this time Coleman was determined to keep Westin on track. If a quality report wasn't in the NSC's hands by September twenty-eighth, he could kiss a full bird promotion and a promising Marine career good-bye.

Halfway to the airport Coleman liked what he heard. Westin and Commander Tanner were somewhat behind getting information from Admiral Kamikura, but a subtle nudge from President Temple to the Prime Minister should correct the problem. Coleman could take care of that, his now having more presidential access than ever before.

Now, it was Westin's turn, and Coleman guessed the subject. Correctly.

Westin accelerated over into the left lane, letting thirty seconds of silence elapse, then asked, "Anything new on *Banto*?"

Coleman grimaced, thinking Westin almost obsessed with this *Banto* Society thing. In Westin's digging around for the missing chips, Westin met and was later approached by a high-level Japanese businessman. The Japanese national put his trust in Westin stating he wished to trade information for U.S. citizenship and a new identity. For starters, he told Westin where to find the unaccounted NIQE chips.

With that information corroborated and proving so valuable, the Japanese businessman's incredible story began receiving serious attention. He'd told Westin of the existence of a secret society comprised of Japan's top vice-ministers, politicians, and industrialists. The twenty-one member group called itself the *Banto* Society—Caretaker Society—stewards of Japan's future. An expansionist future.

Banto, he said, was behind Japan's NIQE-based weapons development.

The Japanese, himself a *Banto* member, said *Banto* wanted him dead. The man was willing to provide what he called the LIST in exchange for anonymous sanction. The LIST was supposed to contain the names of every prominent American figure residing in *Banto*'s pocket, including people at "the highest levels of U.S. government." The CIA and FBI agreed to the deal. However, arriving at the rendezvous site on the day of extrication, his CIA handler found the man's body, brutally mutilated. Again, President Temple took more than cursory notice.

Another Westin diversion, Coleman had noted.

Approaching San Francisco International Airport, traffic began to thicken. As John slowed working his way to the right, he listened:

Coleman explained that there was nothing higher on the President's list of priorities than *Banto*. And that President Temple ensured that both the FBI and CIA shared the same sense of urgency; and that Vice President Reed, personally, was tasked to coordinate the involved agencies; and that Westin shouldn't worry himself over it. Okay?

"Okay."

That evening, City of Berkeley police officers Jake "J.C." Clinton and Tom Ward sat in a police cruiser heading east on Telegraph Avenue. It was a Tuesday evening and they could tell by the increase in traffic that classes at the University had just let out. Both men had agreed that at their dinner break in one hour Italian sounded good.

In his rental car, Westin spotted the inverted "U-shaped" strip center, engaged the left turn signal, and stopped, waiting for oncoming traffic to clear. Beth had said that the Berkeley Fitness Center was located at the first interior corner of the "U."

Dressed in a dark blue and silver warm-up suit, Beth Storey descended the stairs from the fitness center.

"Excuse me. Do you have the time?"

The fitness center was one of those two-storied glass-paneled fish bowls where an already sculpted body seemed required for membership consideration. Beth's mind was in that netherworld somewhere between self-congratulation having gotten herself here to the center this afternoon after classes, and enjoying the report from her physical senses: warm, limber, spent.

Beth strained to see John's rental, a white Mustang. There it was forty yards away turning from Telegraph Avenue into the parking lot. She waved, then said, "I'm sorry?"

"The time," the man said again. She looked up to see a tall nicely dressed man pointing at his wrist, then referenced her watch.

Zap! High voltage, low amperage in the side of her neck. She collapsed unconscious. She hadn't seen the second man approach from the side, holding a black two-pronged stun gun. Hadn't seen the high-speed car braking to a stiff stop. Hadn't seen the trunk lid open to receive her limp body.

But John did. He'd been thinking absently about his father, wondering what kind of man he had been. Wondering if he were indeed a rapist. And if he was, what that said about the man's son. Beth was being carried to the trunk of a BMW, when the bizarre reality sunk in. The BMW had just arrived in front of the fitness center, pointed to head down his parking access lane. He floored the engine's five liters into action.

Once the two men had Beth in the trunk, they quickly bound her with pre-cut strips of duct tape: mouth, ankles, and wrist at her back. The tall one slammed the trunk, then bolted for the car's passenger door. Before the second man ducked into the back seat, he saw young people pouring out of the fitness center. Then he spotted a white Mustang barreling down the access lane toward them. "Back up," he yelled.

Westin already had a plan: block forward movement, crash the front end if he had to, especially if the car tried to back up. He was halfway there when he saw the BMW backing up. *So be it.* He steeled himself for the crash. Kids! Three times a week, the Berkeley High School swim team used the fitness center for evening practice. Two dozen, some now in front of the BMW, ambled their way to a parked yellow school bus.

Westin slammed the brakes...burning blue smoke. The anti-skid wasn't holding the lurching mass of metal true. The spin began counterclockwise. Kids everywhere, ducking between parked cars, screaming, some stood frozen. Then he hit. The thud was sickening, throwing him hard against his shoulder restraint. Water geysered toward the fitness center stairs.

The BMW sped backward, brushing one of the students, positioning itself to escape up the access lane parallel to the one John had just traversed.

"J.C., check this out." Officer Ward just spotted the speeding Mustang. Before Jake Clinton could make the right turn into the parking lot, Ward watched the skid lose control. Ward flipped the overhead lights on. "Get on it, J.C."

John had hit a fire hydrant. The engine remained on but he couldn't steer. A bent ball joint. He slammed the door open only to find a security guard rushing toward him.

"You okay, Mister?"

John knew his mutterings were incomprehensible, especially in the noise of the gushing water hitting the building. He gave the guard one second to understand the situation and offer help.

Times up. With a heel-of-palm blow, John popped the surprised guard under the jaw. The man collapsed, stunned, still. John grabbed his pistol, a police .38 special, then bolted passed the double-rowed parked cars and out behind the now braking BMW approaching Telegraph Avenue and its escape.

While sprinting to position, John made his plan. He had to avoid the trunk. Tires made a tougher target. He'd aim for the rear window, knowing the first bullet would probably deflect—but still shatter it. The second round would be meant for the driver. A half-second later, he was in a crouched Weaver stance, aimed and—

"Police! Freeze!"

CHAPTER 5

NASTY STUFF

"What's your plan?" asked the CIA Deputy Director of Intelligence Marshall Douglas. Douglas stood stuffing folders into a black leather business case. His secretary, in before four this morning, stood holding his suit coat; it was her boss that called this early-bird meeting with the President, and if he left right now, he just might make it.

The other man in the room was Douglas' counterpart, Deputy Director of Operations, Jordan Barr. Barr was a bit rough around the edges, an ex-Marine who could at times be quite irreverent. A trait the polished Douglas considered to be career limiting; though Barr, the DDI had to admit, knew more about the ins and outs of special operations than anyone of recent memory. But still, blue jeans and Reeboks?

Barr answered, "We're ready. Wanna bet he's got the balls?" Douglas grunted noncommittal. "So, tell me, how'd they get in."

"Ride with me. I'll fill you in on the way over," Douglas

offered, then slipping on the suit coat, said, "Nancy, stick around. I may need you when we get back."

Douglas' driver took a side entrance out of Langley Headquarters, then picked up the light George Washington Parkway traffic south. This impromptu meeting with the President turned out to be the culmination of a unique sequence of recent events: A middle eastern terrorist group had, two days ago, attempted to steal spent nuclear fuel from the Hanford Nuclear Power Plant in Washington state. With a little prodding, the only terrorist captured alive provided an incredible story. A story laced with opportunity—if they moved fast. It was this perishable opportunity that called for today's early morning meeting with President Temple.

"Like I said, Marshall, I've been tied up for the last seven hours with my Covert Action Group. So, tell me, how the hell did the ragheads get in?"

"Well, first, it seems they'd been waiting on a fuel cell accident to occur. They had about fifty of the hundred and six U.S. nuke power plants selected as potential targets. The first of these to report a handling accident became the final target of opportunity. That happened to be Hanford. The plant had a fuel cell rod damaged during scheduled refueling. Inside the fuel rod are small uranium pellets. Procedure calls for them to collect the pellets from the damaged rod and dump them into some kind of bucket."

"Let me guess. They're after the bucket?"

"Yep. The plant guys fill it up, hook it to a rope, and lower it to the bottom of a spent fuel storage pool of borated water. Borated water absorbs the neutrons, prevents fission."

"Fine, Marshall. How'd they get in?" *Mr. "Slick" and his pompous bullshit.* With a background in special operations, Jordan Barr had more than a casual interest in techniques regarding surreptitious entry.

Before speaking, Douglas let his fingers run the sharp crease in his trousers. "With the laundry," Douglas said flatly, enjoying the tension.

"They call that security?"

"Four-by-eight foot containers full of clothes go out to a local outfit for washing and decontamination. Our boys break into the laundry's lightly secured storage holding area, find a clean container scheduled for return the next day, remove the hasp lock, and crawl in. They brought food, water, and oxygen bottles if needed, even ziploc bags for their waste. A fourth man secures the loose-fitting lid, then sets up near the plant with a small airplane waiting for his buddies to come busting out.

"Plant security checks the vehicle, a health physics tech checks for residual contamination, *outside* the container, not inside. That's done later inside the plant when they need the clean laundry."

"I get it. Eventually someone opens the lid, and surprise. Slick." Barr had to admire the planning. Execution seemed to have lacked though.

"Slick is right," Douglas added, "Seems as if they didn't bring enough bags. Shit all over. Preliminary report said they stank to high heaven."

Their driver had already crossed the Roosevelt Memorial bridge; two minutes later, they arrived at the West gate.

In the President's secretaries' anteroom, the two CIA deputy directors joined a third man. This early morning saw only one secretary at her desk, along with a Secret Service special agent "at station." The President arrived two minutes later followed by another agent, a personal bodyguard who at first glance bore an uncanny resemblance to Jean-Claude Van Damme.

In a business suit, the fifty-two-year-old John Adam Temple seemed taller. This morning, dressed in a Polo knit shirt, slacks, and deck shoes, the President measured a scrappy five feet, eight inches. His features were the kind that blended: hazel brown eyes, and a lined forehead from which thinning brown hair retreated on all fronts. The three men noted the sour look on his always determined face. He came straight through waving them into the Oval Office; they each filed in behind as "Van Damme" peeled off to check the visitor's register.

Once inside and doors closed, each man sat as comfortably as he could. The President looked for his Chief of Staff and then remembered he was out of town for the week. Lieutenant Colonel Coleman, standing in for the National Security Advisor, was here for continuity, mostly. Today, this would be a CIA show. It was at Jordan Barr's insistence, before Temple departed for this morning's two-day trip out of the country, that they meet at this early five A.M. hour. Barr didn't have two days.

"I hope this is worth it," the President opened crossly. "Who goes first?"

Marshall Douglas rose to hand President Temple a hard copy transcript. The DDI was the quintessential CIA "gray man": so non-distinguishing, so inconspicuous that in restaurants he invariably had trouble catching the waiter's eye. Douglas had just turned fifty-two, and if the police had to identify a distinguishing feature, it would be his dark brown hair combed straight-back from a receding hairline curling a bit at the collar of his white button-down shirt. This morning was no exception.

Douglas placed the folder on the President's desk, then returned to his seat, Coleman and Barr sat to his right. "As you know, Sir, late morning on August fifth, two days ago, a theft of spent material from the Hanford Washington Nuclear Power facility was attempted." Douglas gave a short version of the break-in.

"How were they stopped?"

"It seems the so-called experts missed that one too. Nuclear power facilities are designed to keep unwanteds out. Not a lot of measures in place to keep a person in. Long story short, Hanford security was on the ball, and a firefight ensued. FBI reports two of the three infiltrators were killed, one taken unharmed. Hanford security lost one man, one wounded, with local police losing two more. As for the terrorist, he won't last the week, having exposed himself to a massive dose of radiation. Allah and all that, I guess."

As Douglas spoke, Temple read the transcript, giving his DDI no feedback. Jordan Barr loved it, watching Douglas adjust his tie, a sure sign of nerves. Douglas needed feedback to adjust his spin, if not his conclusions, all depending on the direction presidential winds blew. Always cautious, never too close to a risky recommendation.

"In general, we find captured terrorists usually talk and this one was no exception. He identified himself as a member of the Islamic Action Front—FIA. FIA, our Middle East analysts tell us, is not backed or controlled by the Iranian government; but rather by an independent fundamentalist hard-line group.

"It seems FIA's plan was to deliver half of the nuclear material to Seattle, where the Egyptian registered *Ruh al-Asr* would dock for pick up early August tenth. The other half would be used against selected U.S. cities."

Temple looked up, then asked, "Marshall, you sure FIA's not sponsored by the government itself?" Over the last three months, the Iranian president had initiated two communications with President Temple. The overture's purpose was simple: the Iranian president needed to stimulate a faltered economy. To open dialogue on opening markets with the West, Temple had requested a gesture of good faith: rescind Salman Rushdie's death sentence.

"FIA is backed by an Islamic radical faction opposed to what they consider to be Iran's current soft government. It seems the hard-line group's purpose is to change state law to read identical to Islamic religious law. This radical group itself is loosely structured and has no name. That makes it difficult for their government to identify its members and round them up. We do know its leader's name, a very capable Abu Hakim, but not much more." Temple gestured the answer satisfactory, wishing to get on with it.

"As we briefed before, Mr. President, just one gram of plutonium in the water supply could wipe out an entire community. It's the nastiest substance known to man.

"The freighter, the *Ruh al-Asr*, it turns out is nothing more than a floating terrorist camp and staging base for FIA activities. The captured terrorist provided FIA's plans for spent fuel transfer and a layout sketch of the vessel itself."

"And what is it you want, Mr. Douglas?" Temple asked as if he didn't know.

Douglas deferred to Jordan Barr.

The DDO opened, "It's a unique opportunity to send our Iranian friends a quiet message. But whatever we decide, Sir, it must be done quick. Early August tenth, means the *Ruh al-Asr* makes the Straits of Juan de Fuca in two days."

The President diverted his eyes from Barr down to his fingers cupped around the edge of the hundred-year old desk, he drummed them once and with an audible sigh, "Proceed Mr. Barr."

Jordan Barr was CIA Deputy Director of Operations. Barr was a sturdy man standing an even six feet tall, bronze hair parted high on the right side matched the color of his always alert eyes. His complexion was a bit smoother than one-twenty grit sandpaper, and one got the impression he may have boxed in another life. He was the kind of man who seemed just as comfortable in a business suit or in full Marine gear taking a beach. He knew fieldcraft first hand, and in matters of the national security, he applied a focused professional mind and took no crap. He loved games, serious games; he could not have asked for anything more out of life. For Barr, this operation seemed fairly routine.

After Barr explained the plan, President Temple asked, "And what do you call this operation?"

"SCARAB, Sir."

CHAPTER 6
SCARABAEUS

Navy Lieutenant Don Creed stared out at the dark ocean rushing beneath *Hawk One*'s starboard crew door. Creed didn't like the idea of using two birds. But two birds it was, to handle logistics and ensure stealth. Creed, a lean hard-cut man with short blue-black hair, looked at the five other men dressed in dark cammies, each carrying fifty pounds of gear. Most of the time, his men called him "El Tee" and sometimes "DC" like high voltage, quiet and lethal. He, himself, couldn't ask for a more capable team of men. Men who tonight were devoid of any identification, including the trident insignia, Naval Special Warfare, Sea, Air, and Land. SEALs.

With two minutes to the target vessel, his mind went over Operation SCARAB's objectives: no comm from ship, secure whatever FIA intel possible, snatch the FIA leader, Safi Kahurak, alive, then scuttle the freighter leaving no other survivors. The anxiety he and his SEAL Team Three platoon now felt came as much from the little time for rehearsal and preparation as from the difficulty of the mission.

Skimming fifty feet off the water twenty yards behind *Hawk One*, *Hawk Two* held a tight Echelon Right formation. The two HH-60s raced due north three hundred miles off the coast of Oregon. In *Hawk Two*, Rick "Bloodhound" Bedlund sat leaning up against a tightly rolled and deflated Zodiac boat, its fuel bladders saturating the small cabin with gasoline fumes, including Bloodhound's hyper-sensitive nose. Relief came from an occasional cold gust blowing in through the open doorway. To Bloodhound's right sat Tripod, his head bobbing, saliva drooling from his oversize lips. Next to Tripod was Milkman, outstretched flat on his back, legs nearly reaching the open doorway. Bloodhound saw the crew chief adjust his helmet mike and say something. Bloodhound couldn't hear over the sound of the wind and the rotors, but he knew.

The Egyptian-registered *Ruh al-Asr* freighter headed north-east for the Straits of Juan de Fuca's deep channel that led into Washington's Puget Sound to Seattle. The *Ruh al-Asr* was virtually indistinguishable from any of the thousands of freighters in the North Pacific that early morning. Captain Shahan had the watch on the bridge from 0400 to 0800, and he lit yet another cigarette while trying to discern by the pattern of light where the sun would first appear.

His helmsman was a young seaman from the small coastal town of Kohneh. "Captain," he ventured, "how far to Seattle?" For nearly two hours, he'd wanted to ask the sometimes irritable captain. It had been a long journey from Hong Kong.

The Captain grunted, then rose from his cushioned chair to check the chart. He fingered the paper with a stubby finger, then looked at the LORAN receiver above the chart table. "Five hundred miles," he said, taking a long drag on his cigarette and dropping himself once again into his chair.

In *Hawk One*, adrenaline pumped. Chief McCullough checked the fast rope's attachment points once again, then flicked his charging handle to load a subsonic 9mm round into the chamber of his MP-5 SD submachine gun. Lieutenant Creed nodded to Phil Richards, who loaded his weapon, then motioned for everyone else to do the same. When the suppressed MP-5 fired, the only sound made would be the working of the weapon's mechanism. Only when each had cross-checked the others did they wriggle their hands first into wool gloves then thick leather welder's gloves. Chief eyed Moondog, his platoon's second sniper.

Moondog, or Chucho Muñoz, was junior to Bloodhound in rank, but many argued he was a superior shot, especially in adverse conditions like wind or darkness. What Bloodhound had in smell, Moondog had in sight. Moondog saw better at night than most people in broad daylight. It was indeed an oddity and when sent to a Navy ophthalmologist, he concurred: Moondog was blessed with an unusually high density of rods in his retinas. "*Chúngate*," whispered Moondog. Chief had often thought Moondog's controlled passion made him a natural, a skillful killer.

Two miles out from the *Ruh al-Asr*, *Hawk Two* broke off from the formation, then banked hard right bleeding airspeed off to a steady five knots descending. Tripod felt the foamy spray pelt his face as the rotors whipped the sea just ten feet below. On the crew chief's signal, Milk and Tripod shoved the tethered Zodiac boat out the door then hopped out after it. In the water, Milk yanked the inflation cord as Tripod tried to hold on. When the boat was ready, Tripod cut its nylon lifeline to the helicopter, then signaled the crew chief above. *Hawk Two* rose a few feet, then accelerated again toward the target vessel. Inside, Bloodhound unfolded his sniper rifle's bipod and set it on the helicopter's deck, then slid down in behind it and brought the stock into his cheek like a violin.

One mile out, *Hawk One*'s pilot nudged his craft down until its wheels were just twenty feet above the water. Stealth was his only weapon now. Rushing toward the target at nearly one hundred and fifty miles per hour, the pilots fixed their eyes, catlike, on the black silhouette ahead, six men in the back crouched ready.

The *Ruh al-Asr*'s helmsman heard it first, growing louder, the noise now thundering in his ears. The gray bird blasted in over the starboard side and flared deftly to a hover over the freighter's number two cargo hatch, just twenty-five yards from the seaman's face. The Captain leapt from his chair disbelieving as he stared into the visored face of the helicopter's port door gunner. He didn't see the real threat, Moondog's M86 floating barrel steadied two feet behind. The helmsman reached up grabbing for the ship-to-ship radio handset.

Crack.

Hawk One's pilot had held a perfect platform for Moondog. The 7.62 mm NATO caliber round pierced the glass entering the helmsman's right side just under his raised arm. It tore through both lungs and heart, lodging in the inside of the dead man's left bicep.

The captain lunged for the shipboard intercom. He never saw the flash from Bloodhound's rifle off the freighter's port bow. The back of the Captain's head came apart like a split coconut.

Seconds later, a thick green rope dropped from *Hawk One* to the deck of the slightly rolling ship. Within five seconds, six black-clad men were on deck, shaking the burning outer gloves from their hands. Pulling their submachine guns to their shoulders, they moved out into their assigned sectors, muzzles sweeping the deck for movement. *Hawk One* swung around to starboard and was gone.

In complete silence, each two-man pair began executing the plan with precision. Chief and Moondog vaulted up the external ladder to the third level. They burst in off the starboard bridge wing and fired two silent rounds apiece into the two bodies as they lay. After a quick search, Chief pulled the bodies to the port side bridge wing.

Finding the leather captain's chair still warm, Chief spoke, "Bingo. We got the captain." Chief then checked the ship's heading. "Take her right to one eight zero, slowly." Moondog took the helm and began the gradual turn, but not without thinking this is what he'd joined the SEAL Teams to avoid. After dropping their backpacks onto the floor, Moondog pulled the LORAN receiver and radios from their mounts while Chief smashed them on the deck with quick buttstrokes from his MP-5 submachine gun.

Exactly two minutes after coming aboard, Chief keyed his throat mike and spoke into his MX-300 radio: "Bridge quiet and secure."

Phil and Johnny heard it in their earphones as they entered the ship's superstructure through a forward-facing hatch, moving one-at-a-time in quick short sweeps, covering each other. They carried C-4 explosives in their backpacks, and several "flash-bang" stun grenades on their web gear. Their objective: set charges on the vessel's diesel fuel tanks.

The two men worked their way aft down the unfamiliar passageway, visualizing details from the ship's layout sketches they'd studied. As Phil began a dash, Johnny spotted movement from an intersecting passageway. Johnny sent two rounds past his buddy's left ear into the crewman's head before Phil realized what was happening. Phil looked at the unarmed body, then with a nod of thanks proceeded to the top of the first ladder. The ladders, really steep stairs, descended through hatches in the deck; in two steps, Phil bounded down to the second deck while Johnny gave the above first deck one last sweep. "Clear," informed Phil, then Johnny followed.

The closer their destination approached the less sleep he would need. Shafi Kahurak left his quarters, first checking with his guard stationed nearby at their two "shipping containers." The two men had just lit cigarettes when the guard heard a strange noise, a muffled rhythm he could not identify. Helicopter?

Kahurak acknowledged, then said, "We are changing course. Something is wrong. Investigate topside," the FIA leader commanded, "I will take the bridge."

Creed and Swede moved forward on the main deck. Their

objective: find FIA's main living and training quarters, grab Kahurak, recover available intelligence, and set charges.

Chief's announcement had disappeared in the sound of gunfire. Swede ducked for cover getting off a shot at a shadow. Missed. From his position forward, Creed couldn't tell where the shots came from. He dove for cover behind a life boat, only to look up into a barrel of a nine millimeter held by a man with confident, professional eyes. Creed reacted instinctively, swinging his MP-5 SD up. Too late.

The round found its target, with precision. The Iranian's body twisted, blood-red at the chest. Bloodhound had caught a glimpse of the developing scene and directed *Hawk Two*'s pilot back to station-keeping. From his perch Bloodhound quickly lined up, then "reached out and touched someone." Creed looked up at his guardian angel, then double-tapped the downed body's head—insurance.

Two more, Creed saw. From the hatch he and Swede were headed for. The two SEALs dropped down behind the edge of cargo hatch number one as rounds began to pop over their heads. The eighteen-inch high hatch cover hid the men, but not their backpacks, each loaded with a thirty-five pound satchel of C-4 explosives. "Move!" Creed shouted, and Swede scuttled painfully across the non-skid deck to a cable winch on the ship's port side. From *Hawk Two*'s steadied platform, Bloodhound dropped one of the terrorists, but the other, with a shoulder-fired Stinger missile, took aim at the HH-60. Creed hit him in the leg from behind, and hopped to a crouch to finish him off. The deck washed with smoke and flame as the missile ignited and lifted up into the sky. Swede took one well-aimed shot and brought the Iranian down, the Stinger's canister still shouldered. *Hawk Two*'s tail rotor spun the missile's bright exhaust into eddies as it passed just behind Bloodhound and its crew. The terrorist had acquired a tone but not a lock on the too close helicopter.

"Chief. Eltee and Swedie need a hand," Moondog alerted, watching the firefight from the bridge. Chief came to the glass in time to see two more terrorists appearing from below the bridge. They ran forward on the main deck below, putting heavy fire at Swede and Creed. Chief stepped out to the bridge wing, and from three decks up, took out one then the other with careful shots.

Swede rushed forward to the hatch, dropping in a flash-bang, then bolted down into smoke. Creed make a quick body count, then hopped down after Swede.

Chief engaged his MX-300 radio: "*Hawk Two*, Bridge, Blood, nice shootin'. No casualties down here. Now move your ass." Too much traffic was always a hazard. *Hawk Two* rose up and headed south, crossing the freighter's main deck.

Kahurak eased open the wooden door that separated the bridge from an interior ladder. He could see two camouflaged men, but not the captain, none of the crew. He could take them both, Allah willing.

Creed and Swede found themselves on little more than a catwalk bordering the ship's huge cargo area. Little light filtered up through the hatch, and it took the two a few seconds adjusting to the dimness. The smoke and stench from Swede's grenade still lingered in the air as they looked around for movement. Moving cautiously aft, repeatedly sweeping both their eyes and their muzzles around the gymnasium-sized hold, the pair took stock of the hold's contents. Two forty-foot shipping containers, what Creed and his platoon called "milvans," were placed side-by-side in the forward part of the hold, their aft most doors standing open. Light from the milvans trickled out onto the dirty deck. The faint, pungent smell of a locker room met their noses. The aft part of the hold looked like a terrorist playground, complete with a sand-bagged small-arms range, realistic human targets, a small weight set, a climbing rope hanging from the tall overhead, and several tables and chairs in front of a freestanding green chalkboard. Cots were scattered about, and duffel bags of clothes and personal gear dotted the deck near the bulkheads. Creed and Swede covered each other as they stalked first to the ladder that led down to the deck of the hold, then dropped down, one at a time.

"We gotta find Kahurak," Creed reminded. They moved quickly around the hold looking for signs of life. A cigarette on the deck smoldered, its butt still wet. Three tiny cups of heavy black coffee steamed on a table. Muzzles silently swept the hold area for signs of life. "Clear."

Outside the bridge, Kahurak made his move. He kicked the door open, dropping Moondog on the first shot. At the sound, Chief ducked and spun as Kahurak fired two more quick shots, smashing the glass above Chief's head. A instant three-shot burst from Chief's weapon dropped the terrorist. Seeing the man still conscious and still grasping his pistol, Chief leveled his MP-5 at the man's head before recognizing the face from the photographs. "Kahurak," Chief muttered, then sprang to kick the weapon from the terrorist's hand. Blood spilled slowly from the Iranian's thigh and stomach. Chief leaned in for a closer look and watched Kahurak try to spit at him. Only frothy blood managed to emerge running down his lip. Chief watched Moondog approach his side, then asked, "You okay, Doggie?"

Chief got his answer as he watched Moondog do what Chief had only a moment before thought himself: With his good right hand, Moondog slowly raised his MP-5, then put a single round into Kahurak's face.

"Humm," Chief pondered, "Let me look at your arm." Chief pulled a bandage from Moondog's web gear and tore the plastic wrapper.

"I can't feel it."

"Good. You'll live." Chief wrapped the left bicep tightly with the green bandage and watched it turn slowly crimson. He took another bandage and wrapped it again. "You let me know if you get thirsty or dizzy, all right?"

"No problem, Chief."

Chief reported status into his mike, "Hold, Bridge, we got Kahurak. Moondog's hit, flesh wound in arm. He's okay."

"Roger, Bridge. Almost ready." Creed sounded relieved.

"Kahurak's dead." Long pause.

"Roger. Take pictures."

Chief pulled out an 8mm video camera and recorded the mess. "Mr. Kahurak died trying to be a hero," he narrated. "He shot Moondog in the arm, Moondog shot back. Allah's problem now."

Below, Creed removed his backpack and took his satchel out, securing it to the foot of the starboard ladder he'd come down, shoving it up tight against the ship's skin. The deck of the hold lay just a few feet below the water line outside. Against the port side ladder, Swede repeated the procedure. Creed then ran a detonating cord (detcord) line from his satchel across the hold to Swede's port side satchel tying detcord to detcord. He pulled from a pocket a coil of fifteen feet of timed blasting fuse, a fuse igniter, and a blasting cap. From a pouch on his web gear, Swede pulled out his firing device and carefully handed it to his boss. Creed taped the blasting caps to a small loop of detcord, then set the assembly on the deck.

Swede produced his video camera and began recording. Creed moved to the milvans and began to narrate. "You on? All right, forty-foot milvan configured like an office. Two file cabinets, one safe, four desks and chairs, *Playboy* centerfold on the wall." Both men moved to the next milvan. "Forty-foot milvan, some sort of weapons shack," Creed monotoned, "armorer's tools, grinder, vise, workbenches, weapons racks with various weapons, small crates, look to be explosives. Swedie, get a good shot of these weapons then give me a hand with the demo."

Creed and Swede carried the milvan's explosives to the satchels to enhance their effect. Then while Swede provided cover, Creed went to the office milvan and began stuffing maps, papers, photographs, and files into plastic bags. "Nobody mentioned a fuckin' safe," Creed mumbled. He knelt testing the handle, trying the dial. "Swede, see what you can do with this."

"Give me a minute." Demolition was Swede's expertise.

Swede ran out into the hold and fished in his backpack. He returned with a fragmentation hand grenade and what looked like the water tower from a model train setup. He secured the legs of the "water tower" to the face of the safe with duct tape, then slowly unscrewed the fuse assembly from the grenade.

"You got ninety seconds, Swedie," Creed warned as he provided cover. Swede's toy was a shaped charge, similar to the payload of the armor-piercing round fired by tanks. The "water tower" was packed with C-4 and its bottom indented in the shape of a cone. The legs held the "tower" explosives a calculated stand-off distance from the safe. Focused energy created a powerful jet of heat and pressure, the Monroe Effect, which pierced heavy steel with a relatively small amount of explosives. Swede finished his improvised charge, then announced:

"Fire in the hole." Swede yanked the pin from the fuse assembly and holding his ears dove out the milvan's door.

The explosion sounded louder than it was, echoing off the hold's steel walls. Smoke poured out of the milvan and quickly filled the air. Creed emerged from the other milvan and Swede checked the safe amid the explosive's toxic fumes. He kicked open the blackened door, a clean hole blown through it and the single dead bolt inside. "Shitty safe," said Swede.

"Cover my ass." Creed cleaned out the safe and stuffed its contents into more plastic bags, then went out placing the booty in his backpack.

With everything stuffed back into backpacks, Swede picked up the fuse igniters and waited for his Eltee's signal.

Into his radio Creed spoke: "Bridge, Hold, Ready."

"Roger, Hold, Standby."

Alerted by the noise, three crewmen came down towards the engine room to see if something was wrong. Something was. Coming down the passageway in a tight grouping, Phil dropped the unarmed men in a burst of automatic fire—no survivors. Orders.

It was hot near the deafening engine room; both men mopped their brows. They had found fuel lines and followed them back forward through the twisted maze of pipes and cables that covered the bulkheads and overheads of the old ship. Finally, the fuel line led the two SEALs to the ship's big diesel tanks just forward of the engine room, one huge tank on each side of the ship. Phil placed his satchel against the wall of the starboard tank, then began running detcord lead to port. But there wasn't a direct route to the other tank.

"Let's just blow one side," Johnny said.

"Roger that." Phil wiped the sweat from his forehead and pursed his lips as he tied the two sacks' leads together. He and Johnny produced their firing assemblies and Johnny taped them in, his hands sweaty.

Phil took Johnny's grenade and along with his set them both next to the satchels. They scanned the area identifying the fastest exit, then Phil called in. "Bridge, Tanks, ready."

"Roger, Tanks. Standby." Chief went to the starboard bridge wing and looked aft. One hundred yards off the ship's stern was the black Zodiac, following in the wake. Chief keyed his mike: "Duck, Bridge, bring it in."

"Roger, Bridge. Bringin' it in." It was Tripod.

Milk gunned the Zodiac's engine, hopped the ship's wake, bringing the boat up to the freighter's starboard side.

"Hold and Tanks, standby," called Chief on the MX-300.

"Hold, standing by."

"Tanks, standing by."

"On three. One, two, three, PULL! Gentlemen, time for a swim."

Simultaneously, all fuse igniters pulled, then the back-ups. All had smoke. Creed started his stopwatch.

For insurance, Phil pulled the pin on his grenade and held the spoon while he placed it gingerly underneath one satchel. Johnny did the same. In the hold, Creed and Swede also set their "anti-tampering devices" then scurried up the ladder to the catwalk. One more ladder and hatch led them through the deck into the dawn's early false light.

Phil and Johnny had the harder exit. They went up two decks before the ladders stopped. They ran forward and across the ship, found another ladder, and climbed up one more deck. Phil pulled open a hatch and found himself looking into the crew's mess, with seven scared faces staring back at him. We're fuckin' lost, Phil muttered to himself. He tossed in a flash-bang to stun, slammed the door, then turned.

"*La Tatahrk!*" Do not move!

Creed and Swede hopped off the bow next to cargo hatch number one. Tripod quickly pulled them into the Zodiac. Creed had a bloody nose. "Goddamn water's freezing," swore Swede.

Seeing Creed and Swede jump, Chief bagged his video camera and said, "Let's go. How's the arm?"

"Stiff." The two ran down the same ladder they took up, then paused at the rail.

"I'll go first," Chief said. "I wanna be in the boat before the sharks smell that arm of yours."

Moondog grinned, hopped the lifeline and jumped. Tripod had them both in the Zodiac within sixty seconds. "Where's the raghead?" Milk shouted over the sound of the engine.

"Talk to Moondog," Chief smiled.

"*Cabrón.*"

Below the main deck, Phil turned to see Johnny with his hands raised, a pistol at his head. Only one man, yet he looked capable, and very determined. He seemed not to speak English communicating with gestured commands.

Phil laid down his weapon and raised his hands. He figured they had four minutes before fireworks began. The man, of Middle Eastern descent, ordered Johnny to open the hatch Phil had just slammed shut. Johnny could hear the men in the crew's mess still coughing amid the smoke now beginning to clear. The gunman gestured the two SEALs in.

The gunman stepped in shouting orders in Farsi. The men swarmed both Phil and Johnny slamming them against the bulkhead. While the gunman covered, the men picked over their captive's bodies stripping the two SEALs of every unattached item on their web gear and cammies. Johnny figured less than three minutes. Phil stayed alert, looking around, then whispered to Johnny, "The door on dark."

"*Esmet!*" Silence!

Phil let his hand drop as far as he dare, then slammed down on the nearby light switch. Dark. Simultaneously, with all his strength, Phil rushed three men like a tackle, pushing them toward the gunman, then pivoted and dove low for the light beyond the open hatch. Slamming into the bulkhead opposite the hatch, Phil heard the nine millimeter discharge followed by a groan.

"Behind ya," came Johnny's straining voice, his body tumbling hard in Phil's footsteps.

They scrambled to their feet sprinting down an unknown passageway, found a ladder and scampered up. One minute, Johnny figured. Phil tried a hatch, opened it and looked: The main deck and fresh salt air! "This way," yelled Phil, "Go!" Johnny jumped the lifeline and fell. Phil was right behind. Halfway down the thirty-foot fall, they both figured it out— they were port side, the wrong side of the ship, but neither cared.

Phil and Johnny bobbed in the ship's wake as its black hull slowly rolled along through the swell. Nine millimeter rounds tore at the water around them. But Phil's mind was on more pressing matters. "Move it Johnny! Or we'll be sucked under when she goes under."

If we survive the blast, Johnny thought, now swimming for his life.

"Tanks, this is Duck, Over." Still no answer.

The main body of the platoon was still at the rendezvous point alongside the starboard bow. Creed checked his watch. "No more time. Move it Milk. We got sixty seconds, max."

Phil had made his move before they managed to remove

his plastic knife sheath. Bound to it with duct tape was his Mark Thirteen flare. Now he struggled to remove the duct tape from the skinny beer can-shaped flare. Freed, he held it up pulling the ring on the upper end. The smoke ignited immediately, and soon he and Johnny were bathed under a thick orange cloud.

"There!" Chief yelled spotting the orange cloud. "About fifty yards off the stern." Everyone looked, then heard a suppress thud. "Shit. Get down!" yelled Chief.

The six-minute fuses had burned down setting off the charges within three seconds of each other. There was no doubt which explosion was which. The dull thud of the first was followed by a short silence and then a sudden, massive fireball and a powerful roar pressed their lungs and sinuses. Amidships, smoke and flame spilled skyward, obscuring all but the very stern of the ship. The propeller continued, driving the frothing sea into the forward hull's gaping holes. In sixty seconds, the sea breached the bow, listing to starboard. Four minutes: the *Ruh al-Asr*'s stern stood one-third ass up. Five minutes: nothing but flotsam remained as her giant rudder disappeared.

Their platoon mates' orange flare disappeared in the fireball. In a situation like this, procedure had the two swimmers follow the ship's wake backwards until detonation. Milk sped up overloaded Zodiac into the now sinking freighter's wake. Each member of the squad watched over the Zodiac's bow as they sped south. Four minutes later Moondog spotted them. Alive.

On the deck of the *USS Tripoli*, ten miles south of the *Ruh al-Asr*'s last position, helicopters spun up for the extraction. The pilots tracked on the freighter's black smoke.

The speaker on the bridge wall growled. "Bridge, Combat, surface contact Charlie Tango just disappeared."

The *Tripoli's* C.O. stroked his chin. It was his second SEAL action "that he never saw."

CHAPTER 7

TOP TALENT

Westin found himself driving south on the San Mateo Bridge stretching across the southern quarter of San Francisco Bay. The second time today. It was late Thursday morning two days after Beth's abduction. The night of the incident, he'd spent quite a few hours at the Berkeley police station answering questions. To them, it smelled of drugs, they suspected revenge, a lesson, a deal gone bad. Liberal Berkeley professor and all that.

For John, it played like a bad movie. Not only could he not deter their suspicions, but his actions at the scene made him look like someone's accomplice: the fire hydrant, manhandling the security guard, the "borrowed" gun. Finally around midnight they informed him charges were being pressed by the security guard, for starters. He called Craig MacIsaac instead of a lawyer. Two hours later, with bond posted, he was out of there.

Yesterday morning was more of the same. Shouldn't have

snapped at that Berkeley police lieutenant, he now figured. But the afternoon was his, and he used it digging for information, for reason. Nothing. Finally, he called Beth's parents out in Walnut Grove. That's what put him on this long narrow stretch of a bridge this late morning. He had just left their modest three bedroom suburban home, their having no clues whatsoever as to what was going on.

Beth had mentioned nothing of him to them, so at first they were a bit wary. They warmed up, though, as he spoke of her. Beth's mother reminded him of a full-featured Katharine Hepburn with graying silky dark brown hair. But it was her father she favored, especially the green-blue eyes. He thanked them for their time and promised them he'd do what he could to find her. Strange, he now thought, he rarely made promises.

In the light traffic, the bridge and its expansive water view had a lonely feel to it. John remembered Beth's dad thanking him.

A dad. John had never known a complete family, a father and all that that was suppose to mean. Would he have gone to a father that time, that time of the incident? Without a father, he had never felt quite as good as the other kids in the neighborhood. It seemed all his life he'd pushed himself to make up for it. Now, pushing was something he didn't know how not to do.

Especially when it came to airplanes. For John, it all seemed to start with childhood dreams—dreams of flying faster, closer to the ground, higher in the sky, pushing through the clouds. Even in the swing under that old Texas pecan tree, at seven years old he would swing as high as he could, jump off and fly. In 1957 the Russians launched Sputnik I—the word meant peace. The Americans read war. Westin knew then, at the age of eleven, that he was destined in some way not only to fly, but to play a critical role in man's quest to reach the stars.

An honor student in high school, Westin played football and ran track. The football taught him teamwork. The mile taught him endurance and revealed an inner strength. He was not a quitter and never understood those that did.

Flying A-6 Intruders for the Navy in Viet Nam, Westin was a natural. That was something he really missed. It was a simpler life then, either boredom, trouble, or catapult physics: "If the front legs of a dog are going forty miles an hour," his B/N would say as they cleared the deck and got the flaps up, "then how fast the back legs going?" To which Westin's ready reply still echoed in his ear, "Haulin' ass!" He smiled, *Yep, things were simpler then.*

As much of a high as his naval aviator career was for Westin, his wife leaving him was equally as low. He put most of it behind him, eventually joined NASA's Space Shuttle Program at the then Manned Spaceflight Center—now Johnson Space Center. Specializing in software was very unlike the typical test pilot recruited. When the Shuttle program began, software began driving the program as much as hardware. Westin found himself uniquely qualified and applied to become a Shuttle pilot.

The program was full at the time, so Westin joined the Shuttle Flight Software Group in JSC Building 30 to apply his computer software expertise. There he learned the ropes and waited for an opening. While in the Flight Software Group, he was instrumental in working with the Astronauts' Office to get the flight software and other systems to a state that all parties—astronauts, software contractors, NASA program office—could live with, no small task. A talent that did not go unnoticed.

During that time, Westin got to know the crews. He learned from them and tried to find a common denominator. There was none. Some were exceptional human beings, with a sharp head on their shoulders. Some thought with their other head. And some, although flight ready, had social IQs of zero. But most important to Westin, they were all dedicated, and lived on the edge—just where he wanted to be. It was the ultimate team, "Team America" he used to say to himself.

Four years later, just after the first Shuttle Approach and Landing Test glided off the back of a specially modified 747, Westin was accepted for Shuttle pilot training. Two years after that, Westin flew the right seat as co-pilot. Another two years he had the left seat, Shuttle Commander, and three more flights.

His entire life went into a tailspin when the T-38 accident occurred. It happened the same year the U.S. quietly signed the Joint JAM Agreement with Japan. After recuperating and being medically discharged from NASA's astronaut program, Westin, determined to make the best of it, got himself assigned full time to the NASA's JAM Program.

As powerful as the dream was, Westin figured the Fates had other plans for him. For Beth Storey, that was something he willed himself not to think about.

She was in Iran, more specifically, the city of Esfahan. That much she knew for sure. When she'd arrived eight hours ago she was scared out of her wits. Who were these people? What was their purpose? Would they kill her, or worse?

From Berkeley, she'd been taken to an air field. Emerging from her kidnapper's car, she was blindfolded and led to a small jet aircraft which took off immediately. Aboard, she was drugged, eventually awaking here.

There were other hostages, too. Over a three month period, including herself, a total of nine had been kidnapped, three now dead. Yet since her arrival, everyone seem civil enough, except for the leering Dr. Dech; one of the early hostages, Dech's manner gave her the creeps. Ever-present, were the AK-47 toting guards, two of them at the moment, and the lab director Ali el-Shafii.

Shafii said he was a native of Esfahan. He typified the people of Iran's central plateau: handsomely dark, hook nose and dark-ringed intelligent eyes glinting an evasive humor. Shafii wore western clothes whose drab and obsolete cut, Beth thought, did little to complement his Assyrian bas-relief profile.

The lab, too, was drab and obsolete, isolated somewhere in Esfahan's desert outskirts. Definitely a ragtag operation. Yesterday a sandstorm billowed waves of reds and grays across the eddied landscape. Beth now looked out the window past the only other building, a smaller guard's quarters. After the storm, a wayward herd of goats had appeared. Now, nomadic women, skin blackened by the sun, were leading them away to God knows where. She wondered how the poor animals had survived the sandblasting.

The lab itself was located on the first level of a two-story building. An outside staircase led to the living quarters located overhead. Surveying the lab's layout, Beth saw racks and racks of test tubes atop tables which were arranged in a crossword puzzle fashion mostly toward the center spaces. Equipment and desks were lined up against the perimeter walls: a centrifuge, baking ovens, a small refrigerator, and an electron microscope which had malfunctioned three days ago.

Looking back to the window, she saw not her reflection but John's white Mustang coming to pick her up at the Berkeley fitness center. Then that man wanting the time, then a shock, then nothing. She'd awaken bound in the trunk of a car. *Defenseless.*

She remembered John's wanting to teach her how to handle a gun, combat pistol shooting competition being his hobby. She'd always been perfectly capable of taking care of herself, so why on earth would she want such a violent weapon? She spurned the offer. His Navy SEAL buddies had taught him some basics in karate or whatever, and he offered to teach her some moves, as he put it. No thank you, again violence wasn't her thing. She could almost hear John's baritone voice come back, "Violence tends to find those who are not prepared to deal with it."

But non-violence was what her parents always preached. She more or less bought into their philosophy. Her father was a decent man who used to work a farm growing wheat and a little sorghum outside Norman, Oklahoma. After two successive crop failures, he packed up a young Beth and her mother, and moved to California. They wound up in the slow rolling hills of Walnut Creek forty miles east of San Francisco, now wall-to-wall suburbs. Her father joined up with his brother's new and growing print shop located near Oakland. It was a good life, yet Beth was eternally thankful for her mid-western values, never losing her identity amid California's fast and loose life styles.

Her mother thought she'd made an awful mistake, though. Not marrying Mr. "Investment Banker," managing hundreds of millions of dollars. Now reflecting on the whole thing, she wasn't sure she'd ever loved him. He was definitely attractive, him being ten years older, but there was an attitude. He thought he owned the world controlling all those millions— controlling her. What was it he said, "When we get married, I want you to quit the university, then join the country club and the Bay Area Historical Society—good for business. *Right...and don't let the doorknob..."*

It was only after they'd split that she discovered he'd been seeing another woman all the while. Three months after their break up, Mr. Wonderful married the woman. How on earth could she ever again trust her own feelings, she had sincerely wondered then. Trust another man? *Trust John?*

Feelings. She turned from the window. Sure enough, there was Dr. Dech, leering. She fixed her eyes, shooting a cold blast at the bastard. *Just try it, you sonofabitch, and be ready for a octave change—soprano*. Dech she could handle.

And why was she here with the likes of Dr. Dech? Because the Iranians had stolen the blueprints to something called STAIRCASE, an engineered virus targeted for specific human genetic characteristics. Now they wanted to develop a batch. When the Iranians needed expertise, they kidnapped it. So when some of their machines developed a computer virus, they grabbed an expert. Just like that. Nothing personal. Enter Beth Storey.

Indeed their computers had been infected with a computer virus. She recognized it as *Michelangelo*. If she had access to her "de-virusing" programs, this would be cake. She didn't. Erratic power was another problem, its having dropped off twice in the eight hours since she'd arrived.

To her, it was clear that Shafii and his masters would not

succeed, especially in this ill-equipped, primitive work environment. Yet the Iranians seemed impatient. They seemed not to appreciate the complexity of the task and the time it would take—even under *desirable* circumstances. Time. It would run out on her too. She wondered how much of it she really had.

CHAPTER 8
BIG NUMBERS

NAME DROPPER SLAYS GANG LEADER

A bizarre yet intriguing gang-related shooting occurred in South Central Los Angeles early this morning.

The acknowledged leader of what is known as the Eight-Tray Gangster Crips was slain at a convenience store located at the intersection of Western Avenue and Imperial Highway. This was the 186th gang-related killing in Los Angeles this year.

The victim, Lewis Cane, nicknamed Tiger Lily, a senior O.G. (Original Gangster), seemed to be the victim of a rival gang-related vendetta. On his person police found a MAC-11 machine pistol and a nine millimeter semiautomatic. He was twenty years old.

This killing was unusual, said Police Lieutenant Pat Mantle, member of LAPD's Metropolitan Specialized Gang Unit. "It was definitely a payback killing,"

Mantle said, "but the style, different, almost profes-
sional."

And style it was. The assailant sat in the window of
a vacant building two hundred yards away. Using a
rifle, he took one shot and left the spent shell casing
behind, deliberately. Etched on the casing was the
victim's moniker, "Tiger". An officer on the investiga-
tion team quipped "Name Dropper," thus coining the
term.

—*Los Angeles Times*, 08 August

"Okay, Ross, I'll go over the numbers later," CEO Glenn
Thielken said closing the report before him. They were in the
conference room adjacent to his executive suite office. The
west-facing fortieth story windows revealed a hazy view of
the Los Angeles basin below.

"Just net it out for now." Thielken already knew the gist of
the numbers and couldn't help thinking of their double-edged
meaning *for him.*

Thielken watched his Chief Financial Officer thumb
through the remaining charts, finally selecting one toward the
bottom of the stack. The CFO placed the summary chart on the
overhead projector, then continued with Shiraki Industries'
projected third quarter financials, "Okay, Glenn, state of the
business, net-net." Pointing only at the significant revenue
bullets on the chart, the somewhat portly CFO summarized:
Aircraft production: down twenty percent; Avionics systems:
down eight percent; Fire Control Systems: down thirteen
percent…"

A double edge sword, Thielken grimaced as he listened to
the numbers: thirteen percent of one-point-eight billion dollars is a fair sum. So thought Wall Street's analysts, the
stockholders, and now even some of the directors. The breakup
of the Soviet Union and the resultant military drawdown was
why his CFO now reported such dismal numbers: the U.S.
military wasn't buying the dog food, pure and simple.

But that was the past, Thielken mused hearing Ross get to

the future. "Next our two new business ventures: Commercial Systems Integration: It'll be another five years before that group can hope to turn a profit. Right now, they're in the red 'buying' a lot of business.

"Next, DOE Services: That's our only hope. Mainly MRS." The CFO spoke of DOE's proposed Monitored Retrievable Storage facility at the Nevada Test Site. Most everyone referred to the project by the name of the mountain under which the nuclear wastes would be buried.

"Yucca Mountain. Humm." Thielken leaned back into black Italian leather.

"Step up the timetable, Glenn, and it'll save your ass. At current contract, we just limp along. But we get the 'go' then it's a gold mine, a cash cow well beyond the year 2030. The Board will kneel and kiss your Stanford ring."

Thielken almost grinned at that, his hazel eyes darkening to deep brown. They narrowed when he was thinking, scheming, planning—always narrow, but without furrow lines. His dark brown wet-look appeared as if every strand of combed hair had its permanent place. He had a strong jaw, set, not chiseled, and looked an easy ten years younger than his fifty-four. Today he wore a California light-pink shirt, all-cotton, pin-point, sleeves rolled up one fold, his gold Rolex very visible. The tie, Italian silk, a perfect match with the power-blue suit coat hanging in his adjoining office. He had everything a man could want—a thought he sometimes indulged—even his wife, Carrera—*and now, if he could just hang on to it all.*

A double-edged sword: going after the DOE's Yucca Mountain had been his idea—even before the Soviet's demise when he was but a junior V.P. The company finally agreed to pursue, and gave him the new business opportunity. He was up against the best, but Paxton International wanted it the worst. A spy here, a kickback there, a political ace-in-the-hole, and presto, he brought it in. And none too soon, either, for just after contract award, the attempted coup finished the "Evil Empire." DOD contracts dried up, and numbers turned sour. The pressure was on, golden parachutes donned, and rip chords pulled. From the heavyweights left, including some very senior V.P.s, Glenn Thielken snagged the CEO's office.

But Ross' analysis pointed to the sword's other edge. Site approval. Even though DOE awarded Shiraki Industries the Yucca Mountain development and operations contract, final decision on site approval had yet to be made. Final decision on where the nation would dump over seventy thousand tons of its nuclear waste had the gutless politicians scared shitless. Result: study and wait, study and wait. Ross was right, this thing needed a push.

"Thanks Ross," Thielken dismissed, then stood pacing, finally turning to the other man in the room. Jack Crimm was Thielken's Administrative Assistant, a corporate euphemism for executive secretary. Crimm had black hair, flint black eyes, and a too serious face for a single man of thirty-two.

"Jack, I think its time we get out to DOE's Yucca Mountain dump. Arrange a site visit and a meeting with DOE's Project Director on the morning after. Next subject: Find out what's happening with that, what's it called, environmental award."

"The Green Globe," the AA responded evenly.

"Yes, I want that award this year. It'll be good for the business. Let's get a new ad. Environmental. You know, show some whales, squirrels, that kind of thing."

DOE's Yucca Mountain complex, two miles down into the heart of nearby Rainier Mesa: The dusty, roofless metal cars screeched and clanged their way deeper into the blackness. For the two men riding in the lead car, the dark and deafening ride was quite routine. Occasionally, an incandescent bulb revealed closed-off entrances branching from the rough-hewn walls of G-Tunnel's main shaft. Farther still, they reset their mental bearings from a dim yellow glow illuminating an array of signs warning of radioactive contamination in a side tunnel.

Fourteen hundred feet underground the train slowed as it

reached the laboratory. Up an incline the tunnel widened to a large chamber where workers drilled and sawed into volcanic rock, the area cluttered with tools, instruments, and heavy machinery.

Out of the car, wearing ear protectors, the two men approached the right side of the cavern, then stopped a healthy distance behind a thick sheet of Plexiglas, shielding rock and debris shooting relentlessly against its other side. They watched as an eight-foot, remote-controlled, diamond-tipped chain saw ate effortlessly through the welded volcanic tuff of the cavern floor. It was the second side of an eight-foot cube, which when finished would look like a huge square peg in a slightly larger square hole, but still left attached at its bottom. The process was going well and would be finished and ready for the heated block experiment in another three weeks. The taller man tapped the second man's shoulder, motioning him to a side tunnel. Twenty feet down and around the first intersection, it was quieter, they could talk without being heard.

"You sure?" the stouter Redbone stressed.

"That's what the lab guys said," confirmed Bill Henry still looking nervous. "Didn't let on where it'd come from, though."

"But everything looks okay here," Redbone said, still not quite believing.

"But here ain't there," Henry declared, his eyes scanning the tunnel ahead. "The sample's from the mountain, sure as shit." Yucca Mountain, less than a mile away.

"Shit. You turn that sample in and DOE'll plug this hole forever. Shiraki Industries, and our jobs—hell, fourteen hundred jobs—flushed just like that. Shit, Henry, whatcha gonna do?"

"Don't know yet."

"When's Shelby back?"

"Tomorrow…Maybe I'll show it to him."

"Smart. That's what I'd do."

Awake. The Apache's first reaction was to think of the tribal elders, to ask them to interpret. Such things were taken very seriously in the life of an Apache. But that was another life, a simpler life. Fifteen long years ago. His second reaction was to deny, to deny his heart. But how could he deny the only thing he'd ever trusted to give clarity of mind?

Three-ten A.M. The Apache pushed himself and pillow up against the headboard, clasped his hands behind his head and recounted the dream—an important dream.

Instinctively, the Apache knew the ancient scout was a messenger from the bright vision, not from darkness, though it forebode a dark task. The spirit had used his Apache name, Coyote Shadow, then spoke of his Grandfather's most sacred place, a place to which he must now go: the solitary Yucca Mountain one hundred and thirty miles to the desert west. The spirit did not speak of reason.

He would fast: he would not trap, hunt, or take life. Instead, like the deer he would forage the leaves of plants, and like the mice he would lick dew from the rocks and sticks. He would live without tools, fire, clothing, or shelter. Not since before college had he done anything like this, and at this moment the only thing the Apache could be sure of was that after one moon he would find for himself new limits.

CHAPTER 9
TAKARA

Nagasaki, Japan

Time: 11:01:57. Date: 09 August 1945:

Fifty yards to the northeast of "ground zero": Miyo Takara, dressed in a bright blue *mompei*, stands outside her timber roof and frame home. A tough-minded woman, Miyo has, throughout her nineteen year marriage, devoted herself to her family's needs and comfort, and is especially proud of her four children and their accomplishments. Today, she is outside hanging laundry, now chiding their cocker spaniel, Pochi, who just overturned the laundry basket and is making a hasty retreat...

Time: 11:01:58. DETONATION!

Death now takes control, dominion over both time and space. *A wall of violence surges: Near its origin, at fifty million degrees Centigrade, asphalt and steel burn like rice paper! Miyo Takara looks up at a traveling sheet of sun! There is no sound. Her neatly kept home violently disintegrates behind her. Her liquified brain has not the means of sensing the crushing blast wave that assaults her very being out of physical existence.* Death rushes on as Miyo's and Pochi's ashen cells become part of the roiling dust mushrooming upward into a darkening yellow sky.

Shiroyama Primary School sits five hundred yards west of ground zero. *At two miles a second, the surging tidal wave becomes a monstrous fireball slamming the concrete structure full force on its roof and eastern side.* Tomaka's first grade class is learning to write Kanji...*Tomaka's senses register the flush of heat...his paper booklet bursts into flames. The wooden desk ignites. His body snaps in a malevolent fury tossing children like leaves before the approaching storm... On the fourth floor Tomaka's seven-year-old sister, Miwa, now lies trapped under the collapsed reinforced concrete ceiling. Death has its choice: it chooses fire and asphyxiation over the loss of blood aspirating from the puncture of her right lung.* Eight hundred and forty more broken bodies lay charred under steel-reinforced debris.

At that same instant to the southwest, Chinzei Middle School catches the blinding edge of the white hot assault. Ten year old Kyoko is at recess with his fifth grade class. Dressed in a neatly pressed dark blue and white school uniform, Kyoko stands in the batter's box ready for the pitch. *Kyoko did not see the runner at first make his move for second, did not see the pitch arcing into his strike zone; Kyoko sees only the magnesium-bright flash—the pika—as his upturned eyes melt into a glutinous mass. Dark uniform erupts into flame, white bone clings to the bat, and a shredded body slams to the ground— another leaf in the raging firestorm. Kyoko is now but a shadow burned onto the crisscrossing chain-links of the backstop behind home plate.* Death retires the side and marks its scorecard: no hits, no runs, no errors...no one left on base.

Twelve hundred yards to the northwest: Decelerating to one mile per second, the pinkish-black shock wave now rushes Urakami First Hospital. Nurse Yoko steps out into Dr. Kofuji's crowded waiting room; she could not have known about Chinzei Middle School and her only child's fiery death only milliseconds before: *CRASH! The window by which she stands explodes with blistering heat. Her face, her eyes, are peppered with thousands of tiny slivers from what had been a window with a view. She cannot see, but senses herself down on the tile floor...the searing heat! At eighteen hundred degrees centigrade, the tile bubbles beneath her fallen body. Her hair and white uniform explode into flame...against the floor, her bare skin sears amid her seething blood turned black. Her struggle is but an instant.* Death continues its rounds...

At the north end of the hospital, Mitsu is dressing after having just completed her prenatal examination. The report on now her third child was a good one. She was thinking, "childbirth had come easy for—"

FORCE! against her body...catapulting across the room. Unconsciously, she places both arms around her protruding stomach. Her body slams against a coat-rack permanently affixed to a light green cinder block wall; the base of her skull impales into the metal protrusion, lodging up through her brain to the top of the cranium; Death leaves her body hanging like an empty garment and has little concern for her six-month baby taking radiation, beginning to miscarry. Death wastes little time, now to call on her husband.

Thirteen hundred yards to the south of "ground zero" stands the massive Mitsubishi Steel Works. A foreman in the pipe fitting department silently curses an empty pack of cigarettes. *BLAST! a deafening, torrential roar. Subsiding. He becomes aware of heat and a different, haunting sound replacing the shock's echo...the slow motion groan of twisting, bending support beams now chill his senses. Mitsu's husband looks up, in time to see an avalanche of two hundred and eighty tons of steel girders, pipe, and reinforced concrete filling his vision. Crushed and decapitated.* Death plies its skills with efficiency: recovery crews will find sixty-two hundred more Mitsubishi workers killed or injured.

Two miles out, now subsonic, the shock-wave continues its relentless siege. To the north, Akiko and Toshiko Takara are in the study area at Nagasaki Normal School. Akiko is daydreaming of becoming a civil engineer; he wants to build great bridges and become famous the world over. Like her Aunt Yoko, little Toshiko wants to become a nurse, a surgical nurse. *They both feel...the school's foundation shudder. The thunderclap! Instinctively they duck under the table. To their right, the blackboard bucks off the wall crashing to the floor. Toshiko knows she isn't supposed to cry, but fear of a direct hit from one of those evil American bombers has her terrified; she grabs Akiko and they hold each other tight...Finally after a minute, they assess themselves okay, fear subsiding in each other's arms. Their brother, Hiroshi, will come, they both agree.*

They were wrong. Hiroshi Takara had sat in Biology class at Nagasaki Medical College, just five hundred and seventy yards from "ground zero." Nor would he be present for Death's final lesson: How the human body reacts to a momentary penetration of liberated alpha, beta, gamma, and neutron radiation: In two days, Akiko's and Toshiko's young bodies would give in to the relentless siege of fever, deteriorating bone marrow, and a depleting white blood cell count. In three weeks, Toshiko's tormented body would wither and mercifully die; Death would claim her brother's decayed body the following day. Radiation burns and the latter effects of radiation disease, Death's new allies, would claim another seven thousand tormented souls before the year is out—

Death now looks back at the apocalyptic scene: *Thousands of tons of roiling dust and debris darken the day. For two square miles devastation is complete—a Buddhist Hell. A scythe in Death's hand had just cut down forty-nine thousand people, another forty thousand injured. Huge trees, like the twenty-five thousand homes and buildings, lay in the limitless rubble. A black rain of condensed water vapor and radioactive dust pummels more horror onto future generations.*

Slipping out of *meditation's* nightmare, Kenji Takara senses his face tingling, his breathing deep, nostrils flared. As in the previous forty-eight anniversaries, Takara sits on the consecrated "ground zero." His iron-black eyes refocus, but his mind is oblivious to the curious crowd parting as it makes its way around him. Once again, an all too familiar raw emotion flushes through his body: powerlessness, desolation, and the guilt at being spared. As he slowly rises to his feet, his head begins to clear and perspective returns: The utter emptiness had long since been filled with something from which he now derived power, a clarity of purpose, *a destiny! This would be the year things change*, the last surviving member of the Takara family told himself, his fist clenched white. Takara measured years from one solemn anniversary to the next. *This year we do it!*

CHAPTER 10

THE ALMIGHTY WHEEL TURNS

Today was August tenth, the day after the anniversary of the second American atomic blast. Nagasaki, laying in the urbanized and industrial Urakami Valley, had been Kenji Takara's childhood home. Shimizu, his aide, had seen it before, the days after Takara's annual pilgrimage seemed to darken his spirit-soul, hardening the man's unyielding face deeper still. A mood making it truly unwise, Shimizu reflected, for anyone wishing an appointment.

Yet there he was this late Friday morning, Setaka, the NIQE Director of Udon Software. Setaka, a frail little man in his early fifties, sat there braving the onslaught. Setaka's one saving grace, thought Shimizu, was his longstanding relationship with Takara's *kobun*, Takara's sole protégé recently deceased.

"That is correct, Takara-san," confirmed Setaka, "Unknown to the Americans, we still have three $NIQE_3$ chips left."

"Status?" Takara demanded, shifting his rock-hard frame

forward. For a moment, Setaka found himself distracted by the refection in Takara's polished ebony desk. He saw two flat-black eyes fixed from a rough-cut granite face. His hair, more pepper than salt, resembled a flat top. They were on the top floor of Misawa Group's recently completed fifty story New Misawa Building. It was a magnificently stark office.

Setaka went on to explain how breaking the American encryption system had proven most formidable, even for the $NIQE_3$ chip. Work was progressing though. Training the Military Strategist NIQE chip had just begun; the intelligent chip would learn all known battle tactics and strategies of every key American military figure.

"I expected better than this," Takara leveled, then characteristically Japanese, drew a slow contemptuous breath through his teeth. "Next time I want better news, Setaka-san. Bring it to me in ten days. You may go."

Setaka bowed his head nervously, then ventured, "There is something else, *sempei*." Setaka glanced anxious over at Shimizu, Takara's assistant. Or henchman, as Setaka thought of the man whose face reminded him of a fixed *kabuki* mask, a mask of a cunning fox, a ruthless fox.

"Make it quick," snapped Takara. "I have little time."

What Setaka wanted to say concerned his schoolboy friend, also Takara's *kobun*. It concerned the truth behind his death.

The strongest bond between two Japanese men is called *oyabun-kobun*, a traditional term. The *oyabun*, more than just a "father," possesses strong influence and power over his *kobun*'s career, and gives advice on important decisions. The *kobun*, in turn, is ready to offer his services whenever the *oyabun* requires them. A man's attachments and hopes are often directed to his *kobun* rather than his own sons. Such had been the case with Takara and his *kobun*, Kojima.

Setaka wanted to tell of what Kojima had said to him two days before he died. Wanted to tell of Kojima's plan to face his lifelong nightmare. Wanted to tell him that Kojima did not commit *seppuku*—ritual suicide—as it appeared. Wanted to tell of vengeance due. Setaka wanted to speak the name of the man responsible for Kojima's death: the American named "John Westin." But seeing Takara in such a foul mood, Setaka judged that now was not the time.

"Nothing, *sempei*." After a quick deferential bow, the fox showed him the door, passing him off to bodyguards in the outside anteroom.

Takara swiveled his chair to stare out to the west. From his fifty-story perch he could see the Imperial Palace in the foreground; in the background he saw the National Diet Building and other nearby government buildings. Close in, throughout Tokyo's central Marunouchi district, his New Misawa Building towered above some two dozen other head-quarter buildings, most belonging to his Misawa Group *keiretsu*.

Takara's giant Misawa Group itself was structured like an onion. Takara, himself, rose through Misawa Systems, one of three companies at the inner core of the powerful Misawa Group formed during the prewar industrial state; the other two were Misawa Bank and Misawa Corporation, the major trading company. The next layer was comprised of a close knit base of twenty companies; and if broadly defined, the number of corporate links listed into the hundreds. For Misawa Group was not simply a single corporate entity with a central "brain," Misawa was a *keiretsu*: interlocking directorates, cross-holdings, joint ventures, and long-term business relationships—all underpinned by interpersonal ties, common educational affiliation, or historical links. The resultant family of companies did not depend on formal controls, but rather on recognized mutual interest. *Keiretsu* was Japan's contribution to modern capitalism, beating the West at its own game. Misawa Group's revenues last year totaled two hundred billion dollars, ranking second worldwide behind the giant Mitsubishi Group.

Takara was Misawa Group's CEO.

Beyond Misawa Group, Takara had another role. He was the understood leader of the most powerful group of twenty-one men in all Japan, the secret *Banto* Society. It was this "Caretaker Society," not the official government, that set policy and steered Japan's ship of state through international waters. But as its leader, Takara now had a problem. *Banto* was in trouble. The coming October election of House of Councillors spelled trouble for *Banto* and its goals. The high state of tensions with America and the resultant downturn in Japan's economy pointed to a failed American policy by the Liberal Democratic Party, the LDP. Time for a change, came the opposition. In this case, change meant putting the secret *Banto* members out of government. As *Banto's* leader, he could not allow that to happen.

Struggle and sacrifice, Takara thought, seemed to best describe the path the sixty-seven years of his life had taken. Before *Banto's* difficulties and the death of his beloved Kojima, he'd already known more hardship than any man should expect to bear: being shot down over Manchuria, escaping the Russian pigs, stealing his way back to a broken Japan, a devastated Nagasaki, and a decimated family. So many sacrifices.

Staring out the window, Takara pulled out an object made of tin, always there in his pocket. Clenched tight within his fist, he knew every edge of its disfigured shape. Found after the Atomic blast, it was a toy soldier from his childhood, an arm missing, legs melded together, face deformed. Yes, thought the last survivor of Nagasaki's Takara family, many sacrifices. It was time to even the scales.

Takara swiveled back to his desk, then spoke, "Shimizu-san, your handling of both the *Banto* traitor and the American President's National Security Advisor was quite impressive. Who is the assassin?"

"The best, Takara-san," Shimizu spoke confidently. To protect Takara, he was duty-bound never to speak the assassin's name.

The answer was sufficient. That could be only one man, *Shiro Kage*—the White Shadow—now a legend within Japan's most closed circles. "When will he handle the station chief?"

"The terms stated by August tenth. That means tonight, probably early morning." Ever since the *Banto* traitor's untimely death, Takara had become aware of a very disturbing situation: large sums of money and effort were being spent seeking intelligence on the existence of his *Banto* Society and its aims. Shimizu's well-placed sources informed that the man behind that initiative to be the CIA's Tokyo Chief of station.

"Good. That will take care of the immediate problem." Takara stood, again looking west. The sun was near its zenith. "But not its cause. Shimizu-san, I have one more job for your man." Takara turned back, then spoke with cold arrogance, "The American President has become a liability, in more ways than one." It was time to share the sacrifice.

Shimizu simply looked up, by now in stride with his *sensei.* "When do you wish it done?"

As quiet as the dark, the assassin left the Tokyo night entering the sumptuous apartment, entering a place of dreams. He knelt beside the western-style bed, near the pillow of the man's sleeping body. He confirmed identification: CIA's station chief. The man and woman both breathed deeply, a sake bottle and cups sat on a night stand. Her black hair was tossed in telltale disarray, deep in the netherworld of sleep and dreams.

The matte-black figure had found a flower vase and emptied a small quantity of water into a dish. Now, he produced a sheet of thick brown paper and laid it atop the plate, letting the cool liquid soak it throughout. He then slipped a thick leather ring onto the index finger of his right hand. With movement as purposeful as a surgeon, he reached inside his sleeve, produced a four-inch assassin's needle, and placed it between his lips.

Finally, the assassin spread the wet paper on the *tatami* mat at his knees. He watched, observing quietly for thirty long seconds, again studying the woman's breathing, studying the man's polished face against light tracing through the translucent *shoji* screen behind him.

Suddenly the assassin moved. With ferocious speed, his left hand picked up the sheet of moist paper and plastered it over the man's face. Eyes flew open! With superhuman strength, the assassin pressed harder, removed the needle from his teeth, and with one fluid motion penetrated the needle deep into the right ear.

Without sound, the man's body twitched once, his mind barely registering death's dark eyes burning from a ancient light. The figure observed the silence, verifying the woman undisturbed. Twenty seconds later, the thick brown paper removed, he studied the still body before him. The one drop of blood present, the assassin removed with a swipe of the moist paper. Then, quiet as the night, the black-clad intruder left.

New York City: Takara's basic plan, Dr. Mitsuru Zenjuro had to admit, seemed sound enough. Coopt the American Vice President Reed, eliminate President Temple, then put the new ascending President to good use. There was a time constraint, of course.

Reed had to be sworn in by October sixth, eight days before Japan's House of Councillors elections. Give the man five days in his new Oval Office, then let him announce his support of Japan and a new bilateral agreement with the Prime Minister. Then, with only three days before Japan's Sunday elections, the opposition could not possibly respond adequately. With increased credibility, his fellow *Banto* members, those in the House, plus the Prime Minister would remain in power. Yes, a solid plan. And eight weeks to execute it.

Takara's "transition plan" to remove President Temple entailed two approaches. To Zenjuro's knowledge, he was the only other *Banto* member who knew the entire "transition plan," both primary and backup. Zenjuro's role was key in both, but today it was the backup plan he would initiate. Truly a brilliant plan, he mused. For in the offing, it coopted the vice presidential heir to the presidential throne it was designed to vacate.

Zenjuro spotted the limousine, the one with the small

placard wedged visibly on the right-side dash, on it a large four-leaf clover. Briefcase in hand, he left the United Nations foyer and stepped to the curb. Beneath the constant flutter of national flags, Japan's Ambassador to the U.N. opened the rear door himself and quickly stepped in.

"Good afternoon, Mr. Ambassador," Glenn Thielken greeted, as the driver accelerated smoothly heading north on First Avenue. Thielken regarded this man who seemed not to fit the stereotypical modern-day Japanese diplomat. What little hair left at the sides of his head, had long since been shaved giving the appearance of complete baldness. He had a rather large five-feet, ten-inch frame and wore thick gold rimmed glasses encircling alert pearl black eyes. That, and the studied wrinkles on his forehead gave him a very scholarly look.

Zenjuro returned the greeting, again wondering why people from California looked so perfect: perfect clothes, teeth, vision. Zenjuro further inspected the interior, mentally appreciating the tinted windows and driver's privacy window, then inquired about time constraints.

"Then I will, as you Americans say, get down to business. Without proper formality, but nevertheless, with complete sincerity. Is this satisfactory?" *No Jap bullshit, now there's a change.* Thielken nodded, glancing at the burning cigarette.

Zenjuro extinguished the offense, then continued, "You are familiar with the Trans Bering Strait concept?" Thielken affirmed, a four hundred billion dollar engineering project to link Alaska with Siberia: bridge the Aleutian Islands, then tunnel under the sixty-feet-deep Bering Strait. "I can tell you now that it not simply a concept. It is a fully thought out and economically feasible project. A decision to pursue is much closer than anyone thinks. *And*, Mr. Thielken, I am in a position to ensure Shiraki Industries is selected as prime contractor."

Thielken tried to maintain his composure, both at the enormity of the project and at Zenjuro's confidence. He waited for the driver to complete a left turn, then asked the obvious, "That is very generous, Mr. Zenjuro. Is there anything I can do in return?"

Zenjuro indulged a look at Rockefeller Center, a Japanese asset, then responded, "Japan wishes a favorable inclination from Vice President Reed. If you can deliver this—"

"What does favorable inclination mean?"

"His support lobbying President Temple on matters concerning Japan's interest." Thielken motioned for more. Zenjuro did not like doing business this way, rushing things left little room for the art of negotiation. "Two things: one, a publicly stated policy of warmer relations between our two countries. And two, U.S. support for Japan's bid to secure a permanent seat on the U.N. Security Council."

"Humm. Don't think Temple will—"

"The possibilities are enormous, Mr. Thielken, both for your company and for your career." Zenjuro paused to elucidate, "There is always a possibility that a U.S. President could step down from office. You have seen it before. We have certain information, if disclosed, would ensure Temple's early retirement. Put this information in Vice President Reed's hands, and who knows, a beholding President Reed may respond in kind, Secretary of Defense, perhaps."

"I've always delivered in the past, but this time, what you ask. I'm not sure."

Zenjuro produced a sealed envelope from his briefcase. "Deliver this still sealed to the Vice President. It will help him make up his mind. I understand you and Mrs. Thielken are hosting a party in his honor. In two weeks, I believe. That would make an excellent opportunity, don't you think?"

Just like now, Thielken marveled, Zenjuro always had his shit together. Well, Thielken had to admit, he'd always wanted a shot at the back room game. But with the Japs dealing the cards? Somehow that didn't settle all that well. *Scruples?* Whatever, the price of poker just went up.

The limousine pulled up to the U.N. front entrance and stopped. Zenjuro extended a hand, then wished the man on *Banto*'s LIST a pleasant flight back to Los Angeles. Then quickly, Japan's Ambassador to the U.N. stepped out onto sunlit sidewalk. As he watched the limousine depart he indulged himself a smile, thinking of the plan, and its boldness. Thinking of the contents of that sealed envelope, thinking of the sheer audacity.

Carrera Thielken wasn't used to picking her husband up at the Los Angeles International terminal building. It wasn't much fun either, dealing with the heavy Friday evening traffic and limited curb access. Yet problems with the Shiraki corporate jet at La Guardia Airport necessitated Glenn's taking a commercial flight. In keeping with her name (used to be Carol back in Kansas), she drove a white Porsche, whose stick shift at the moment had become a further inconvenience.

Carrera was a woman of acquired taste, a veneer barely concealing a lust for power, power through men as her talents had directed her. She had carefully cut features and deliberate China blue eyes. Eyes as engaging as a siren's song, and, it was said, were never seen to blink. For tonight's opera, she wore a short-cut gold metallic body dress with handbag to match. Just flashy enough to be noticed, she had decided, but short of full-blown "gliteria."

Third time around the World Way terminal ellipse, she spotted her husband, a little worse for wear, she appraised. But still, he'd remembered to wear a darker Brooks Brothers, suitable for tonight's performance. She picked him up and as they had little time, she headed straightaway for the Dorothy Chandler Pavilion.

Except for his extramarital forays, Glenn Thielken withheld little from Carrera, especially information of strategic value. He had long since recognized her possessing the innate mind of a strategist; from the mold of Niccolo Machiavelli himself, he'd often thought. But not the balls to execute the strategy once formulated, only he had the balls. He told her of his meeting with the Japanese U.N. Ambassador. He told her of Zenjuro's proposition, the quid pro quo, the possibilities, then watched her smile as she accelerated through a red light.

CHAPTER 11
LISTING

Special agent in charge Jim Rhodes watched the two men enter the Oval Office anteroom. Both CIA deputy directors, one he liked, one he didn't. He thought of Jordan Barr, the DDO, much like himself: former marine, no nonsense, no shit kind of a guy. If in a barroom things went to hell, Barr was the kind of guy he'd want backing him up. Not so with Marshall Douglas, DDI. Douglas's idea of backup was having the Company's general counsel at his side.

The two men had yet to notice Lieutenant Colonel Coleman had already arrived, seated, waiting. Rhodes saw a lot of Coleman lately, especially as it'd become more apparent that the President's National Security Advisor wouldn't be returning. Strange, Rhodes thought, Rennick perfectly fit one day, and a slammer illness the next, might even die, he had heard.

Rhodes himself stood a solid six feet tall, a hardened face revealed nothing of his thoughts of these two men. A definite recession of his sandy brown hair belied his mid-fortyish age.

Jim Rhodes had made the Secret Service his civilian career, rising through the ranks to the senior field man in charge of the President's security team. He was the special agent in charge (SAC) and usually got the President's out of town trips where his charge was the most vulnerable.

This early morning, the SAC stood at one of the secretary's desks checking her edited version of the President's schedule against his. As the two Company men entered, he appraised them in unusually good spirits, at least until Barr asked the question:

"Any word on the Donahoe thing?"

Douglas frowned. Barr referred the mysterious death of the Chief of their Tokyo station. "Just got the forensics out of Tokyo. Foul play. Puncture into the brain. Through the right ear, while he slept. No marks, no struggle."

"And no clues, I take it." To Barr, it sounded like a technique employed by Japan's ancient assassins. "What's hot over there?"

"You know the answer to that. Lotta irons in the fire, but this *Banto* and their LIST has had top priority for three months now." Marshall's political caution didn't allow him to comment how fed up he was with this fictitious "LIST hunt."

"And what does this do to the effort?" asked Barr, knowing, but not sharing Marshall's sentiments on the matter.

"Using Okada, blind (a blind asset, unknown to the local station). Also covers Westin's ass when he puts it on Jap soil."

Barr approved, "Yes, if anybody can…Yes."

"The President will see you now," the secretary broke with her always cheerful voice.

The three men walked into the Oval Office, each a bit surprised to see Dhillon Reed, the Vice President, already seated. That meant one thing to the grimacing Marshall Douglas: Dhillon Reed had the point on the LIST, the fucking LIST hunt. Add one more item to today's agenda, he mentally noted.

Temple came around from his antique oak desk, "How the hell are you, Jordan?" The tone was almost jubilant, his knowing of SCARAB's success.

"It's a bitch, Sir," Jordan Barr deadpanned. "Keeping the peace can be dangerous." Temple returned the wry smile, welcomed the rest, then motioned to the DDO. "Okay, Jordan, let's have it."

Jordan Barr recounted the heliborne assault, good execution, one man injured, flesh wound, and all but one mission objectives met. "We were unable to extract Safi Kahurak, the FIA leader. He died in a firefight. However, SEAL Team Three found a safe and were able to secure its contents. Marshall's analysts have had the stuff for three days now."

The DDI took the cue. "The reason for FIA's attempt to steal spent nuclear fuel at Hanford has come to light. Sir, among other things, we found a list. It was an inventory of all temporary nuclear waste storage locations supporting the United States' one hundred and six nuclear power plants. That's not all. Contamination points for the plants themselves, major city water supplies, and aquifers were charted."

"Holy shit." Temple paused leaning forward, "What have we done about these targets?"

"All nuke sites have been alerted," Coleman answered, "Security has been tripled at those facilities and stationed at the target contamination points. To date, Sir, we've seen no additional activity, untoward or otherwise, at these locations."

The President digressed, "Tell me, if this nuclear waste is so dangerous, then why do we have so much of the stuff scattered over God's half acre?"

"DOE's got that ball, Sir," Marshall broke taking back the floor. "They're trying to consolidate it all. Some place out in Nevada called Yucca Mountain, I think. As I understand it, permanent storage is a complex issue, a very slow process."

"Humm." Temple made a mental note to see his Energy Secretary on the matter, then turned to Coleman, "Very good, Colonel. Stay on top of it," Temple directed. "What else, Mr. Douglas?"

"Sir, we hit the jackpot. We found a list of Islamic Action Front members and operations going back twelve months. We got a break on the kidnappings too." The DDO watched

Temple remove his reading glasses and lean in even more.

"As you remember, the government of Iran was on the short list of suspects. Instead of the Iranian government, FIA documents seem to leave no doubt about Abu Hakim and his radical fundamentalist group. We now have proof that FIA was responsible for abducting two of the missing scientists. A Bob Watt, microbiologist from Chem Tech out of Cambridge, and a Ms. Storey, a professor at Berkeley University."

Coleman's head snapped back. "Beth Storey?" Coleman broke. Douglas looked at his notes and affirmed. "Mr. President, you remember John Westin, the man who nailed the Japanese for holding back NIQE chips, then discovering their NIQE-based weapons program."

"Yes, but what's Wes—"

"Sir, Beth Storey and Westin are an item, as they say. Westin was there last week when it happened. Tried to stop it."

Temple did indeed remember the ex-astronaut. The man smelled a Jap rat and started turning rocks. Temple liked initiative like that. He also liked the straight talk he got from the man about the Japanese NIQE program and possible agendas. Temple expected Westin's NIQE-base Weapons Report to make some interesting reading. But now a troubling thought wouldn't go away: why did John Westin's name keep popping up in the middle of…chaos. "What's Westin know about the kidnappings?"

"Other than Ms. Storey's, nothing. He halfway suspects it's the Japanese in retribution for his exposing their secret weapons program." At that, Barr exchanged a look with Douglas. "Local police think its a drug matter, a deal gone bad, vendetta or something."

"Okay," Temple said drawing the word out as if not knowing what to think of what he'd just heard, then motioned Douglas to continue.

"Ms. Storey is now the ninth known abduction. Six days ago. But her case was different. The common denominator in the disappearances is their each being experts in their respective fields. Most microbiology related, although one from

Paxton International was a missile payload specialist."

"And what is Ms. Storey's specialty?"

"Two, Sir. At Berkeley, she teaches fractal geometry. Tracking down computer viruses is her second skill. As it was explained to me, she's developed a fractal algorithm to simplify the identification of old and new viruses for irradiation."

"What else?"

"STAIRCASE." Each visitor watched the President's face tighten.

Whenever he heard that bye name, Temple's mind always cast back to his pre-inaugural briefings. As president-elect, of all the things he'd heard, it was STAIRCASE that disturbed him the most. It seemed that his predecessor had covertly acquired the technology from a highly successful surreptitious operation on foreign territory. The result was that now the U.S had in its arsenal the most deadly weapon humankind could ever hope to envision. STAIRCASE was a lethal genetic virus. Determine the target's racial characteristics, say all balding Chinese of Mongoloid origin, locate the corresponding genes, then mix up a batch. Skin contact was all it took to spread it, like a common cold. But unlike the common cold, its targets never recovered from a deadly bout with STAIR-CASE.

Then, three months ago, Temple's worst nightmare came to fruition. It involved a briefcase being transported from the Center for Viral Disease located in Fort Collins to a government lab in Los Angeles. Everything one needed to develop a designer batch of STAIRCASE was contained in that briefcase—Pandora's briefcase, someone had later called it. During its transport, in what appeared to be a random gang-related robbery, the briefcase was stolen. And with it, the doomsday genie was out of its bottle.

The DDI continued, "After looking at the disappearance pattern, CIA analysts tried to determine what a collection of this sort of scientist would be up to. Independent of the SCARAB findings, and not knowing about STAIRCASE, their conclusion was some sort of genetic engineering project.

Since a missile delivery specialist was also included, they deduced the this genetically engineered product probably had an offensive intent.

"Now knowing Iranian hardliner involvement, it's starts to make sense. We speculate their first target to be Jews, probably Israel."

"And the second?"

"Sub-groups within the Caucasian race. Most likely starting with America."

Temple slumped back into his chair, fingered his thinning brown hair and muttered, "Holy shit." He took a long breath, eyes darting between his DDI and his DDO. "Gentlemen, find this goddamned STAIRCASE, destroy it and neutralize any possibility of proliferation. Do I make myself clear?" Both men nodded. "And when that's done, I want it removed from U.S. Government labs and destroyed."

The DDI ventured first. "Sir, we have reason to believe the Israelis know its location. Speculation. But last night, my MOSSAD counterpart informed me at home that soon Israeli commandos would infiltrate Iran, and destroy a facility producing what he termed to be 'a substance posing a grave threat to the Jewish people.' My guess, its the STAIRCASE development lab."

"Why'd he tell you this?"

"Ever since 1956, Israel has sought our consent to its major actions. They get our consent, we prepare for the political fallout. I have a good relationship with Israeli intelligence, especially MOSSAD's director. Director Amit doesn't particularly trust the U.S. government to keep a secret, but he does trust me. As a matter of courtesy, he keeps me informed of imminent insurgent actions in the Middle East. I do the same. Keeps us from stepping on each other's toes.

"Sir, I agree, the last thing we want is proliferation, even to the Israelis. If we go in with them jointly, under some pretext, we could ensure STAIRCASE destruction and avoid a technology transfer. A joint op, Sir."

"Jordan?" Temple wanted the DDO's skin in this.

"Special Ops guys don't particularly like joint ops. But if what Marshall says is correct, what choice we got?"

"Okay, I like it," jumped the President a little too quickly, "Don't tell the Israelis what we're after. Marshall, develop a plausible cover. Ensure they know it's important to me. Colonel Coleman will coordinate NSC from my end."

"Israel will want something in return," added the DDI.

"They always do," replied the President with exasperation. "I'll deal with that when the time comes. If there's nothing else, let's—"

"Sir," interrupted Vice President Dhillon Reed, "you said you wanted to cover the LIST."

"Oh...yes." He'd asked Reed to honcho that one. Temple was convinced that this secret Japanese society called *Banto* really existed. Sources, albeit tenuous sources, seemed to corroborate. And he had to go with what John Westin had discovered: *Banto* had a strategic LIST of prominent U.S. citizens, coopted, and always available to do *Banto's* bidding. And obviously, *Banto's* bidding would be to seek Japanese advantage. All reason informed Temple's practical mind that there were names on that LIST close to him. Names capable of doing immense damage to him and to the United States.

Until two minutes ago, the LIST was one of his two top priorities; America's long-term economic health being the other. All that paled now. He had an honest-to-God crisis. He had to stop this STAIRCASE menace from proliferating, from being unleashed. *Christ, what have we done?*

"Well, David, your man in Washington, it appears, was correct. I had no idea his CIA sources were so well placed." The man speaking was Yitzhak Cohen, Israel's Minister of Defense. The two men were in Cohen's modest Tel Aviv office.

Cohen, himself, was a political animal. An animated no-nonsense man, he presented a high forehead pushing back thin white hair with washed out gray eyebrows over piercing, intelligent, brown eyes. His nose bulbed at the end atop perfectly arranged white teeth.

"The American response virtually confirms its existence," Cohen continued. "Still, to believe is difficult. And possessed by the Iranians. The cursed Iranians."

David Amit, Director of Mossad, kept a serious tone, "Yes, the American response to our menacing substance ruse is convincing. And the request came yesterday from my counterpart, Marshall Douglas. Joint operation, indeed. Said it had been stolen from a U.S. storage facility: highly toxic, highly dispersive." Amit wanted to indulge the moment for this was indeed an intelligence coup. Manipulating the CIA Deputy Director of Intelligence was a feat for which he was justly proud, though its message was as ominous as the young state of Israel had ever encountered. Amit watched his long-time friend assimilate this new and dangerous reality.

"You told Marshall Douglas we knew where it was?" It was more of a statement of admiration than a question. Cohen, over the decades never ceased to be surprised at Amit's cunning and resourcefulness, not to mention his bravery. Cohen himself also rose through the ranks of *MOSSAD Letafkidim Meyouehadim*, specifically the Operational Planning & Coordination branch. With multiple assignments around the world, he made his mark as a top operative and master strategist.

He and Amit went back to 1981, coordinating and executing the attack on the Osiraq "research reactor" at Tuwaitha just outside of Baghdad. Shortly before its completion, fourteen Israeli fighters executed a precision bombing raid on June seventh, putting Saddam Hussein's nuclear ambitions on indefinite hold. Back then, what the world hadn't known—but later came to suspect—was that MOSSAD saboteurs had infiltrated the building, placed radio-controlled charges around the core itself and simultaneously with the raid, ensured the reactor's total destruction.

"Yes," the MOSSAD director replied flatly, "and now we must find this Iranian facility."

"Or tell the Americans that it has just been moved, and let them find it for us. In the meantime preparation for this joint operation should commence."

"May I suggest we have Zvi humor the Americans."

"SAYERET MAT'KAL?" the Defense Minister spoke. The Israeli Defense Force's ultrasecret General Staff reconnaissance force. Finally he affirmed, managing a slight smile. "They will like that. I will take care of it.

"But," Cohen continued, warning, "understand how critical this is. Israel must at all cost possess this substance. David," Cohen raised his short frame from the chair, hands braced against its edge, eyes fixed like bullets, "David, I am depending on you. Israel depends on you. We must locate the substance before the Americans do. And we must be ready to act quickly when we do."

"I understand, Yitzhak. If it is there, I will find it."

Eight days in this god forsaken place, thought Beth Storey, again. After cleaning up her captor's lab computers, her programming skills and experience in human disease spread patterns proved of further use to them, sparing her life. Three of the nine abducted captives hadn't been so lucky.

It was evening in the living quarters above the makeshift lab. It was a scene starting to look familiar to her, a troubling thought. The two guards, and the other five kidnapped hostages were scattered about. Ali el-Shafii, the lab's director always left in the evenings.

The second story living quarters was separated into two make-shift sections: the larger area housed the sleeping and dressing area; the other, separated with just a gauze-cloth, contained the bathroom, including the one bathtub.

The bathtub. At first she resisted. But it was so incredibly dirty here that finally two days ago she relented. This was her time for a bath, and she regarded it as a bitter-sweet experience. With just the gauze cloth partition between the "living quarters" and the bath, she had to endure the drooling eyes of the guards and stealing glances from the rest. Of the other five hostages, Dr. Dech was the worst. She liked the name the others had given him, Dr. Death, with that slicked back hair, goatee and all.

Even now as she slipped her well-curved form into the soapy water, she could feel Dr. Dech making little effort to divert his eyes. *Fuck him. Fuck them all*, her mind screamed. She put her back to them and choked back a tear. She purposely worked to disregard modesty, refusing to yield her captors the smallest satisfaction of control—control this time derived from successfully demeaning her self-esteem. Beyond defiance, at times like these, she tried to consciously blot out the bastards. Especially now as she felt the warm soapy water push above her breast. She did this by thinking of John and their last time together.

She thought of John's all-American grin, boyish, almost pranksterish. She liked the way he laughed at her childhood stories. John really liked the one she'd told when he asked about the scar on her shoulder. In the warmth of the water she let her mind drift to the story, inwardly smiling at the memory of her mother's reaction.

Back in her Oklahoma grade school, she never really warmed up to the boys, choosing to fight with them instead. She still remembered her mother's reaction the day she came home from her sixth grade classes, her blouse ripped, blood-stained, and a deep gash across her left shoulder blade. Beth didn't say a word, just sat there, while her mom cleaned her up. Later her mother found out a local bully had pushed her down into a rocky ravine. As told to her mother, it took a full minute at the bottom of the ravine for Beth to recover. After gaining her senses, she bolted up and out like a cheetah, charged the surprised boy, and when it was over, he lay sprawled at the ravine's bottom with a compound fracture of his upper leg. Such behavior, not the way her mother was raised—ambulance and all.

Stirring in the water her mind drifted back into the present, into her living nightmare. All her life she'd taken care of herself, stood up for herself. Until now. A stand here got you killed, or worse.

"Enough time," came the guard's heavily accented English breaking the reflection. Half startled, she looked up then stood, at first unaware that the room was empty, save the one guard...

In a flash, Dech had his arms around her nude form. She reflexed twisting free, her slippery body working to her advantage. She caught a glance at the guard. He was in on this too, him and his chummy Dr. Death. She was totally alone. Her eyes searched for a weapon, anything. Dech came at her again. Backing up, she almost slipped, her hands catching herself against the side of the tub...the soap dish—with pronged legs.

He forced her against a wall. She struggled with one hand, the other grasping the soap and dish, its legs facing outward. "Time to give in," he said, almost drooling. With all her might, she arced the soap dish around, his face turning to see the distraction.

"Aaaah!" came his cry. She'd stapled his eye, cheek and lip, at the same time caving his nose. She thought of swiss cheese as she watched him stumble back. He looked at his hand, disbelieving the blood pouring from his bug-like nose.

"Never!" she screamed defiantly.

Both men sensed the irony, meeting in this place. It was the old Hilton Hotel just off the old aristocratic Pahlavi Avenue near the northern Embassy district. It was his leader's, Abu Hakim, idea, always to meet under the Iranian government's noses. But Rashid liked it all the same. It showed cunning and courage, the two traits he valued most, especially in his leader.

Colonel Mohammed Rashid was from the north. Typical of a Turkomen, he presented a stalwart image looking through brown slant-eyes, as though nothing were beyond his power, noble or atrocious, as though they'd never known fear or revealed a secret in their entire fifty hard-worn years. It was an image that easily could have fit into the past of his ancestors wearing a black fleece hat, sitting bolt upright on his spirited imperial gray. With such a heritage, Rashid today would have preferred wearing his military uniform; instead, he now sought anonymity in the form of casual Western costume.

Abu Hakim himself had the look of a fisherman, face weathered before its time, a strong body beginning to bend. At fifty-two, he was ruggedly handsome, his thick hair and mustache showing no signs of gray. Hakim was a leader. His black eyes seemed all pupil, foreshadowing a destiny for even greater power, yet giving away nothing of the man's capacity for ruthlessness.

Hakim longed for the day when he and Rashid could work as a close team, openly. But at present, Rashid, a colonel in the government's Islamic Revolutionary Army, could never be seen with the revolutionary outlaw his government so desperately sought to put behind bars.

Hakim turned from the window, leaned forward and pointed his finger almost accusingly. "Shafii has not said any of this to me. Why do you?"

"Because we go back a long time, Abu. Because I am your friend. Because Shafii is afraid of you. Because I am not." Rashid waited for Hakim's face to soften, then continued, "Shafii may be capable, of this I do not know, but he has told me he has not the facilities, has not the equipment—"

"But I gave him the best experts in the world!"

"Yes, Abu, but even the best carpenter does not build a house with a club."

"Hmmm. Shafii and I will talk. Now, what of the mission?"

"Still no communication from Khayyam and his group. Nor is there any news in the American press about Hanford or any other nuclear power plant. Attack, theft, or otherwise. It does not look good, my friend."

"And the *Ruh al-Asr*?

"That one worries me even more." The STAIRCASE project was rising in importance.

Westin wheeled his '65 Nassau blue Corvette convertible into the assigned slot under his condominium building, the radio's last tune still playing in his head, "I heard it through the grapevine"… In the hot, muggy month of August, John had to remind himself why he called Houston home. The answer that came was good enough: Houston was sort of a loose, live and let live kind of town, full of good friends too. His kind of place.

John removed the mail from his box, then ascended the three flights. Inside, women usually judged his place as neo-modern male sparse. That lasted until they saw the far-end floor-to-ceiling glass revealing a spectacular top-floor view of a sun-glistened Clear Lake.

John found a cold one from the near-empty refrigerator, then almost stumbled over Earl's bowl. Since he went over to Paxton, he'd been spending the majority of his time on the West Coast or in Japan. With so little time for Earl, finally last month he gave the dog to his only grandson out in Oregon. He thought it fitting, naming the Labrador Retriever "Earl" after the Earl of Malmesbury who originally named the breed. Earl had a smooth taupe-gray coat and deep brown understanding eyes. The bowl sat empty.

He continued on through the living room stepping out onto the thirty foot covered balcony. It was a breezy summer afternoon, and the lake teamed with hundreds of boats: power, sail, wind surfers, and a lone canoe; jet skis, like mosquitos, pestered the bigger boats. From the patio table John picked up the binoculars (every bachelor has a pair) and focused on a sleek schooner cruising by under power. Fifty footer, "Texas law," someone once postulated, "the older the captain and the bigger his belly, the longer the boat and the younger the girls."

Girls. He thought of Beth. He hadn't been very good with lasting female relationships. He figured his wife was fully justified in divorcing him, his being wrapped up in a Naval Aviator's career and all. The others, since, seemed not so different: him on AM, them on FM. Result: not much communication, not much chance.

So who the hell is Beth Storey? This woman he couldn't get off his mind. One sharp cookie, there. As a professional, she definitely knew her stuff; and, as a woman, definitely had *his* number. He'd toyed with the idea of commitment once, yet another part of his mind invariably chimed in, cautioning against losing independence. *Independence of what?* a more sobered mind-corner now kibitzed. *Control?*

Eight days now since Beth's abduction. Westin had been lucky in that people in the fitness center "fish bowl" saw the abduction, saw the entire thing. Evidently, yesterday, Coleman made a call. A call, mentioned this morning by the City of Berkeley police lieutenant handling the case, mumbling something about friends in high places. The heat diminished considerably, although the guard he'd chopped still wanted charges pressed. Beth Storey and drugs—*give me a break.*

The telephone. John took the call in his back study, hoping it was Coleman returning his call. It was.

But instead of answers, John hit a U.S. Marine stone wall. He did get that Coleman's buddies had an idea where Beth was—and "not to worry." *Shit.* John was scheduled to leave for Japan this Monday. But now, he decided, he wasn't leaving until he met with Coleman, face-to-face. Answers. Finally, he wrangled an invitation the day before he left: Sunday afternoon backyard barbecue, Coleman's house in the Washington suburbs. He'd get answers then, he swore to himself as he hung up. *It's the Japs.*

John took a long deep breath, staring absently at the bookcase on his left. On a shelf about half way up, the A-6 Intruder Model caught his eye, it sitting next to a pair of plastic longhorns.

It was at the University of Texas where he learned about aircraft and the emerging discipline called spaceflight. Westin learned how a spacecraft works, about guidance, navigation and control. Navigation told you where you wanted to be. Guidance told you how to steer to get there. And control is what you did to make it happen. Back then, Westin had seen his life in a similar metaphor. His goal was to fly spacecraft, and he set career "navigation points" to that end. He graduated with a B.S. in Aeronautical Engineering, then married Laura Halston.

Quickly developing events in Viet Nam made Westin's path, or "guidance" strategy clear to him: First, the Navy needed pilots; second, a war meant opportunity to advance and be noticed. The third was the kick: working with such a professional team in the hottest spot on the planet, a real kick.

A year after joining the Navy, he won his wings and became a father to Stewart Kreuger Westin both on the same day. Another year later he qualified for carrier operations. He spent two years carrier duty on the CVAN 65 Enterprise off the coast of Viet Nam as a squadron fighter pilot driving an A-6. Toward the war's end, he went inactive, worked around aerospace for a few years trying to establish a stable environment for the family. Then entered MIT's graduate program. A year later he had under his belt an M.S. in Aeronautics and Astronautics and Engineer of Aeronautics and Astronautics. The path was not unlike that of the Apollo astronauts who had just finished the moon program, except he took every computer course he could schedule.

Just before graduation, Laura separated taking Stewart with her. Back then, he thought he understood it all, but didn't know how to deal with it. For John Kreuger Westin, "control" helped him stifle the pain and something called emotion. His son, Stewart, was the one loose end, a loose end, at the time, he had decided to deal with later. *Later.* Over twenty years, now, and he hadn't. Something he couldn't control.

Now here he was again. *No control.* In locating her. In wanting her. He emptied the beer.

CHAPTER 12
Lat 36 50' 12" 6N
Long 116 28' 50" 4E

For the short hop from Los Angeles to Las Vegas, Glenn Thielken and his Administrative Assistant (AA) took Shiraki Industries' smaller corporate jet, a computer stylized "SI" emboldened in red on the tail of the gleaming white aircraft. Fifty minutes after receiving LAX tower clearance, the pilot taxied off runway 25 R onto the tarmac west of the Las Vegas' one-story McCarran International Airport's terminal building.

The Lear's pilot pulled up near the Page Avjet Building, some sixty feet short of a ASTAR 350 helicopter sitting readied to receive the Lear's passengers. The jet's left door opened. Thielken's AA stepped out first to retrieve their two shoulder carry-ons and the communications briefcase. Thielken, himself, hesitated to watch a sandy-haired man, solid football physique, dressed in boots, jeans, and a white long-sleeve western-style shirt—a classic home developer look—approach the plane. As Thielken stepped out, he fixed a no-nonsense look on the man now extending his hand.

"Good morning, Mr. Thielken. Good trip?" said Tom Shelby, his grip as firm as his boss'. Shelby was a geologist by training, Colorado School of Mines, but also showed an extraordinary aptitude for management, both project and personnel. After Shiraki Industries won the Department of Energy's prime contractor bidding, Thielken "bought" Shelby away from Paxton International, his major competitor. Shelby, as his Yucca Mountain on-site project manager, now coordinated up to fifty-six sub-contractors totaling an overall fourteen hundred personnel.

Thielken noted his AA already stowing the bags into the leased helicopter. "Ready?" he replied.

"Yes, Mr. Thielken, though I don't know the pilot. We'll talk later," Shelby said gesturing his boss to the right side of the Air Wolf-looking ASTAR 350, its engines and rotor blades already beginning to tense.

With his distinguished visitors all buckled in, and receiving clearance to fly into the Nevada Test Site's tightly restricted airspace, the helicopter's pilot deftly applied power easing up on the collective. The ASTAR rose slowly then turned to the west. Thielken watched the Las Vegas strip fade quickly to the east, then got down to business. "Everything okay out at the dump?"

"Everything's proceeding per our last agreed-to schedule," Shelby replied dryly subtly casting an eye in the new pilot's direction.

Thielken knew and trusted his project manager's judgement. The evasive reply meant trouble, they would talk at the site. Thielken was not so much a hands-on man as he was a tactician, always looking after the SWOT, as he liked to called it: Strengths, Weaknesses, Opportunities, and Threats. He admired the late great American retailer, Sam Walton, and the way he looked after every aspect of his business: he may have destroyed the commercial heart—and vitality—of every small American town whose outskirts he placed one of his cutthroat Wal-Marts, but business was business. Thielken understood that.

Tomorrow he would be in the DOE Project Director's

office back in Las Vegas. He wanted that man to see him as a CEO on top of this project, that Shiraki Industries was in his court and that the converse should continue to be true. He'd spoken with Vice President Reed yesterday, and especially wanted the DOE Project Director to know that.

The thought of Dhillon Reed made him think of Japan's U.N. Ambassador Zenjuro's proposal. He himself wasn't so sure; but his wife, Carrera, was all for it and he trusted her judgement. As Zenjuro pointed out, he and Carrera were hosting a party in Vice President Reed's honor in two weeks. Maybe he'd do it then.

Business. Thielken handed a single sheet of paper to Shelby. "Give me your gut on these."

Shelby did a quick scan, all only too familiar. "No problem. Just remember DOE's objective: To find out whether the volcanic rock at Yucca Mountain can provide a stable and contained repository for seventy thousand tons of nuclear waste to last at least ten thousand years. That's how long it will take for slowly decaying material to lose its toxicity." Thielken's quick nod communicated annoyance.

Shelby sluffed it off and began at the top:

"Water table looks good: measures seven to fourteen hundred feet below the repository. That's good. At that distance any dissolved radionuclides created will never reach it.

"As for weather in ten thousand years, NOAA climatologist look to the past, ten thousand years in the past. And that's not good. The last ten thousand years, they say, huge ice sheets covered this part of North America, as well as Eurasia. DOE doesn't know what to do with that. I suspect they'll let that sleeping dog lie.

"Geochemistry: The tuff is holding up well to the stress tests and heated block tests—"

"Tuff?" To his query, Thielken noted Shelby's quarterback shoulders stiffen. He let it slide, for now.

"That's the volcanic rock that actually makes up Yucca Mountain, it's at least thirteen million years old. The region has two kinds: good tuff and bad tuff. The good stuff is called welded tuff, a strong dense rock with twelve times the compression strength of concrete. Nonwelded tuff, however, is made up of volcanic deposits that cooled much more quickly; kick it, and the spongy compacted ash crumbles away—not at all what we want." Shelby's fixed eyes said it all: *Later on this one.*

"Let's see, yes, volcanic activity: Geologist are beginning to agree that the Lathrop Well Volcano twelve miles to the west is only five thousand years old, increasing the likelihood of another eruption during the project life. Another dog DOE will keep in slumber-land.

"Next, earthquakes: there are thirty-two faults at or near the site. In the last hundred and fifty years, since the region was settled, there have been eight major quakes."

"Intensity?"

"Six-point-five or higher on Richter. Not a problem. My guys tell me tremor intensity diminishes significantly that far below the surface. The 1992 quake east of L.A. tends to verify that opinion. Repercussion, if any, would be small, DOE says, even the opposition's scientist agree on that one.

"But if you ask me," Shelby continued, looking back at a stare that made men doubt themselves, "If this area gets a another quake within the next year, you can kiss this project's ass good-bye—experts or no experts. Public opinion—right or wrong—would kill it."

Thielken understood Shelby's logic: DOE maintained a hundred twenty-seven facilities, their watchdogs estimated ninety percent of them leaked. Growing disclosures of DOE's mismanagement of nuclear facilities, especially those producing nuclear weapons material, had eroded public confidence to a new low. "Yes," he said, taking back the paper.

Over the Amargosa Desert of southern Nevada, Thielken watched as Shelby pointed out the six-mile stretch of Yucca Mountain's ridge coming into view. They were ninety miles northwest of Las Vegas on the southwest corner of the Nevada Test Site. He felt his body press against the left wall as the pilot banked then aligned himself for a straight-in approach into the

DOE's operational base located at the foot of near Rainier Mesa.

On the approach, Thielken reflected on the brief he held in his hands: Beneath this god-forsaken place was a subterranean maze that once thundered with explosions signaling the dawning of the nation's nuclear age. Fifty years later, nuclear technology had come of age, but so had its radioactive legacy. DOE was spending two billion dollars just to identify a suitable site for the nation's overflowing stacks of spent fuel from one hundred and six licensed nuclear power plants and deadly spoilage from its nuclear weapons factories. Finding proper storage space for the now thirty tons of highly toxic waste material had become a massive problem, and an ever increasing dangerous one.

More than anybody, Thielken knew, the DOE wanted Yucca Mountain to work out, they wanted this thing put to bed, a thirty-five billion dollar bed by official account. Internal Shiraki estimates weighed it in at closer to sixty billion, of which the lion's share would go to the prime contractor, Shiraki. With the rest of Shiraki's primary market sectors shrinking, Thielken needed a "go" on the Yucca Mountain project, and he needed it now. The only thing that could stop full funding was if site feasibility proved unsatisfactory. Shelby's current discretion bothered him.

Thielken watched the towering Rainier Mesa engulf his view as the helicopter descended into the DOE operations camp. The thing that struck him was that everything was brown, dry, a no-mans land. And the dust: Immediately upon landing, for the sake of his air intake, and passengers, the pilot chopped the engine to abate the huge billowing brown swirl. And finally, as the ASTAR's door opened, Thielken felt the dry hot air sandblasting his face.

"Most of the testing is still being done here at Rainier Mesa," Shelby informed as they walked toward the trailers, "but the actual repository will be located under Yucca Mountain, that ridge there. Shafts will honeycomb an area of more than fifteen hundred acres inside the mountain. All total, one hundred and twelve miles of tunnel."

Shelby loved this place and his job. He couldn't help thinking how out of place his boss looked, his pressed L.L. Beans and all. Thielken, already beginning to sweat, followed Shelby to a dusty creme-colored double-joined trailer, with a satellite dish pointing skyward at its far end. Taking Shelby's cue, Thielken directed his AA to another trailer thirty yards away, its weathered sign read, "Mesa Cantina."

On the inside, Thielken found a fairly spacious office setup in three distinct areas: a somewhat large combination secretarial station and lounge occupied the front, and toward the rear were an office and adjoining work room complete with table, computer and file cabinets. Shelby introduced Thielken to his secretary, Mary, whom he credited as the one responsible for getting anything done around here. Mary knew the routine, explained the errand she had to run, and was gone.

Shelby poured two large glasses from the freestanding water bottle, pointed to a chair and handed Thielken a glass, "Out here, you can't get enough of this stuff."

"So what's up?" Thielken began.

"The second exploratory shaft dug into Yucca Mountain bore small pockets of nonwelded tuff. That's bad. We know some water will penetrate the repository and corrode the containers. That's where we count on the welded tuff to contain such an event, transmits heat well too. But this nonwelded tuff, it's too porous. Dissolved radionuclides'll run through that like a dose of salts, as my granddad use to say."

"How bad, and how long?"

"When this gets out, DOE'll shut this mother down, you can bet on that."

"Don't fuck with me, Tom," Thielken iced, "How bad?"

"Nonwelded tuff. Shit. It'd be like a sieve, radionuclides leaking right into the regional aquifer beneath, flowing down to Death Valley. Insects, birds, animals drink the valley's contaminated springs, and walla, you got the stuff in the biosphere. Also, there are geologist who think the aquifer feeds into local public water supplies."

"When?"

Shelby almost blinked at the assumption behind the question. "Well. Rainfall reaching the repository is estimated at point-zero-two inches per year. At that rate, the canisters are designed to last one thousand years. So, after a thousand years, the canisters would eventually give way to corrosion, and allow the water to dissolve the waste into liquid. Now when its mobile, its dangerous. With welded tuff, the federalies count on ten thousand more years before any dissolved waste penetrate the saturated zone and reach the aquifer. But after ten thousand years, who cares, the waste is neutralized. Of course, that's barring a major surface fracture."

"English."

Shelby stood pouring more water, then said, "With nothing to stop it after it liquefies, one thousand years. That's worst case."

"One thousand years. Goddamned planet won't be around in a thousand years. Christ, I could live with a hundred years." Thielken's stare turned stone-hard, then summed, "I've got no problem with it. Do you?"

Shelby turned away half-focusing on a plastic insulated coffee mug. Someone had once set it next to a hotplate, deforming its Shiraki logo. Tom hadn't anticipated such a question, but knew this man could be deadly ruthless with anyone who stood in his determined way. Shelby thought of his wife, of his two kids, one about to enter college. He thought of the principle of the issue and taking a stand. He thought about the consequences, his career, his family, his very life. "Yes, Mr. Thielken. I can live with those numbers."

"Good. Who else knows?"

"Bill Henry and Redbone, that's Reid Gaver. Their Shiraki men working the Yucca shaft number two. They've kept their mouths shut, except to bring the matter to my attention. I wouldn't worry. Those two know who butters their bread. They're good men, they'll keep it zipped."

Thielken stood. "Good. I'll count on your word for that. Let's get on with the tour." They walked out, picked up the AA, then headed for the Tunnel G Complex, with a few introductions along the way. Reaching the rail car at the mouth of the tunnel, Thielken looked up to read the entrance sign overhead. "We Recognize No Substitute For Safety."

That night, atop Yucca Mountain. The Apache's fast now progressed into its twenty-seventh day. The dream that brought him here was now all but a distant memory.

He had remained awake until at times unconsciousness took him, and tonight everything on the barren moonscape below appeared distorted, unreal. He began to doubt himself, and his ability to lift the veil, to pass into the void of nothingness—of oneness. He had possessed the sacred skill once, that was before entering the white man's world, some fifteen years ago now.

He was nearing the end of his one-moon quest, nearing the end of his time in his Grandfather's sacred place: an impressive appellation called Yucca Mountain—a six-mile-long ridge pushing up at its summit fifteen hundred feet above the surrounding canyons and desert flats. The mountain itself was barren: mottled, grey bedrock laced with thick veins of creme-colored crystalline calcite deposit throughout.

Standing at the summit of its weatherworn ridge during the day, under the purist of blue skies, he had seen an unbroken panorama extending more than fifty miles in every direction. Here, life was as sparse as the land was arid: drab green creosote bushes, sagebrush, and tan tufts of grass cast a patchy fuzz on distant hills. Only an Apache, he had thought, could call this unyielding land, home. Indeed, he'd seen little evidence of civilization except for activity on a dusty trace of a road cutting across the brown valley below, a road that split to convey traffic to the bases of nearby Rainier Mesa and Yucca Mountain itself.

Tonight the view, indeed the feel, was different as a full moon began its ascent on the eastern horizon. Again at the summit, the Apache sat naked in new reverence as he now listened to the ridge speak of a violent past. He could see Yucca Mountain's fault line which long ago created sheer cliffs plunging nearly a thousand feet from the summit into Solitario Canyon. Five miles to the southeast stood Busted Butte, its noble peak sheared by ancient earthquakes, its eastern side lifted several hundred feet upward. Twelve miles to the west, rising above Crater Flat valley, he observed the graying Lathrop Wells Volcano, and farther out, its three perfectly symmetrical sister cones beginning to cast their night shadows across the high valley.

He remembered the dream, the ancient scout, who had called him by his Apache name, Coyote Shadow. He remembered his Grandfather's voice of long ago, the wisdom of his instruction, "Trying creates limits, letting go creates."...*an equilibrium of existence and nonexistence...a limitless void...absolute nothingness...*" The veil removed..."

Coyote Shadow opened his eyes, and understood an eternity had passed in but a moment. He felt a deep sense of relaxation wash over him as his being transcended mere senses. He recounted the knowledge given him:

The same ancient spirit had appeared, rising before him from within the mountain, creating an open crevice. The heat from within was intense, extreme. With a tear, the spirit pointed down into the inferno, then looked directly at him, with purpose, with destiny: *Our Earth Mother is being violated here.*

Coyote Shadow stood looking at the mountain's ridge line receding in the distance. He felt himself move within the mountain and the mountain within him. He became aware of his body's mooncast shadow: taut, fit, feeling its strength fused with mind, where mind controls body, where body controls mind. Coyote Shadow looked up at the heavens and released his namesake's long primal cry of loneliness. He could leave now.

CHAPTER 13

GATHERING FORCES

Los Angeles: Central Avenue and Vernon. They called him Major, a serious O.G.—Original Gangster—claiming the Outlaw Crips. Major liked the respect he got from his gangster set and the neighborhood. Like now, as he looked around the McDonnalds quick eat. He wore the set's uniform: black sweatpants, blue T-shirt, a vintage black Oakland Raiders cap, and hundred and fifty dollar Nike shoes. Over the uniform, he wore a heavy link-chain gold necklace called a "Turkish rope." The uniform got the respect, the "ropes" got the attention.

Lace watched Major finish the remaining fries. Lace was an Outlaw Crip homie and wondered how Major could be so calm. Tonight—early morning—they and five others would hit a national guard armory, their biggest mission yet. The two guards at the gate would die. Major would handle them. They didn't expect more than two or three inside the warehouse either. Might have to kill 'em all, Lace thought, watching

Major lick ketchup from his fingers. Major was down, the downest he'd ever seen.

"We outta here," Major announced. Lace, Major and two others headed for the door. Major looked crazy at the full-time security guard, a clear challenge. The young rent-a-cop looked away.

Into a hot humid night, they stepped through the glass doors onto the fractured sidewalk. Major groused, "Fuckin' para-pig." Lace laughed, then acknowledged Major's mental conquest holding up a high five. Lace expected a confirming slap, but saw instead Major's left eye turn red, then felt the red spray of—

Crack!

Lace watched in horror as a hole larger than a baseball emerged from the left side of Major's head. Then, like startled predators, Lace and the others were gone.

"First Tiger Lilly over at Rollin' Sixties," G-Rake went on. "Last night, Outlaw Crips get it, and Major at that. He O.G. He bad." Most of the set were here in their adopted South Central L.A. hangout this Friday afternoon. They called themselves the AK Gangsters Crips.

"News say they find a shell, got Major's name on it."

"Just like the others. We talkin' major escalation in war over there."

"And East Coast Six-Deuce. The baddest rep there, he get it too," Cage added, "Shit's happenin'." Cage, like most of the rest, wore some variation of gray cords, faded black sweatshirt, and expensive running shoes. Above the designer sunglasses, each wore a blue baseball cap sporting the initials AK embroidered in white; massive gold chains and rings for each finger were the norm. Some wore ear rings, mostly the shape of a Cadillac emblem inlaid with sapphire and diamonds. Cage himself wore a Presidents-model Rolex on his left wrist.

"Ain't war," El Cid finally spoke. All eyes turned. G-Rake looked over at El Cid regarding one cool dude there. Raised just east of Inglewood, El Cid talked the talk and walked the walk just like any of the local gangbangin' brothers. It always amazed G-Rake that El Cid, an Essay—Hispanic—commanded such deep respect where all the other homeboys were brothers. But of them all, in an unnerving sort of way, El Cid was the ghetto star, with one very serious rep.

El Cid, himself, presented a look matching his rep. His eyes were flat, reptilian, hooded liked a cold snake. Tattooed under the outer corner of his left eye were two black teardrops. His brown Hispanic head was shaved, all giving the appearance of life on the line. And never was it clear whose.

The AK Gangsters hung out in an abandoned taped-windowed storefront on Western Avenue, just off Imperial Highway. Their AK letters, shaded and shaped, superimposed over the form of an AK-47 assault rifle, dominated the graffiti. Everywhere up and down the street it proclaimed the neighborhood: "This is AK Gangsters Crips' 'hood." Several of the buildings along the street looked as if a bomb exploded from within, windows blown outward, heavy streaks of carbon splayed across exterior walls. The kind of street where kids stand on corners watching time pass.

El Cid continued, "You take down some S.O.B., you want 'em to know it's comin'. You wanna see the mother's eyes. Even if just a drive-by, he know it comin' and who doin' it." He took an experienced drag off the cigarette. "This Name Dropper, buster's no Crip. Blood either."

"Who then?"

"Don't know, loc. All I knows is we gotta be down for the buster. We got firepower, we be down."

"Ye-eeeeeh. Magic briefcase take care of that. You down, El Cid. You down for the 'hood." Several raised their hands displaying the AK Gangsters' gang sign. They each possessed AK-47s, and any other weapon they desired, especially handguns. That was because of El Cid's good luck.

Three months ago El Cid had to get his anger out. The day his girl dumped him, he went out in broad daylight looking for a fight, anything to get her of his mind. He was walking across Century Boulevard, when her voice began scratching inside his head—and there it was. A taxi stopped for the light. He just did it. Smoked the cabbie, and the passenger with the hand-cuffed briefcase. Anything worth handcuffing, he had thought, must be worth having. With his AK-47 on full auto, he pummeled away at the dead courier's forearm until it fell away. Slipped the briefcase cuffs passed the bloody stub and walked away.

El Cid always kept contacts. Unlike most of the 'bangers dying over a street they didn't own, El Cid had other ventures, grander goals. He had relationships with companies, very lucrative companies, relationships with people with foreign interests. As it turned out, the right ones. Recognizing that he might have stumbled onto something, El Cid went to Abdullah. Abdullah took two of the documents and said he'd get back. One week later, El Cid and Abdullah struck a deal: In return for the "golden briefcase" and its contents, El Cid received forty thousand dollars worth of any weapons desired, and fifty thousand dollars in cash. His set got the weapons, only El Cid knew about the cash. And only G-Rake knew about Abdullah.

El Cid now stood looking at his reflection in a taped storefront window. He concentrated on the two tattooed teardrops under his left eye, then smiled at his good luck. He refocused, now looking through the glass, admiring his pride parked by the curb. It was his bomber, a fully restored cherried-out '64 Chevy Impala, made possible thanks to Abdullah. Luck. He wondered what kind and where it would turn up next.

They called him *Shiro Kage*, the White Shadow. His house stood in the lower mountains of central Hokkaido, Japan's northernmost large island. Although the house looked very average, two things were not. The forty-acre wooded land that surrounded it was, by Japanese standards, expansive. Also, closer inspection of the house revealed that no expense was spared in its construction. The retreat epitomized the austere taste of the ancient warrior class, a class which scorned ostentatious displays of wealth.

As the powerfully-built assassin stood from meditation, so stood the product of the mountain mystics, spiritual ancestors of the ninja some nine hundred years ago. In that tradition, *Shiro Kage* was a product of his upbringing, his training.

At the age of five, his master turned children's games into exercise, particularly balance and agility. At age nine, body conditioning started using yoga-like movements known as *junan taiso*. Around the *dojo* training hall, jumping, rolling, and exercises brought about muscle limberness and joint flexibility.

In his developing teen years, he learned about the ninja's secret fighting art *ninjutsu*: he learned the skills of *taijutsu* (unarmed combat) including *koppojutsu* (bone-breaking) and *koshijutsu* (muscle and organ destruction); *shinobi ri* (silent invisible movement); *tantojutsu* (blade fighting); and *hojutsu* (firearms work). In addition to the many and varied weapons, he learned the use of subtlety and illusion, mainstays of *ninjutsu*. In his late teens, he developed the skills of acting, disguise, practical psychology, hypnotism, chemistry, and medicine. He learned even more specialized combat techniques. Above all, he developed a sense of duty, learning *always* to complete an assignment—without fail.

Before he was twenty, he had reconciled himself with his own mortality. Only then, possessing his philosophy and deadly skills, was he fully prepared to navigate in the dark world of the elite, the assassin.

Today, for travel, he wore a blue business suit, tailored to downplay his powerfully-built body. His dark eyes were somewhat large possessing little of an epicanthic fold characteristic of Japanese; they burned fierce from a fire within, yet were strangely disarming as they displayed an absolute assurance that comes with competence, the competence of a professional at the pinnacle of his career. Over his left eye, his forehead possessed a highly unusual scar: an undulating line, like a heartbeat on a CRT, but instead of tracing across horizontally, it traced vertically upward. Today, the scar would not be seen, expertly masked behind applied makeup.

The assassin looked down at the crate officially marked for transit. At the irony, he allowed himself the ghost of a smile. In his mid-thirties, this assignment would test his skill, would test his resourcefulness, would test his place on the Inner Path. For this was his most challenging target yet. Within seven weeks, he would kill the President of the United States.

His Apache name was Coyote Shadow, his American birth certificate read "Teal Coro." Teal Coro walked down the concrete steps of the University of Nevada-Las Vegas J. R. Dickinson Library building. His steps were those of a man in control, powerful, graceful, quiet. Power was the word one's mind unconsciously filed when they met Teal Coro. He had deep clear brown eyes, eyes of a powerful cat, always alert, always aware. He wore a somewhat long, defiant crew cut, resisting casual attempts to finger back into a presentable look. To many, his facial features, plus the flint-black hair, possessed an Italian bearing: solid nose and chin, a good looking man. There was a reason for that.

Before Teal Coro attended UNLV, he had, all his life, lived around Arizona's northwest canyon territory. His people never lived on a reservation. He had known no parents, and for some reason never asked why. All he had known as a child was his Apache Grandfather, a descendant of the Hualapais Apache, a scout and later a shaman.

His other grandfather was Italian. He'd met the man once, a good looking high spirited man who spoke many European languages, as well as Apache. His European grandfather had told his grandmother that he had a University degree from some European University, and left books to prove it. Books Coro read. Asked how he came to the land of the Great Canyon, the Italian made vague reference to his part in a failed attempt to overthrow a European despot and his ruthless government. Finding the American Southwest to his liking, he settled in, dying when he was but thirty-two.

It was his Apache Grandfather who gave him his Apache

name, Coyote Shadow, for Teal Coro possessed the stealth, cunning, and the courage of the canyon's coyote. Back then the two of them were inseparable as Grandfather taught him the coveted skills of the Apache scout, inseparable as he began to learn of the shaman's way and its power, inseparable as the old one died. Inseparable.

Looking out at the library's courtyard, table and chairs scattered about, brought back memories: the culture shock, basketball mania, more knowledge from distant peoples, knowledge he was determine to acquire, and that he did: Magma Cum Laude, Masters, Political Science...and more, much more in an abbreviated career with his country's Federal Bureau of Investigation.

"Excuse me." From behind, a harried student's voice broke the daydream into his now new reality. A reality that had just printed itself onto his searching mind. It would have been nice to have a CD ROM reference search computer when he was a grad student here. But still, nice to have it now, entering in the keyword search: "Yucca Mountain." Within three seconds, he had found twenty-three references, the most recent having to do with the Department of Energy. It seemed, he discovered, the DOE had chosen Yucca Mountain as its primary site for all the nation's spent nuclear fuel and irradiated materials, a nuclear graveyard. "Finally, a decent burial," one article had said.

Now it made sense, the vision: the ancient Indian scout, and his message up there on the mountain's summit, Grandfather's sacred place. The scout spoke of man out of balance with nature, on Grandfather's sacred ground. Teal Coro's heart still spoke true, and now he knew. He must find a way to stop the planned desecration of sacred Earth Mother.

But how? he wondered, as he strolled over to the large evergreen, towering over the smaller olive trees scattered about. A whiff of a breeze rustled its leaves. It was under this tree in the spring of his junior year that he met Serena, and knew at that moment she would be his wife. She knew it too, communicated in her almost vulnerable brown Indian eyes amid the proud lines of her lean face. Her hair, black silk.

She hadn't wanted him join the FBI. Why had he accepted the on-campus interview? Why had he accepted the next interview in Washington? Why did he accept their offer? It was clearer now: Back then arriving at this University, he had somehow left *Coyote Shadow* back in Arizona. In the white man's world, he'd lost the greater perspective.

She had hated the Washington beltway life, she'd hated the artificial people, she'd hated the hours. The hours…It wasn't just him, he knew, but through him, the entire Apache Nation was being measured. He toughed it out, he would never quit, shame his people, validate the white man's expectations. He'd done well, though he was, and always had been, a loner: such was his training as an Apache scout, a most important tribal position only a century ago. In the end, it was his skills in survival, resourcefulness, and ultimately, shooting, that attracted attention. To his FBI superiors, he was a natural sniper; to himself, he reasoned: Does not the coyote kill the snake to protect its young? Does not the assassin kill his country's enemies to protect…*it had seemed so clear then.*

Ten years and a promising career…and then the end. The FBI's investigation of the Japanese mafia, *yakuza*, taking hold here in America. Coro was the agent in charge. After a lengthy investigation, he nailed the yakuza leaders. And *yakuza* got revenge. He quit the Bureau three weeks later.

Now Teal Coro stood surveying the eastern sky. Since returning from his fast on Yucca Mountain, Coro had again begun to practice the ways of his Grandfather, regaining his keen sense of awareness, learning to again trust his body sense. It was that body sense that suddenly struck discord, as he looked eastward. A far East. An ancient East.

CHAPTER 14
PHOTO OP

"Hey, we could use a shooter like that on our side," USMC Lieutenant Colonel Judd T. Coleman said after hearing an on-the-hour new report. After the weather man confirmed another sweltering August day, the radio continued with its light-rock Sunday afternoon programming.

Westin had to agree. While L.A. officialdom were appropriately horrified and "applied all resources possible" to get the "Name Dropper," Westin thought Coleman's comment reflected a more prevalent sentiment. Westin sat in a lawn chair watching Coleman put steaks on the charcoal grill, wondering why black men seemed to keep muscle tone with apparently little effort. The two men were in the modest backyard of Coleman's Alexandria home, and for a few moments, they were alone while Sally prepared salad inside.

"How many more trips to Japan?" Coleman wanted to get business handled before his wife returned. With only six weeks to get the NIQE-based Weapons Report done, John was still very much behind.

"After tomorrow morning, one more, mid-September. Got a draft worked up. I'll leave it with you if you like." It was a bone, albeit a skimpy one.

"Damn straight. And that last trip, John, I'm riding shotgun." Coleman ratcheted up his best don't-you-just-love-me smile, stood and turned the seared steaks.

"Fine, Judd. Now it's my turn," John leveled. "You guys know where Beth is." Coleman grimaced. "So what am I, a fucking spy or something?"

"Look, John, I can't—"

"The fuck you can't. Jap's got Beth, don't they?"

"Where do you get off? Already said more than I ever should have." Coleman stood spinning a half-turn looking skyward, than back. "Do you have any fucking idea the position you put me in?"

Westin stood, himself pacing. The answer was yes, and right now he wanted to grab something and break it.

Coleman drew a heavy breath, releasing it as if cigarette smoke, looked at John, then lowered his voice, "Sit down John. If this goes beyond—"

John threw up his arms submitting his promise. Both men sat, Coleman collecting his thoughts.

Judd T. Coleman knew how Westin felt. He too had hired on to push bayonets, not paper. But in the last twenty years, he'd done his share of both: When he wore his uniform, a pair of Jump (Recon) Wings headed an impressive array of campaign ribbons and medals, including Silver Star—testing his courage was no longer an issue for him. Yet in situation like this, courage took an entirely different form.

His extended tour in Washington had taught him well. How and when to take risks. When to distance yourself from a losing cause. The lesson he'd yet to fully internalize, was to separate the job from human emotion. Yes, what he was about to do did have a certain logic: get the Japanese "chip" off John's shoulder, at least long enough to get this goddamned report out. But it was something else. Even with Westin's penchant for detours, Coleman liked the man on some gut level. Something to do with country and being a player. Because of that, he wanted Westin to get a sense of the truth, without his compromising classified STAIRCASE information.

Coleman reached over cranking up the radio's volume for privacy. He told John about the Los Angeles gang incident last May, the stolen briefcase, and its contents—"a blueprint for the deadliest toxin the world had yet developed." He told him of an Iranian radical group's effort to develop the "toxin," and of their kidnapping scientific experts to help them do it.

"What I'm saying, John, it's not a Jap thing. So get off it with them. Just do your job, okay?"

"Why Beth?" John asked fingering back errant strands of hair. He needed a haircut.

"Computer expertise, maybe to cure virused computers. Just not sure. Believe me, the man's working it hard."

"How long to develop?" John asked knowing the answer would give the upper bounds on her life.

Coleman hesitated, then answered, "With outside talent, CIA estimates three to four months."

"Which means?"

"Worst case, six weeks from now." October first.

"I'm going to find her, Judd." The steaks were starting to burn.

"*We'll* get Beth and the others out, John." Coleman's voice hardened with each word, "*You, mister*, will do what your President has asked you to do. And that's the weapons report. Is that clear?"

The veins in Coleman's neck had stiffened. John responded, "Tell you what, Judd. You keep me updated on Beth's situation, and I'll get you that report on time, guaranteed to stiffen their britches. Okay?"

Coleman shook his head slowly. "John, you keep running red lights, sooner or later you're going to get hit."

"Deal. Say, you keep a fire extinguisher around here?"

As the now dusty black Mercedes 560 SEL approached

the remote building on the outskirts of Esfahan, Abu Hakim sat deep in its rear seat, and not in a good mood. There was no question now, FIA had not only failed, but had disappeared. The Hanford team, the Egyptian freighter *Ruh al-Asr*, its crew and FIA members, all vanished from Allah's earth. But by far, the tragic loss was in loosing Safi Kahurak, his personal friend, FIA's most capable leader.

For two years, poisoning America's fresh water supply had been Hakim's dream. He conceived it, planned it, and finally with the proper backing and resources, initiated its execution. *Only to see it fail?*

But the more his enemies moved to thwart him, the more it increased his resolve. Not the Zionist, not the American infidels, not even Iran's current weak-kneed government would stop him. For who stops Muhammad's *jihad*. No one.

Indeed Allah now showed another way to strike at his infidel enemies. A way so efficient, so eloquent, so...final. The briefcase. The key to the American genetic virus called STAIRCASE was now in his hands.

But with the failure of Kahurak's mission, he felt the need to press, to accelerate the virus's development. The first virus targeted for Jews. While unleashing STAIRCASE on the Jews, at the same time he needed a batch for the Caucasians, just in case the West got righteous again.

But Hakim had a problem. His trusted friend, Mohammed Rashid, was right, Shafii and his lab were clearly behind schedule. As yet, he was unsure of the reason. Today, he would find out.

As the Mercedes pulled to a stop behind the lead car, six of Hakim's personal bodyguards joined the lab's security personal cordoning a tight perimeter around the grounds. Hakim, himself, was out of the car before Shafii could reach it. To Shafii the hard weathered lines in his leader's face seemed deeper still. Not good. They greeted each other with a traditional embrace, then Hakim spoke, asking but one question, "Which of the scientists is the least productive?"

Shafii's dark eyes reflexed away, then sought to regain

composure for a direct answer. "The one called Bob."

With Shafii in tow, Hakim turned and entered the building. "Which is he?" Hakim commanded. Shafii pointed to a rather obese man, thinning hair, already sweating profusely at the eleven o'clock morning hour. Hakim motioned for the frightened fat man to approach, then pulled a Browning HiPower from his belt holster. When the shaking man was but five feet away, Hakim raised the pistol firing a nine millimeter round into the man's fleshy head.

Beth heard herself let out a yelp, then chastised herself. She wondered if she'd be next as she focused on the executioner's eyes, totally devoid of empathy. Shock turned to disgust. At her helplessness, for doing nothing. Disgust turned to surprise as she became aware of her feelings toward this little man hiding secure behind a coward's gun. She wanted him dead, and at that moment she thought she could do it herself.

Hakim stood watching the remaining five scientists. They each diverted their eyes, except the woman. There was defiance there. It made him want to explore, to tame, but that wasn't his purpose at the moment. He'd seen Colonel Rashid look at her with interest. Well Allah had nothing to say about fucking infidels, did He, so who was he to interfere.

"Listen to me," Hakim demanded breaking the uneasy silence. "We have gone to great trouble and expense to bring you here. You are here to help us achieve our goals. It should be clear to you by now that we do not have time for those who do not cooperate fully." Hakim signaled two bodyguards, then waited the half-minute it took for them to drag Bob Watt's body from the room.

"If you cooperate with Shafii and his team, I promise that you will live and in time be set free. If you chose to impede our progress, I promise you a slow death. Is this clear?"

Following the quiet, Hakim exited the door waving Shafii into the privacy of his Mercedes. "I will get you more scientists, Shafii, just make a list of what you need. Is there anything else?"

Even with what just happened and the resolute eyes he now faced, Shafii decided to speak his mind. "Abu Hakim, all the living Nobel Prize winners in the world will not complete the project." He paused, letting Hakim watch him flick a spider from the leg of his trousers, then drawing more courage, he continued, "We still do not have the proper facilities. We need a clean room, free from the environment, free from dust. Free from spiders. We still do not have all the equipment requested. This place is not adequate."

Silence. Shafii pressed on anyway.

"Ali, we must have the government's secret biological warfare lab complex at Tajrish. It is the only way to create the Jewish targeted virus." Shafii was surprised by Hakim's tranquil response.

"I will see what I can do, Shafii." Just maybe the time to act was now, Hakim allowed himself to consider. *I think yes, Allah willing.*

It was afternoon now, four hours since Abu Hakim had left. All Beth could think of was how to get out of there, her rational side continuing to caution against desperation. Indeed Hakim's object lesson had her and the others on edge, except maybe Dr. Dech, Beth noticed.

The more Beth Storey looked at Dr. Dech, the more he began to look like their Iranian captors, especially with his dark slicked-back hair and goatee. At the moment, Dech sat with a guard near the door, smoking a slim, black, foul-smelling cigarette. She had reason to despise Dech, but foremost was the way he cozied up to his captors, seeking to curry favor. And sometimes, she was sure, at the expense of the others—like maybe Bob this morning.

"Dr Death" knew the most about STAIRCASE, and well he should, Beth knew. He was the only one of the now five of them who had actually worked on STAIRCASE back in the U.S. Government's Center for Viral Disease located in Fort Collins, Colorado. Two years now.

A week ago, she'd asked Dech if the Iranian's could target

a race gene with STAIRCASE. He delighted in explaining his subject of expertise. Actually, he had said, there is no race gene, per se. What we call a race turns out to be nothing more than a common set of physical features, traits, and characteristics. For any given "race," this common set is well known. For instance, to target a set of Negro characteristics, look in the dictionary, which he did: skin pigmentation: dark brown to black; shape of nose: broad and flat; lips: everted; and hair: short, thick, curly. Once the dominate characteristics are selected, he had said, then each gene responsible for their presence is identified. That's the tricky part. For instance, in the case for everted lips, that gene is located on the long arm of chromosome five; that's one of the forty-six chromosomes that carry the genetic blueprint.

No doubt in her mind, Dr. Death was a menace to the planet. One of those scientist who didn't care how his work was applied, just as long as he was able to continue with it.

Of the other three captives, she had gotten to know two of them fairly well: Jamil and Bill Sanborne. Bob hadn't associated much with anyone; all she knew was that he had had a family in Cambridge.

She looked across the makeshift laboratory at Jamil Velayati standing over the spinning centrifuge. Jamil was by birth an Iranian, a slim, fine-featured man of chestnut skin; coupled with a slight slouch, the image conveyed academic rather than scientist. After the fall of the Shah, Jamil's family fled the Islamic revolution, taking residence in Paris. There he studied microbiology, a subject for which he had a natural affinity. He specialized further, becoming one of the world's first molecular geneticists; his brilliance was rewarded in 1991, the Nobel Prize.

It was from Jamil that Beth came to understand what was happening. Jamil knew the history, the current politics, and spoke Farsi, useful in understanding their current situation.

It was the *tondro*, the hardliners, he had informed, that kidnapped them. Not the Islamic Revolutionary government. Over the weeks, he had seen *tondro* leaders come and go from their remote facility, but it was Abu Hakim that scared him. Beth now had a much greater appreciation for Jamil's warning, "Never make Hakim angry with you." Hakim had a reputation for being exceedingly ruthless and a staunch anti-Zionist, a hate second only to a greater Satan, the American infidels who supported them. Jamil knew this project would serve one purpose, and one purpose only—*jihad*, armed struggle against the infidels. If successful, it would be the ultimate victory of Islam over the unbelievers.

The other man, Bill Sanborne, had arrived a week before Beth. A rangy, long-limbed perfectionist from Virginia Polytech, Sanborne was an oddity here. He was a missile payload specialist from Paxton International. At first, he'd thought their intent was to deliver biological or chemical warheads. Then, after he discovered the true nature of the project, he wondered why he was there. Delivery by a handshake was just as effective, and much cheaper.

"Break. Ten minutes," announced the guard in broken English. While the others headed for the bathroom, Beth approached Sanborne seated at a 1950s-like "contemporary" sofa away from the other guards. "Think they know where we are?" Beth asked irrelevantly, pushing back strands of hair.

"They have eyes but don't know where to look."

"Why not?"

"First of all, they probably don't know we're in Iran. And second, if they did, what would they key off of?"

"You mean, like patterns?" Sanborne nodded. "Footprints like airstrips, silos, and what-not?" Bill continued nodding affirmative. "How big a footprint?"

"If it's a known pattern and a clear day, six inches. Something unknown, to get a photo interpreter's attention would need to be twenty feet at least."

"You mean we make a readable footprint, and they get the message." It was a question.

"Well, yeah. Iran's a priority for the photo-op crowd. I know the pass-by schedules."

CHAPTER 15

WAR STORIES

John Westin emerged from Narita Airport's baggage and customs clearing area with ease. He now stood next in line to exchange dollars into yen. "Mr. Barr wishes to know the time, Mr. Westin," came a voice from behind. The English was quite good, yet unmistakably from a Japanese.

Westin turned, the man was surprisingly tall, his own height, about six feet, more lanky though. Thick, but short-cut black hair, trim mustache, and sharp features were all but noticeable against friendly disarming eyes. The man pointed at his watch. Westin responded, "four-fifteen," then stepped up to the exchange window. There, he felt a hand in his coat pocket. He'd only met Jordan Barr, the CIA's DDO, once but somehow this method of communication seemed in keeping. Receiving his exchange he proceeded to a toilet, then read the note.

He emerged scanning, printing faces in his mind. He proceeded to buy a ticket, then boarded the next Kiesei

Skyliner train for Tokyo. He sat down near the door, carry-on under his knees, still watchful…*There, with the newspaper, scared eyebrow.* From the window's reflection, Westin watched the man sit center coach. Westin waited for the conductor's warning call, then looked back at the man. His paper instantly raised to avoid. *Yep, that's him!* Westin listened for the final call, then grabbed his bag and slipped through closing doors. Through the accelerating windows he watched the man lower his paper and smiled as he watched composure turn to panic.

"Very nice," came the same voice, "Come, I'll explain later." Westin followed the tall Japanese man back into the South Wing terminal and on out to the adjacent parking lot. Once on the Higashi-Kanto Expressway, he spoke, "My name is Shuji Okada. I work for Marshall Douglas. I used Mr. Barr's name because I understand the two of you have met."

"Back there, who was that man?"

"I do not know. He picked you up on your previous trip, two days before you returned to the States. Where are you staying?"

"Tokyo, the Shinbashi Daiichi. Your English sure is good. How long you been following me?"

Shuji Okada had good reason for his fluent English. In the 1982 his father, an executive with Honda Motor Company, was sent to Marysville, Ohio, to run Honda's new American venture. Okada attended Stanford University and eventually fell in love with unstructured life in America. CIA recruiters appealed to his more daring side, and made him an offer he couldn't refuse. "What's your schedule?" he asked his left-side passenger.

"I'm here for ten days now, and back again in mid-September. Tomorrow I see Takara, CEO of Misawa Group." Okada returned a look. "Then I tag up with U.S.N. Commander Stan Turner. We'll spend a few days at Udon Software in Nagoya, guy's name is Setaka. Then a visit to Yokosuka to see Air SDF General Kamikura; we'll board the *Yukikaze*, a destroyer equipped with technology I've been sent here to assess." Westin decided to try again, "Again, Okada-san, who was that: *yakuza, ninja*?"

"*Yakuza* are Japanese mafia. They have no interest in you, unless paid to kill you. *Ninja*. There are no *ninja* as Hollywood would have you believe. Today's *ninja* are teachers and businessmen, and study *ninjutsu* for developing personal power. There are assassins here, as in every society; the most lethal are those trained in the old *ninja* ways, the ways of infiltration and assassination. They say there is nothing on earth more adept at finding and killing its prey—a thousand ways of death."

Coleman had told Westin about his having a guardian angel looking after him in Japan. Coleman indicated the angel may or may not make direct contact. Well he just did. It was his safety, the Washington crowd worried about, after his involvement uncovering Japan's secret NIQE-based weapons program. No one knew if Japan actually knew of his involvement in that little ditty; but since his current assignment was so important to the President, NSC, and the Joint Chiefs, the powers opted for a little insurance—now sitting to his right.

At the moment, Westin didn't mind it either. It seemed that Japan wasn't a very good place for the Westin family to visit. Certainly not very healthy. There was Kojima's attack and his own brush with death. And back in 1946, his dad's accident resulting in his death. On that score, while in Japan, John had decided to dig deeper. He'd investigate post war records, trying to piece together his dad's tour of duty here, trying to prove or disprove the rape. Either way, he had to know.

Westin was chewing on Okada's answer as the expressway became a four lane road and the first traffic light illuminated yellow. Coming to a stop, Westin heard a loud speaker blaring from a white van at the right, waiting for the cross-street light to change. He asked about it.

"Election. Every three years Japan elects half of its House of Councillors, this year on October fourteenth. Seven weeks, I'm afraid, before peace returns to the neighborhoods." The van accelerated into the intersection.

Crash! A car on the expressway had failed to stop in time. The two vehicles deflected away from each other. Westin watched, incredulous, as the responsible car, sporting a newly smashed left-front fender, hesitated, regained composure, then accelerated away. "Shit d'you see that! Hit-and-run. What an asshole."

"In Japan, that motorist is not an asshole," Okada stated flatly.

Like he told Tanner the day after Kojima's attack, anything to save face: that man fleeing the scene saved face by avoiding blame—while the injured bled to death. And to reinforce it all, in Japanese courts, the man responsible gets no consideration for sticking around to help. Just the opposite in America. A good reminder, Westin mentally noted, to adjust his thinking while in Japan. *When in Rome...*

Okada pulled the four-door Toyota up next to a parked cab. "He will take you the rest of the way. Just remember, Mr. Westin, you are being followed. I will find out why, but in the meantime, please be careful."

"One other matter, Takara-san." Shimizu, the fox, watched Udon Software's NIQE director, Setaka, work up courage. Setaka had already presented his progress on Takara's special NIQE projects. Things were looking up. Yet it was obvious to Shimizu that the frail timid man was clearly nervous. About something else, something about to be said. They were in Takara's penthouse office atop the Tokyo's New Misawa Building, the evening sky still bright.

Setaka glanced nervously over at the fox. "I have nothing I wish to hide from Shimizu-san," spoke Takara. "What is it you have to say?"

"It concerns Kojima-san's death." Setaka avoided direct eye contact, preferring to catch Takara's reflection in the highly polished ebony-surface of his desk. Studying the reflection, Setaka saw the edges of Takara's mouth deepen. This was taking more courage than Setaka had imagined. "There is something you should know."

"Yes." The tone was guarded.

"I do not believe your *kobun* committed *suppuku*."— ritual suicide.

"Yes."

"I have a story to tell." Setaka's mind would never forget that night hearing Kojima's horrid story. Half-focused on Takara's image within the desk's polished ebony, Setaka began:

"Three days before Kojima-san's death, the two of us were in a small basement bar somewhere in the Shinjuku district of Tokyo. He was in a strange mood, his eyes different, sterile, lusterless. At first, I thought it was because of his uncle's having just passed away. It wasn't."

As Setaka told the story, his mind relived that night, and his listening to Kojima's even, measured tone:

"Setaka-san, remember Numazu?" Kojima asked his old friend. "Remember the B-29's, and how they found us again? Setaka, when your family left for Kofu, I missed you, more than anything in my entire life then or since." Setaka echoed the sentiment with a nod and an uttered sigh. "It was even harder after the war. If it were not for my grandmother's vegetable garden, I think we would have starved.

"Setaka, something happened after you left. It was a horrible thing. A thing until now kept secret, even to you. It was August, almost a year after the war's end, occupation troops were everywhere, even in Numazu. The American soldiers reveled in their glory and our submissiveness. I was only five, and remember being very frightened in their presence.

"It was late evening, a rainy Saturday, August third, when three American soldiers came to my grandmother's house. We would see soldiers patrolling during the day, but usually not that far out and never after dark. My mother had just returned from the city only minutes earlier; they must have followed her home. They were loud and drunk, banging on the door. It seemed that my mother knew one of them, a tall fit man with close-cropped light brown hair. My grandmother was in the back bedroom, weak, not feeling well. I was in the front room and watched them barge in not bothering to remove their muddy boots. My mother was respectful in pleading with the one she seemed to know. She wanted them to leave. I knew something was very wrong, and now know that it must have been very difficult for her, a Japanese woman, to stand up to these men, especially three giant conquering *gaijin*.

"The larger one moved in behind her; he had thick black hair, a bear—yes, like a bear. All of a sudden, he grabbed her arm. She struggled, kicked and bit him on the hand. The tall American GI laughed brashly, then grabbed her frail body, and pushed her down onto the *tatami*. In the back room, in a weak, crackling voice, my grandmother began yelling, screaming. The third soldier quickly entered her room and kicked her hard across the face; It was as if in slow motion, her head bouncing down and off the soft *futon*. Where I sat on the floor, I could see her still body, her eyes staring at me—eyes filled with fear, anger…disgust. I cowered down." Kojima grasped his glass with both hands and swallowed hard. "The third man returned; he had closed the *shoji* screen, but not my grandmother's judging thoughts. This third man had unbelievably angry eyes, a flat face that seemed…Oriental.

"None of the three men seemed concerned with my presence. I did not think my legs would move…as if a dream." Setaka's eye contact with the waitress quickly brought two more to the table. Kojima stubbed out the cigarette's luminous source, then spoke distantly as if to a listener inside the glass before him.

"The tall American tears off my mother's gray *kimono*. She lays back perfectly still while the vulgar beast removes her underclothes. Her eyes are closed. Her lips move as if repeating a chant. The American pulls down his pants, and stands over her with his erect penis in his hand. It is huge and I am somewhat awed by the sight. He spreads her legs and rams it in. I cannot close my eyes. Her body tenses, her face writhes with pain. His smelly clothes, his filthy body, a grotesque creature pressing against my mother's pure blanched skin. Strange, at that moment my mother became even more beautiful to me, in spite..." Kojima paused for a minute, then took a stiff shot.

"The big bear and the smaller Oriental man meanwhile find a bottle of *sake* in the living room cabinet. It is a very old and decorative bottle, my grandmother had kept for many, many years. The two barbarians take turns drinking from its open mouth.

"The tall American finishes with my mother. The bear moves in to take his turn. My mother's face is stoic. He is sweaty. The savage grunts, pants, and does not last long. The third man's eyes show rage, yet he does not touch my mother. I sense that if he had he would not have been able to stop himself from killing...from killing her, from killing me, from killing...the world. He throws the precious *sake* bottle through the closed *shoji* screen, ripping its rice paper, the bottle landing in pieces beside my grandmother's *face*. Before they leave, the bear grabs jewelry, treasures of our ancient ancestors. He laughs derisively, then kicks me in the ribs. They leave...but not their muddy tracks. Not the nightmare."

Two more rounds arrived. Setaka felt he needed a brace almost as much as Kojima. He thought he knew Kojima, thought he knew pain, but this was deeper than anything. Kojima wiped beads of sweat from his forehead, then intoned:

"My grandmother lives in my head. Her words haunt me still, they echo at this very moment, 'Your mother is disgraced,' her voice says to me, 'and like your father is probably dead. You must avenge, you must kill the American and his family. You must save face for the Kojima family and its ancestors. You will, Atsuko, for it is your destiny!' Those were the words I heard each and every day she was alive. On her day of death, she added four more words: 'Promise me you will,' her voice filled with as much disgust as anger. I gave her my word." Kojima reached into his pocket and onto the tabletop, tossed a GI dog tag. The sharp clatter broke the room's quiet, and Setaka's mind-lock.

"Is this the soldier?"

Kojima answered, "I found it the next day outside my grandmother's house near the front steps. It could be no one else. I showed it to my grandmother. I remember with one eye swollen shut, she took it into her hand and burned those words into my brain. Earlier that same day, my mother had quietly packed some things and left. I never saw her again. As you know, we found out my father died in a bombing raid in Nagoya, and when I was nine my grandmother died."

Kojima's mood suddenly lightened as he picked up his half-full glass and said, "As you know, my uncle wanting a son adopted and brought me to Tokyo. We can thank the fates for that, my friend, for bringing us together again as freshmen at our Tokyo University." The two men clinked their glasses.

"Why do you tell me this now?"

"My uncle. When I arrived at his home in Tokyo, he saw how consumed I was with the dog tag and my grandmother's curse. He seemed to imply that she was a little crazy, but that did not help. After a while he took it from me, and said, 'So much hate is not healthy for a growing young man. My task, young Kojima,' my uncle said, 'is to make your body and mind strong so you can choose the path for yourself, lest the path choose you. Do you have the will to make the necessary sacrifices to attain strength, to attain mastery? Then I will keep this dog tag of yours, and you will receive it when my task is complete.'"

The fine whiskey chasing so much beer was beginning to take its metered toll. Setaka had watched Kojima's mood shift throughout the one-sided conversation from somber to now melancholy. "Now, Setaka, to answer your question. From my uncle's estate I received a box. It is a very old box and shows the wear of caring hands. It is made of mahogany, thirty by forty centimeters square. On its top is centered a hand-painted ring encircling a three-leaf clover, all painted black on the dark wood.

Three weeks ago I opened this box. Aside from my uncle's important papers, the box contained two items. Items finally revealing to me the path I must take. The first you have before you, the American dog tag. The second was a letter addressed to me. In that letter my uncle wrote,

My work is done. You have strength. Your body and your mind are one; listen to them both, always. You have your duty. You have your will. Now you have means.

Kojima picked up the dog tag. "I am the oldest son." Setaka witnessed Kojima's mood once again shift, stiffening to bitterness. Kojima held the dog tag at eye level as if inspecting for imperfections in a precious stone, then continued, "Setaka, I hired a private investigator. The American is dead. But his son lives. He has the same name."

"What will you do?"

Kojima answered: "It is not *what* I will do, Setaka. It is *when*. And the Fates indeed smile on me. This man is in Japan as we speak."

Kojima mockingly read the name from the metal plate; a name with a serial number, a name that now could be traced, a name echoing from his grandmother's deathbed ever scratching at the inside of his skull. A name that would free his blighted soul. The name stamped into the metal read, "Westin, J.K."

Setaka's small eyes slowly refocused to the polished surface of Takara's ebony desk. Takara's reflected face had gone ashen. The story told, Setaka fell silent.

Finally, after what seemed minutes to Setaka, Takara spoke stiffly, "I will look into it. Thank you for coming." Setaka quickly bowed and left, passing bodyguards in the outside anteroom.

John Kreuger Westin. Takara felt energy drain and rise simultaneously. It was the first time in forty-eight years that he felt off balance. And, he would see this man tomorrow morning. "Shimizu-san. Take what you've just heard and look into Kojima's death. Make it thorough. If anyone gets in your way, refer them to me."

It was eight-fifty the next morning as Westin stepped from

the immaculately clean cab, paid the driver, and proceeded into the mirrored-glass edifice called The New Misawa Building, Misawa Group's headquarters. While at the elegant reception station, he heard a sharp voice from behind. "You are Westin-san." Westin turned to see a medium-built Japanese man impeccably dressed out. It was his eyes that caught John's attention, brilliant, probing black, the eyes of a predator.

"I am Westin-san. I am to see Takara-san." Westin wondered why whenever he spoke to these people, he spoke slowly sounding like a *Weekly Reader*, and louder as if they were all hard of hearing.

Westin followed the well-dressed fox to a private elevator and up to the top fiftieth floor. They entered Takara's expansive office. Sparsely positioned on light plum carpet, the furniture consisted mostly of black leather and ebony. Two small alabaster conversation tables provided a quiet contrast.

Takara came around his desk to offer greetings; Westin reciprocated the polite bow, and the handshake. "I see you have met Shimizu-san," Takara said, gesturing them all into black Italian-leather chairs. Takara took the one under a Sesshu, a painting from the Muromachi-period: 1400-1500.

Takara took a moment to reassess John Kreuger Westin. Watching the American closely now, Takara saw a different John Westin altogether. For starters, he noted Westin's slate blue eyes, taking in everything about him and his office, seeming to miss few details. He had underestimated the American and now sought to figure out why. Becoming an astronaut and performing its duties required more than just a pilot's skills; it required intellect, savvy, political adroitness, and perseverance. Why had he not relied on that assessment, instead of his impression? *He'd been disarmed. How?* In Japanese company, Westin had been a very unassuming man, quite un-American. That was it. He now viewed this man in a very different way, he now considered him very dangerous.

Setaka had been Kojima's long-time friend since before primary school. Takara had no reason to doubt Setaka's recounting of the barroom story, nor Kojima's story told of the American rape during their occupation. That raised a thousand questions: Did this Westin-san actually kill his *kobun*? And under what circumstances? Why did NASA's Project JAM liaison suddenly leave the agency? Why did he join Paxton, a company in financial trouble? Did he have a hand in exposing Japan's NIQE-based weapons program? Who was this man? CIA?

For Westin, normal Japanese business etiquette required him to pay a courtesy visit at the top. Since Misawa Systems was Japan's NASDA's prime contractor on Project JAM, it was Takara's companies that were responsible for the NIQE chip moonlighting. His six years working with the Japanese had brought him to love the country and its people, but not its leaders like Takara. In Japan people like Takara were considered gods, and like most gods with clay feet, they tended to abuse their power.

John felt the average Nippon Joe busted his butt seventeen hours a day, and got in return zip for quality of life. Hardly any libraries, parks, or museums. The infrastructure was falling apart, especially the roads. And all too little personal time to enjoy life.

Over the years, John had taken the time—and *sake*—to talk with the people he met, to understand their personal feelings. It seemed that Buddhism taught them the way to reach nirvana—the divine state of release from physical pain and sorrow—is through correct living and self-denial. For the individual it was Buddhahood, not economic gain, that was the prize to be gained through selfless devotion to one's work. A "work ethic" easily exploited, and that it was, thought John.

Japan's government had used this personal religion in a skillful way, fulfilling its national aims: not only to catch up but to surpass the West. Japanese culture was unique, in that a citizen's primary source of self identity and dedication was with the group; and the ingrained goal of any Japanese group was to be number one, for that determined social status among their peer groups. People not unlike Takara wove religion and culture together binding the individual to a greater goal: the economic growth of the ultimate group—Japan. In the offing, the people subjugated their individuality for the "greater national good." That was just one of the reasons John had less than total respect for the "god" now sitting before him.

First Takara not sitting behind his power desk, and now a friendly warm-up chat. Westin's antennae went up: Takara was seeking a warmer, friendlier atmosphere than ever before. Finally, came the reason.

Takara leaned his stiff frame inward a bit, then asked, "Westin-san, do you know Atsuko Kojima?"

Oh shit. He knows. How? Probably a thousand ways—if someone were looking. Japan's forensic medicine took a back seat to no one. But still, even if he had evidence of foul play, he could only conjecture, only suspect. Westin stuck with his rehearsed story, pausing:

"Why yes. Thank you for introducing us. A very nice man. Director of NASDA's OREX (Orbiting Reentry Experiment) project, I believe he said." When he'd arrived at the airport last night, Westin half expected the National Police to pick him up for questioning. Getting the question from Takara almost jolted him.

Takara had forgotten Kojima's coming upon him and Westin that day in one of Tokyo's parks. Was that event really happenstance? Indeed it was himself who introduced the two younger men. "Kojima-san died."

John noted Shimizu, the fox, shift his weight. *And how did he die, pray tell?* He knows damnit. Or thinks he knows. "I'm sorry to hear that. Was he a close friend of yours?"

"He was my *kobun*," Takara informed, his eyes narrowing with a corrosive contempt barely veneered.

"I am deeply sorry. My respects, Takara-san." Westin liked the term, "bolt hole," a place through which a spy calculated he could make a hasty exit should a situation turn to shit. Right now, during the long silence, Westin thought of bolt holes.

"That is kind of you," *but we shall see the true extent of your sorrow, soon enough.* "Have a good stay in Japan, Westin-san. I trust you will find my staff cooperative as you conduct your survey. Thank you for coming."

After customary bows, Westin was shown to the door where a bodyguard escorted him down to the lobby level.

"Shimizu-san, do not lose him." The fox returned a confident bow. "I wish to know his every activity, who he speaks with, and what is said. Is that understood?" Shimizu affirmed. "And Shimizu, remember, Westin is not to leave Japan."

"It should not be difficult as we know his itinerary. The men are instructed to seize him just before he leaves."

"You say you know the identity of the man Westin met last night?"

"Yes, *sensei.*"

CHAPTER 16
SHADOW BOXING

The assassin stood next in the LAX customs line, briefcase in hand. He wore a tailored dark blue suit, and combed his lacquer black hair neatly parted to the side—a presentation designed to stereotype. He wore no disguise, save makeup covering the scar above his left eye. That was a risk, he knew, for suspicion might be aroused in a trained inspector with a studied eye.

He let his powerful arms hang to his side minimizing possible stress exerted against the suit coat's fabric. Looking like any serious Japanese businessman, he stood pensively, his mind considering the entry procedures before him.

The crate would be in a freight office stored in a bonded cage. He had made all the proper arrangements with a local customs service broker including faxes of invoices and letters of authority. All was in place. Now to process past the rather serious looking customs inspector ahead, then call the broker. The broker in turn would call the freight office, give the carnet number, and request the crate's inspection and release.

With luck, all would be cleared and in his possession by this afternoon. Then on to Washington tomorrow morning. A clever plan, the assassin had to admit to himself. Him, in the guise of the Kyoto Museum's Director, proposing a public exhibition in selected museums in the United States. And of course, he needed a sample of the would-be collection.

Pete Tarrance loved the U.S. Customs Service. It was the perfect job for him; he had a computer-like memory and never forgot a face. At the moment he was at LAX Inspection Station number two, filling in for today's short staff, as most were in an all-day class learning more about the new breed of weapons—hardened plastic, undetectable by normal airport metal detection scanners. He liked being supervisor, but times like this made him realize how much he missed being on the front lines.

It was the fifteenth Japanese businessman in a row. Always this way following the arrival of JAL's ten-twenty A.M. flight, Tarrance knew, as he wondered if they ever took their wives or families along. Pete observed the next man stepping up. He was taller, a bit broader, than the rest of the businessmen. "Passport, please." *Yasuo Okabe.* The passport's photo bore a fair resemblance, except for the eyes: these were ancient, ink black, both intelligent and primordial at the same time. The brow furrowed in with an intensity, the likes Pete had never experienced. It bothered him in some oblique way. Nose a bit larger than a typical Japanese, broken once, badly reset.

"How long will you be in the country?"

"Three weeks," came a resonant knell.

Pete looked up, *something* lurking in the shadow of his mind. "What is the nature of your visit?"

"I am curator at Kyoto National Museum. I am making proposals to American museums for a special exhibition. Ancient fighting weapons of Japan, artifacts."

"Which cities?"

"Los Angeles, Chicago, and New York."

"Where to first?"

"Los Angeles."

Tarrance looked the man over, then again at the Declaration form. "This exhibit sample. Have you made special arrangements?"

The assassin handed Tarrance the broker's confirmation letter. "As this states, the carnet is already in local LAX customs files."

"No business materials otherwise?" The Japanese shook his head, negative. There was a long pause. Then Pete said cheerfully, "Enjoy your stay in the United States, Mr. Okabe."

Last night Pete Tarrance hardly slept. It was because of that Japanese national he'd let through U.S. customs yesterday. Pete's mind never forgot a face. The name, maybe, but never the face.

This morning he'd called every major museum in Los Angeles. None of the directors had heard of a Yasuo Okabe nor expected anyone proposing to show Japanese artifacts. A ringer got through, Pete finally decided. That, plus the fact that the man's face was filed somewhere in his memory, warranted a closer look. The look took him to his bottom left-hand drawer, where he'd just removed the third binder. Scrapbooks, he called them, containing descriptions, photos, drawings, and composites of every man, woman, and child who over the years was ever of interest to a U.S. federal agency.

He'd started keeping the scrapbooks as a rookie Customs Inspector back almost seven years ago. Now, he was in the original book…and there he was! Pete slammed his fist to the desk in triumph. Another alias, he was sure, Yasutaka Ishigura. The only difference his memory informed was that Ishigura's photograph showed a thin almost meandering scar tracing down above the left eye. He'd asked for a rush development on yesterday's film on station number two. That would leave no doubt that this was the man.

Tarrance read the bio:

Agency: FBI

Wanted: Yasutaka Ishigura, Japanese national
Description: 5' 10", 170 lbs, muscular build.
Dark eyes, Black hair
Distinguishing features: irregular scar traversing down
over left eye.
Reason: Capital Murder—Federal Agent
Contact: Special Agent Ryan Voight 202-324-3000

"Hmm." Tarrance picked up the telephone receiver and punched in the number.

Ever since his arrival yesterday morning, the assassin assessed the operation so far to be an efficient one. Retrieving the tools of his trade from customs, he had transferred the crate's contents to a golf club bag, then inserted it into an airline baggage carton. That evening he stored the brokered shipping crate in a mini-storage shed not two miles from Los Angeles International Airport. Last night was spent at a too-soft hotel on Century Boulevard near the airport. To sleep, he laid a blanket on the carpeted floor—still too soft.

Now, the flight attendant had just announced their beginning descent into Washington D.C.'s National Airport. He had been in the air for six hours, time enough for a thorough review of the report on President John Adam Temple. He'd memorized the President's current calendar and habits, along with the White House layout and security measures. He needed more information on Secret Service procedures, but that would come from his Washington contact. Other than that, the assassin mused, he saw no insurmountable obstacles.

Ryan Voight, FBI Deputy Assistant Director, returned Pete Tarrance's call. That was one U.S. Customs Inspector really on the ball, Voight had thought. Voight reported Tarrance's findings to his boss, the executive assistant director (Investigation) and for more than one reason was assigned the case. This was a high priority case, just as sensitive as it had been six years ago.

As part of FBI standard procedure, Voight put the incident

on the FBI teletype network, Top Secret, Priority. By the next morning every flavor of FBI agent would have a hard copy of the incident report on his or her desk.

"Good morning, Mitch," greeted the FBI Director's driver. Mitch Kendall was a morning man. He had already read the Washington Post and was ready for a sport commentary, if asked, which his driver often did, dispatches permitting. Kendall did not depict the stereotypical blend-in-the-furniture FBI man. His gray hair was cut short, military style, wore silver rimmed octagonal glasses and stood all of five-feet-five.

Slipping into the back seat, Kendall quickly made it through the dispatch box's cipher-lock, then devoured its contents. Skimpy, he thought, until he read the very last item, the lowest priority.

Kendall picked up the secure telephone receiver, punched familiar numbers, then asked his secretary to have Ryan Voight in his office at nine this morning. The next call was to a friend.

It was five until nine when Ryan Voight arrived at the Director's large seventh floor office. It was an office display-ing traditional furniture, with many of Director Kendall's personal antiques placed about.

"Glad you could make it, Ryan," Kendall greeted, then turned to the Oriental man seated to the right. "Dr. Tom Nakamoto, like you to meet deputy assistant director Ryan Voight." Voight assessed this Japanese man with hawk-like occidental eyes. Make a good center fielder, Voight thought, well built, quick and easy to his feet. They exchanged greet-ings.

The alert blue eyes were the only clue one had that Ryan Voight merited a second look. Like many at the Bureau, Voight presented an appearance that was the epitome of American normalcy: husband, father of three, dedicated to the office. He stood five feet seven inches tall and weighed in at one hundred and forty-five pounds. But on second look, one saw revealing signs of the unordinary, like today, in the stressed fabric of his suit coat's dark gray wool blend, especially around the upper body muscle groups. Voight's sense of pride in being fit at forty-eight years of age had its roots in his Marine Corps upbringing. Even though Voight was now in management, on the high profile cases like this one the Executive Assistant Director (Investigations)—sometimes at the request of the Director himself—would assign Voight to coordinate with the field and bring the case to a fast and orderly closure.

"Ryan, I've explained to Tom your role in the Ishigura case," Kendall began. This was Voight first clue explaining this morning's summons. "As for Tom, he's the best damn expert on Japanese culture and affairs I know of." The FBI, being a domestic law enforcement agency, had no permanent foreign affairs specialist on staff. Kendall and Nakamoto were old Georgetown University classmates and close friends ever since. This wasn't the first time Nakamoto sat in this chair consulting.

Kendall glanced again at a memo atop his desk, then began sternly, "Gentlemen, no one else is to know of the discussion we're about to have. When I explain, I think you'll understand why." Voight noticed Nakamoto cross his legs and relax. "CIA Director Miller tells me they have reason to believe that elements in Japan have targeted President Temple for assassination. Ryan, I've shown Tom the photograph from LAX Customs and covered the museum director's ruse. Tom, want to take it from here?"

The Japanese gentleman began, "I cannot be one hundred percent sure, but it is a strong probability that the man who passed through LAX customs yesterday is *Shiro Kage*. That means White Shadow. In Japan, he has no name, only aliases; those who know of him refer to him simply by *Shiro Kage*. He is widely respected as the most accomplished assassin of all time. It stands to reason that only the best should be sought and dispatched for such an assignment." Nakamoto hesitated focusing on Kendall. "Pardon my saying so, old friend, but your FBI has not the skills to stop such a man."

Kendall cast a look at Voight, then to Nakamoto, and stated flatly, "I don't buy—"

"It will take training, yes. Intelligence, yes. Resources, yes. But it will take much more to stop this man. I know I'm out of line, Mitch, but I'll say it anyway. *Shiro Kage* works on a different plane than you and me. He not only operates on this plane from a higher state of consciousness, but looks down onto our plane like an eagle views a rabbit."

Kendall pushed back almost amused, "C'mon."

Nakamoto uncrossed his legs, leaned forward, then said, "I'm deadly serious, Mitch."

Voight broke the silence. "Teal Coro."

"What?" replied the Director, a hint of irritation all but missed.

"We were classmates at Quantico, sir. He's an American Indian—well, three-quarters Indian. I got close, as close as one could to Teal Coro. He spoke of such levels of consciousness to me. He said he used this sixth sense to anticipate, to outmaneuver the man he was assigned to bring in. And that he did, commendably. Medal of Valor, too."

"And?" The director sensed more.

"And, sir, he's no longer with the Bureau."

"Free-lancing?" Kendall was a fairly recent appointment and didn't yet know the Bureau's history as well as his predecessor.

"Not really. There's a bit of irony here that needs explaining." Kendall motioned for Voight to explain even though his own patience was beginning to thin. "Almost seven years ago we busted a Japanese mafia ring operating in Los Angeles."

"In Japan, the mafia is called *yakuza*," Nakamoto offered. "If I recall, that one was the Omata *yakuza*."

Voight continued, "That is correct. The key player busted was the brother of the head of this Omata *yakuza* in Japan. Agent Coro was the man who secured the key incriminating evidence and brought the brother in. Three weeks after the brother's conviction for racketeering, Agent Coro's family—wife and child—were brutally killed. Coro, himself, found their bloody bodies, their throats cut."

Voight watched Kendall wince, then continued, "CIA agents in Japan were able to ascertain that the head of the Omata *yakuza* had hired this so-called White Shadow to do the job.

"Obsessed, Coro left for Japan looking for White Shadow. Working on his own, he disregarded the National Police. He was arrested twice and finally deported, politely, of course, and asked not to return. The State Department apologized. Embarrassed, the Bureau reprimanded Agent Coro. Shortly after that, he resigned. But I might add, sir, he told me the second time the Japanese police came down on him, he was within an hour of finding White Shadow. That was his last shot, National Police held him in custody until his deportation."

"He would be the first." Nakamoto spoke in an impressed tone. "No one has ever gotten close to *Shiro Kage*."

"Sir, in spite of the history, that's precisely why I mention Coro's name."

"Can this man remain objective?"

"I don't know, sir."

Kendall stood, turning, his hands clasped behind his back. He stared blankly at the Justice Building across Pennsylvania Avenue, pondering what he'd just heard. His politically sensitive mind considered another factor: how would a Presidential post mortem judge this moment? Finally the FBI Director spoke, "Deputy Assistant Director Voight, I want you to use all means possible to locate and apprehend this probable Japanese agent."

CHAPTER 17

MEASURING DRAPES

The assassin spent his first night in Washington at a cheap
hotel in Maryland, just outside the District. He'd paid cash for
two nights and now left early; it was the evening of the second
night as the taxi pulled up to the front lobby of the Hay-Adams
Hotel. The assassin paid the driver while the doorman retrieved his suitcase and airline-boxed golf bag, then proceeded passed a gray stone and freshly painted black wrought
iron exterior.

The assassin was again a successful businessman, an
image more than confirmed by his initial survey of the hotel's
interior: ivory-colored walls accented, massively, with rich
polished walnut, a seventeenth century Medici tapestry, and
everywhere appointed with fine English antiques, polished
brass and leaded glass. He checked in and proceeded to the
seventh floor and on to the reserved room with a view to the
south. He tipped the bellman—not a custom in Japan—then
approached the far antique writing table and indulged the view

across Lafayette Square. There it was, just across Pennsylvania Avenue, the White House, bathed in an array of aimed floodlights, the north lawn fountain reaching for a cooling evening sky.

He wondered what people were doing at this moment: the target, his protectors, his adversaries, his friends, the local residents. A job as challenging as this one would take time to study. But in spite of the strengths, there were always weaknesses and opportunities. Breaching a castle, he knew, was always easier that defending it.

The assassin returned to his bags, quickly unpacked, and donned a loose-fitting street version of his matte-black assassin's uniform. Next, he carefully unpacked the golf bag and its hidden compartments, laying its contents out across the bedding's quilted cover.

It was rare to take this many weapons, but this was indeed a rare assignment, demanding tools with which to effect his unique skills—a thousand ways of death. When finished, before him lay a most lethal array of weapons, weapons of his master's ancestors: sword with a plain hilt, a shorter hidden *katana*, blowgun, *shuriken, tantos, kamas*, knife, smoke bombs and blinding powders, throwing spikes, caltrops, and two sturdy four inch needles. Satisfied, the assassin secured the deadly array, keeping what he would need for this night.

Wearing black soft-soled toe-fitted shoes, he took the service elevator to the kitchen level, surveyed the routine and uniforms, then moved quickly for the service entrance and out. Unnoticed. Unseen.

The Indian observed dust kicked up in the vehicle's slip stream, now two miles out along the north fence. He knew who it was.

In two directions, north and east, he could see the fence and its adjacent access clearing, each diminishing to a point against distant mountains. Dotting the plain itself were mostly sagebrush, mesquite bush, and few piñon pines. His pickup sat just fifteen feet away, its bed loaded with coiled barbed wire, several four-inch round posts, and a crosstie.

Teal Coro had just finished digging the new hole, and now had the one crosstie balanced on his shoulder as the four-by-four Toyota light truck came up to a halt. Emerging from the driver's side was a familiar face, a face from a distant past, a distant world.

After his noon arrival into Las Vegas, Ryan Voight had rented the vehicle and took Interstate 15 heading northeast. Eighty miles later, just outside of Littlefield, Arizona, he turned south entering the huge Triple Bar Ranch. It took his badge to get him onto the property, heading for the ranch's southwest corner. Being FBI trained, Voight couldn't help studying the physically fit man before him. The Apache wore a red bandanna around his forehead, well-worn jeans, work boots, and no shirt. But his attention stopped at the man's eyes: clear lucid and dark, like wellsprings after the winter's thaw. Now, as Voight approached his old friend, he sensed a smile would appear disingenuous. "Hello Tonto."

"Hello *kimo sabe*." They'd been roommates back at the FBI's Training Center in Quantico. The greeting was an old joke. But this time the levity was gone, the words carried a weathered edge, almost somber.

Teal Coro let the bridging moment work its way, then asked, "In the neighborhood?"

Ryan shrugged.

"They send you," Coro continued, barely making it a question.

"Something like that."

For the next twenty minutes, no words were spoken. Voight held the crosstie upright straight while, into its surrounding hole, Coro tamped red rock and sandy dirt into a solid pack. After nailing the two cross-braces in place, Voight wiped sweat from his forehead, then broke the silence, "Teal, the director sent me out here."

"And what's on the director's mind these days?" Coro asked without malice, now working a strand of barbed wire to the new corner post.

"We got a situation, Teal. All hands on deck. I convinced him that he should consider all his resources."

Coro snapped back, "*His* resources!"

"Coro. A man's been sent here to kill the President."

"So. We'll get another one." Coro had a crowbar notched secure into a barb, its neck braced against the new corner post. He pulled back on its handle tensing the wire across the black creosote of the square post.

"Let me explain," Voight came back evenly, while holding wire cutters, ready to cut the overreach. "It's Yasutaka Ishigura, the White Shad—"

Snap! Up the fence line, the wire broke under the sudden surge in strain. The barbed strand came back at them, like a sidewinder gone mad. It coiled about both men leaving them loosely entangled, their clothes and skin nicked and slightly cut from the unyielding barbs.

"Hope you didn't give much for that city shirt," Coro finally deadpanned.

"Lands End. What the Hell," Voight came back wiping blood from his chin. Standing and looking at each other, they both began to laugh, and laugh.

Coro was the first to free himself from the tangled mess, then assisted Voight. When freed, Coro put the conversation back on course, "What d'you come to offer me, Ryan?"

Offer. "The offer's simple. You get another shot at the man who killed Serena and your child. You get it as a contract employee under the aegis of the Bureau and access to its network and investigative resources. I'll be your primary contact."

Coro studied his friend. Not since before attending college had his spirit-heart spoken with such clarity, such intensity. He now understood what the spirit atop Yucca Mountain had meant. He now knew what he must do.

"I will remove White Shadow's threat against your president, but I seek something in return." Voight gestured to hear it. "Some hundred and fifty miles from here," Coro pointed due west, "there is a sacred place. It is called Yucca Mountain and is being made ready for storing your nation's nuclear waste. This is my offer to you, Ryan: I stop the White Shadow, you stop the desecration of Yucca Mountain."

Coro turned back to the task of securing strands taut around the post. Voight had miscalculated, badly. Allowing an opportunity to avenge his family's murder wasn't enough. "I'm not sure I can sell that to the director."

"I'm sure your president would buy it, especially if I save his worthless ass."

"I'll see what I can do," Voight finally said with a hint of resignation.

"Can you do it or not?" Coro snapped back.

"Yes," Voight reflexed, regretting it already.

Returning to Las Vegas' McCarran airport, Voight passed a small bar near the strip. It was Friday evening and Tom Shelby needed a drink before heading home. During the week at Yucca Mountain, he stayed at a Shiraki on-site trailer; on weekends, he flew to Las Vegas to his real home, wife and the kids.

It'd been exactly one week since Glenn Thielken's visit. Since then, he'd not been able to get his boss' words off his mind. The callousness. The ruthless manner. And Thielken's call today didn't ease matters either. Shelby ordered another drink.

Paxton International had hired him right out of college. He was the key technical lead on Paxton's bid to win DOE's Yucca Mountain project. With Paxton's loss, there were no other projects suited for his skills. He was about to be laid off. Then Shiraki Industries, the winning prime contractor, made him an offer: Shiraki's on-site Project Manager at Yucca Mountain. He took it, albeit with misgivings leaving Paxton, and especially his long-time mentor Craig MacIsaac.

Tom's mind reflected upon MacIsaac, a man with an easy manner, sharp rawboned face, short reddish hair, and tobacco brown eyes. MacIsaac had taken an interest in him, fresh out of the Colorado School of Mines. On Tuesday nights, they'd play racquetball, Craig's wide lean body always in position for the shot: finesse not power.

It'd been awhile since he'd seen Craig MacIsaac. His being Shiraki Industries' Yucca Mountain Project Manager, and MacIsaac, now Paxton's JAM Project Manager, kept them both plenty busy. That's Craig, Tom mused, always working, keeping to the highest standards of excellence, of integrity.

Funny, Tom thought, before joining Shiraki Industries, issues of corporate integrity, corporate morality, had never really crossed his mind. Yet lately, he found himself thinking about them, a lot.

Carrera Thielken looked beyond her husband and his Saturday morning paper. From the pool side deck, she looked out at the Los Angeles basin still clear before the afternoon haze. This morning she had orange juice and plain toast while making last minute plans for next week's party. It was in honor of an old friend and associate made good, Dhillon Reed, now Vice President under John Temple.

Glenn, being Dhillon Reed's most generous financial supporter, left Reed little room to decline her invitation to a party in his own honor. It would be her most important party since they moved to their new home in Hollywood Hills. As she looked over the invitation list, she figured she had the perfect mix of people and now mentally went over who she intended to introduce to whom. Introductions that later turned lucrative for those introduced was what political networking was all about. Not to mention, she knew, the political and social credits she herself accumulated for creating such a prestigious environment.

And then there was John Westin. She had taken a fancy to Mr. Astronaut, a good-looking, fun, and like herself, a bit irreverent man. She wouldn't mind a toss in the hay with the man, if only she could corner him. Like next week, he'd still hadn't RSVPed to her party. Well that would have to change, she plotted, pursing her lips.

"Did you read this shit?" bellowed Glenn Thielken, tossing the paper onto the table's glass top. "Police giving the goddamned gangs protection! Now that's a switch. These fuckers carry Uzis, AK-47s, MAC-10s, you name it. Hell, we should be asking *them* to protect the police. Goddamn nerve." Carrera grinned at the outburst. Glenn continued anyway, "Fuckin' punks. If it's not murder, or raping an eighty-year-old-lady, then they're ripping off your car. Shit…Me, I put my money on the Name Dropper."

"C'mon honey. I hate it when you play coy like that. Don't hold back, just tell us what you *really* think." She grinned.

He looked over at his wife of now five years. There in the morning's light flashing those china-blue eyes he loved so much. Yep, he thought, makes grown men cry, and strong men weak. He loved her body, and respected her mind, which at the present looked ready to get serious.

"Glenn. When are you going to talk to Dhillon about Ambassador Zenjuro's proposal?"

"I'm not sure," he answered knowing he'd just shifted the issue to from "when" to "if."

"I think you should, Glenn. You'll never get another opportunity like this." And Carrera, born Carol Ann Cooke, knew about opportunity. When she was fifteen she teamed up with a man passing through Topeka, Kansas. He offered her a ride to Dallas and she took it, never looking back. After a couple of months in Dallas, the man drifted on his way; she found a job at drug store. There, she met a young aerospace engineer and married him. It was the most stability she'd ever known. It was in the process of their buying their first home that she saw the opportunity that lay in real estate sales. And it didn't require a rocket scientist, either. She got her license, got herself established, and began making money. Money, she quickly came to understand, meant power. Very quickly, she found herself wanting more of it. More than her husband could ever provide. She left him, and headed west to the land of opportunity. In California, she established her reputation in exclusive properties. A few years later, she locked in on a wealthy man, whom she convinced to divorce his wife. Years after their marriage, he died in a tragic accident. Less than a year after the funeral, she married Glenn Thielken, a comer at Shiraki Industries.

Carrera reached over and gently pulled down her husband's clutched newspaper, then pressed the issue. "There are a lot of things in life just there for the taking. Some require effort to pry them loose. Yet others require opportunity. Lotta people playing in the majors, but not many move on up to the front office where the shots are called.

"The way I see it, honey, is if you open this door for Dhillon, and he walks through it becoming President of the United States, you could name your ticket. You mentioned Secretary of Defense, but to me, Vice President has a better ring to it. You ask for it and you'd get it, I could almost guarantee you that—you're that good, Glenn. And once that ticket's punched, all totalled," she dramatized looking at her watch, "in less than ten years, Glenn, it's yours." *And I'll be measuring the drapes at the White House.*

He drained the orange juice from the pitcher, then sat staring at the bubbles bursting in the full glass. Finally, he said, "You're right. I'll speak with Dhillon at the party."

Carrera Thielken knew she had an instinct for power. At this moment, she smiled inwardly, for again, she'd married the right man. And now on to the obstacles. "But there's more, Glenn. I know you, what is it?"

A trace of a smile curled the corner of his mouth, always amazed at his wife's power of perception. He leaned toward her, then told her, "Remember our conversation about Tom Shelby out at Yucca Mountain?" Carrera nodded. "Talked to him yesterday. He's beginning to worry me. He could blow the whistle on the whole project, shut it down, possible criminal indictments if all were known. Opportunity's door could be slammed right in our faces."

"Hmmm."

Willie Harman had bought into his mother's logic: education, and only education, would get him out of South Central Los Angeles. Yes, he claimed a gang, but that was more because they claimed him, "jumpin' him in" when he was ten years old. And as they say, "Once you in, you in."

This Saturday Willie Harman headed for the library at Exhibition Park. On his bicycle, he was cutting through the AK Gangsters Crips' 'hood. He'd done it before just like today, in the bright afternoon; sometimes he'd gotten looks, some challenging, but never had any real trouble, as long as he kept his head down making no eye contact. But today, Willie Harman made a mistake: he forgot to remove his ball cap, a "62" emblazoned in crimson across its front—Six-Deuce Brims Bloods.

"Fuck that name droppin' buster," El Cid yelled. El Cid and Cage were in the bomber, his cherried-out '64 Chevy Impala, "cruisin' the 'hood, showin' the colors." On the street were mostly houses, some boarded up empty. They'd spotted a couple of homeboys and stopped to check out the action. The Name Dropper, that's all his homeboys could talk about, and El Cid was getting tired of it. But there was more to it, he could see, his homies were getting jumpy, jumpy took over instincts, causing mistakes.

El Cid had just gotten out of the bomber when he heard a screech of tires. Quickly, he scanned the street, the people beginning to gather—they always gathered in his presence—the parked cars, the moving...black Dodge van screeching its breaks. He reached in the window grabbing his AK assault rifle from the inside door panel. Still searching...*bam!*

A bicycle on the cross street clipped the old van. El Cid watched the wobbly bicycle and its scared rider careen off, and head for them. Too late. *Crunch.* It plowed into the Impala's rear left panel catapulting the kid onto the polished red-cherried gloss of the trunk.

"The nigger's a Blood!" shouted Cage, holding the baseball cap. "Six-Deuce Brims." The black van didn't stick around and was gone. "What the fuck slobs doin' here?"

"Ain't believin' this shit," El Cid screamed, AK-47 still in hand, "A dent!" He reached over, grabbed the back of the kid's collar, jerked him off the car slamming him down onto the pavement. "And a goddamned scratch!" He kicked the Blood, then kicked more, and more, wildly. Finally Cage reached down, holding the kid's arms at his back, he pulled him up to face the torrent of fire in El Cid's eyes.

Willie Harman, still a little dazed, looked up at the tirade. What he saw scared him. First, the blue cap, a Crip. Second, the initials, "AK", the notorious AK Gangsters. And third he'd heard of their ghetto star—an O.G. with a very, very serious rep—the Essay with the shaved head and black tears tattooed under his eye. He'd heard of El Cid.

"Put 'em in there," El Cid said, calmer now. He pointed to an abandoned house across the street.

"Ye-eeeeah," came Cage's approval. Willie tried to believe nothing bad would happen. Willie's mind knew otherwise.

Inside, the front living room was charred and smelled of urine. Willie found himself tossed to the floor, center room. El Cid walked up, pointed the assault rifle at the boy's crotch, flipped the selector switch to "three-shot burst," then pulled the trigger. The others looked away. The second burst in the head mercifully ended Blood homeboy's life.

El Cid motioned to one of the baby homies, wannabes ready to "put in work" for the set, ready to prove themselves worthy to claim membership in the AK Gangsters Crips. "Dump him over by the freeway."

CHAPTER 18
VICE ADMIRAL ONISHI'S IDEA

They called it the Jungle, Blood territory. Just before dawn he had scaled up the back alley wall of a small Korean dry cleaning establishment located on the eastern fringes of South Central L.A. It was but one in a string of one-story buildings on this and the next block, ending at the park.

Last week a Blood baby homie had told him of his set's picnic plans in the park this Sunday afternoon. He'd made a careful survey of the immediate area surrounding the park, finally selecting this site for a variety of reasons:

Being Sunday, the business below was closed, footsteps above would go unnoticed. With the afternoon sun now at his back, his crouched position fell into a deep shadow cast by a huge dryer outlet just behind him. And looking east, he estimated his line of sight to cover a full sixty percent of the sun-cast park before him. A perfect shooting aspect. And finally, the alley-way itself offered a perfect escape cover and alternate routes, if necessary. He doubted he'd need use of the alternates as more than once he'd watched, after a gangbanger went down, his buddies scatter like roaches under a just turned-on light.

The shooter now studied the site picture through his 20-power scope, waiting for the desired head profile: The reticles crossed on a head coifed in bright red rubber bands on corn-rowed hair, a gold ring hung from the target's right ear. Minutes ago, as the massive buffed-out man approached a picnic table, the shooter observed the infamous razor-sharp hatchet looped within his belt—no mistake, this was the Butcher.

Down in the park, Butcher now sat at the picnic table surrounded by homies and baby homies. He held the circle rapt as he pulled out a gold watch chain, on it hung last night's trophy. It was the ear of a man, gold earring still looped through the fresh purple-colored pliable tissue. Representing previous gangbanging revenge kills, the chain held six other studded ears, each darkened over time possessing the feel of dried apricots.

The shooter mentally judged the increase in wind, then felt for the scope's adjusting screw, turning it one click to the right. As if on cue, Butcher turned his head. The shooter took a deep breath, let part of it escape, steadied his sight picture, and softly, steadily...

Crack! He quickly realigned his site picture on his target, now flopped backward over the bench. Perfect, blood gushed from the visible right ear. He couldn't see what replaced the disappearing left ear, a golf ball-sized mass of red erupting outward. But he visualized it all the same. Satisfied, he pulled back the bolt ejecting the .308 shell casing. He located the hot brass and with a handkerchief moved it into the light, the etched "Butcher" now clearly visible.

"Welcome aboard the *Yukikaze*, Commander Tanner, Westin-san," greeted the military man in dress uniform. Handshakes followed formal bows. They were at Japan's Yokosuka Naval Base, near the U.S.'s Atsugi Naval Air

Facility, Tanner's base. The *Yukikaze* was Japan's latest and most modern destroyer. Their host was Japanese Self-Defense Force Admiral Takuji Kamikura.

Kamikura was a tall, physically fit man with thick black hair cut less than an inch long. He possessed an Electrical Engineering degree from the University of Tokyo, making him well qualified for his current assignment. Befitting his family's long military heritage, Admiral Kamikura at fifty-four had just received his second star. Next week, he would take on a new assignment, a tour at the Boci Cho—Japan's National Self-Defense Agency Headquarters, an equivalent to the U.S.'s Pentagon.

The second star had come with his commanding the SDF's Advanced Weapons Research, Development, and Evaluation Center. It was under his direction, that NIQE-based weapons were developed with Misawa Group companies. Kamikura was sure John Westin was the man who exposed Japan's secret NIQE weapons program, and now appraised the man he would love to see dead.

From the quay, Kamikura led his guests up the ramp and on to the bridge. There the two Americans were introduced to the destroyer's captain, a small man in a foul mood. Later the two Americans would disagree as to which one of the two Japanese had a more disagreeable attitude.

Kamikura led his two guests from the captain back into the CIC—Combat Information Center. As their eyes adjusted to the darkened room, Kamikura wondered just how much these men really knew about his program, about him. They had requested a briefing on two NIQE-based weapons systems. Today, they would see the modified surface-to-air HyperVelocity Missile (HVM-J2).

Both Westin and Stan Tanner had read the technical reports on both NIQE-based weapons systems provided by Kamikura on Westin's last trip out. But, this was their first look at the system's actual test and firing control panels. Kamikura turned the details over to the civilian contractor who explained the details, answered systems and procedural questions, but deferred tactical issues to the admiral.

The technical briefing lasted three hours, well into lunch time. They ate a light Japanese meal in the officers' mess then proceeded to a small ward room.

The room's walls were covered with flow diagrams, pert charts, and schedules, none of which could the Americans comprehend. Center room held a table, six chairs, and a video tape player and monitor. The civilian contractor removed four video cassettes from his briefcase, placing them on the table before Westin. "Per your request last trip, Westin-san, the narrative and superimposed text were converted to English. As we proceed, please ask questions."

This afternoon they would see the HVM-J2 tape, including footage of the physical missile itself and its test and control system supporting an actual test. Westin noted his host had made no effort to hide the test's location, Penjantan, Indonesia.

"What kind of fuse?" Tanner asked.

"With access to the intelligent NIQE technology, we realized that accuracy was no longer a problem. We removed the heavy American proximity fuse and went with a kinetic impact design; the one-hundred and twenty pounds in weight saved went to the high-energy compact carbon dioxide laser generator."

"And the other sensors?"

The civilian described the sensor pod located behind a telescopic lens integrated into the tip of the nose cone. It contained up to four sensors of the seven developed: radar, sonar, vision, hearing, olfactory, infra-red, and ultraviolet. Simple movement of a mirror directed incoming energy to a selected sensor wafer, which then via CCD array sent a continuous stream of energy "snapshots" to the NIQE neural-net computer. The beauty of this design, Kamikura knew, was that like the human brain the NIQE computer processed and "knew" about the sensed information the instant it arrived in its neural circuits.

Tanner asked about the NIQE chip's training.

The civilian explained how knowledge engineers repeatedly showed SAM the things they wanted SAM to learn. SAM learned how to fly, identify and destroy enemy aircraft. Through its sensors, SAM was shown every aircraft known to exist in the world and asked to identify. At the beginning, SAM would guess and when wrong, was told to try again. Over and over SAM was presented images and tested until his neural network had properly configured itself and the error rate became infinitesimally small. Next, aircraft images were rotated to present a myriad of possible profiles, SAM's associative abilities, along with his ability to fuse sensor input made this task a simple one. In time, SAM's neural network connected and programmed itself to identify visual, laser, and close in thermal images of any of thousands of aircraft in millions of situations. Next SAM was taught mission objectives—how to kill. He was shown the most vulnerable locations of a given aircraft; he learned how an aircraft flew, protects itself, its tricks, and how it evades; he learned about closure rates and optimum intercept solutions. He learned about the thousands of natural and man-made situations and obstacles to expect along the way.

Technical questions answered, Kamikura described the test scenario: Two of Japan's Air SDF's Mitsubishi-built F-15 Strike Eagles flying over the Kamimata Strait were the targets. The aircraft were eighty kilometers to the west of Penjantan Island when the test began. Bearing one-eight-zero degrees, speed five-five-zero knots.

At an optimum fifty-two hundred knots, the HyperVelocity Missile would find its target in less than fifty seconds. The video showed two computer displays flanking the status panel. The voice-over explained that all HVM-J2 systems on the three-man console indicated "ready." "Standby to launch. Five second count on mark. Ready...Mark!" a voice broke.

The fire control technician flipped the switch to "Activate." His monotone voice synchronized with the digital display, "Five, four, inertial, two, one, missile away. Forty-nine seconds to target." Kamikura noted that the narrator would refer the HVM-J2's NIQE processor as SAM. That was because the knowledge engineers affectionately referred to the HVM-J2 as *Samurai*, or SAM.

Once fired, SAM's HVM-J2 required no further instruction from Fire Control computers. No guidance assistance, no communication of any kind from Pejantan, save a self-destruct command by the Range Safety officer if events necessitated. Other than transmitting telemetry, the HVM-J2's sensor systems were totally passive and hence "nonexistent" to listening electronic ears.

Ignition: The men watched the missile bolt out of the launcher under the power of a tandem "kick-start" rocket booster, off into a late afternoon light. After launch, the video changed to a split screen: HVM-J2 telemetry on the left, radar on the right. The telemetry showed the results of critical parameters superimposed on a sequenced background of passive sensor playbacks: vision, laser scan, audio frequencies, and infra-red heat patterns.

Westin sat there watching the telemetry feedback, trying to comprehend what it meant to be SAM. Trying to comprehend SAM's *thinking* as he progressed through the mission profile.

SAM assessed his situation, then adjusted fins one and three to plus eight degrees, to achieve the necessary eighty-degree turn to the right while staying within structural stress limits. SAM referred to his holographic memory, comparing expectations with the actual terrain of Pejantan Island quickly sliding away to his right. He rectified the visual image with his "mental" map, then recalibrated position and bearings. SAM now knew where he was, where he was going and he knew how to get there.

SAM activates his carbon dioxide laser set to coarse beam for target detection, and analyses the reflections. The sea's surface looks smooth, no land masses or ships in his direct intercept path. A total of three airborne solid surfaces show up within his laser field of view: one at thirty-thousand feet, SAM switches the laser to fine beam and "paints" its profile. Not a fighter aircraft, he concludes with the assistance of his holographic memory. *Probably a Boeing 767.* SAM assesses the multiple: *two F-15Es flying close formation.*

SAM calculates 3-D ranging: ten seconds in flight, 66.702 miles to target. SAM estimates target heading three-hundred degrees at five hundred and fifty knots; Doppler velocity: 5986 miles per hour. SAM replots an intercept solution. He moves fin two minus point-six degrees for 656 milliseconds.

Sensor threshold EXCEEDED. SAM analyses overheating in the ramjet burners. He throttles down eight-percent and recalculates range and closure solution. *Well within operational and mission limits.*

Thirty seconds later, SAM maneuvers to circle in behind the target, now 19.423 miles southeast of estimated intercept. 12.692 seconds. He switches the carbon dioxide laser to fine beam for terminal guidance, and estimates the two craft at eighty percent military power. His doppler input indicates he is now moving six times faster than his helpless prey. *New input!* SAM feels radar energy picked up by his sensor: it is the sweep of the F-15's powerful on-board Hughes APG-70 synthetic aperture all-aspect radar. SAM deduces that the weapons systems officer—the F-15's backseater—of the second aircraft activated his attack radar. Now that his prey has detected his presence, SAM expects evasive maneuvers, part of the game, said the knowledge engineers. A serious game, *he knew*, for he had *his* orders, and now he had the scent: speed, cutoff angle, and most importantly, a superior intellect.

The second aircraft drops back.

At 15.303 miles, SAM's attention is drawn to what his Fijitsu high resolution vision sensor "sees" through the telescopic lens: From the lead F-15, chaff and a flare are ejecting from its right ejector. SAM's fine-beam laser sees the chaff forming a metallic cloud; he discounts it for what it is, ignoring the radar decoy, and concentrates on the new heat source. SAM watches the flare exit the tailcone. His infra-red confirms what his vision observed, thermal characteristics in the wrong wavelength and intensity magnitude too high: *another decoy.*

SAM watches the F-15E's aerosurface configuration begin to change: right aileron trailing edge down maximum, right horizontal stabilator four degrees down, left horizontal stabilator four degrees down, the twin vertical tail's trailing edges do not move; the fuselage blocks SAM's view of the left aileron, he makes a high probability assumption: *trailing edge up maximum.*

SAM focuses on his forward looking infra-red sensor and sees two thermal vector plumes pushed out by the huge Pratt and Whitney F100 series twin turbofans. From each engine, he sees the infra-red heat vectors lengthen: *One-hundred percent military rated power.* SAM knows the pilot's reactive tactic even before the aircraft begins to respond: a violent roll to the left; SAM further estimates the pilots intention based on the severity of the repositioned aerosurfaces, and engagement doctrine called up from his holographic memory: *a "Split-S": one-hundred and eighty degree left roll inverted and dive vertical.*

SAM refers to the current intercept estimate: range: 15.211 miles, time to intercept: 9.941 seconds, then re-calculates the intercept: Estimating a five thousand foot drop before the pilot can pull out and complete the mid-half of the "S," SAM recomputes the lengthened intercept: range: 15.447 miles, time: 10.096 seconds. SAM then adjusts his cutoff angle by three degrees and forty-four seconds.

Each sensor locks onto the changing profile of the startled F-15 Eagle. SAM's vision sees the trailing edge of both horizontal stabilators rotate up to maximum and both ailerons go to detent. *Split-S maneuver confirmed.* The F-15E drops a thousand feet, still inverted pitching downward at twenty-six degrees, pulling positive Gs throughout the entire maneuver. For a brief moment the F-15E presents minimum cross-section as the aircraft pitches through the HVM-J2's attack angle; the HVM-J2 is now at the inverted pilot's eleven o'clock. SAM re-corrects the intercept solution: 7.444 seconds now.

SAM's vision sees the F-15 nose-up pitching moment continue at maximum design limits as the pilot continues with throttle back beginning to climb horizontal. SAM catches the glint of sunlight reflecting off the pitching canopy, *wrong wavelength and intensity* and ignores the distraction. He fine tunes the closing intercept: range: 4.122 miles, time: 2.691 seconds.

SAM sees the target approaching horizontal, louvers opening to maximum; infra-red senses the thrust exhaust vector lengthening to maximum. *Afterburners.* Olfactory confirms the exhaust mix; Audio confirms maximum RPMs. Vision sees both stabilators still full up, ailerons detent, twin horizontal tail trailing edges detent. *He* expected the kick out of the split-S and has already compensated. SAM evaluates the tactical parameters: closure rate: 1.5332 miles per second; distance: 2501.66 feet; time to impact: 0.309 seconds.

Sensors see more chaff emerging, and a flare purging, this time from the left ejector. He ignores the decoys and concentrates his four locked-on sensors on the aerosurfaces, each giving him information to assimilate: range, cutoff angle, closure rate; all sensors fused to his NIQE "mind" giving him a tactical "feel" for the situation, for the kill. The pilot pulls the throttle back to the max, pulling a hard six-Gs: sun on his right, SAM high on his left. Time: 0.22 seconds...

SAM knows this maneuver. *Too late.* SAM would be deadly accurate. SAM would make his kill with a direct hit; at Mach 7, the kinetic energy of his inert warhead of dense depleted uranium would more than devastate the structural integrity of the aircraft. SAM makes a minute fin adjustment to correct for the 295 feet error that would have resulted from the pilot's last action. Intercept in 0.070 seconds...Fins to detent, closure solution is now perfect...*INTERCEPT!*

Time to clean out the britches, Westin mused, as the video tape ended.

Kamikura commented, "The HVM-J2 just screamed past the pilot's left wing at a relative Mach 7, twenty-meters off and nine-meters high—all within the minimum margin of safety prescribed by the test and its stringent mission parameters."

Westin reflected: The F-15 Strike Eagle was a formidable foe, with its power, range, maneuverability, and sophisticated avionics. But all that wasn't enough when it encountered HVM-J2, everything a missile of tomorrow could dream to be. Christ. It had precision guidance, speed at mach eight, and non-detectable passive sensor systems—truly a "fire and forget" weapon.

Kamikura felt proud as he knew what the Americans now felt and tried to grapple with—a quantum jump in the tactics of warfare. *And only Japan could have accomplished this—* the ultimate *kamikaze*.

The rest of the afternoon was spent with more questions; the ASR-J3 briefing would resume tomorrow.

No obstacles, thought Westin, they'd gotten what they came for, *with no hassle*. Westin signed for the videos and two more technical manuals, thanked his host, parting company back on the quay.

"Can you believe it?" Tanner still not sure he did himself.

"What, the weapons or the attitude?"

Out in the parking lot, the two men finally reached Tanner's car. Westin stared absently toward the entry gate. He did not see the man street-side with binoculars focused directly on him. Finally, Westin spoke, "Stan, you know, you and I used to be one hell of a team—"

"The best," Tanner interrupted, fond of their Viet Nam record in the A-6 warhorse.

"Yeah, but just the same, I'd sure hate to have that thing on *my* ass."

"Roger that."

Esfahan, Iran: She remembered seeing it in some old WWII movie, or "Hogan's Heroes", or something: American POWs alert overflying recon planes that the ball bearing plant, or munitions, or something, had been moved to a different building within their large secure complex. Once a day, the POWs got to exercise in a large open area amidst the many on-site secure buildings. The idea cooked up by the hero was to align the men, profiling an arrow, its "V" pointing to the culprit building.

Bill Sanborne had described the satellite pass-by schedule in effect before his arrival. Valid, he said, unless the orbit was altered or a replacement bird's been inserted. Well, a shot, any shot, was better than sitting on their hands. The only satellite pass that synchronized with their outside activity was at eleven in the morning. That's when they'd return from an early lunch served at the second building, forty yards away. That building, much smaller, housed Shafii and any guards rotated off security detail. This was their third clear day, and thus their third attempt to execute Beth's tenuous plan. All the captives, except Dech, knew of it. No one trusted Dr. Death.

Returning from the second building, the group formed a loose line, with two guards flanking the front, and one guard bringing up the rear. Dech was usually up front making friendly conversation with the guards; Beth hung nearby. Twenty yards out, they executed their plan:

Beth stepped out a couple of paces in front of the flanking guards—this formed the arrow's head. Dech, unknowingly, began the arrow's shaft, followed in line by Sanborne, the other two captives, and the rear guard. The entire moving formation stayed solid until reaching the outside staircase, where they ascended to their quarters for a thirty minute rest before returning to work in the lab below.

Beth watched those participating. Trying anything, even a hairbrained scheme like this, seemed to lift their spirits beyond the ever-present feelings of despair. She smiled.

CHAPTER 19
ALLAH'S WILL

Yesterday he had marked it "NI"—No Interest, and forgot about it. At least he thought he did. The night before, he and his wife went to a dinner party attended by three close couples: good food and too much wine. He should have slept better. He didn't. It was something from the office, swimming at the edge of his consciousness, not quite making it to shore.

That explained why Pete Townsend flashed his badge to the CIA's main gate civilian contract guard this early Sunday morning, much to the chagrin of his wife who earlier just groaned and rolled over. There was little traffic this morning as spies, his mind quipped, didn't like working weekends.

Once in his office, he pulled his back-data file. He kept a rotating month's worth of photo/data on hand for this very reason: handy reference and cross checking. Pete's area of expertise was the Mideast, in particular a geography known as the Islamic Republic of Iran. He found the folder marked Iran, Aug 24-KH18, and studied its contents once again. There:

photo number sixteen, east of Esfahan, 11:39:02 local: *those people.*

In reverse chronological order he pulled files, studying the same area. There it was, what his unconscious mind refused to let go: Aug 21 and Aug 23, same peopled configuration. So what? *Ain't going to the boss on…* There, the lead person, a woman… So…

"That's it!" he said aloud, unveiled, lot's of, he guessed, brown hair! A Westerner. *Okay, what else?* He went back to the peopled configuration, *like an arrow, maybe.*

Pete spent the following hours looking at what real time moving imagery the bird had captured during the time period of interest. At noon he left, feeling as if he'd just been laid and gotten a great night's sleep.

The place was called *Kirya*, home to Israel's Ministry of Defense. Located on Tel Aviv's Shaul Hamelekh Boulevard, the unmistakable government buildings within the compound stood in drab contrast to its modern, steel and glass highrise neighbors. They were in Defense Minister Yitzhak Cohen's modest office. He and Mossad Director David Amit waited for the third man to arrive.

"So, David," Cohen began, stroking his chin absently, "what does your agent in Washington tell us now?"

The MOSSAD director motioned toward an open folder. Visible atop its ten-page contents were the photocopied words, "STAIRCASE CLASSIFIED: Copy # 9." He placed it on Cohen's rather small desk. "Our first hard evidence. We must assume our friends in Iran are designing a batch targeted at Jews."

Cohen stood pacing, then spoke as if lecturing, "We are but six million people, as the Prime Minister keeps saying, crowded on a small strip of land. This STAIRCASE unleashed here would mean certain death for the state of Israel." He came around behind the MOSSAD director's chair, then full circle. "We must have this genetic virus, David. Do you understand?"

Amit did understand. He understood that Cohen and the

Prime Minister had become paranoid about this STAIR-CASE. They blamed him and his MOSSAD for not locating the Iranian lab. Finding a government lab and its purpose was relatively easy work since many people were required to support such a thing. But an underground operation run by a wanted anti-government radical group was quite another.

Amit sighed, "Yes, Yitshak, I understand."

There was more to understand. Israeli leadership desperately wanted the ultimate weapon in case the tide turned against Israel, which meant its enemies overrunning Israel's sovereign territory. Enemies, of course, meant their Arab neighbors, even distant ones like Iraq or Iran. Israel already possessed the ultimate weapon, had for over a quarter century—they thought. Yet the atomic bomb proved impotent in the face of the world's wrath, sure to descend upon them if they ever used it. But a virus was different. Designed for Arab genetic characteristics, it would be quiet and impossible to trace.

"Anything else?"

"Just that Zvi was correct. Nine hostages. They are experts in their fields: microbiology, molecular genetics, missile payload specialist, and a person specializing in computer viruses. Abu Hakim is pressing hard."

Cohen closed Amit's STAIRCASE folder, then answered the knock at his door. A solid, sure standing man in his early forties entered, greeted his peers and took a seat. Colonel Zvi Eitan was the SAYERET MAT'KAL leader of operation TALON'S GRIP, the label given by the Americans for the joint Israeli-American commando strike. Eitan looked through his dark eyes like a man who'd paid his dues, and needed little excuse to collect in kind. He was an extremely capable commando and now led the Defense Force's ultrasecret General Staff reconnaissance force. He held a special, dark place in his heart for Arabs, especially those calling themselves Persian.

Cohen spoke. "Zvi, I know that you are busy training your men and working with the American SEALs, but some things have changed." *What now?* thought Eitan. "First of all, how did the joint exercise go?"

"We have compartmentalized the operation. The SEALs secure entry and retrieve the hostages. My SAYERET MAT'KAL clear out any remaining on-site personnel, set charges, and destroy the lab and its contents. Obviously, it's very difficult to dry run, since we as yet do not know the lab's location and layout." No slight to the MOSSAD director intended, none taken. "Personally, sir, I do not see the need for the Americans. SAYERET MAT'KAL can handle it alone."

"Politics, Zvi. The Americans want credit for the hostage rescue, and they are more than a little concerned about their precious 'toxic substance.'"

"Zvi, on this matter of politics, I hope you appreciate the grief I endured from Colonel Hatfield from U.S. Special Operations Command. He says this should be a SEAL Team Six operation, their counterterrorist unit. He further says you refused their services, preferring west coast SEAL Team Three instead. I backed you up and agree with your reasoning. But Zvi, please, in the future, especially with Colonel Hatfield, exercise a little more diplomacy with your request."

Eitan smiled. "Of course, sir." His reasoning was sound. Operational security had to be maintained at all cost, lest lives lost and governments embarrassed. Eitan's problem with Team Six was that it currently had two foreign-exchange officers from the *Kampfschwimmerkompanie*, the German combat-swimmers. Each man in the room knew German companies freely sold offensive technology and materials to any Arab state that could afford them, including chemical and biological. And each man knew that any international transactions by German corporations surely had the support of the German Republic's government.

"Zvi, God willing, you may get your wish. If we find the lab before the Americans do. But just in case, is SEAL Team Three working out?"

"I know their Lieutenant Creed. He has an enviable record. Also, he led the raid on the *Ruh al-Asr*. Clean job. FIA never knew what hit them. I must admit, I've never seen any commando team as proficient in amphibious missions as this particular SEAL team. They can go from a wet environment to a dry one, and back again without difficulty. Very quiet, clean and tidy. My team will have little difficulty working with them."

"Thank you, Colonel. Just keep your men in your sight and ready to move on a moment's notice."

Eitan rose from his seat, then hesitated at the door. "And the hostages?"

"They are no concern to us."

The second line manager down at Photo Analysis had called this morning. Said he had something to show him. Important.

Marshall Douglas now stood in front of one of the lab's image analyzers. Next to him was the manager; seated at the controls was a young photo analyst, Pete Townsend. Pete began the brief like a detective solving a crime. The crime the DDI wanted solved was where were the missing scientists.

Townsend began with the stills, five days, three of which showed people aligned in an arrow configuration. Two of the stills showed a loose line, with no particular pattern. In all five, Townsend noted the woman, unveiled. Probably Western, not unlike the photo of Beth Storey now on record. He also pointed out the three men holding what looked like Kalashnikovs. Guards, Townsend speculated.

Next Townsend queued up the KH-18 sat real time imagery recorded on the same days. Like everyone else, Douglas watched the loose knit line, as if on cue, form into an arrow moving toward the two-story building. But Douglas saw more.

"I've seen enough. Excellent. Look, Pete, I need five copies of each of these photos. Can you condense the sat imagery into a three minute clip, packaged on standard video tape?"

"When do you need it?"

"Two hours."

Abu Hakim sat before the television watching Iran's president sell out everything Islamic fundamentalism stood for. And for what, Hakim boiled, so Iran can do business with the Great Satan.

The way Hakim saw it was that a true fundamentalist could pursue the Prophet Muhammad's word in one of two ways: either within or from without the current impure government. Many of his old influential colleagues, they would say, chose working from within. These, he knew, had simply been co-opted by plums of office offered by a government all too willing to compromise Islamic law, Islamic perfection. Hakim himself chose to work outside the corrupt government, seeking to replace it with a pure Islamic state.

Hakim knew that under this president, the Islamic movement had stalled. The current regime knew what it was against, but not what it was for. But even at that, *jihad*, armed struggle against the infidels of the world, had turned luke warm. Indeed, supporting the *umma*, the Islamic community of nations, had waned as well. And the economic troubles Iran now experienced, the president chose to blame on the *tondro*, the hardliners, his favorite whipping boy. The man blames anyone but himself, Hakim bristled, this man who now on the television before him, proselytizes himself and Iran before the entire world.

The Khomeini regime had tried to exterminate all opposition, especially the militant hardlinners. His wrath turned fiercest against the People's Mujahideen of Iran, killing or imprisoning a quarter million of its supporters. That was fortunate for Hakim, for, unnoticed, it allowed him and his militant Islamic followers to grow and strengthen. And strengthen they did. Hakim now garnered the sympathy from an impressive percentage of the *Majlis*, Iran's parliament. Now he would take control, Allah willing. Now he would have the means to handle the Zionist problem once and for all.

Hakim looked at his watch, then leaned forward, listening to the president lead up to his reascending Salman Rushdi's death sentence for blasphemy against—

"Pop, pop...pop," he finally heard, then watched the

president slump to the floor. *If Allah wills it*, he prayed.

The DDO was the first to notice an increase in Presidential security, and he understood. The Secret Service SAC, himself, Jim Rhodes had the post in the secretary's anteroom. It was axiomatic: the assassination of a head of state spurred ideas in every would-be crackpot assassin in the world.

Temple remained at his Oval Office desk motioning the three men to chairs. Accompanying Jordan Barr was Lieutenant Colonel Coleman and the DDI, Marshall Douglas. "Okay, Marshall, it's your meeting."

"Good news, bad news, Sir." Douglas briefed everyone on the KH-18 reconnaissance find and CIA photo analysis.

"Other than the scientists, anything on STAIRCASE?"

"Sir, there's a subtle twist to this human arrow. It doesn't just point to the building. Specifically, it points to this staircase leading to the building's second level." Douglas repeated the word, punctuating the two syllables. "Gentlemen, let me repeat, STAIR-CASE."

"Humm. It fits. Ingenious. Now what?"

"Now the bad news, Sir."

"Don't tell me, Temple usurped. The assassination."

"That's correct, Sir," said Barr. Coleman nodded his agreement. "The country's in a very unstable state. The military's on alert and everyone's tense. I wouldn't recommend an operation for at least a month, at least not until they get their new leadership worked out."

"Ideas on whose behind it?"

"Not really," answered Douglas. "The man was part of the president's personal guard. After he fired on the president, he turned the gun on himself. Who stands to gain? The extreme fundamentalists have made significant inroads over the last five years. They want a pure state run only by Islamic religious laws. I've even heard Abu Hakim's name mentioned as a possibility."

"Recommendations?" asked the President, leaning back into his chair.

Coleman answered, "Put TALON'S GRIP on hold, but keep the SEAL and Israeli teams on a high state of readiness. Gather more intelligence on the lab and its location so a more detailed mission profile can be worked up."

The President, though not a simple man, followed a few basic and simple rules. The one on which he never flinched was "tit-for-tat," applying it to all his interactions with the external world. For each "tat" received, Temple would always respond with his version of a "tit"—usually of greater magnitude than the incoming "tat." If the "tat" were hostile, his response was with greater force and impact. Much to the chagrin of a newfound enemy. Although he didn't necessarily agree with them, Temple always admired Israeli methods: an attack on Israeli sovereignty was always answered with considerable force directed at those who ordered, as well as executed, the attack.

If the incoming "tat" was a gift or the result of a requested favor, the "tit" was always more than appreciated.

Simple rules, Temple thought, made for the best working environment. It had been that way since he could remember. The one glaring exception had been the Carter Administration. The ground rules, if there were any, kept changing. No one knew which way was up; no one had their feet on the ground. Sort of the same thing happened to Reagan. When he veered from his simple rule, "I will not deal with terrorists." Guess what? The conflict in Reagan's mind, Temple was convinced, showed up as chaos in the American psyche.

The ground was stable as long as everyone knew the rules. So here he was, his rules required him to slam those responsible for taking the hostages. Problem was their identity was still unknown. Certainly he could forget overtures from the Iranian government for awhile, if not indefinitely. Douglas says cool it, but still.

"Okay, we know where they are. Find out whose behind that operation, and make it fast," said Temple. "Meanwhile I'll be talking to our U.N. Ambassador looking at ways we might get at the Iranian bastards through the U.N.—without revealing the nature of STAIRCASE, of course. Maybe if the government hurts enough, they'll fix this problem." With no other comments, Temple brought it up again.

"New subject. The LIST. Where do we stand? Marshall."

"Sir, as I said before, it's a tall order. The assassination of our Tokyo station Chief has me worried. I've chosen to cool the pressure exerted by our Tokyo station for fear of driving the LIST down even deeper. Sir, we've had a blind agent in Japan working this. If anyone can dig it out, it'll be him. But I must remind, just like I tell the Vice President each day, it *will* take time."

Temple knew the LIST wouldn't be pretty. But more of late, he began to realize that more than scandal and embarrassment, his pursuing *Banto*'s LIST risked undercutting his very own political career. For the more he pressured *Banto*, the more apt they were to call up the LIST and exercise influence against him. Plus, Temple knew, Japan was now the world's banker, and their money spent well in the Senate and Congressional offices on the Hill. A place, it seemed these days, he had few friends. It was almost like a gunfight, the first one hitting his target, wins. The trouble with this gunfight, he grimaced, was that at the moment the only visible target standing in the street was him.

"Stay with it, Marshall." For whatever reason, John Adam Temple had to know.

CHAPTER 20
STRANGE ATTRACTORS

Seven days had passed since the assassin's Washington arrival. It was his intent to study every inch of the White House grounds and its three block radius, especially at night. Tonight he stood in Farragut Square looking at a bronze statue of the park's namesake. He took the time to study the Union Civil War admiral, telescope in hand, surrounded by cannon, one at each major point of the compass.

Japan, herself, was a nation of the sea, he thought, but a much older one. Admiral Farragut was celebrated for his victory at New Orleans and breaking the Confederate blockade at Mobile, fighting for a nation still searching for its identity well less than a century in age. The Japanese cultural community traced back to its Joman Period, some ten thousand years ago. Even *ninjutsu*, the *ninja*'s secret fighting art, originated five hundred years before the first European set foot on this new land. America was but a young teenager, lacking grace, lacking focus.

The assassin's heritage, itself, could be traced back some three hundred years. His roots were from Tokushima, a city on the eastern shores of Shikoku, the smallest of Japan's four large islands. At a young age, the assassin learned of an ancestral grandfather. The grandfather, as a young boy, escaped the local Shogunate's vengeful killing of his entire family for their aligning themselves with the Shogunate's enemies. Hunted himself, the boy made his way inland up into the mountains. There, he remembered Sakuma-san, an acquaintance of his now slain father, whom he'd visited once just two months before the attack.

The local villagers left Sakuma and his group alone, for it was said the old man practiced magic, especially magic tied closely to the practice of *ninjutsu*. The young refugee made his way to old Sakuma's house and was accepted. There, he melted in quietly with Sakuma and his obscure *ryu* of twenty.

The members of the *ryu* were experts in assassination. Each job was executed with quiet precision sometimes against well-fortified and protected noblemen. They were highly successful and their reputation spread. With the consolidation of his power over Japan in 1603, Tokugawa Ieyasu began two and a half centuries of peace. Early in this Tokugawa period, fearing the *samurai* as potential destabilizing threats, these feudal warriors were transformed into a governmental class: *bushido* became *kanryodo*—the way of the bureaucrat.

In co-opting the *samurai*, the *ninja's* usefulness increased. And so did Sakuma's deadly fighting machines who believed "in the old ways"—the ways of infiltration and assassination with ancient weapons. It was through this lineage that the assassin came to stand before this American admiral on this crisp moonless night. His special skill was killing people—a thousand ways of death. The death of the American president would pose few problems.

Through his *bujutsu* martial arts training in this ancient ryu, he'd learned a different way of perceiving reality, body sensations unverbalized, *haragei*—what some might call extrasensory abilities: extraordinary perception of hearing and feeling one's immediate surroundings. It was this total inte-grated "sense" that now warned him of danger. *Two of them...behind the tree over his left shoulder...watching, now moving.*

The assassin reaches inside his loose-fitting black-matte shirt, pivots and steps toward the on-coming figures: teenag-ers, both black, one nine millimeter now pointed at his stomach; the other taller one is producing a Mac-10 from under an expensive black leather jacket.

The two teenagers hesitate inexplicably under an intense black gaze. FLASH: the night goes nova, retinas shut down blind. A blur, and a homeless man lying on a nearby bench stirs. And the assassin becomes the night.

Through the back kitchen entrance, up the service elevator and back into his Hay-Adams Hotel room, the assassin quietly checked for unauthorized entry and listening devices. Just as in the last five days, the room was "clean." The encounter tonight had been the first untoward incident since his arrival. It did not disturb him, especially since no blood was drawn. Senseless violence was something foreign in Japan.

Tonight, for three hours, before retiring, the assassin sat under the writing desk facing the door. Watching, sensing. Tomorrow, he would call this Washington contact with a 212 Area Code. After that, John Adam Temple would die.

Eariler in the afternoon, Teal Coro had spoken with Ryan Voight back at his Washington office. It seemed the FBI hadn't a clue where the Japanese national called White Shadow was. Voight went over the L.A. customs agent's statement. Nothing there except fabrication. It was part of their arrange-ment. Voight funneled anything of interest to Coro, Coro reciprocated.

Tonight, Teal Coro knelt on the hide of a bison, facing the sweatlodge. Tonight, Coro would listen with Coyote Shadow's heart, not with his ears.

It was customary for his people to enter the sweatlodge

seeking purification of body, mind, and spirit, especially in preparation for taking a life. Tonight, he would trust only his heart for clear thinking. It would allow him to get closer in touch with the primal animal within him, closer to his basic instincts he knew he would need against this dark product of ancient Japan.

Coyote Shadow paused reverently before the sweatlodge in front of him. It was constructed of things pure, built by hand using only carefully selected materials of the wilderness: saplings, skins, and stones. A place that was pure.

Coyote Shadow entered the lodge securing the door from all outside distractions. He found his position among others in a darkness ladened by the translucent glow of red-orange, hot rocks. At first the heat was oppressive, sweat pouring from his body. But in time its notice disappeared as his mind drew groggy, then began to expand. Expand beyond his body, beyond the lodge, filling the universe of all things.

Hours later someone placed cedar, sage, and sweetgrass on the rocks. The fragrance mingled with flesh and mind. Applied water turned dry heat to superhot steam. It became too hot for clear thoughts, too hot for focused...

Coyote Shadow traveled through the veil, and beyond the veil time as a barrier did not exist. It became a path down which one could travel. He became aware of Greek-columned architecture. An old woman was studying it, taking pictures. It was a place he knew. The Treasury Building next the White House. But it wasn't a woman at all. The "woman" walked toward him, looking directly at him, but of course she could not see his form. *It was him.* The White Shadow.

Conscious thought began to intrude, and the image was gone.

Before paying the Japanese taxi driver, Westin again looked out the rear window. There he was, on the black and chrome motorcycle, pink stripes flanking his gray-visored helmet. Some days Westin spotted him, some days he didn't. Yesterday morning he was there, following him to the Tokyo train station. Yet Westin hadn't seen him at all during his stay in Numazu, but now there he was upon his return, as if on cue. That meant he had more than one tail. Westin wondered if his guardian CIA angel was out there too; he'd not seen Okada since his arrival ten days ago.

Between briefings on Japan's impressive progress in developing NIQE-based weapons systems, Westin had scheduled a couple of weekdays for himself. He'd spent yesterday in Numazu, where his father allegedly assaulted Kojima's family. The trip was just as fruitful as his researching the World War II achieves in Tokyo. Zip. No official Numazu records survived the July 1945 firebomb raid on the city, and none kept until September the next year. That left out August, the critical month.

Upon his return, this time he decided to stay in a western-style hotel in Yokohama, located central to most of his activities. He threw his bag onto the "real" bed, opened it, and found his father's military service record. He read it again for the hundredth time: He noted the Pacific theater campaigns. He read from the forms filled in by his Dad's officers, their fitness reports, a couple of commendations, the fateful reprimand, *loss of dog tag, Numazu, July 29*. His duty in Japan: stationed Yokohama, May 05, 1946…Numazu, July 19, 1946…Accident, August 01: pinned under an overturned Army jeep. Chest crushed, lacerated kidney. Taken to Yokohama Army Base Hospital same day. Died August 07, 1946. Cause, internal injuries and bleeding. Westin studied the photograph for a long time, unaware of the pitched ringing building in his ears. *A rapist?*

On the third ring, Westin finally picked up the telephone receiver. It was Coleman. Coleman promised he'd let Westin know if something broke on Beth's whereabouts. It was a short, somewhat cryptic call, just enough for Coleman to make good on his promise, yet stay clean over an unsecure line.

John understood very well the veiled references: They had found Beth, and as Coleman suspected, she was with the other missing scientists. And evidently working on that "most deadly toxin this world has yet developed," as Coleman put it over Sunday afternoon barbecue. The bad news: the group had moved, destination unknown. Even worse was what John had read in the newspaper yesterday: Abu Hakim had been quickly appointed Iran's new president, the man Coleman suspected as behind the kidnappings and the biological project. Coleman didn't want to speculate on when they'd find them again, much less attempt a rescue. A month maybe?

Westin sat pondering Coleman's cryptic words and their ultimate meaning. What did Coleman say while tending those backyard steaks two weeks ago: CIA's worst case netted out to October first, the earliest estimate when "borrowed" scientific services would be no longer needed. Today was August thirtieth. *At best, a month before a rescue attempt.* His stomach churned at the deduction. She wasn't going to make it!

The telephone's ring startled him from his ominous thoughts. He answered, then heard the unmistakable voice of a temptress, "Finally tracked you down, Mr. John Westin. How are you going to make my party when you're stuck way over there in Japan?" Carrera Thielken. He begged duty to the seductive voice six thousand miles away. "You know you can't resist me, John Westin," she purred coyly. "Besides, I have someone special I want you to meet." *Someone special*, rang in his ears as he thought of Beth Storey and the last time he saw her—*the last time? What could he do, he didn't know. But for damn sure he couldn't do it from here.*

"Carrera, do I get a prize for 'traveled longest distance'?" John shifted.

"A prize you'll never forget, John Westin," came a voice wrought with sensual interest.

"That's what they said when I won 'Best Camper' back at Camp Little Watonga."

"And what did the little camper win?"

"Lunch at the local woman's club. Had to read a poem to the biddies."

Carrera laughed goodheartedly. John followed, "Carrera,

looks like I'll be in L.A. this Saturday night. I promise. See you then." *Well, Carrera, chalk up one token astronaut for your party.* Ole Craig MacIsaac was right—sort of—one doesn't refuse Carrera Thielken. Hmmm, the beverage of his choice—that'll be a bottle of scotch, J&B.

John looked at his watch, then called Tanner at the Atsugi Naval Air Facility. "Commander Stan, this is important. Can you meet me in Yokohama, a small restaurant next to the Holiday Inn…Yeah, the Holiday Inn…Thirty minutes then. Thanks Stan."

John called the airline, rescheduled his departure taking the five-ten out this afternoon—two and a half hours. He retrieved his tickets and passport, zipped the bag and left to check back out. At the small eatery, he took a booth with a good view through the street-front windows and door. No one suspicious followed him in and he paid little attention to the two men seated at the center table.

Like clockwork, Stan joined him. Over iced *kohii*, John explained the situation and what Coleman had just said. He told Stan too much, he knew, but he had to tell someone he trusted, and besides he was about to ask his friend for a little covert and possibly dangerous help.

"So, Stan, I need two things. First, can you do that interview tomorrow, solo? Send me the transcripts and any material you get. Second, as I said, I'm being followed," Stan leaned in closer, "and it's occurred to me that they might not want me leaving their country."

"How can I help, ace?"

"I don't know how many there are. But I do know the motorcycle. Think that cheap-shit car of yours can loose it long enough for me to jump out, hide, then grab a cab for Narita?"

"John, remember that time in North Nam. We had a missile hot on our six, and you fly under that bridge to scrape it off. Sucker took out the bridge to boot." John grinned. Tanner pushed back his chair, then said, "Son, now it's my turn to show you how a professional does it."

As John walked out, something clicked, something his eye just took in but his mind had yet to register. He looked back at the center table. One man removed an earplug, its wire connected to a mini-boom, the kind private detectives used to eavesdrop on distant conversations. The second man, scarred eyebrow. *Shit!* The tail at Narita Airport. *Just great!* He stepped up even with Tanner and in a lowered voice announced, "Stanner ole buddy. Two of the fuckers are behind us, heard the plan, too. It's me they want. Plan B." Westin bolted for the door and into the street from between parked cars. The motorcycle, at high speed, rushed towards him...

When John made his move, Tanner turned to look back. He saw two men heading for him, shoving a waitress, now at a sprint, their eyes focused beyond him...at John! As they accelerated for the door, Tanner stepped to the side, grabbed two chairs swinging them hard around into the thugs' oncoming path. It worked, clipping both men, tangling their legs in the chairs' ironwork. The eavesdropper went headfirst into the doorjamb, bouncing off unconscious. The second man careened into an empty table, cascading further into another table, occupied by two businessmen. That's when Tanner saw the pistol tucked away in the tumbling man's belt. Tanner took the cue, and outside seeing no sign of John, sprinted around the corner.

John felt like he'd just dodged a bullet. He'd ducked back between the parked cars feeling the motorcycle's heat as it tried to run him down. Once by, he tucked his airline carry-on under his arm, then like a running back with the ball, bolted for the hotel doors across the street. He found himself in the Satellite Hotel Yokohama's extravagantly elegant lobby which seemed to go on forever. His civilized mind told him to slow down, act normal; his instincts said run. He ran. To the left, the lobby narrowed down to a sumptuous hall, several doors flanking the gilded splendor. In mid-hall, he stopped, again hearing the high-pitched sound.

John couldn't quite believe his eyes: a black and chrome motorcycle tearing black rubber on the gold-patterned persimmon-red carpet. He took the nearest door, and almost stopped to stare. A banquet for two hundred stretched out in four long rows, each comprised of fifty separate floor chairs and accompanying lacquered tray tables. Two hundred blue suits sat amid cypress woods and red accents; at the far end was a stage with a huge silkscreen draped across its back wall.

John dashed for the opposite stage end. As the room fell silent, the entry doors crashed open with a deafening roar of eight thousand RPMs. Near the stage, a blue suit stood to challenge John's obtrusive presence. John shoved him aside as the bike closed in, hitting brakes. John ducked through a side door to the right, a service hallway. He took the shortest path heading for the double-doors at the its end, now hearing the powerful engine reverberate against the cinder block walls, closer...closer. He threw his body against the hinged double-doors, the roar blotting out all sanity. Crashing through, he lost his footing, slipping down hard onto a completely wet terrazzo tile surface. It was the service entrance into a Japanese bath, naked men about in various stages of scrubbing, rinsing, most in the far large bath, soaking. He scrambled wildly, unable to regain his footing...then just rolled to the side as tires streaked across his left arm and carry-on. In the blink of an eye, the bike was down on the slick surface, sliding at tremendous speed toward surprised men submerged to their necks. John watched as bike and rider hit the water, surging a wave of hundred and ten degree water onto the far wall. Bodies scurried amid more steam. In the confusion, John wasted no time finding the bath's guest entry, another hallway, and exit.

A minute later, he sat in a cab, carry-on beside him, nurturing a sore left arm.

The man at the Yokohama eatery, recognized by Westin, had regained his composure. He followed the motorcyclist into the hotel across the street. Seeing the commotion stirred and that he couldn't keep up, he returned to retrieve his colleague, come to, but definitely not up for another round.

Having listened to the American's conversation, the man

knew Westin was leaving Japan early. That, could not be allowed to happen, per Shimizu's orders. Which meant Takara's orders. And no one failed Takara. He put his colleague into a cab, then raced off to Narita. He would stop the American at the airport.

"Concourse B, down the escalator over there. Have a pleasant flight, Mr. Westin." Westin turned to clear his battered carry-on through the airport scanners—

"Westin-san, please come with me." Westin looked up. It was the same Japanese man, scared eyebrow, he'd left back in the Yokohama eatery. A discrete gun barrel in his ribs made his request quite reasonable. In tandem, they walked out passed the front row of brightly lit South Wing duty free shops, and on outside the main entrance. It was busy and Westin considered a quick move, perhaps back into the terminal, when—

"Good evening, Mr. Westin." It was Stan!

The Japanese looked shocked, then blurted, "*Omae*—"

"Before you get excited, Mojo, look behind you." Two rather fearsome-looking men met the gaze. "You may walk away now, or you may not. You have three seconds to make your choice. One, two—" The Japanese turned and walked briskly toward the close-in parking lot, disappearing into the evening. He didn't see the third man fall in behind him.

"John Wayne and the calvary," John said looking relieved, "Who the hell are these guys?

"Called a friend of mine. He's a Technical Services guy with the Company. He brought friends. Look John, they're not suppose to be here. You didn't see 'em, okay?" John had to smile. Tanner looked at his watch. "Let's get you moving. They'll stay with you as far as the security scanners, then you're on your own."

Takara was furious. His fox-like aide, Shimizu, and the man whose hands John Westin slipped through stood respectfully listening to the tirade leveled at their competence.

They were in Takara's remote summer residence located two hours south of Tokyo. A virtual fortress, compliments to its CEO from the Misawa Group. The exterior of the house was patterned after the *shishinden* within the Imperial Palace complex in Kyoto. The *shishinden* had once been the residence of the head of the royal household, often used for special celebrations. That's where the similarity from the nine thousand square-foot classic rectangular building ended. Two things differed significantly: first was the location, embedded in a mountainside, the fortress offered three majestic views, one including the Pacific Ocean; the second difference was the interior, totally designed to suit modern taste contrasted with a visual richness offered by appointments from ancient Japan.

Pacing behind a wide Chinese couch, Takara had them at attention in the east sitting room. The room itself depicted a noble splendor dominated by an enclave. Within the enclave, atop a cabinet's reflective surface sat a black *okidai*—sword holder—standing like an archway. Beneath the two meter curved arch, two swords lay in the *okidai's* holding slots, their sheathed blades bending in gentle synchronisity with the crowning arch. Visually together, their curved silhouettes cut into three equal spaces the intensely stark background: the flag of Japan—the rising sun, bright blood red against its white silk background. This was Takara's favorite room.

Shimizu, he trusted, totally, but this fiasco merited his wrath, and that he'd just given in ample quantities. The one with the scared eyebrow briefed Takara on Westin's movements: the NIQE-based meetings, and the subject's personal excursions.

Takara was now convinced Westin killed his *kobun*, Kojima. Kojima's body had already been cremated, but analysis of the ceremonial knife present with Kojima's body confirmed Setaka's warning: foul play. In addition to the *katana*, traces of Kojima's blood and guts were also on the nearby knife. Takara now wondered if Westin sought revenge against the entire Kojima family. His digging around in Numazu would indicate so.

Two things softened Takara's wrath this Friday morning. First was that in mid-September, Westin was scheduled to return. He'd deal with his *kobun*'s murderer then. Second, was the description of the two Americans' conversation, and this "most deadly toxin the world has ever developed." Takara pulled the disfigured tin soldier from his pocket, his fingers unconsciously rubbing it's deformed face.

Takara waved his thick hand, dismissing the incompetent, then walked over to a large display encasing a seventeenth century Japanese warrior's costume. He stared at writing on the breastplate while giving instructions to his aide, "Shimizu-san, begin opening channels with the new Iranian government and its president. It will take time, but your goal will be to ascertain the nature of this toxin he possesses. After that, if it can be of use to us, then proceed to secure it as soon as possible."

CHAPTER 21
ALL DRESSED UP

Traversing the quarter mile circular approach to the Hollywood Hills mountaintop estate, Westin passed a never ending display of exotic "metallica," valet parked curbside. Finally, he pulled up to the front of the strikingly simple Thielken estate. The home took a quiet and somewhat eerie feel from soft shadows created by floodlights pointed skyward against its white adobe facade. Simple yes, small no. To John's eye, the estate disappeared only when it cascaded out of view down the gentle slope of the rear-side hill. John surrendered his rented Chysler Acclaim to a not too enthusiastic valet, then began to wonder what the hell he was doing here.

Inside, the men split evenly in business suits—John's blue was passable—and California hip, which defied a consistent description. It was nice, John had forgotten, to survey the women, all decked out in glitter clinging to sparse quantities of fabric. John found one of the three bars, then walked into the expansive living room nursing a scotch and water.

Around the room the play of light against totally neutral tones gave the appearance of rippled fields of wheat. Each tasteful piece in the room reinforced an atmosphere of sophisticated simplicity. John cruised the room admiring the large bronze sculpture along the way. He hardly knew anyone, though he recognized a California senator, and L.A.'s mayor. Spotting an encircled Vice President Dhillon Reed over by the grand piano, he sauntered over joining the circle in time to hear someone ask Reed's thoughts on the Name Dropper.

Reed, a broad-shouldered fit man, towered above the cluster. The characteristic feature exploited by political cartoonists was his stern trying-to-be-serious scowl plastered strangely on a boyish face. To Westin, his commentary always sounded prepared, memorized.

"I believe the mayor and the Chief of Police have set the proper policy tone and are doing everything possible to stop the person who slays Los Angeles' underprivileged youth." *All dressed up*, mused Westin, *and nothing to say*. He peeled off catching a Midwestern mush-mouth in mid-oratory.

"Godless commies. Finally got what's comin' to 'em. Starve in Hell in the end. God's prophesy, I tell you." Westin moved on, keeping an eye out for Carrera or her husband, Shiraki Industries' CEO. John felt a little odd, on leave from Paxton and being here in their archenemy's castle.

John walked over to the window. He looked down at a four hundred and sixty square mile carpet bejeweled and shimmering under thermals rising from buildings patterned on its asphalt fabric. It was as if by providence, he thought—or better still, "by Carrera's" will—that a night like this, without haze, presented itself for the party. He didn't really know Carrera Thielken all that well, except that she invited him to all her parties. MacIsaac was right, Carrera was a woman who wouldn't take "no" for an answer—there was danger there too, his mind continued to caution.

"Hello, Mr. Westin." It was Carrera. John turned to see a most stunning contrast: Carrera wore a simple tuxedo pant suit, with wide-notched brushed satin lapels. That was it, nothing else, except for the Mikimoto pearls: three matched concentric circles snug around her neck, matched bracelet, and finally resting on her right hand ring-finger, nestled amid small diamonds, was a perfect South Sea pearl. Somewhere deep within this display of elegance and power, Westin, as before, sensed a hint of little girl's insecurity—and they both knew it.

"Saw you over there with Reverend 'Righteous,'" she continued, smiling, moving closer.

"Tammy here too," John deadpanned.

"I know. That's Glenn's doing, not mine. I would have rather you met Raja Ajar. He is a mystic, an enlightened master, teaching me how to attain transcendental oneness, perfect harmony." John tried to look interested. "He couldn't come tonight, sent his stockbroker instead."

"Hmmm," he took a sip, "How many Elvis sightings has this Raja Ajar had?" John's grin communicated shamelessly: Take's one to know one.

"Don't forget, Mr. Astronaut, one man's bullshit is another man's Revelation."

"What does Raja Ajar reveal to you?" Westin said, feeling as if on the edge of a whirlpool threatening to suck him in deeper, faster.

"My desires," Carrera came back, her deep China-blue eyes displaying an uncertain hint of tease.

"Now that's some answer." *Deeper, faster.*

"But answers can be dangerous, John. Questions, I've discovered, are much more interesting," she said, her voice softening, moving closer still, "For instance, you ever wonder what's on a woman's mind?" She paused strobing his chest.

John willfully refrained from moving closer. "Yeah. Except a question like that invites more," John ventured, not knowing why. "Tougher questions."

"Yes," she said triumphantly, a conquering smile tracing her lips.

"Uh-oh. I've seen that look before." It was the Vice President.

"Dhillon Reed, this is John Westin, astronaut, now with

Paxton," Carrera introduced.

Reed indulged, then said his time was short and reminded Carrera she'd wanted to show him something. They excused themselves, leaving Westin alone again with the Los Angeles basin below.

Carrera led Reed out to the pool, ringed by Chinese-style iron lanterns. She made conversion, "Now what was that banker's strategy you promised to tell me?" Reed's background was banking.

"Okay," Reed said, his face lightened up a bit. "The problem for an established bank is that it's difficult getting new customers. So it becomes critical not to lose the ones you've got. And that boils down to customer loyalty. So in the banking game, we build customer loyalty by establishing relationships with the customer." Carrera nodded to the Shiraki security guard as they proceeded down the hill to the greenhouse. Reed did the same, motioning his Secret Service escort not to follow.

"The way it works with relationships is, more is better, better bonding with the customer. For instance, if we have a customer with only a checking account with our bank then we figure we have a fifty percent loyalty factor; that is, a fifty percent chance our customer may come in tomorrow and close his account—goodbye relationship. But if you have a second relationship, say a savings account, loan, or safe deposit box, then loyalty goes to seventy percent. And if you have a third, like if we're involved in his portfolio management, then we're at ninety percent—he's practically locked."

They'd reached the greenhouse, Carrera locking its door behind them. Reed finally asked, "And what is it you want to show me?"

She took his hand moving him to a closed tool locker. She moved closer, her wide sensual lips parted gently, her tongue playful. He pulled back. Her lips pouted to a point, as she wrapped her hands around his ears, through his hair. He responded. Her tongue became a snake, searching, hot.

She stepped back, slipping off the black tuxedo pants. He watched them fall coiled like a silent serpent. He watched her hungry eyes while her hands plied his buckle, while her hands worked wonderful magic.

He grabbed the silk pulling it down, then powerfully, he pulled her to him, his arms entwined tight around her waist. She responded by lifting her athletic legs, wrapping them around his back.

He turned pressing her body against the wooden locker, both moving in concert, heated, wanton, lusty, convulsive. Her back arched as she whispered a primal, "Yes, yes!" Her ankles locked hard against his spine, tension reaching the exquisite threshold of pain. Her loins rolled upward in powerful thrusts…and yes, he felt a muffled groan against his chest, feeling tenseness dissolve from her peaked body.

Moments later, with the intensity still an echo in his relaxing body, Reed turned to lean against the storage locker side-by-side with Carrera. His breath subsiding, he wondered what thoughts might be going through this woman's mind right now.

Tell me again, Mr. Vice President, about relationships and customer loyalty.

Westin found himself in the media room snagged by a personal injury lawyer; classic stereotype, he thought, playing his personal life as close to the vest as he did his professional life. The attorney had just boasted of a case just won; it was against the man to whose party his client had attended, drank alcoholic beverages, then on the way home, he'd run a light killing a young mother of two.

"Whatever happened to personal responsibility?" Westin leveled at this lawyer who himself had had too much to drink.

"Oh, I get it," the lawyer defended, exaggerating mocked surprise, "Lawyer bashing!"

"Not really," Westin lied. "And besides, where do I get off bashing the top of the food chain?" *Shit.*

Westin turned for another drink again trying to remember why he'd bothered to come in the first place. The phone. It was located in the middle of twenty people, segregated in clustered conversations. He picked up the receiver, entered his account number followed a 619 Area Code and number. "You ready to collect on that beer I owe you?"

"You a little dressed for this place," said Navy SEAL Lieutenant Don Creed, motioning a seat next to Chief McCullough.

Westin had had no problems with Creed's telephone instructions: from the Thielken party to San Diego and over the bridge to Coronado took a little better than two hours. The place was called McP's, a kelly green, brass and oak kind of place. Not too big: a few booths, some two-foot round tables scattered around the fireplace and a massive Irish bar. Even though food was served, unmistakably, this was a drinking place. The Saturday night C&W band had just knocked off for a fifteen minute break.

Back at the Thielken party, his encounter with the drunk lawyer made him think of vultures, and the joke: Where one of two vultures perched in a tree turns to the other and says, *Patience, hell. I'm going down there and kill somebody.* That's exactly how he felt, and why he'd made the call.

Westin looked at a lean hard-cut man with short blue-black hair. It was the same look, a look of supreme confidence, of the two Navy SEALs that pulled his aviator ass out of the drink off the coast of Nam. Ever since that time, John kept up with the West Coast SEALs, especially those in Team Three. He'd made new friends over the years, abruptly losing some too. The thing he liked about these men was their attitude: They lived by a different set of rules, rules that included, if necessary, breaking the ones that the rest of the world lived by. That's what brought Westin here tonight.

"Chief" was the name Sean McCullough took when he was promoted from First Class Petty Officer, and immediately the name seemed like it always was and would be. "Fifteen years ago," McCullough would say, "he was bored with his first two years in the Navy stationed at Yokosuka, Japan." Then he joined the SEALs. "Now," he was fond of saying, "when I get up in the morning, I don't know if I'll be jumpin' at sixteen thousand feet, running fourteen miles, or takin' a walk in someone else's backyard. Life ain't dull no more!"

Creed, in his "before" life, had worked at a steel mill in Johnstown, Pennsylvania. His fateful day turned out to be just another Saturday after payday waking up in the drunk tank, again. Focusing his eyes, he looked up to see an older co-worker, and as if a portentous dream, saw himself twenty years in the future. As Creed would tell the story, that scared the shit out of him and as soon as he was released, he walked straight out and into the Navy recruiter's office and said, "When can you get me outta here?" After Navy boot camp, he entered Basic Underwater Demolition/SEAL (BUD/S) Training and graduated a SEAL, one of the elite. He quickly excelled at the important things, like getting the job done, especially the quiet art of death.

Westin thumbed his tie, then quipped, "Knowing you guys were here, I just assumed this had to be some swanky place."

"He tellin' us this ain't swanky?" Chief asked Creed in mocked puzzlement. Westin grinned, removed his tie and ordered beer.

After some catching up and another round, Westin got down to business. He swore his two friends to secrecy, then summarized Coleman's story about the L.A. cab shooting, the stolen briefcase, and its deadly contents—a new deadly toxin or something. He talked of the missing scientist, Beth Storey, and the likely link to the stolen briefcase. As Coleman had relayed to him yesterday, he described what satellite reconnaissance revealed; at that, Westin thought he saw a look exchanged between the two SEALs, but couldn't be sure. He went on telling of the group's movement, probably the work of the suspected mastermind Abu Hakim, a hardline Islamic fundamentalist, ties to FIA, too.

At this point, Westin felt the mood change: from guarded curiosity to guarded sensitivity. They knew something. He knew it, but decided not to push it for fear they'd withdraw from the conversation, from his request for help.

"Let me get this straight," Creed said with a sarcastic lilt. "You waltz in here, buy us a couple of beers—which you owed us anyway—and ask us to help you find this gang-Iranian connection. And you're going to use this connection to find this woman of yours." John nodded slowly, unabashedly. "And why should Chief and me give a rat's ass?"

John leaned in, both forearms flat on the table, his face almost centerline. "Creed, in some ways you and me are a lot alike. You and Chief, when you sign up for a job, you don't quit 'till you see it through, right? Well, same here."

Creed didn't blink as he studied the pilot. Yeah, in some ways they were alike, mostly unconventional ways. Ever since he'd known the flyboy, he never saw Westin on the sidelines; definitely a player, maybe that's why he liked the man, Creed wondered. And right now, this player, sure as hell, wasn't going to let it go.

Throughout the silence, John held a steady determined gaze, a look acknowledging that only from a friend would he ask such a favor.

Finally Creed looked at Chief. Chief returned a shrug—what the hell. The band approached the small stage, settling in. Soon conversation would be impossible. John, wanting to offer something in return, asked, "Sneaking into other people's backyards, that's your bag, isn't it?" No response. "I've got something to show you sometime," John continued, pushing his chair back. "Think you'll find it interesting."

Westin paid up their bill and then some, then left as the band cranked up "Drop Kick Me, Jesus, Through The Goal Posts of Life."

Creed leaned toward Chief, "Whadaya think?"

"L.A., Moondog came from there. Got a brother there, I think."

"How's his arm?" Creed asked. After SCARAB, the base physician gave Chucho Muñoz a month limited duty to nurse back the wound.

"Moondog's healing good. You want me to talk to him?" Creed nodded.

Beth Storey stepped into the grayish morning. They had been moved to a compound somewhere north of Tehran. A converted Army Aviation Command Hospital, one of her guards had said. The previous regime had converted the old compound into a secret biological warfare research and development center. Now, under the new Islamic fundamentalist regime, the hardliners moved her and the others here, dedicating the compound solely to developing a STAIRCASE targeted for Jewish characteristics. After that, efforts would shift to other selected Caucasian traits.

Beth had just stepped out of Ward Number Two, where the five remaining hostages were kept. Adjacent to that, was the larger Ward Number One, which now housed the a platoon of the elite Islamic Guard. She stood studying her new home.

About one hundred yards long and wide, the inside fence was surrounded by an outer fence, thirty feet of mined buffer lie in between. Four guard towers at the corners, each mounted with a machine gun and manned by a submachine gun toting soldier. Wards One and Two were located to the rear, behind where she stood now. As she looked to the front, the old brig building stood straight ahead, and beyond that was the building housing administrative offices, mess and a isolated security control office. Off to her right was a modern lab in which she and the others would work during the day. In front of the lab was a helipad, currently unoccupied, near the only entrance.

Ever since she witnessed Abu Hakim murder Bob, she had thought of nothing but escape. And now this maniac ran the country. She had to get out. Her "arrow" maneuver, she figured, had gone for naught. With a modern lab like this one, she suspected, her captors just might accomplish their goals. All they needed, Jamil had said, was some updated equipment. It was now early September and she wondered how long.

Another military plane climbed for gray skies, catching her attention; nearby, there had to be an air base. Occasionally she had also seen smaller commercial aircraft activity. When the rest of the others had joined her on the grounds in front the

Ward One, they all moved off double file toward the mess.

Mohammed Rashid stood near the Ward Two barracks, baton in hand. All these years, he had indeed supported the right man. His assistance in the previous president's assassination yielded a nice promotion: from Colonel to General of the Armies. One of his highest priorities set forth by his new President Abu Hakim was the security of STAIRCASE development here at the compound. *Jihad's* effectiveness just increased a billion-fold.

Located just outside of Tajrish, the lab had been chosen by Ali el-Shafii, the project's director. For Rashid, it was nicely fortified—compliments of German technology and engineering. Just a few changes, he figured, and it would be virtually impregnable.

Impregnable…he almost said aloud, while watching the American woman walk toward the mess. *I think not*, he smiled.

CHAPTER 22

A THIRD APPEARANCE

"Get me Glenn Thielken!" demanded U.N. Ambassador Zenjuro into the box.

"Right away," came his secretary's instant reply.

He was fed up. Here he was, Dr. Mitsuru Zenjuro, Japan's Ambassador to the United Nations, sitting hamstrung as the world's self-appointed privilege had their way, again! Try as he might to prevent it, the Security Council had voted to sanction the Indonesian Government for their dismal record on human rights violations. Indonesia was one of Japan's major trading partners, especially oil. And yet all he could do was watch the others undercut Japan's interest, again.

Japan must acquire a seat on the Security Council, Zenjuro knew. The stakes for Japan were enormous, for a permanent membership on the Security Council was tantamount to belonging to the World Board of Directors. And that Board of Directors made the world's most consequential decisions: war on Iraq, peacekeeping, sanctions. That meant major business opportunities for those able to steer decisions and thus position themselves beforehand.

Also, the Security Council all but controlled the World Bank and its right arm, the IMF. It was the World Bank that determined where global economic growth would flourish, or wane. Strictly business. Business Japan could cash in on.

The telephone buzzed harshly. He punched a button activating the speaker-phone. He needed Thielken's help. He needed Vice President Reed in Japan's pocket before White Shadow made his move.

"Dr. Zenjuro, how are you?" It was a good connection and Zenjuro thought the man too cheerful.

"Not very well, thank you. It has to do with our conversation now almost four weeks ago. What is your status on that?"

"I've yet to discuss the matter," came Thielken's firming voice.

Zenjuro audibly sucked air through his teeth. "Then he does not have the sealed envelope," Zenjuro imputed, pushing his thick gold-rimmed glasses up into place. "May I ask why, Mr. Thielken? We've discussed the possibilities for both you personally and for your company."

"I haven't had the proper opportunity." A lie, Zenjuro knew. *Unreliable Americans!*

"Then I suggest the next Business Council Meeting coming up Tuesday next week. If not by then, I will assume our relationship has come to an end. Thank you, Mr. Thielken. Give Carrera my regards." He punched the button severing the line, severing any possibility of excuse.

"Was it good for you, honey?" Carrera teased, affecting the obvious.

"Terrible, as usual," Glenn Thielken came back, smiling, satiated.

She leaned down straddling his spent body, playfully beat his chest with her fist, then rolled over. She let a few minutes elapse, then asked, "What gives on Tom Shelby?" She'd heard he was to be in the office tomorrow.

Glenn rolled to his right, propping his head on his anchored hand, then said, "Funny you should ask. He's doing a Yucca Mountain status tomorrow. Plan to get him to the side, get a reading, and have a 'Come to Jesus,' if necessary."

"So you're still worried he won't keep quiet about this rock quality problem?" Glenn affirmed with a nod. "Then I suggest you have Kransky have him watched, bug his phones, that kind of thing. Insurance is far cheaper than the cost of the possible disaster."

Eddie Kransky was the head of Shiraki Industries' Security. "Yeah," Glenn finally said, "Tomorrow, after I've seen Shelby." He let a few moments pass then said, "Zenjuro called." He watched her body tense, eyes widen. "The bastard's pushing."

Carrera knew her husband to be ruthless enough, but needed direction, a little push was often all that was needed, then there was no stopping him. "Don't know why you're hesitating, Glenn. It all lines up, the downside risk is minimal, the possibility limitless. Why *are* you hesitating?"

Pleading patriotism seemed shallow at the moment as he looked into those mellow China-blue eyes. Finally, he replied, "The annual Business Council Meeting's in Hot Springs this Tuesday. I'll do it then." She reached up to kiss him, then slid down his bronzed body, nibbling all the way.

Hot Springs, Virginia is a town of less than twenty-five hundred people, fifty miles from Washington. It is here at the Homestead Hotel under an aura of secrecy that the power elite meet regularly to forge the general policies that will benefit them as a whole. The event, called The Business Council since the 1950s, has been the major contact point between the corporate community and the executive branch of government. This is what brought Vice President Reed and Shiraki Industries CEO Thielken to today's lavish event.

It was two o'clock, the formal program had just ended. A potpourri of social events—golf tournaments and tennis matches, all suited for this first Tuesday in September—was to begin a half hour later. Thielken had arranged to meet Reed in his vice-presidential suite after the two o'clock sessions ended.

In the sitting room, Thielken took the small Empire sofa, Reed a chair at the writing table. After five minutes on pleasantries and remembrances, Thielken got down to business, handing Reed Zenjuro's sealed envelope.

"Dhillon," Thielken began, "I have a message from Dr. Zenjuro, Japan's U.N. Ambassador." Thielken watched Reed break the seal and open the envelope as he spoke. He watched Reed's face drain completely white, then heard the Vice President's strained voice:

"Before you continue, Glenn, have you seen the contents of this envelope?" Thielken shook his head negative. He suspected a bribe, maybe blackmail: sex and money were always ready staples. Thielken waited for a few studied moments to pass, then watched Reed return the envelope's contents and secure its flap. Reed then signaled for him to continue:

"Zenjuro seems to think that you have an excellent chance at becoming the next U.S. President, even before Temple's current term is out." Thielken watched Reed's large athletic body stiffen, then relax as if on mental command. All Japan asks in return for their assistance is a favorable consideration on two points: a) a declaration of renewed friendship and cooperation between Japan and the United States; and b) U.S. support for Japan's permanent membership on the U.N. Security Council. Dhillon, don't get me wrong. What I'm doing here, that is, playing courier, is simply paying back an obligation to Ambassador Zenjuro. Nothing more, nothing less. What you do from here on is between you and him."

"You sure you don't know what's in here," Reed responded, pointing to the envelope.

"No. Should I?"

"For this *service*, let's call it, Glenn, what can I do for you?"

Thielken uncrossed his legs, a little taken aback by the rawness of the offer, but instincts told him to take his best shot. He leaned forward. "Accelerate DOE's approval of their nuke dump site out at Yucca Mountain. Also, the Green Globe Award next month. I want that to go to Shiraki Industries."

Reed leaned back, his rather placid face revealing nothing, then said, "Let me work it. Anything else?"

Thielken sensed advantage, and positioned. "We can discuss career opportunities later."

Reed pushed his chair back rising. "Then I'll be in touch with you with my response to Zenjuro's proposition. Thanks for coming." Thielken thought it a cordial salutation after so many years of support and friendship. He left.

Reed pulled the contents from the envelope again. He studied the three photographs: all of himself and Carerra Thielken naked, making love. He figured the Bahamas last year. Reed knew how to separate the principle at stake from the actual stakes. Fuckin' Japs. What balls. And Glenn Thielken seemed to know nothing—*at the moment*. He looked at the cryptic message on the fourth item. *In seeking new employment, Senator Calhoun can be of assistance.* Sonofabitch.

It had been a week since his fateful conversation with Glenn Thielken. Before taking the office of Vice President, Dhillon Reed had come from the Senate. In his current capacity as the Senate's fifty-fifty tie-breaker, Reed kept close tabs on his old buddies. So on this Friday afternoon it was not at all unusual to see him on the short underground rail between the Capitol Building and the Dirksen Senate Office Building.

Reed and his Secret Service escort proceeded to the fourth floor and into the private suite belonging to the North Carolina Senator John C. Calhoun. Just as Reed hoped, his appearance surprised the overstuffed Senator. After the secret service escort gave the office a quick look-over, they left the two men alone to conduct their business.

Reed felt this office hadn't changed a bit in the last twenty-five years, just like the old man who now occupied it. At the end of the rectangular office sat a massive dark oak desk, complete with three multi-line telephones. Behind the desk, was a floor-to-ceiling window, flanked by wall plaques and awards. It seemed every square inch of wall space was dedicated to an ego just as inflated as the man now motioning him to a green and white striped couch under the "photo wall." Reed took the seat facing a somewhat anxious cigar-chomping man. And beyond, another wall, this one filled with political cartoons, all of which depicted the heavy-jowled North Carolina Senator in various shades of guiled caricature.

Reed reminded Calhoun of a cigar-store Indian, stiff, wooden. The Senator remembered the old political joke about vice presidents: Typically you see them twice within a four-year administration: once at the announcement that he's on the ticket, and once at his acceptance speech. If you saw him a third time, he'd gotten himself into trouble. And this one, Calhoun assessed, was in plenty deep.

Calhoun watched the man unconsciously playing with his wedding ring; broaching this subject seem to petrify the man's wooden facade. He'd always thought of the VP as a light-weight, so dispensing with the small talk, Calhoun took the lead, "For what it's worth, Mr. Vice President, I do appreciate how difficult this is." Reed acknowledged the mitigating gesture with a half-nod. "I know what you want and I'm prepared to scratch your back. Mine itches for a cabinet position; Secretary of Commerce might take care of that itch."

"I'm not—"

"I know, Mr. Vice President. Just give me what you can, and I'll take care of all our itches." Reed produced a manila folder, handing it over to his future Commerce Secretary nominee.

CHAPTER 23
"CATTITUDE"

"So, David, CIA analysts agree with your MOSSAD analysis." A routine cabinet meeting would convene in ten minutes. With familiar people filing by, entering the large conference room, Defense Minister Yitzhak Cohen held his voice deliberately low. For here, the enemy was not anti-Semitics, but the left wingers looking to topple, factional elements looking for advantage, and his own right wing colleagues looking for more power, power at his expense.

MOSSAD's director, David Amit, nodded. "This is correct. We estimate five probable locations. They include one at the University of Esfahan, one in Tabriz, two locations in Tehran, and one outside Tehran, a place called Tajrish."

"And your man in Iran, what does he say?"

"He has investigated three so far, the ones in and around Tehran. He says all are in a high state of activity. It seems Hakim has stepped up Iran's biological and chemical programs, using every available resource and facility now at his disposal."

"Speculation?" The Defense Minister was speaking to Amit, but his eyes scanned the hallway, observing who was talking to whom, always noting the body language.

"There is no doubt that the lab at Tajrish is the most secure. I believe STAIRCASE is there."

"Penetration and neutralization?"

Amit sighed. "Its security is the best German engineering can build. We have a hand-drawn layout and there exist systems we do not know how to defeat. Besides perimeter mine fields, towers, and ground patrols, it has a very sophisticated electronic surveillance system: ground pressure sensors, laser beam detectors crisscrossing the grounds, microphones and motion detectors strategically placed, especially in the lab and other buildings. Also an electrically activated interior mine field. It's all centrally monitored and controlled from a security-control room located within the compound itself. To complicate the mission, there is a medium-sized Iranian air base and army contingent adjacent to the compound. The compound itself used to be an Army Aviation Command Hospital."

"How does it compare with Dimona?" Cohen's question addressed Israel's maximum security measures installed in its Dimona nuclear reactor in the Negev Desert.

"On a par or better. Yitzhak, only an air strike could do the job."

"Warplanes draw attention, and repercussions. This must be done quietly, David. And besides, an air strike deprives us of the prize, this STAIRCASE." Cohen referenced his watch. It was September seventeenth. October first, the American CIA estimated, was the worst case time-line for Hakim's developing a Jewish targeted STAIRCASE. "Two weeks, David. We must find and destroy the correct laboratory within two weeks."

"Or laboratories," Amit said heavily.

Cohen stroked his chin, then asked, "Any new ideas from the Americans?"

"None that they have revealed."

Westin stood in the modest San Jose airport terminal this Monday morning watching the 8:23 from San Diego taxi to the gate. There they were, the two men he'd asked for help, now two weeks ago. They carried no luggage, for this would be a quick show-and-tell and back they'd go.

Westin wanted them to begin thinking of the NIQE technology and how they could use it. He wanted to return the favor. For they'd sure come through for him. He had a name:

Westin had no way of knowing how that name surfaced. How Chief approached Moondog and asked him to poll his brother, sniff around his old L.A. neighborhood. It seemed a gangbanger called G-Rake when drunk liked to talk. Talk gets on the street. Seemed that G-Rake's set, AK Gangster Crips, was the best armed gang in Los Angeles. Reason: a fellow named El Cid, busting chops one day for the hell of it, was rewarded for his effort. Turned up a "golden briefcase," and cashed it in. The cashier turned out to be a man named Abdullah.

Westin was given Abdullah's name and how to find him, compliments of the two broad-shouldered gentlemen approaching him now. It made sense. An Arab connection, probably Iraqi or Iranian. Could be an agent, a well connected freelancer, or just a cheap two-bit hood got lucky. Whatever, he'd made the call and eventually the contact. He was to meet the man in Los Angeles this coming Saturday. And then what he'd do would be illegal as hell.

He greeted Creed and Chief then made off for the parked car. Their destination was but a mile and a half from where they stood, as the crow flies; the earthbound route took Westin fifteen minutes to drive.

After parking, they entered the grounds of Mission Santa Clara de Asis. Nestled among tall palm trees, the adjacent two-story church presented a soft blend of beige stucco and reddish-brown tile.

"Where's Slaughter?"

"We're a little early." Just then a tour group passed; they listened in on the guide:

"The Spanish Viceroy Antonio Bucareli's plans called for two missions. The purpose of the one in San Francisco was to strengthen New Spain's northern frontier and secure the valuable port against Russian or British expansion. The Santa Clara mission was named for St. Francis' childhood friend, St. Clare of Assisi. Its purpose was to convert the many Indian villages nearby."

Chief looked at a punker sporting a purple mohawk, then quipped, "Don't think the friars were too successful."

They walked under an arbor intertwined with pale yellow banksia and purple wisteria, finally stopping at the Sacred Heart statue. Creed was bored. Restless, really, and had been since that Iranian assassination put TALON'S GRIP on an indefinite hold bringing them back to the states.

Chief read one of the statue's inscriptions, translated as "Come to Me." Just then a cat, a domestic black and white short hair sporting a black Hitler mustache, rubbed against Chief's leg. Five seconds later the cat was in Chief's arms.

Westin looked around, then saw Dr. Slaughter enter the mission garden area heading toward them. John made the introductions wondering what Slaughter would do next.

"I see, Mr. McCullough, you've met Fritz."

"Call me Chief. Yeah, Fritz's got what I call 'cattitude,'" Chief said examining Fritz's long whiskers and a few eyebrows.

"Very well. Chief, would you like me to inform your next of kin?" Puzzlement. "That is correct, you expired two minutes ago." Slaughter reached for Fritz, pointed to the statue's second inscription, translated "Learn of Me," then looked down stroking the cat.

"Whadda you mean? The cat?" Chief looked at Westin, then said, "What's goin' on?"

Slaughter explained Fritz's capabilities: understands ten thousand English words, her goal orientation, faithfully obeys commands, and when her hypodermic-like claws are loaded with strychnos toxifera, is quite deadly.

"A command like, 'Kill that woman in the yellow dress',"

Creed said, pointing to a young woman walking toward the nearby St. Joseph's Hall.

"That is correct," Slaughter replied, "something less severe, perhaps." Then the doctor spoke to Fritz. "Fritz." The cat meowed acknowledgment. "Zee-tirf." Another acknowledgment. "The woman in yellow." Slaughter pointed at the target. "Have her pick you up, then ten seconds later jump out of her arms and return."

The four men watched the cat trot over to the young woman, rub against her leg, meowing, then allow herself to be picked up. Ten seconds later Fritz tensed and freed herself, then returned to Slaughter's side.

"Well fuck me," mumbled Chief, scratching his head.

"Can *anyone* give her, uh, it instructions?"

"For Fritz to execute an order, she must recognize three things: an authorized voice, a code word, and an intelligible English language command. The command could be a pre-learned set of complex instructions invoked by another code word."

"You thinking what I'm thinking?" asked Creed.

"Infiltration," came Chief's answer.

Westin smiled.

Five days later Westin found himself in one of greater Los Angeles's small incorporated communities called Downey. He'd had no trouble finding the two-story Spanish-style motel located near Rockwell International's huge L.A. aerospace complex. Safe enough, he assessed. Briefcase in hand, he knocked on the door whose room number he'd been given a week ago.

No answer. He tried again—

"No turning," came passable but broken English from behind, "Allow me, Mr. Westin." Two large hands started at his chest and worked their way down outside then inside his pants. "Your briefcase."

"Inside. You can inspect it inside."

After hesitation, "Very well." That's when John felt the

barrel in his back, followed by a room key. John took the key, opened the door and was relieved to find the room empty— visibly anyway.

The barrel eased him inside. "Place the case on the table there, then step to the wall and face it." John did as he was told stopping at the hint of a mirrored reflection. He heard the latches snap open, then he looked to the right at the wall mirror. From his vantage he caught a double reflection from it and a dressing mirror attached to an angled closet door. He saw a handsome, thin man in his early thirties, with black neatly combed hair and mustache. "Turn. You have five minutes. What is it you want?"

And penetrating, aware eyes. Gun now not visible. "Last May, you acquired something I want. I believe I have something you may wish to trade it for."

"Who sent you?"

"That's not important. What's important is the technology I offer in exchange." John assessed the guy as a light weight, but not a dumb one.

"Exchange for what?"

"The golden briefcase." Abdullah blinked—*the right man.* John now wished desperately that he knew more about "its deadly contents," to establish some semblance of credibility, anything beyond pure bluff. "I wish to acquire a copy of its contents."

"I do not know what you are talking about."

"Fine," John walked over to his open briefcase and pulled out a video tape. "Tell them my interests wish also to possess the briefcase technology." John handed over the tape. "Give this to the people you gave the briefcase to. Tell them I can deliver the weapons technology on this tape. Tell them it's a win-win for both parties." Westin closed his briefcase, opened the door, and left.

When John was sure he wasn't being followed, he doubled back to the Los Angeles International Airport. In time for a stiff drink before boarding for home.

CHAPTER 24
SUBTERFUGE

LETTER TO THE EDITOR
Who Represents L.A.'s Disadvantaged Minority Youth?

For the last twenty years, homicide has been the leading cause of death among minority youths, especially young African American men. And now we have the "Name Dropper." The obvious question is, "Whose's doing anything about this travesty?" Or better yet, "Why hasn't anything been done over these two decades to stop such a tragic loss of young talent and potential?" I'll tell you why:

To protect himself, a youth living in the ghetto today is forced to band together with others like himself. Our society labels the result of this survival action, "gang." And we (society) all know a gang is nothing more than a bunch of hoodlums. Right? And what does society care about a bunch of hoodlums?

*Not one rat's ass—as the proverbial saying goes—
especially as long as they stay out of society's face.
Benign neglect is the catchword used in more rarified
circles. But it's not benign anymore, it's devastating,
as the facts above so clearly show.*

*In this, the greatest of all societies called America,
there is still one group without representation: the
ghetto youth. And I don't see that changing without
impetus. That's why I support an ACLU class action
suit on behalf of the disadvantaged minority youths of
Los Angeles for greater and more effective police
protection. Such an action would go a long way in
breaking the gang culture and the stigma that goes
with it.*

—*Los Angeles Times*, 24 September

It took longer than Eddie Kransky expected, *Los Angeles
Times* newspaper in hand. That explained why Eddie had read
just about the entire paper, including the column under "Letter
to the Editor." What crap, he muttered to himself, as he flushed
and pulled up his pants. Eddie knew better.

Eddie Kransky approached the mirrored washroom on the
thirty-fifth floor of Shiraki Industries' L.A. headquarters
building. It'd been a long, roundabout and bumpy road getting
here. This was big time for Eddie Kransky, and Eddie intended
to stay. To that purpose, being head of Shiraki Security offered
opportunities, opportunities in that murky realm called discrete information.

Eddie looked into the mirror, rinsing his hands. Yeah, a
roundabout road: stint in the U.S. Marines; Cleveland P.D., too
enterprising for their taste; L.A. private detective, that's how
he first met the now Mrs. Carerra Thielken, her trying to get
something on her previous husband. He'd worked at that one
for six months—nothing, nothing she could hang his shorts
on. Then the old fart tragically upped and died. *Imagine that.*

The rest of his journey was easy: Her marriage to Glenn
Thielken, a phone call, innuendo—subtle, you know—and

walla, head of security for Shiraki Industries, a fuckin' fifty billion dollar company.

Not bad, he judged looking at the mirror's reflection. He'd always had a wrestler's physique, no neck, taut skin over a wide, flat-featured face, good teeth and still a good head of chestnut hair. Good enough to still get laid. *Enough of that, Kransky. A couple of minutes and "Spider Lady'll" be here.*

Eddie had just gotten back to his desk, when he turned at the sound of his door closing. The lady taking a seat wore a pale persimmon linen jacket, collar turned up, a gold Porche emblem broach pinned to its left side. Not much else, he thought, except the black skirt now hiked up approaching dangerous territory. *A rich and sexy bitch. Jesus, what a deadly combination.* He gave the briefest moment's thought to those athletic legs wrapped around *his* back—

"And good morning to you, Eddie." She smiled at the lecher, wondering if Eddie ever polished his shoes.

"Uh, yes. And that it is. What can I do for you Mrs. Thielken?"

"Don't have much time, Eddie."

Not much time, like with Mr. Vice President. Like three weeks ago, at the party right there in the greenhouse, or in Chicago two months ago, or the Bahamas four months ago. Vice President Dhillon Reed's time would come, he knew. For anyone who went to bed with Carerra Thielken eventually got fucked. He himself kept his place there. Why screw up a good thing, being head of Shiraki security offered unique revenue opportunities?

Eddie reached into a desk drawer producing a covered report, its contents read like a crime sheet. "Okay, our last checkpoint was Monday, a week ago. Monday, seven-ten A.M. Left home arriving office at eight o'clock. Ten, left for…" Eddie recited Glenn Thielken's every movement he and his special security team were able to trace. Carerra listened pensively, until she heard the Saturday two P.M. address. He watched her re-cross her shapely legs. That was Glenn Thielken's ex-wife, Eddie knew, and always wondered what the Spider Lady thought of that. He ended with this morning's routine, same as a week ago.

"Glenn's meeting with Shelby Friday, what came out of that?"

"We were able to record it. Basically read the man the riot act about some Shiraki exposure, as Mr. Thielken put it, out at some mountain. After the meeting, he asked me to put Tom Shelby on full surveillance, tail, phones, mail, the works."

"Any results?" she asked coldly.

"Why yes," Eddie replied obviously impressed with himself. He pulled another folder from his desk and produced a transcript dated Friday, September 21, 3:30 P.M. Eddie pushed it across the modest desk.

Carerra read the text highlighted in yellow. *Hertz rental car mobile telephone: I-405 North. Shelby to 408-223-4658: Craig MacIsaac.* "Something hot, Craig. I think I'm in some pretty deep yogurt. Can't talk over the phone. Craig, gotta talk to someone I trust..."

Three days after his Saturday encounter with Abdullah, Westin found himself approaching yet another hotel. This time a fleabag in North Hollywood. The dark lobby was like a cave, appointed in green and gold furniture, original 1950s, faded and frayed. It smelled of stale cigarette ashes, and when Westin saw the front desk temporarily unattended he moved quickly through, watchful. Westin didn't exactly trust the elevator straight ahead, its scissored collapsible gate warped inward as if a *sumo* wrestler had had a run at it. He went for the stairs to the right. At the top of the third floor, what had to be a hooker looked him over approvingly, then descended. He found the room number and knocked.

He hadn't exactly appreciated the hospitality in Abdullah's last welcome. This time he had a nine millimeter Beretta tucked within his belt under the windbreaker. If it had occurred to him, he'd have thought it strange that Beth right now was the last thing on his mind. He heard the voice from within:

"Come." Abdullah's? He couldn't be sure. Opening the

door, he saw the briefest silhouette of a form behind its hinged slit, then Abdullah sitting at a brown laminate-top table, arms folded, *right hand not really visible*. He could still duck outta there, part of his mind offered...

John lurched into the room slamming the door open hard against the unseen form, while kicking upward catching the small table's edge. It toppled toward Abdullah throwing him—and any line of sight—off balance. Westin kept charging, coming around the table's left while pulling at his nine millimeter, its front sight hanging on his belt, *pulling...* He heard the door slam shut; his eye caught movement, an arm, a gun rising. Westin reached the seated Abdullah, who'd begun to recover his balance. Finally, the pistol pulled free, a solid grip. Crouching low, he jammed the barrel hard against the Abdullah's retreating head.

Westin kept sliding in low behind Abdullah's back, putting a barrier between him and the man at the door, then yelled, "Drop it!" Hesitation. "Okay. Who wants it first?" *Shit,* John's mind echoed, *you sound like a bad late night movie.*

Abdullah dropped a nine millimeter Browning. It clattered onto the thin green carpet. The doorman, again of Middle Eastern descent, still hesitated. Westin's eyes fixed eternally on the doorman's fury, then he pulled back the hammer, the barrel now in Abdullah's ear. The doorman finally held out his free hand, stooped and laid down an Uzi machine pistol. Westin started breathing again, not quite believing this, where he was, what he'd just done.

What the Hell do you do now, John, he asked himself, pissed. "You assholes! I come here to do business. You come here to fuck around. Wasting my time, wasting my client's time. Shit." He kicked Abdullah's pistol toward the door, then pointed his own at the doorman, "You. Move to the bed." As the doorman came by him, John moved back and toward the door, then carefully picked up the two guns.

Reaching for the doorknob, he displayed the two weapons, then said, "For my trouble. And forget the offer."

"Wait." John ignored the plea, leaving. "Wait. Maybe we

can do business." It was the doorman, a stocky man with mustache and cold coffee-brown eyes. John hesitated. "We are interested, but need more information, proof of your technology's existence, what it can do."

Westin fixed a glare on the hard man, then said, "I know President Hakim is your ultimate contact. Tell him I too need proof. And understand this. My instructions are to see for myself the development facility. Implement whatever security measures you deem necessary to protect your asset, but I must see it demonstrated."

"But—"

"*But* is no deal." Westin pulled another videotape from the pocket of his windbreaker, hesitated as if possibly changing his mind, then stepped watchfully, placing it on a nearby dresser. "This is the proof Hakim will need. I suggest you move quickly. This deal is perishable." John turned and left.

He would be followed, Westin knew. The trap was set, now to authenticate the cheese. He had made a luncheon appointment with a man at the L.A. British Consulate General. Reason: potential high-tech business opportunities with Paxton International—innocuous, yet luring.

It was now ten-thirty, plenty of time to play coy. And that he did as he meandered his way to Willshire Boulevard, then parked and entered the reddish-lustered marble building.

Abdullah and the other Iranian national followed the American using a less conspicuous two cars. An hour later, Abdullah observed the American enter the British Consulate General, then emerge with another man, a Brit it was speculated. The American and the Brit were observed having lunch at a nearby restaurant. Forty-five minutes later, the American left for the L.A. airport, ticketed for Houston.

Before the day would be over, the two Iranian agents would have two names: The man with whom the American had dined would be identified as the British Consul for Commercial Affairs, also Deputy Consul for the entire consulate. The American himself would be verified as John Kreuger Westin, ex-NASA astronaut, living in Houston, now with

Paxton International involved in a highly secret advanced computer chip research and development. Later in Tehran, they would deduce the "interest" John Westin represented to be either British SIS or MI5.

CHAPTER 25
RODENTS

Jim Rhodes, special agent in charge, had missed Charlie's retirement party last night and wouldn't get a chance to say goodbye to his old mentor unless he did so now. Now, because he'd be leaving within the hour, back out to California-land conducting another site survey. Rhodes was the lead man on the President's G2 trip, G2 being the acronym the advance team had given the "Green Globe" Award in Los Angeles, less than two weeks away.

Approaching his old friend, today stationed in the hall outside the Oval Office, Rhodes saw that it was "show time." The Vice President and Coleman had converged to enter where Charlie stood; and as usual, the Secret Service veteran looked them over as if he'd never seen the two men in his entire life. The third man, a rather serious-looking DDI, came down the hall from the west entrance.

Once all three had settled in, Temple kicked it off with little fanfare. Marshall Douglas quickly sensed the chief's irritation, and mentally noted today's watchword, "discretion."

Douglas covered his items on the President's agenda, closing with the missing scientists and Operation TALON'S GRIP, now on hold. He had nothing firm from his field assets nor did the Israelis. Pursuing all avenues with diligence.

"And TALON'S GRIP's readiness?"

Coleman took that one. "Both SEALs and SAYERET MAT'KAL report ready as can be without a definitive target and its layout. The U.N. food relief program is in the planning stage. I would remind you, Sir, that we should not announce U.S. participation until it's a 'go' on TALON'S GRIP. Then we'll coordinate. It's a good cover."

Dhillon Reed reported on the secret *Banto* LIST, avoiding direct eye contact, often deferring to Douglas as if to shed blame. The blind agent in Japan was still working on it. Nothing new.

Nothing new! Temple groused, chewing down on his well-gnawed temple-tips. One more item remained on the agenda: the two stories that broke in this morning's *Washington Post*. He slapped a two-page photocopy of an article on the desk for all to see, then almost accusingly, asked, "Any ideas where this came from?" Silence.

Finally the Vice President spoke: "Six years is a long time to keep a story like this under wraps. Especially since some of the insiders on the Hill aren't exactly our fans."

"Fine. But I still want the bastard." It was the NIQE technology. Since its inception NIQE coded projects carried the highest compartmentalized classification. Actually, thought Temple, Reed was right about keeping it under wraps for so long. But there was more to this, his political mind sensed, a mind superbly prepared for such situations like this.

Temple was born in Missouri, and when his father wanted to move back to his native state of Alaska, his mother said, "Fine," filed for divorce, and kept the kids. Growing up, Temple spent each summer with his dad in Anchorage, and had developed a soft spot for the majestic beauty that was Alaska. When his father ran for the State Senate, a young John Temple came up only to help, but wound up virtually running the campaign. After that, he never forgot the sweet taste of political victory.

And indeed, since, he had never experienced the bitter taste of defeat. Why? Because he knew people, their issues, and he could smell a political rat. This morning he smelled a rat.

"Page two." Temple shoved another photocopied *Post* article across his desk. "Another DOE environmental mess in Colorado. Is this true?" Coleman nodded, thinking his standing in for the National Security Advisor wasn't all that much fun after all. "Goddamnit, gentlemen, now I get my news from the *Washington Post.*" He hit a button, "Anne, get Blancher at DOE, have him in here ASAP." Turning back to his stirring guests, Temple directed, "Gentlemen, I've already got Kendall over at FBI on this. I suspect it's the same leak. Work that angle."

"Yes, sir," the room chorused. With nothing else, the three men readily filed out.

Yes, a very large rat. Some one person had leaked both those little tidbits to the *Post*. Someone whose name, Temple's political instincts sensed, was on that fuckin' Japanese *Banto* LIST. Someone close. *Very close!*

John Calhoun felt pretty good about himself returning to his office from the last vote: All totalled now, one hundred million dollars for the tobacco industry in the form of price supports, credit guarantees, and crop disaster insurance. He'd come through for the tobacco's special interest, the people of North Carolina, and most importantly, *himself.* Sustaining a twenty thousand dollars a day inflow building up the next campaign's war chest wasn't difficult when you delivered. Today, he delivered.

He'd traded his votes deftly, bullied the junior members who dared not cross him, and debunked arguments of those trying to show the absurdity of the bill: government subsidies allowing its citizens to kill themselves more cheaply, not to mention the lung-related medical cost to the nation.

He spent the next half hour on the phone reminding his benefactors of his worth, then reached for the in-basket.

Sorting, he chose the one marked "Personal and Confidential" from the newly infamous "J. Smith" alias.

Yes, from Vice President Reed. Humm, he smiled to himself. He could use this.

The next day Secret Service SAC Jim Rhodes was in Los Angeles. From the thirty-first floor, he looked absently out over northeast view of the Hollywood hills while his mind played "what-ifs." He stood in the luxurious Huntington suite, atop the Westin Bonaventure's Green Tower, one of five gleaming glass cylinders rising out of the heart of L.A.'s downtown business district. He'd just replaced the telephone receiver and now let his mind mull over what FBI Deputy Assistant Director Voight had just said. The Fibbie had no direct knowledge or evidence, only some tenuous lead from CIA's Tokyo station. And so what, the President received real threats every day, some from very serious people, like Iranian state sponsored terrorist groups—the "Great Satan" and all that.

And more so, this was L.A., this was California-land. Here, the boys from the Office of Protective Research had compiled an extensive list of would be threats. Most on the list had already been visited by one of his agents. Those deemed a solid threat would be watched by an agent or local policeman until the President was safely out of town. And of course, photographs of dangerous individuals were already in the hands of all law enforcement allowed near the President. From Voight, Rhodes already had the L.A. customs photo of what the Fibbie called White Shadow. *Enough.*

The major problem his men reported was the range of their communication system. Their earphones picked up transmissions from the same floor just fine, but not from other floors. Working the problem, he would have technical support from the local field office there shortly.

Other than the few loose ends—there were always loose ends ten days before a Presidential arrival—Rhodes felt pretty good about this one. His team from the Presidential Protective

Division, and boys from OPR came in four months ago working with members of the President's personal staff and local officials to develop a security plan: arrival, route layout, exposure assessment and mitigation measures, facilities security, departure, and emergency response.

The circular suite itself seemed okay. An entry door entering a seven hundred square-foot hospitality parlor, itself flanked by the library and dinning room/serving bar; and on around, count 'em, five bedrooms. Jim Rhodes paced the twenty-five hundred square-foot ring of penthouse suite, looking, playing assassin. Satisfied, he stepped into the interior circular hall. This hall formed an inner doughnut ring to the circular suite area surrounding it. The "hole" in the doughnut hall housed the stairwell. He walked the doughnut hall, repeating his mental assassin's game. Off the doughnut hall, a "spoke" hallway led out to the elevator clinging to the building's chrome and glass exterior. Pacing this elevator hall, Rhodes felt comfortable with the floor below as it was fully reserved by his team. But it was the loft above that bothered him, with so many nooks and crannies. It'd be searched again on arrival day, he knew. But just to ease his professional mind, he mentally noted, he'd double check it himself.

The place was the Old Ebbitt Grill, one block east of the White House. Neither man new the other, however another Japanese man wearing a bright green tie indeed would be rare. The assassin spotted his Washington contact entering the old Victorian gray stone-front between F and G Streets on fifteenth.

Satisfied with the situation, he followed, stepping onto white marbled Italian tile. Progressing to the back, the scene before him assaulted his spartan *shibui* taste. He passed a well-worn watering hole rich with deep mahogany, etched mirrors, glass and brass; the dining area to the left seemed to him overstuffed, over-ornate—soft. It was early afternoon, only a dozen patrons throughout; all seemed normal as he continued on back to an small enclave called Grant's bar.

There, in the last booth on the right, the man spotted his

contact. He was a rather large, but distinguished-looking Japanese man having shaved what little hair left at the sides of his head. He wore thick gold rimmed glasses encircling alert pearl black eyes, narrow epicanthic slits of wisdom, seeming to know more than they should.

"You're late," the seated man tried to admonish while studying the most notorious Japanese legend of his time. He had wondered how this would work, for no man had knowingly laid eyes upon *Shiro Kage*'s face and lived to describe it. Before him moving carefully was not the White Shadow he'd expected, but an elderly Japanese man, in the mid-seventies, he guessed. An elaborate disguise. The elderly man's head also was completely bald and he wore thick black-framed glasses. Glasses obscuring little of the cold omni-science radiating from this "old man's" dark stealthy eyes, two black gemstones.

Still standing, observing, the assassin forced the conversation to Japanese, then insisted on switching seats to face the door.

While the businessman begrudgingly moved to the opposing booth seat, the assassin studied the man's movements, observing stresses in his suit coat's fabric, and scanning the benign contents of the attaché case.

Once settled, the establishment personnel delivered requested tea, then left the two men alone in the still early afternoon hour. The assassin did not know this man, nor did he care. What was important to him at the moment was listening to his developed senses: now acknowledging this man and the situation to be authentic.

The assassin watched the businessman reached for his briefcase producing a manilla folder. Japan's Ambassador to the U.N., Dr. Mitsuru Zenjuro, began cautiously, "It cost a small fortune to get this information, information I believe you cannot use."

The assassin studied the papers, then unfolded the schematic of the grounds, leaving the architectural drawings in the folder. "Yes, I have spotted cameras on the roof, under eves, and about the grounds. Motion detectors?"

"Yes, and pressure sensors, both calibrated to signal when anything larger than a squirrel crosses their sensors. Invisible laser "trip beams" also, placed in strategic locations throughout. It's impossible. The grounds are constantly watched and patrolled."

"Yes," replied the assassin, "even the grounds keepers look fit, more like marines than gardeners." He had already ruled out surreptitious entry over the seven-foot slightly spiked wrought-iron perimeter fence. "There's nothing here about daily access. Where does the President enter and exit by car?"

"There are seven official gates. In addition, there are underground tunnels to nearby buildings providing access to street level, all well-lit and highly secured. There's no predictability, as the Secret Service let the roll of a die select the exit. Routing is also random. As for outside exits, snipers are hidden within the stonework of nearby government buildings." The assassin concurred having spotted three perches already: two in the Treasury Building, one in the Old Executive Office Building.

"I see air traffic follows a route over the Potomac, just two kilometers away."

"Forget it. Hidden away, Washington, and especially around the White House, has the highest concentration of anti-aircraft and anti-missile missile batteries than any place in the world. As I said, penetrating the White House is impossible."

"Food?"

"Selected suppliers, transported in secure vehicles, examined for poison, radiation—tampering of any kind. Food preparers have the highest clearances." Zenjuro seized the silence, "Here," finding a stapled two-page paper with editorial marks, "this is the President's calendar, everything publicly scheduled for the next two weeks. This item, here October sixth, seems most promising. It is—"

"No. Here, October two." The assassin pushed the paper back at Zenjuro to read.

Zenjuro's forehead wrinkled pulling the bald line that used to be hair down towards the furrow, then answered, "'ASEAN State Dinner. Seven P.M. Foreign Ministers, aides, and wives.' That's the Association of South East Asian Nations: Philippines, Indonesia, Malaysia, Singapore, Thailand, Viet Nam, and Brunei, I believe. I cannot get you invited to that one, sorry. Los Angeles on the sixth looks better. Security while traveling is never as tight as it should be, and nowhere near the level of the White House itself."

The assassin grunted, then acquiesced, "Los Angeles then. I'll need the President's schedule, logistics, landing sight, route, hotel, all details." Zenjuro responded exhaling a long slow breath. The assassin continued ignoring the resistance, "And a trusted man to assist."

"You will have it," responded the U.N. ambassador pushing a telephone number across the linen. Ten days and it is done.

Six blocks away, FBI Deputy Assistant Director Ryan Voight sat in his sixth floor office at the FBI's Washington DC headquarters, staring at his computer screen. He'd just requested a search on all FBI message traffic regarding Yasuo Okabe, alias Yasutaka Ishigura, alias *Shiro Kage*, alias White Shadow. This man now ranked "most wanted," Director Kendall saw to that. Yet looking at the results of the computer search, "0 Messages Found," it was as if the man had dropped off the planet.

Voight felt the urge to loosen his tie. He'd always thought of himself as a man of his word. It was one of the bonding elements between him and Teal Coro back at Quantico. *So what if Coro comes through?* How in the hell could he ever stop DOE's plans out at Yucca Mountain? Coro knew he had not the clout nor the authority to make such an absurd commitment. Yet Coro asked. *And what did you say, asshole?* Why did he ask?

He should have called Coro again by now, the FBI man knew. But there was another truth in the matter: His FBI and all its resources had yet to turn a probable sighting, much less a positive one. Not one solid lead. Not a clue as to where this White Shadow might possibly be.

The Washington noon hour turned pleasantly sunny. Young staffers brown-bagged on benches paralleling the circular driveway approaching the Rayburn House Congressional Office Building. Few paid notice to the young Federal Express delivery man approaching on foot from South Capital Street. Even fewer noticed he was Oriental. The man breezed past the circular concrete barriers and entered the granite building. He continued, passing through the airport-like metal detectors, turned right, read the directory on the wall, and proceeded to a California Congressional Office on the first floor level. Confirming previous noon-hour observations, he saw no secretary conspicuously in sight.

The assassin quietly stepped through the open door displaying the seal of The Great State of California. Voices emanated from the right, another open door revealing a large work room with banks of wide chest-high filing cabinets. He noted the congressman's office behind the closed door to the left. He opened it. It was a reasonable calculation: the representative out of the office, most likely for lunch; otherwise, sorry, wrong California congressman and off he'd go.

The assassin quickly surveyed the rather sedate office with its high-ceiling and worn pea-green carpet: a large neatly arranged desk sat in front of a window flanked by two flags, walls covered with memorabilia and awards, bookcase opposite the window, and door—*to where?* He tried it: a coat closet, bare hangers, an umbrella and poster cylinders stood in its corners. The assassin stepped inside closing the door behind him. The entire infiltration took six seconds.

As he stood in the black, the assassin reflected on his previous trips to America. The turmoil stirred from his last job had left the United States off limits, until now. He had killed an FBI agent's family in revenge for the arrest—and later conviction—of a prominent member of Japan's *yakuza* mafia family. Later, he was told the FBI had focused every resource it had, along with support from the CIA, to solve the case and apprehend the killer. They had gotten close, too; that is, the man called Teal Coro had.

That was over five years ago. A cool trail, but still a trail. He had been and would be extremely careful. The only chance taken was entering LAX with little disguise, but that had to be, lest the suspicions of a highly trained and observant inspector be raised. The only reason he'd entered the United States was because his client required the best.

He had left his Washington contact thinking he would strike in Los Angeles. Indeed, he would fly to Los Angeles, meet his new accomplice, devising a plan and support requirements. But that was just a ruse for no one would know his real plan, his greatest challenge. The White House. In five days it would be done.

That evening, the assassin heard the last staffer finally leave and lock up. The California congressman had never returned. He opened the coat closet door standing in the silent dark for five minutes, listening, feeling, sensing. Satisfied, he opened the door to the secretarial entry area from which he had arrived six hours ago. He turned on the light, business as usual for any passing security personnel.

A week ago he was here under the ruse of a constituent dropping by. It was then he learned the White House tour reservation procedures. It would be in the secretary's desk before him. Locked. Fifteen seconds later, the lock picked, he had the center drawer open. Luck was with him. There, on top of a melee, lay the general appointment book. He leafed to the week of October first. *Excellent!* Tuesday, October second: "Mr. and Mrs. Tanabe/San Francisco" scribed in pencil along with their telephone number. The assassin looked at his watch calculating a four o'clock California time. He picked up the multi-line telephone receiver and keyed numbers.

"Yes, Mrs. Tanabe," he began in very-good English, "My name is Jack Thomas from Congressman Elliott's office. I see here that you and your husband have requested a White House tour on October second. Yes. I'm afraid that date is no longer acceptable. We just received a call from the White House and all tours for that day are being canceled due to some last minute event and rescheduling. How long are you to be in Washington? Good. The White House can re-schedule you in at eight-thirty on October fourth, two days after your planned Tuesday tour. Very good. Don't forget to pick up your tickets the day before. Thank you for your understanding, and we'll see you then."

The assassin noted the White House provided sequence numbers penciled under the Tanabe's name. He searched the center drawer until he found the pre-stamped White House tour tickets bound by a rubber band. He took two. Mimicking previous notations, he penciled the calendar as if the Tanabe tickets had been collected by its requesters. Two minutes later, the desk-lock picked secure, he exited the building walking out into a cooling autumn evening.

CHAPTER 26

NONBELIEVERS

It was nine-thirty P.M. when Israeli Defence Minister Cohen's staff car pulled to a stop at the second armed checkpoint. This one in front of the Prime Minister's reinforced concrete three bedroom home nestled within a quiet neighborhood west of Jerusalem. The hillside residence, set fifty feet off the street, was well secured by a contingent of highly trained, fully armed soldiers.

Five minutes later, Cohen was inside seated in the Prime Minister's comfortable study, door closed. The Prime Minister presented the look of a classic jewish businessman, savvy, spry, intense. Indeed Ibrahim Maklef had come up through the business ranks, of sorts. Before being drafted into the Begin Cabinet, his first foray into party politics, he was the head of the Israeli Military Industries, builder and exporter of the highly successful Uzi line of weapons. Physically, he was a short man, with snow white hair flanking a continuous smooth scalp. Thick lenses over keen blue eyes tended to reveal little of the man's raw compassion, nor equally still, his notorious iron will.

Maklef poured small measures of cognac from a cut-glass decanter. With time running out, Cohen knew, Maklef's summons had one primary intent: a decision on what to do about STAIRCASE. Cohen described the probable Iranian sites noting Tajrish, the odds-on thinking, being virtually impenetrable.

Maklef reached across his desk for a silver-framed photograph, handing it to Cohen. After Cohen's compliments, Maklef began like a mentor, "Yitzhak, you too have granddaughters, yes? The longer we wait on this, the greater the chance neither yours nor mine will ever live to see their own daughters, much less granddaughters. The longer we wait, the greater the chance Israel's very existence comes to a horrible end. The longer we wait, the greater the chance Herzl's Zionist dream dies fruitless on this barren land."

"What is it you wish, Ibrahim?"

"An air strike." The Prime Minister's words rang with finality. "On the primary target."

Cohen took a sip of the warm dry liquid, pulled a map from his briefcase, then spoke, "Very well. Do you wish also to attack any or all of the other four suspected locations?"

"For now, just overview the other four."

"Specifically, they're not unlike other infiltrations. From a friendly freighter, SAYERET MAT'KAL or naval commandos insert into Iran from the Persian Gulf, make their way to their designated target, destroy, and quietly exfiltrate.

"For Tajrish," the Defense Minister continued, pointing at a map and red hand-drawn arrows. "Coordinated with strikes at the secondary targets, fifteen IAF F-15Es depart from Etzion Air Base. Equipped with extended-range pylons, they fly low around the tip of Saudi Arabia, skirt the uninhabited desert, here, in Jordan, fly just north of the thirty-second parallel—the old no-fly zone boundary—across Iraq into Iran swinging north coming at the Tajrish facility from due west.

"Now let us look at probabilities of success. First, understand we cannot repeat Operation Babylon, my friend (Israel's 1981 air attack on Iraq's Osirak nuclear reactor building). I will tell you why. Arab military and radar stations now cover every square kilometer of airspace from our borders to Tajrish. Saudi AWACS is always airborne and vigilant. Iraq has built up its air defenses again. Iranian air defense is denser than any other Arab country, especially around Tehran, just thirty kilometers south of Tajrish."

The Prime Minister came back, "But we have a friend out there in the dark. *Surprise* is her name." Cohen found it difficult to hide his disapproval at the man's decision already made. "What is your casualty estimate?"

"Eighty-five percent reach the target. Thirty percent return to Etzion. Do not forget the American hostages will die. And, of course, STAIRCASE is lost."

"STAIRCASE, ten fighter aircraft and crews, and nine Americans," Maklef said aloud to himself, then refreshed the glasses. "Versus our daughters. Versus our granddaughters. Versus the very existence of our Jewish state." He sipped quietly. "Yitzhak, work up a coordinated operational plan. Air strike for Tajrish, infiltration for the next two highest priority targets. Pull in whatever resources required to develop the plan. I do not have to tell you the need-to-know list must be kept at a minimum."

"When do you wish to see the plan?" Cohen asked as if he didn't know.

"Immediately." Maklef ignored the audible resistance. "I'll convene a Cabinet meeting tomorrow night. Yitzhak, what I will tell them is if MOSSAD or the Americans do not present a better option before your planned engagement time, then we strike."

General Mohammed Rashid had earlier arrived at the Tajrish compound late afternoon. He used the daylight hours to inspect security himself. All systems had to be fully operational, all measures fully implemented, all procedures fully adhered to. The German contractor had done well, but still it had to be impenetrable.

President Hakim of late had become almost fanatical

about the STAIRCASE development effort and its security. And well he should, Rashid understood. Rashid appreciated the promise this STAIRCASE offered, an awesome weapon clearing the infidel battlefields, leading the way for victory after victory with minimal casualties suffered by his Islamic military forces. Seeing his successes, the *umma*, the Islamic community of nations, would join his campaign for the final victory, *jihad's* objective realized—riddance of the infidel forever. He, himself, the supreme General of the Umma.

After inspection and two reprimands, Rashid spoke with the project director, Ali el-Shafii. It seemed Shafii had an audience with the president tomorrow. And the news was not good: Shafii would tell Hakim that still, a Jewish-targeted STAIRCASE virus could not be developed. He needed more precise machines, and another molecular geneticists. Rashid was glad he'd be away on that one: unrest down in Shiraz was brewing, the economy again. Since it had the potential to be the first uprising since Hakim took power and appointed him General of the Armies, he wanted to take the opportunity to prove his capability. He would squelch the rebellion with an iron hand before a full blown riot erupted.

But first things first. Now after dark, General Rashid approached Ward Number Two, where the scientist-prisoners were housed. He'd had the woman on his mind, now for four weeks. It was time. He motioned for the two outside guards to accompany him inside, then ordered them to fetch the woman.

Beth's cot was next to Jamil Velayati's. Jamil heard the command in Farsi. "Beth, the General has sent for you. The guard is smiling. Beth, I do not like this."

Beth scanned the ward turned barracks, as if looking for the escape she'd not been able to locate each and every day for her twenty-six days here. Her eyes locked on "Dr. Death," having heard Jamil, now leering. Then she felt the hand on her arm, pulling up hard. She had on flannel pajamas, but not for long, she winced, judging the glint in the General's eyes. *Christ! Why couldn't she been born a man? Well, she'd give him a fight. Something he'd never experienced from one of his black-clad concubines. She'd win too, if it was the last thing—*

The second guard, smiling, grabbed her other arm, now forcing them both behind her back. "Take her to the brig," ordered their general. In the nearby brig, the two men took her to the back cell block. Beth noted the cots. She struggled.

Whop! came the fist connecting with her jaw. She fell back stunned. It was Rahid, who then produced a knife, warning, "Your alternative, woman, *is not so pretty.*" He brought the knife's edge close to her reddening cheek. "A face with a hundred scars is not much to look at."

She tried again to free herself, struggling against the two Iranian guards. She kicked at his crouch, missing. Rashid laughed, hit her again, then with both hands, ripped open her pajama top. He stared delighted at her exposed breasts, then ordered, "Put her in—"

"General," came a breathless voice from a soldier just arrived.

"Yes," Rashid snapped still fixed on the frightened woman's undulating breasts.

"Shiraz. Riots. Public buildings being looted. President Hakim wishes to speak with you. He waits on the telephone."

Beth watched Rashid's face flush, brushing his wet lip with the back of his hand, then replied, "Very well." Then left.

The pilot announced their beginning descent into Frankfort International. "You may wish to reset your watches and note the date change. It is now eleven-fifty-five, Friday, September twenty-eighth, local. "Damn," Westin almost said aloud. Coleman's NIQE-based Weapons Report was due today.

It had only been this morning—well this morning Thursday, L.A. time—when he saw Abdullah, his third meeting. The Iranian informed him that waiting at Los Angeles International was a round-trip ticket on the next one o'clock Lufthansa flight to Frankfort. Westin also received ten new business cards; he was now a manufacturer's representative for a large German construction company—one that conducted tens of billions of dollars of military business each year with the Islamic Republic of Iran. The third item was a contact and number within his "new" company who would vouch for him, should the authorities be curious. The fourth item was a hotel name in Tehran.

It was now Friday Frankfort time, approaching noon before touchdown. Once through Frankfort airport's elaborate security, he would purchase himself a round trip ticket on Iran Air to Tehran, representing the manufacturer, of course. That would get him into Tehran's Mehrabad airport at one o'clock early A.M. Saturday.

Twelve hours later, after a short night's sleep in Tehran's affluent north side, John found himself in a government Mercedes being chaffered through Tehran's wide avenues and thoroughfares. During the drive, he was struck by the great variety of buildings—none very tall—each attesting to the Persian Empire's rich and tumultuous history of foreign conquests and expulsions. Into central Tehran, Khayyam Street divided the Bazaar quarter from the administrative and government district called the Ark.

Once within the Ark, Westin was surprised to see fountains in this arid country. His mouth was already dry, and he wondered how anybody around here worked up a spit. He was led to an administrative building sporting tall columns of pinkish marble and a cobalt-blue dome, where, inside, he was told the meeting would begin shortly after the first of five daily prayers. He waited in a large room plush with Persian rugs and walls inlaid with blue tiles. Not at all the paltry raghead existence he'd expected.

Listening to the crier's call to prayer over the building's public address system made him think of how little he really knew about the Muslim faith. About all he did know was that Muslims abhorred nonbelievers, considering them not fully human. Yet they tolerated those infidels who had something to offer, something to benefit the Islamic *jihad*, its struggle for world dominance.

So obviously he *did* have something to offer, Westin mused. Little did they know. Little did *he* know, he cringed.

He'd brought copies of the last two Japanese NIQE-based weapons videotapes. At his request, Abdullah had prepared cassette labels; John found them scribed in Farsi and German for the benefit of American and German customs officials. The German he could passably read: "Project—Verse of the Sword, Maintenance and Training." The tapes, themselves, were clean, Kamikura having translated the audio and super-imposed text to English.

A rather pot-bellied Muslim-robed man wearing a white skull cap appeared and ushered him down and through the hall's last door. Westin took in the place: it wasn't a palace with a throne and all, but it definitely had trappings. The thing that struck John was that there was no furniture on the wall-to-wall Persian carpet blanketing the massive room. On one wall was draped a large gold tapestry, swirling Arabic scripted a verse from the Koran. Hung on other walls were paintings of Iran's more famous mosques.

At the far end, Hakim sat in a black ornate chair elevated on its foot-high platform. A flower-garlanded photograph of the Ayatollah Khomeini hung on the back wall like a halo above Hakim's head. Abu Hakim, himself, wore a brown satin robe over an open-collared white shirt. The white turban accentuated the strong weathered face of a man eternally devoted to Islam's fundamentalist *jihad*. Two Muslim-robed AK-74 toting guards flanked the entry door; two more in opposite corners flanked Hakim himself. John smelled wet sandstone.

"Please give any further evidence of this NIQE technology to General Rashid." Westin noted the president's excellent English—maybe Brit accented, then extended the tapes to the only other visitor in the room, a stalwart military figure. The general hesitated, staring, sizing. Westin knew immediately, this man, now in his face, would be his major obstacle in his establishing authenticity. Finally, baton tucked firmly under arm, the general took the tapes and left.

"Who do you represent, Mr. Westin?" Abu Hakim spoke.

"I'm sorry. I'm not at liberty." Westin answered the

questions directly, standing at military parade rest, hands clasped behind him—stomach tied in a knot.

"Why do you make us this offer, Mr. Westin?"

"Why does Islam struggle against the nonbelievers?" came Westin's rehearsed response.

Hakim shifted his weight, then let the artifice continue, "Because Allah wills it through His messenger Muhammad. Does Allah guide you to seek this STAIRCASE?"

STAIRCASE, so that's the byename. "I follow my personal interest, President Hakim. I haven't always done that. I do so now."

"I see, Mr. Westin. You represent America." John almost froze. *Bolt holes?* "For it is very American to believe in nothing higher than its own interest." John began breathing again. "And what is America's interest in this region? Simple: access to cheap oil. And how do they accomplish this? You keep the region relatively stable, maintaining a balance of power amongst the Arab and Persian nations, never letting one get too powerful, lest it control oil production, distribution and price. So when the scales tip in favor of Iran, America supports Iraq; when the scales tip in favor of Iraq, America supports Kuwait. That, my friend, is America's Middle East policy. And it makes me sick when you declare righteously that your intervention is benevolently in the name of democracy: Kuwait a democracy, hah. Iraq a democracy," he mocked derisively, "Maybe when Jesus Christ converts to Islam, but until then, it is nothing more than selfish interest."

John wasn't sure what to do with this diatribe. "Will STAIRCASE solve the American problem?"

"No. I am told America is too diverse in it's ethnic makeup." *Holy shit! A genetic agent. No wonder there's a full court press on this.* "But I can rid myself of the Zionist, once and for all." John stayed quiet while Hakim seemed lost in thought until finally, he asked, "Tell me, what will your interest do with STAIRCASE, if we share technologies?"

"I represent an interest who does not possess a malevolent nature, and certainly does not harbor ill feeling toward you or the Islamic movement. They simply wish a complete arsenal."

The British, Hakim believed Westin correct, were harmless enough. The answer was logical. They simply wanted the genetic weapon in their arsenal, as any advanced power would.

John continued, "You have a bomb, I offer a highly accurate and most intelligent gun. A gun *jihad* can put to very productive use."

"Why does an American astronaut care about *jihad?*"

"As your Allah knows only to well, I have no choice in such matters of life." Westin appealed to the Muslim belief that everything was Allah will—no free will here.

Hakim rubbed his dark chin with a finger casting a look toward a guard, then said, "Allah's will may be that I do not believe you. Allah may have brought you here so that I may dispatch of one more infidel."

"Or many."

Hakim smiled. "That has been my dream," Hakim finally said, "and dreams, Mr. Westin, are always more powerful than reality."

Later that Saturday at the Tajrish compound, Beth studied the sun's light against the curtains, harsh for a late September. It had been two days since General Rashid made his aborted move on her. It now seemed so hopeless, just a matter of time until…

She had to get out of there. Sometimes she wondered if it were John in this situation, how would he plan his escape. John. Every day she missed him more, wondering why she'd been so guarded with him.

It was only three o'clock, yet a half-hour ago, she and the rest of the hostages were moved from the lab. Now they were in their barracks, curtains drawn, armed guard present to keep them so. Something was up, they all knew. But what?

Then she heard the thumping of helicopter rotors…and felt strangely anxious.

John Westin couldn't see anything either. After the Hakim

meeting, he spent the rest of the morning answering questions about his documents, new videotapes and the NIQE technology in general. No mention was made of the Japanese. After lunch, apparently satisfied with his story, they blindfolded him and drove for twenty minutes, then guided him aboard a helicopter—not American he was sure—and flew for an hour, he estimated. Being a pilot, he could tell they'd not flown a straight heading, feeling subtle turns along the way.

The only sanity available to him during the trip was that he could see minuscule slits straight down his cheeks. It helped keep his mind off Beth and what a dumb-ass stunt this really was. But then again, so far so good. He lost his balance as the pilot banked hard, then positioned into a landing profile. It seemed to take a long time for the pilot to get clearance and actually put down.

A hand guided him out the right door and straight ahead. Concrete quickly went to hard ground, maybe some grass. He counted paces until reaching steps into a building. Inside he heard the sounds of communications, toggle switches being manually flipped, and the continuous hum of electronic equipment. He judged two men inside, now three with his handler. They seemed to be waiting.

He cocked his head enough to see the a control panel. Above each light or switch, a neatly lettered German and Farsi label identified its function. Only the Germans would be so organized. John had to smile. He could make out most of the German: East Mine Field, North Mine Field... He committed as much as possible to memory before the door opened and a hand guided him at a "two o'clock" direction relative to the forward helicopter at "twelve o'clock."

Counting steps, he eventually entered another building. Here, the blindfold was removed revealing a large, windowless, dim-lit modern laboratory. His eyes adjusted quickly, surveying. Present were two armed guards, and a third man, a rather handsome man with coffee-colored features and a hooked nose wearing western-style clothes.

"I am told you wish a tour of our lab," Shafii began. "I will show you our equipment, then show you some rather interesting videotaped experiments."

As John did a quick scan of the lab's interior, he knew this was it; he could almost feel Beth's presence. And two days was all she had left. He went through the charade, mildly impressed with the high-tech dust-free environment and equipment. In addition to the racks and racks of test tubes, he was shown centrifuges, baking ovens, a large refrigerator, an electron microscope, and equipment he couldn't begin to guess its purpose. Actually, John was somewhat impressed with the operation; that was until Shafii showed him a chair, walked over to video cassette player and television, and punched buttons:

The initial video scene showed a lab environment: very clean, white tables, cabinets full of test paraphernalia, monitoring machines and some electrical juryrigging. The next scene showed a table on which sat a placard which read, "TEST # 17", and a test-tube tray containing just one test-tube half-filled with a clear liquid. The video quality was good, but the CAM operator was a bit shaky; each successive scene clipped to the next in a jerky fashion.

The third scene showed a lab technician wearing a white lab coat; a black man stands near. The technician places a cotton swab into the test-tube and withdraws the wet end. The black man, dressed in mere rags, extends his thin arm; the cotton swab is swathed across his open palm. Next scene: the technician repeats the procedure with a working class white man. Next scene: the procedure is repeated again with a fairly large monkey. The next scene shows the three subjects behind a glass wall fronting what looked like an average size living room, with two cots forward on the left side wall. The two men have a couch, two chairs, a table with books and a television. Food and drink are present. On the back wall towards the left corner is a sink and toilet. Five-feet of the right side of the room is barred, housing the monkey. After this scene, the media changed: stop action, time-stamped photographs.

The video now showed one still frame every two seconds, each frame taken at hourly intervals. Just as in the previous sixty-eight frames, frame sixty-nine—nearly three days—shows normal activity.

However, frame seventy showed the black man lying on the couch, obviously in pain. Frame seventy-one showed the black man doubled up, he had lost control of his bladder, his face displayed excruciating pain. John almost flinched at that. In frame seventy-two the black man lay lifeless on the cot, clotted blood caked to the side of his open mouth. In frame seventy-three the black man was gone; the white man was watching television, so was the monkey. Test seventeen ended on frame one-hundred and twenty—five days. The two remaining subjects seemed to be in good health still.

The video flicked a little, then showed a new scene similar to the second scene in the previous test: a table, this time the placard read, "TEST # 22." The next scene showed a different lab technician removing a wet cotton swab from the test-tube and rubbing it in his own palm. He then rubs his hands together and turns to shake hands with a young, healthy handsome black man. The following scene showed the black man alone in the "glass house." The camera pan revealed exactly the same layout and provisions as in the previous test number seventeen. Seventy-three frames later, life was extinguished from a muscular body lying on the floor.

Shafii hit the stop button, smiling. It made John sick. At the moment, what he could not know was that these two experiments, now being passed off as a product of Iranian efforts, were really part of the booty retrieved from the stolen "golden briefcase."

After expressing his satisfaction, a somewhat sobered John Westin was re-blindfolded, then in the helicopter, repeated the time profile, returning back to his hotel after six. He had told them he would report his findings to his interest, after which, plans for an exchange could be negotiated.

"So tell me, Mohammed, what is it that you do not trust about the American?" asked Abu Hakim, after complimenting the general on his quickly suppressing the Shiraz riots.

Rashid couldn't put his finger on it, but *something*. "At present, Abu, I cannot say, maybe nothing."

"Even the American newspapers begin to speak of this NIQE technology. It seems the American indeed has access to—"

"Yes but..."

Hakim put down his small tea glass, placing his hand on Rashid's shoulder, then said, "My friend, if Mr. Westin's intentions are less than stated, then I will personally order his execution in the name of Allah."

"I will review his videotapes again. Maybe then, Allah willing." Rashid emptied his cup, then asked, "Have you spoken with Shafii?"

Hakim slammed his fist on the low table, rattling the tea service. "The incompetent has finally told me what I have suspected." Rashid nodded. "He still cannot develop a STAIR-CASE that will rid ourselves of the Zionist plague. Even with what we have given him!"

"Yes, Abu, but still, bringing this STAIRCASE to us was indeed a blessing from Allah. If the American is genuine, and the technologies are shared, then with these NIQE weapons alone, my forces will be victorious on the *jihad* battlefield. This is indeed better than nothing."

Hakim filled his tea cup, then leaned back. "We may still have it all, Mohammed. Allah has presented us with another opportunity." The general looked up in interest. "As we speak, a representative from the Japanese Misawa Group sits outside in the waiting room."

CHAPTER 27
SMALL NUMBERS

NAME DROPPER SLAYS BLACK
COMMUNITY LEADER

Inglewood— *Last night, the so-called "Name Dropper" claimed his seventh victim, the most prominent gang leader to date. Morris Jefferson, who made his name in the One-Twelve Hoover Crips, died instantly of a gunshot wound to the head.*

At 12:50 A.M. Saturday morning, while leaving the Pussy Cat Lounge on Crenshaw, Jefferson was shot in the left eye by a .308 caliber rifle. As in the previous six instances a shell casing was found at the seen of the shooting. This time its inscription read, "Stone," Jefferson's One-Twelve Hoover gang moniker.

Jefferson had, over the years, become a respected leader of Los Angeles's African-American community. Jefferson's speeches, often punctuated with an-

archist rhetoric, called for a more activist community, moving away from the previous African-American generation who received passive guidance from the church.

Normally, said a fellow member of the One-Twelve Hoover Crips, this would be attributed to a set of the East Coast Crips. But this was different. "We find Name Dropper," he said, "and we be down for the 'hood, down for Stone." Translated, that means revenge.

—*Los Angeles Times*, 29 September

Bill Henry and Redbone were dead. That much, Tom Shelby's fading mind knew for sure. The shaved-headed Hispanic with the tear tattoo was one mean sonofabitch. The other, called Cage, simply did what this El Cid told him to.

It all started yesterday. Shelby usually returned alone back to his family living in Las Vegas. But this was the first weekend of the month. On other weekends, Redbone stayed at Yucca Mountain hunting rabbits; Bill Henry simply drank beer and watched the sports network. Only on the first weekend did they come in to try their luck at the tables. The two men had a pretty good string, too, until last night.

Now it was late Saturday night in a remote house north of the city. Centered within a dim lit room, under a bright halogen light, Shelby sat bound naked and gagged, struggling with consciousness, with pain, with exhaustion.

El Cid didn't exactly enjoy this kind of work, breaking fingers, listening to a man scream. But the pay and contacts were good, the best.

The other two men were easy: a bullet for each, between the eyes. It was a kind of killing that was strangely different, El Cid discovered, not just a quick hit or drive-by; in some convoluted way he'd found himself fascinated being so close to a kill, to the bullet as it had its way, to the blur of the head snapping with the momentum, to the small entry hole and residual powder burns, and finally to the fist-sized exit gutted through the base of the skull. White matter covered with red splayed the wall behind like modern art, he'd thought.

Over the last twenty-four hours, El Cid had gotten one name from the exhausted man, the sixth finger, he remembered. Nothing more since. It was time to bring it to an end. El Cid pulled a switch-blade from his pocket, held it before Shelby's puffy eyes, then depressed the button.

Click. Shelby flinched. The five inch blade glistened under the intense light. "Ain't no thing. Not if you shootin' straight with me."

"Booyah!" Cage pantomimed the report of a shotgun. "Hey Cuz, do him now an we go home." El Cid would rather have had G-Rake here for support, but three weeks ago, he'd heard, G-Rake upped and left L.A.—in a big hurry.

"He live if he straight. We gonna find out now. I cut out this eye," El Cid put the blade within an inch of Shelby's left eye. Shelby tensed, focused on its point. "And I leave the other if you give me the other names you told."

El Cid motioned Cage to hold the struggling white man. From behind, Cage locked Shelby's head with one hand around the forehead and the other around the chin from below; using his fingers, he forced and held the left eye wide open. Shelby went frantic. "Don't worry, *gringo*, you keep the other if you talk."

Shelby's adrenaline spent quickly within a depleted body. He felt El Cid's fingers push in, grab his eyeball from the sides, then pinch in holding it still. He watched helplessly as his eye instinctively tried to focus on the approaching blade's point. Light became pain, a horrendous pain transmitted by a half-million bundled nerves directly to his brain, not three centimeters away. The lids tried to shut out the fluid-pressured resistance, the scraping, the six deliberate cuts. Light faded to a merciful purple-black. He wished he'd pass out, even die. Anything to stop the horrible pain dulling his very soul.

"Cage, what's you think?" Cage came around to look at El Cid's work. Nothing to see as the blood covered the cornea. "Can't see it now; I carved 'AK' right across the blue part."

Cage had maimed and even killed, but this was gruesome.

"Yeah man. We smoke 'em now?"

"Shelby, my man, how ya doin'?" El Cid said in feigned compassion. "Who else you tell about the mountain? Tell us and you keep the right one."

Shelby managed to mumble, "No one else," then passed out.

El Cid turned to Cage, "Okay, man. We go. Wait for me outside."

Cage left.

"One name. That's it. I believe the fucker."

"Very well," came the voice from the shadow. El Cid pulled the .45 semiautomatic tucked in his front belt, aimed at the canted head, and pulled the trigger. Carerra Thielken stepped out to inspect. Blood gouted out a wicked rent in the dead man's skull. "How soon can you be in Sunnyvale?"

"Mr. John K. Westin?" John barely got a word out in response when a second man grabbed his arm very firmly.

"I am agent Ted Woods," the self-assured first man continued with his FBI badge out for identification. "We wish to ask you a few questions, Mr. Westin. Please come with us." John inspected the badge, then scanned the JFK gate area. "You can make this easy or difficult. That, of course, is your choice. Either way, understand you come with us." Their destination, they kept to themselves.

It was eleven o'clock late Sunday night. John had just returned from Tehran, this first step onto U.S. territory being less than hospitable. What's an FBI badge supposed to look like anyway; for a two dollar mail order, he'd bought a genuine KGB badge for his grandson, Jeffery. Finally, their authenticity become more apparent as they brisked him passed normal U.S. customs entry procedures. He didn't see the third man deplane.

The two agents boarded John on a small twin-engine jet, and flew south to a small airstrip outside Washington D.C. There, they took him to a manor cloistered within a clump of trees amid Maryland rolling hills. Throughout the early Monday morning hours, he was questioned about his trip to Iran. He told them everything—save where his two special assists originated.

He explained his intentions, and told them about Abdullah, about the second Iranian, about the copied video tapes. There were many questions about the tapes, about his current assignment, about Lieutenant Colonel Coleman, and the NIQE-based Weapons Report now three days late. He went over the trip and his meeting with Abu Hakim. Lots of questions about Hakim: description, personality, those close to him, any sign of strife or question as to who held the real power. About what he saw at the lab, the questions were incessant, over and over; he described everything his memory recorded. And yes, again, he left Mehrabad airport at eight Sunday morning, Tehran time; no, he didn't have an accomplice, nor did he see anyone follow him back to New York.

Finally, his interrogators left the room, another man entered. A big strapping black Marine Lieutenant Colonel, and he looked pissed.

"You sonofabitch." Coleman's delivery began cold and warmed up super-hot. "Mr. astronaut goes fuckin' solo! If you're looking for me to bail your candy ass out of this one, look again. You know why, Mr. John Westin? Because the NSC Chairman's pissed. You wanna try guessing why he's pissed? The report, John, he didn't get his report like *I* promised. You know what that means? It means Lieutenant Colonel Coleman can't handle the workload. It means he just got passed over for his next promotion. To these guys here, it means he can't keep his mouth shut."

"But—"

"BUT, my ass! I got the buts, John. But I'm not on the missing scientist case anymore. I've been removed." Coleman face flushed as he drew breath looking as he were about to destroy the planet. Thirty seconds later, more composed, he continued, "But I don't give a flying fuck what they do to your ass," he lied. "They could grind it up good, you know. Treason, providing highly classified national secrets to a hostile foreign government. Fuckin' treason."

"How'd they know?"

Coleman just shook his head. Even now, his career just

pissed down the drain, it was hard to generate genuine hate for the man, especially with Beth Storey and all. "FBI had your Abdullah under surveillance, suspected Iranian agent. You mixed it up with Abdullah and picked up a tail for your trouble. You leave the country, then buy a round-trip to Tehran, and let me tell you, shit hit the fan. Then you bring back a tail—"

"What?"

"Iranian national, known agent. Don't worry, he didn't see your reception at JFK. Matter of fact, customs grabbed him, false passport. Should keep you clean for awhile."

"Okay, Judd, how much trouble am I really in?"

"Treason's serious shit...I don't know. Sounds like you stumbled on the lab?"

"STAIRCASE, they told me. Genetic-targeted agent. That's heavy, Judd." Coleman glanced away. "Anyway, I'm sure Beth and the others are there. I saw the lab, everything's written in English. She was there, I know it. I could almost feel her close-by."

"Hope you're right, John. You're headed for Langley right now. You'll be looking at some sat pictures. After that, I think they'll let you go. When that happens, come over to my office. We got a report to finish. You listening: We—"

"Judd, I'm sorry—"

"Shut the fuck up! I don't wanna hear it," Coleman snapped almost involuntarily, then pulled a slip of paper handing it to Westin. Finally, with voice nearing normal, Coleman said, "Better take care of this. MacIsaac's been trying to reach you, sounded desperate the third call."

At Langley, the questions concentrated on his trip to the lab itself. He told them about hearing two aircraft take off very nearby, one a military combat aircraft, his experience told him. Tajrish, they suspected to themselves, having an air base adjacent to their suspected compound. He told them about landing on concrete, then stepping onto hard ground. The helipad, they were sure, as they studied the glossy satellite photographs, one with a HIND-D on the disk. They measured his stride and calculated distances, correlating with the sat photos within a couple of feet. Caucusing away from Westin, Tajrish was it, they agreed. He handed them his hand drawn layout of the control panel he'd peeked at. Everyone agreed, Westin's blindfolded first stop had been the compound's security control building. It looked impenetrable, an operations analyst would later say, even for special ops.

Westin's last meeting was on the seventh floor with the DDO, Jordan Barr, and a few others, including an official visitor from Israel's MOSSAD. Again, he recounted the story: from Abdullah to Iran and back. Barr gave instructions to what turned out to be his Covert Action Staff, then sent them off to work up a mission plan. Barr and Westin were now alone.

"What's going to happen to me?" John asked.

"I'd say that depends. If we come out of this with STAIR-CASE and the hostages, your balls may stay intact. If we don't, Temple will hang 'em from the highest tree in Washington."

"When do you move on it?"

"Hard to say," Barr said, always cagy about divulging timetables. "The President's been cozying up to the bastards. Previous Iranian president said he would drop the death sentence against Salman Rushdie. That was a pre-condition with Temple."

"Fuck Rushdie. She'll be dead by then. Why don't you guys just assassinate these asshole leaders? Saddam Hussein instead of a war, Abu Hakim instead of this STAIRCASE shit."

"It's a moral thing. We go shooting their leaders, their shooters start shooting ours. Makes everybody look bad."

"Still sounds like a good idea to me."

Barr smiled. When he'd found out the real reason, then it made sense. A retiring senator he knew once put it straight. It came down to a governmental conflict of interest: the President wants to dispatch a bad situation before it gets worse; but congressmen want votes. Assassinations cost votes, the old senator had said. Assassinating someone has no impact on the commercial sector. War requires production, material, and logistics; that means jobs, and jobs means votes. All very moral, now that Barr had it in its proper Washington perspective.

"Say, can I use a phone?" John asked, sensing the meeting over.

The DDO punched a button, "Nancy. Mr. Westin needs to make a call, and have Jeff drop him at the nearest Metro station." Barr told Westin he was expected at Coleman's office, wished him good luck, and handed him off to his secretary.

John found Coleman's slip of paper, then punched numbers. MacIsaac's wife answered. Something was wrong.

John had arrived at JFK Sunday night at eleven o'clock. Now fifteen hours later he found himself on Metrorail's Orange Line proceeding toward Washington proper. He leaned back into the seat recalling the conversation. MacIsaac was dead, brutally murdered, his wife had said. She didn't know why, but she did know MacIsaac very badly wanted to talk to him, something about a project...*and you weren't there*. "The Japanese?" had been his first thought.

The girls at Langley didn't tell him shit. Questions, caucus, and more questions. *Shit!* His whole life seemed to be turning to dog shit. Everybody he gave a damn about. After going into the city to handle flowers for the funeral, Westin found himself on the Red-Line approaching the huge cathedral-like Metro Station, Metrorail's major transfer point.

Again, he thought of Beth and what Coleman had said six weeks ago: worst case development time-line CIA estimated at six weeks. *That meant...today! October first!* From this point on, she was on borrowed time. If he'd just stopped her abduction. If he'd just gotten to the lab sooner. More sobering, though, was that if he read Hakim correctly, the man would kill her, like a faithful dog at the end of its useful life. The days in her "useful life" were indeed numbered, it seemed. Small numbers.

And where was he on his father, the rapist. *Shit. Goddamn shit!* He would never find out. Japan was too tight, a society closed to the *gaijin*—the outsider, the barbarian. He heard his northbound Red-Line apply its pneumatic brakes as it came to a smart stop adjacent to a stopped southbound train. As the doors opened, he looked over at the passengers in the opposing train. He saw the face of a Japanese man, looking not at him, but on through the windows at someone on the platform area. What attracted John was the harshness of the Oriental's face, now transforming from distraction to surprise.

John looked around to see a physically fit man probably of Italian decent...*or, American Indian*...wearing a denim work jacket and jeans. The Indian had locked eyes with the Jap, eyes communicating fate. Then John watched the Indian cry out, echoing the waffle-like walls of the station's huge circular concrete cocoon. The backlit shadows from cool white neon seemed to darken more with each reverberation. It was the cry of Coyote Shadow's namesake, a primal cry that sent chills through the now silent crowd. John snapped back at the Japanese, only to see an accelerating blur as electric motors strained under load.

John looked back to the platform. Gone.

One station later Westin got off and walked to the Old Executive Office Building adjacent to the White House. Coleman was free and quickly showed him into his modest office.

"FBI won't let it go, John. Don't want you leaving the country. I got a compromise. They tail your ass here the rest of the week. I ride shotgun with you to Japan Friday, we arrive Saturday morning. I understand you met the CIA's man in Japan; he'll cover while we're there."

"Protection or custody?"

"Both," Coleman hesitated, "mostly custody. You fucked up, John, copying those NIQE weapons tapes, handing them to a hostile foreign national."

"I did some editing, the most sensitive stuff. Does that count?"

"Cut a day off life in Leavenworth, maybe. What's important now is to wrap this goddamned report up and be done with it."

"When we going in?" John asked softening his voice.

"How the fuck do I know? I got taken off the case, remember? One thing. One thing only, John: the NIQE-based Weapons Report. No Lone Ranger stuff. Loud and clear?"

"Let me tell you what's loud and clear, Judd. Test number seventeen and test number twenty-two."

Coleman froze. "You saw the STAIRCASE test videos?"

"And they made me sick. Ashamed to be an American."

Coleman reached back rubbing the back of his wrenched neck, then said, "South Africa. It came from South Africa. A man on the inside couldn't take it anymore. Came to the U.S. Cape Town Consulate, asked for the CIA agent in charge, and told an incredible story. We were able to verify the story, STAIRCASE and its hideous intent. Working with the insider, Green Beret Special Forces went in, destroyed the lab, and brought back STAIRCASE, including videotapes. That was two years ago. One of the tapes was in the briefcase ripped off last May. The rest you know. Anything else?"

This story, coming from a black man, had to be tough. John shook his head negative.

"Fine. We leave Andrews noon this Friday. Thanks for coming over."

"Can't be there." Coleman exploded. Sixty seconds later John was able to explain about MacIsaac and that a wake would be held Friday evening.

"Okay," Coleman had calmed down, himself now the one feeling a little shitty, then looked at his calendar. "Okay, be at Moffett Field by 2130, we push off at 2230.

"Thanks, Judd. I'll be there." Coleman looked down shaking his head, doubtful.

Glenn Thielken hung up the telephone receiver. A nice feather in his cap, compliments of would-be President Dhillon Reed. The chairman of the Green Globe selection committee had just called. Shiraki Industries was selected winner of this year's Green Globe Award. *Congratulations*. Thielken gratefully expressed his thanks and agreed to accept the Award in person this coming Saturday night. *Thank you, Mr. Vice President. It would indeed be nice having you in the White House.*

CHAPTER 28

UNINVITED GUEST

"Where's the other party?" asked the somewhat lethal-looking, uniformed black officer. The question was directed to an Oriental man, elderly, dressed in an old-style loose fitting shirt and pants. The old man had presented two congressional White House tour tickets to this officer who sported a raised scar on the side of his seventeen-inch right bicep, created as skillfully as the work of any tatoo artist: a viper.

"My wife fell ill last night," the old man said, bowing slightly. "But she insisted I not miss this opportunity. She is all right, I think."

Once again, the officer looked at the benign gentleman, then checked off the two names making a note. Keeping the stubs, the officer informed "Mr. Tanabe" that he should be inside within half an hour.

Other than a hardened plastic knife and smoke bombs, the man carried no classic *ninjutsu* weapons—*taijutsu*. The smoke bombs he carried in double-wrapped ziploc bags to defeat the explosive meter just ahead.

He quietly passed through the airport-like metal detector and followed the promenade up the gentle slope to the East Portico. Two weeks ago, twice under different disguises, he had taken the public tour reconnoitering the two-hundred-year-old structure. It would be difficult, he had concluded, but not impossible. Today, happenstance would determine which of three plans he would execute.

The promenade came to a stop in the east terrace pavilion, catacomb-like in its appearance with its crisscrossing curved ceilings above ivory-pink Italian tile floors. While others viewed the period portraits of the White House's evolution, the elderly man studied the ceiling, walls, shadows, personnel, and security measures.

After a short wait, the old man found himself in group of forty, partitioned by a Secret Service guide who then explained tour logistics and more: "Stay with the group," he warned solemnly, "You wander off, you'll just find another police officer who'll shorten your tour, but lengthen your stay in Washington." People smiled, but no one laughed.

The old man hung back to the group's rear, as the Secret Service guide led the group into the Ground Floor Corridor. Passing the Library and Vermeil Room, he followed the others into the red-motifed China Room where past presidential place settings stood for inspection. *The doorway!* He'd missed that before: a metal detector expertly concealed in the door's frame.

The Secret Service guide led them into the adjoining Diplomatic Reception Room, an oval room accented in petite-point yellows against sky-blue hues. As the guide explained that the room used to be the White House boiler and furnace room, the old man shuffled around looking to the room's far end, the South Portico: again he noted the permanent presence of a black-clad Secret Service officer complete with FAG bag slung across his chest. He had seen others like this one patrolling the grounds. The report had covered the fast-action-gun: fast-action meant weapon out, aimed, and fired in less than two seconds;—gun meant Uzi 9 mm submachine gun. Outward another forty yards was where the President's helicopter performed its shuttling duties.

The Secret Service guide seemed to be working a tight schedule as he politely herded the group out of the Diplomatic Reception Room and up a staircase to the State Level. Entering the East Room, the largest of the White House's hundred and twenty-three rooms, the old man spotted two microphones; he'd only seen a few, but listening devices were everywhere, his senses warned. Fewer cameras, but strategically placed, nonetheless.

Adjoining the East Room, was the first of three parlor rooms, each with two parallel doorways eventually leading to the State Dining Room at the far west end. The Secret Service guide split the group into two parallel processions: The guide spoke from the half-group proceeding along the inside wall; the old man took the half-group along the windowed-exterior wall. The first parlor was the Green Room with its Early American Liberty-period furnishings. The old gentleman took in the sight, including the inset window casings and twenty foot ceilings.

Onward, he moved slowly into the oval Blue Room furnished in a French Empire style, the most formal room in the White House, the guide said. The old man wondered if the room had motion detectors beyond the boundaries of public access delineated by perimeter chord attached to the top of brass stanchions. He assumed, without doubt, that under the room-sized blue Aubusson rug lay pressure sensors.

The double-columned group proceeded into the last parlor room, the Red Room. The Secret Service guide began his description. The old man saw not the American Empire furnishings, nor the surprising portrait of John James Audubon carrying a hunting rifle; he saw only his last chance as the tour's end was very near now. The guide called it a state reception room, walls covered with red twill satin. The old man once again studied the red-damask wall sofa opposite the fireplace: low, dark underneath, crowded by two chairs and a small round table. His group was moving on now, into the adjoining State Dining Room, half were already gone; a tour group behind theirs was just entering the previous Blue Room, its Secret Service guide momentarily out of view. He saw no cameras, but that didn't mean…

Form became blur. With the fluid motion of a powerful cat, hugging the wall, the creature crouches down, uncoiling flat on the floor while simultaneously rolling on his back, his hand slipping inside his loose-fitting shirt. A snake, now under the sofa, he produces a four inch hardened plastic knife, and with swift exacting motion, cuts the black underlining down the length of the sofa's rear and a third way up the sides. The resultant flap now hanging just touched the hardwood floor—easily cloaking his body from all but the most oblique angles. Start-to-finish: three-point-three seconds.

For the next two hours, the assassin would lay perfectly still in a highly attenuated state. Satisfied with normalcy, he would then induce a deep meditative state bringing all body functions and emitted heat to an absolute minimum.

North Carolina Senator Calhoun locked up his desk thinking about the Vice President and the third package he'd received today. Counting the day the two of them entered their unholy alliance, he had received information now for two and a half weeks. This last one was good, *very* good indeed.

The environmental issues were nice, *but American hostages.* Now that was something: Crisis kept secret, Iran snatches American citizens, impotent administration lacks will, failure to act, cover up. Yep, he smiled chomping down on his cigar, he knew just the right special prosecutor for the job too.

Before leaving, on his private line, he made the day's last call. He finished and arranged to meet his contact after the White House state dinner this evening. He never thought of himself as a "Deep Throat" leaking political dynamite to the press, but that's what it seemed like now as he switched off the lights. *Eat lightly tonight, Mr. President, for reading tomorrow's Washington Post could easily induce indigestion.*

• • •

President Temple wasn't exactly enthusiastic having Senator Calhoun here in the White House, much less at a State Dinner for one hundred and four. The occasion honored the visiting foreign ministers of ASEAN, Association of South East Asian Nations. But Calhoun was chairman of the Senate's select sub-committee on Asian Affairs and, politically, it just wouldn't do to exclude his name from the invitation list—as much as the thought delighted the more devious side of his presidential ego.

Jim Rhodes, special agent in charge, and seven other plain-clothed Secret Service special agents watched over the eight circular tables positioned about the gilded State Dining Room. Tonight, protesters demonstrated across the street bitchin' about exporting jobs to Asia. Standard fare, just something to be watched; what occupied Jim's professional mind at the moment was loose ends.

Rhodes hated loose ends and tonight that's precisely what he had. There seemed to be one less visitor exiting from this morning's congressionally sponsored White House tour than entered, according to a brief image on just one camera, the others missed it. The visitor's sheet was inconclusive: Uniformed Division officer Wilcox made a "no show" note on a pair of reservations—a pair or just one of the pair? As luck would have it, Wilcox headed out on a one-week vacation just after his shift this afternoon—now on the road somewhere between Washington and Mobile, Alabama. Whatever, he figured, he'd asked everyone on duty tonight to be on heightened alert. For Jim Rhodes, it would be a long night. After this, he'd be on the red-eye for L.A., SAC on that trip too.

The honored guests and "official Washington" now sipped at the last of their coffee, napkins correctly refolded and placed next to empty dessert plates. Temple rose, and as the room quieted he formally announced what was already scribed on the place card before them: after-dinner entertainment, a jazz pianist, would commence shortly in the East room. In odd bunches, people began pushing away from tables.

The Philippine foreign minister and his wife were seated near the doorway to the three consecutive parlor rooms. They were the first to leave, Calhoun saw, choosing the route through the adjoining Red Room. He wanted to talk to the little bastard before things got crowded back there. Now was his best chance, he decided, excused himself and moved in quick pursuit.

Beneath the sofa in the Red Room, the assassin was ready. No man is feared more than one with nothing to lose. And so it was with the assassin's preparation, now counting himself dead—free from all inhibitions or fears. He was now invincible.

Removing the loose-fitting clothes revealed a more elegant layer: tuxedo. He'd pulled the shirt collar up and nestled the black tie snugly in its proper place. He still wore his toe-fitted soft shoes within the patent leather shoes in which he'd arrived. The make-up and toupee he now wore presented an image of a fifty-ish Oriental man with style and stature.

Listening to the background noise in the adjoining State Dining Room, the assassin heard the momentary silence, then chairs pushing away: dinner was over. He moved to emerge from beneath the sofa, but…people, already! Two. Already beyond the fallen black cloth underlining, he froze. The two passed through quickly. Apparently unnoticed, *but for how long?* Clear. He made his move.

"What the hell—"

Senator Calhoun, over halfway into the Red Room, never had a chance and would never glimpse the irony of his demise: Seizing the plastic knife, the assassin leaped toward the astonished man, alone—for the moment. One lightening savage thrust guaranteed silence, the knife penetrating his larynx severing the trachea. Both hands now free, he stepped to the side of the collapsing body, and expertly snapped the neck accelerating death by fifty seconds. With superhuman strength, the assassin spun the overstuffed body around and down almost parallel with the wall-sofa from which he'd just emerged, then jammed it beneath. *Voices!* It would have to do, he decided, as he sprung erect pretending to admire Albert

Bierstadt's *View of the Rocky Mountains* painting above the now notorious sofa.

Increasingly, in groups of twos and threes, they passed through or stopped to admire the room, paying little attention to the apparent not-so-important aide of someone who was. The not-so-important aide casually proceeded back to the gilded splendor of the State Dining Room. Temple was cornered by the fireplace, now telling a joke. The assassin approached his target, slowly, purposefully, eight feet away.

Special agent Baker saw it first, a shoe, a foot protruding beneath the side of the wall-sofa in the Red Room. He grabbed his communicator, "Silver Road, I repeat, Silver Road."

Jim Rhodes was the nearest to the President and responded immediately, looking, looking: There it was, just four feet away. A face he'd not seen tonight, Oriental, approaching, alert eyes—now registering on him, on his heightened alertness, on his physical conditioning, on his tactical posture. Rhodes reached for the Mac-10 under his coat, eyes fixed on the oncoming figure, on his eyes…*something* caused his mind to distract but for the briefest moment, a deadly moment— *saiminjutsu*. Jim Rhodes never really got to the Mac's grip before the rushing figure arrived with a perfectly balanced full power kick—*soku yaku*—to his head. Reflexing, Rhodes's turned head received the full force against the flat bone at the left temple, transmitting an intense referral shock hemorrhaging cerebral blood vessels on a massive scale.

Hitting the soft green and brown Persian designed carpet, Jim Rhodes calmly looked across at the people. He saw forty-three years of his life: he saw his graduating class at Federal Law Enforcement Training Center in Glynco, Georgia, he saw his wife and his children, he saw people he didn't know: people he walked passed at Disney World, strangers standing in a supermarket line. He saw them all, and then he didn't.

The assassin spun around looking for the President. To his right, a woman stood screaming; in front stood another blue blazer shielding his target. He tensed for the attack…then from behind, he heard the distinctive sound of a Mac 10 safely flipping to "off." To his left, someone now rushed toward him. He threw down three blinding smoke bombs and bolted, reaching the Cross Hall, now heading for the Entrance Hall to the main North Portico—and escape.

Surprise was his best weapon: coming around the corner, the nearer agent saw him first; the hurling shadow lunged into a pivoting gun barrel, his iron-like fingers spread. Both men went down as fingers went for the eyes digging deep, scratching the right, bursting the left eye in a spray of blood—threat disabled. The second agent saw barely a target, the shadow moved so fast. On the floor now rolling, the assassin sprung away from the sweeping Uzi gun barrel seeking the best angle for attack. Instantly, knife again in hand, he toe-kicked—*soku gyaku*—the exposed gun armpit, sending a momentary nerve shock throughout the arm. Keeping balance, the assassin slapped the stubby barrel to the right ignoring its staccato discharge, then thrust the knife's plastic point into the agent's solar plexus up and into the heart.

The assassin kicked off his patent leather shoes, and like the wind's shadow glided down the floodlit front steps, angling right and around the tall front hedges. Only thirty meters and a seven foot wrought-iron fence separated him from Pennsylvania Avenue, from the noisy protesters rhythmically moving on the sidewalk across the street. He heard radios crackling—*close*—as he passed a large Red Maple, *twenty meters*. He moved like a cheetah, yet lighter than a cat—not desiring to trip pressure sensors of any sort. He heard the distinctive sound of an Uzi, the muffled crack-crack-crack, coming from his right near the Northeast Gatehouse. Little time now, the fence. Like a nocturnally-sighted bat, he leapt rising to the top. He took balance from the spear-like apex—tripping an invisible beam which automatically engaged more flood lights—and landed near a cylindrical concrete barrier, then sprinted across Pennsylvania Avenue—

CRACK!

Ted Slater refocused through the sniper scope. Sitting in his perch atop the adjacent Treasury Building, he'd received the "Silver Road" alert, and was ready. *Missed!* The target was fast, almost a blur, dodging traffic and now merging into the group of protesters before he could refocus, line up, and squeeze again. The protestors froze at the sound, then panicked, scattering. Ted Slater looked down at chaos, chiding himself, second shots were for amateurs. He grabbed his high-powered binoculars, radioed status and swore he'd find the bastard and get that second shot.

He didn't.

CHAPTER 29

REGROUPING

Beth sat at her keyboard copying a set of infection dispersal data files. October third and a heat wave, Beth thought feathering her khaki shirt for air. The air conditioning wasn't keeping up and no one seemed to care.

Her mind was on yesterday's incident. One of the microbiologist broke down in the sweltering heat. Just started crying, mumbling about his family. He wouldn't stop. After a half-hour of the miserable sight, Shafii called in a guard, and had him shot. That was very unlike Shafii, and she didn't know what to think of it.

The first hostage had arrived over three months ago, Beth, herself, two months ago. Of the nine total, only four were left: two now killed outright, two failed to return after being taken away, and one slipped out at night only to trip an electrically activated interior land mine.

After ridding the virus-infected computers of their maladies, she spent her time writing computer programs for the other scientists. Now, sometimes she helped Bill Sanborne or Jamil Velayati, but most of her time was spent supporting "Dr. Death."

Dech gave her the disease spread characteristics and simulated infection points within Israel, and she calculated fractal spread patterns and kill estimates. It was all so clinical. Yet all too real, the emotional side of her mind kept reminding. Finally, Dech developed a set of infection points that had a kill percentage of eighty-five. He and Shafii seemed please with that.

Staring blankly at the scrolling screen, she wondered what John was doing now. Wondered if he'd found another woman. Forgotten about her. If he had, well it was her own damned fault. The question was innocent enough that last night. He'd asked her what her middle name was. She hated that name and withheld it, like an older sister withholds a favorite necklace. He'd come back disbelieving: No one knows, and never will, ever...never? Now she regretted her petulant reply: Well, maybe. Someone important, I guess. Someone I could trust. To his query she'd told him flatly: At this point, Mr. Westin, all you get is a 'T.' *Why'd she do that?*

Refocusing back onto a now blank screen, she saw an empty reflection, her reflection. Over their months together, John had come closer to her, slowly opening up, trusting. Especially, his telling her about the Japanese man, the attack, and his accusing words about John's father, the rape. The man's death. John had shared that with her, and only one other person. He'd let her see pain, pain a formless enemy now exacted on a father's son. And what did she do? Nothing. *Christ.*

Probably didn't matter anymore, she tried to shrug. Because here at the lab, something was up.

Today they were told to make one copy of everything: files, documents, samples, computer programs and data. Two sets of boxes were brought in. They were instructed to place the copies in one set of boxes, the originals in the other. Jamil was convinced the Iranians were abandoning the effort. If that were true, she knew, their captors would have little use for her and the remaining three hostages.

Except, of course, maybe General Rashid...

Special agent Bob Upton now understood the phrase: feeling the weight on your shoulders. At the moment, his were locked tighter than a steel safe. He'd just viewed the video footage, again. The other three Secret Service investigators present were specially assigned by the Bureau Chief to investigate what happened last night and review safeguards, procedures—and performance. The other three were FBI.

As Upton viewed the tuxedo-clad figure leaping the north fence, escaping, the conclusion dredged at his gut: the Secret Service almost lost the big one, the President of the United States. Strangely enough, the concern of the Secret Service personnel in this room was not so much for President Temple or his life; the concern was about honor and reputation, and measuring up to the charter and sworn oath that makes the Secret Service the revered organization that it is. All of that, badly shaken at the moment, but still in tact.

In tact because one man did his job. Jim Rhodes' quick reaction, they all agreed, delayed the killer, just enough for their men to respond to "Silver Road," the broadcast warning of immediate presidential jeopardy. It cost him his life, and eventually another, along with special agent Bryant who lost an eye.

Who was that man? Upton wondered, again watching the Oriental man, the mystery man on camera number one. Old men don't jump seven foot fences, old men don't take down three highly trained Secret Service professionals, vanish, and avoid the biggest manhunt this town has ever seen. The FBI. Was this the man they flagged back in August? If so, there'd be hell to pay.

Adding to Bob Upton's chaos was his new assignment: SAC for the L.A. trip. Jim Rhodes had that one, until last night. Upton felt uneasy about the assignment. He had not been a part of the "security plan's" development, thus didn't know the thinking behind it: local law enforcement coordination, routes, exposures, measures to minimize danger—the issues, as always, were endless. Compounding the pain now hammering his head was the assassin himself. He was still at large, presumably with an unfinished assignment. *Christ!* And, of course, Temple wouldn't even consider canceling the G2 trip.

Yes, no question about it, special agent—now in charge—Bob Upton felt the pressure.

Mrs. Kim, an elderly Korean woman, waited for the rest of the passengers to deplane. During the flight, she had told the businessman next to her that she was visiting her son in Santa Monica. Called *hensojutu*, this was the assassin's least comfortable disguise, but it had served him well getting through a heavily watched Dulles airport this morning.

During the flight he'd tried to analyze what went wrong the night before. Was the plan too bold? Could he have chosen a better room, or a different place to hide? No. All had gone as planned, even the canine team failed to reveal his presence—*haragei* and his hypnotic power easily overpowering the dog's trained responses. No, it was just bad luck: the fat man's arrival, maybe his body discovered. Bad luck, yes. But Los Angeles was different, he'd always had good luck here. It was such a diverse uncaring collection of people where the sensational was commonplace, and the horrid commanded but ten more seconds on the eleven o'clock news. Yes, he liked Los Angeles.

So his "Washington" contact had been right after all. The assassin was now glad they'd pursued developing the Los Angeles plan; and the man given him to assist was a good one too, dependable. They'd flown to Los Angeles last weekend to check out the Green Globe Awards hotel, the Westin Bonaventure. Indeed, Los Angeles was lucky for him, a convention would end the Friday before Saturday night's award ceremonies. He could expect a low level of Saturday morning confusion caused by the rush to check out and in; this would create a desirable state of disorientation.

It was clear that he'd have excellent access at his target. And he could use his weapons, the "golf bag" now tucked away in an airline carton secure in the hold below—a present for "her" son. That made this job much easier, for weapons increased the efficiency of violence. But even at that, he had to admit, given the certain increase in presidential protection, having an assistant could indeed prove useful.

He planned to leave nothing to chance. During the six-hour flight, he'd memorized the hotel operations and its layout, an entire top floor reserved for the Presidential suite. He studied the freeway system, collector streets, even secondary street patterns. It was a much easier plan to execute, and this time *he would not fail.*

"Ma'am, it's time to go," said the flight attendant to the old Korean woman, "Let me help."

After the assassin's attempt, Teal Coro contacted FBI Deputy Assistant Director Voight. From Voight, he received the President's itinerary, then took the next plane out.

Coro had to check his overnight satchel because of the two special weapons it contained. In addition to his five inch fighting knife with sub-hilt, Coro carried a customized seven inch bowie knife. The longer bowie knife, he chose as his weapon against the Japanese sword he was sure to encounter. Made of the finest 5/32 inch 440-C cutlery-grade steel, its upper false edge had also been sharpened. Its guard curved slightly upward toward the blade's tip; that would catch the sword's edge preventing it from coming down onto his hand.

The plane landed and pulled up to the gate on time. Teal Coro knew Los Angeles fairly well, for this was where he busted the Japanese *yakazu* case. That effort took six months, and not without memories. After deplaning and retrieving his overnight satchel from the baggage carrousel, he exited the airport terminal building. Under a restless sky he waited for the next rental car courtesy bus.

Standing curbside, Coro glanced at the paper being read next to him. He saw the photograph and read the caption: "Shiraki Industries wins Green Globe: President Temple to be in Los Angeles Saturday presenting Shiraki CEO Glenn

Thielken the prestigious Green Globe Award..." He felt his skin flush as he thought of his grandfather, the ancient spirit, and the desecration of Yucca Mountain.

Coro closed his eyes and breathed deeply, letting the sensation pass, only to become aware of different feeling entirely. An ominous feeling. *White Shadow had been here,* the Apache scout's senses informed, and not long ago.

The next day, early Thursday: The assassin had had fourteen hours to prepare.

First, in yesterday's airport restroom, the Korean woman had transformed into a successful Hong Kong businessman. Next he hailed a cab to the Westin Bonaventure, a cluster of five towering chrome and sea-green-tinted glass towers in the Convention Center area of downtown Los Angeles.

Second, checking in, the businessman received a card key to his requested Green Tower room. He was pleased to hear his Latino bellman confirming his prediction, the place was a madhouse: a major convention called URISA, the Urban and Regional Information Systems Association, filled the hotel, and now Secret Service people swarming all over; they've gone berserk, he said, so soon after the assassination attempt and all.

Proceeding to the exterior elevator, the businessman surveyed the massive open atrium with indoor lake, layers of shops and restaurants cascaded skyward, all of it bustling with activity. After stowing his golf bag in his Green Tower room, he spent hours carefully surveying the tower and its activity.

Third, the businessman left the hotel hailing another cab. He instructed its driver to take him to the nearest Oriental market. There, he purchased odorless food and bottled water adequate for a forty-one hour vigil.

Finally, back at his hotel, he slept until midnight.

Now awake, the assassin donned matte-black, selected his *ninjutsu* weapons, slung a nylon rope and triangular grapple around his chest, then proceeded up the circular tower's "doughnut core" stairwell.

At the thirty-first level, the assassin stopped, and for

twenty minutes he listened. Two men paced continually in and out of the suite and its interior doughnut hallway. Secret Service, he had to assume.

At the moment, one agent was in the parlor directly across the stairwell. The agent stood looking out the floor-to-ceiling's south view. The second agent was in the hall, *just feet away.*

"Jake, take a look at this," beckoned the man in the suite's parlor. The black clad figure heard the second man leave the hall. "Two 747s in a side-by-side landing pattern."

"Don't see that very often."

This was it. Their backs would be to the hallway, *to him,* for the briefest of moments. The figure opened the door, confirmed expectations, then silently slipped out. With a blur, he put himself on the opposite side of the doughnut hall, its doughnut hole stairwell now obscuring his presence from the two men now leaving the opposite parlor. He straddled a bedroom doorway, then using its frame to brace, shimmied up to the ceiling, pushed up on a large acoustical square and disappeared into a more familiar darkness.

It was two A.M. Thursday morning.

Coronado in San Diego is where SEAL Team Three, along with Teams One and Five, calls home. Specifically, Coronado Naval Amphibious Base was located directly across the Silver Strand Highway from the Phil H. Bucklew Center for Naval Special Warfare and the Basic Underwater Demolition/SEAL school.

Wiry, intelligent, and an outstanding student, Rick Bedlund got his "Bloodhound" nickname from his sense of smell. Through his three and a half years at Washington State University, Bedlund never thought twice about his nose; he took it for granted that smells came to everyone as they came to him. But during a Basic Underwater Demolition/SEAL (BUD/S) training exercise on San Clemente Island, off the coast of southern California, Bedlund's squad was tasked to locate a friendly pilot who had been "shot down." The "pilot" was Instructor "Chief" McCullough, and the squad was given an entire thousand-meter square in which to search for him. On an overcast moonless night Bedlund led the squad straight to the "pilot."

Sitting in his hiding position, Instructor McCullough asked him how he did it. "It was pretty easy," Bedlund replied, "I'd smelled that Crest on your breath before. I guess you were breathing hard or something, 'cause I smelled it way back there." The squad stood in awe—both at the olfactory feat, and at being that frank with an instructor, a sure ticket to extra "duty." McCullough only smiled and proclaimed, "Bloodhound!" After that, the only extra duty Bloodhound got was an occasional "sniffing" assignment: finding out which girls were hot, juicy, and ready!

Bloodhound knew Chief had pulled strings to get him to SEAL Team Three, then pulled a few more to get him into his platoon. Once there, Bloodhound had been the natural choice for sniper training. The sniper embodies many of the SEALs' most valued traits: stealth, endurance, marksmanship, and "fieldcraft," a sixth sense about knowing how to live and move in the bush. Bloodhound filled the role perfectly. He was patient and calculating: frustratingly cautious, then suddenly bold.

Today Bloodhound had just left Building 616 now climbing the steps of the Quarterdeck. This morning had been pretty routine, his boat crew carrying a three hundred-pound log on a fourteen mile beach run; they'd returned to their base only to be turned around by their instructor and led to repeat the revolution. Team Three was now in a high state of readiness, getting a little antsy for a "go" on TALON'S GRIP.

Now, after the workout, Blood just wanted to rest and let the television do the thinking for him. He sprawled his lanky frame across the facsimile of a couch and fixed on the tuned station, now the five minute noon news already a couple of minutes along:

"And now for California news. The Los Angeles Name Dropper has struck again." Bloodhound watched as medical technicians covered a white man, a clean shot in the head. "Again the bullet was a .308, its casing found; etched on it was

the word 'Asphalt' the gang moniker of the slain Crip leader,"
said the anchor. And now for San Diego…"

Blood couldn't get the scene out of his mind, recounting
other Name Dropper kills…308 caliber. There was something
else he couldn't get out of his mind. Finally, he moved his stiff
body out of the couch, then headed back to 616 to check the
log.

It was nine o'clock Thursday morning, thirty-six hours
since the attempt on Temple's life. Each of the three men now
sitting in the Oval Office had found it a pain in the ass getting
through the doubled security just to get to this meeting.
Temple, himself, was extremely at ease, it was the others that
seemed on edge.

Except for DOE's environmental fiasco in Colorado,
things were relatively quiet. In Colorado, the press smelled
blood; a pack were out there now. But what heartened Temple
of late was no new leaks. That would give him more working
room for the action this meeting would soon demand. Before
him, he'd summoned the two CIA deputy directors, Barr and
Douglas; the third man was Israeli Ambassador Maklef,
brother of the current Prime Minister, Ibrahim Maklef. He
could have been Ibrahim's twin: short stature, snow white hair
flanking a continuous smooth scalp, thick lenses.

In a restricted Presidential staff meeting an hour earlier,
the decision had been made. Still, this meeting was more than
just formality. Temple wanted to remind the Israeli Prime
Minister that America still wishes to work with Israel in
cooperation, though in the past, reciprocation seemed sometimes less than obvious.

After a cordial greeting, Temple got the meeting moving
in quick step, the ambassador having been advised as to the
questions he would be asked to answer. "Mr. Ambassador,
you've seen last night's CNN interview." CNN aired a live
interview with Abu Hakim. During the interview, the Iranian
President declared his intention to solve the region's Jewish
problem once and for all. When asked of a timetable, Hakim

responded with, "Weeks. Precious weeks."

"We wish to execute TALON'S GRIP," Temple continued. "My advisors tell me it will take thirty hours to coordinate and stage assets designed for a joint strike on the lab at Tajrish. Does your government still wish to participate in a joint operation?"

Maklef thought of his brother in Jerusalem, and the rage spewing over the secure telephone line this morning. MOSSAD had let the CIA pull off the intelligence feat, right in its own back yard; Director Yitzhak Cohen would pay dearly, the ambassador knew. Be that as it may, now what choice did he have? It was the Americans with the intelligence, and now the initiative.

"Obviously," Maklef answered, "the state of Israel wants this *toxic agent* destroyed and removed from the maniac's hands as soon as possible. We also feel that our expertise in the region would prove most beneficial to U.S. special forces. I am authorized to commit the SAYERET MAT'KAL unit your SEAL forces have trained with. Colonel Eitan, it's commander, has been advised and awaits instructions from your special operations command."

The old fart knows, Temple just figured out. His political gut said Maklef already knew about STAIRCASE. *Shit.* Well, so be it; they have the most to lose if this thing fails. "Thank you, Mr. Ambassador. We accept your offer." Temple looked at his DDI, "Marshall?"

"Within the hour, the U.N. Secretary-General will be notified that the U.S. will participate in a massive food relief program centered in the CIS nation of Turkmenistan. We'll be staging as planned, from Incirlic air base; Turkey has already consented. I expect no problems having the planes there by the evening of Saturday, October sixth, local."

Temple looked over at his DDO, "Jordan?"

"Colonel Eitan should have his unit ready to move within twelve hours, the DDO advised, "I'll have my staff send our latest intelligence on the lab and coastal defenses. Please ask MOSSAD to reciprocate."

"Very well, gentleman," Maklef closed seeing the President rise. He shook hands around, ended with what Temple always thought as the traditional Israeli non sequitur, "*Shalom*," then left.

Temple remained standing, then spoke to both CIA deputies, "I have a bit a bad news. The environmental mess in Colorado. Politically I can't duck the Green Globe Award ceremony." Temple's schedule called for presenting the G2 Award Saturday evening. That meant he'd be aboard Air Force One when TALON'S GRIP executed early morning Sunday, Tehran time. He'd wanted the Vice President to handle it, but his Chief of Staff thought better of it; besides Reed was giving an address in Chicago that night. No, Temple needed political credits on the environmental front, his Chief of Staff had advised, presenting the G2 Award did just that. In the end, Temple agreed.

"Marshall, set it up remote so I keep informed of status and development, by the minute if it becomes necessary."

"Yes, Sir."

CHAPTER 30
PITFALLS

"Fifteen minutes, huh," Carerra Thielken was impressed. "What's your agenda?" They were at home in their living room, ten o'clock on a Thursday night.

Glenn finally put down his magazine, seeing the questions weren't going to stop. "Three items: accelerate DOE's MRS approval at Yucca Mountain. The Senate's Abbott Bill, it'll cripple American business. And relax tensions with the Japs, that'll stimulate American—read Shiraki Industries—business."

"Wish I could be there." Four months ago Carerra had accepted an invitation to keynote at United Way's Annual Convention, her work *and contributions* having opened that prestigious door. "Your star is rising, my dear. Vice President Thielken has a nice ring to it, don't you think?"

"Road's rife with pitfalls." Carrera's attention peaked.

"Shelby's disappeared. Could be in FBI hands as we speak—as *he* speaks."

"Just keep making the right moves," Carerra returned, her finger smoothing a crease in the couch's soft Italian leather. "We'll handle the pitfalls as they arise."

Friday, the next morning: "I'm Glenn Thielken, with Shiraki Industries. I believe you've already met my administrative assistant, Jack Crimm." Thielken's AA had just shown Thielken the Westin Bonaventure's California Ballroom. He briefed Thielken on the agenda and the Green Globe Award ceremony itself. Now they were at the Green Tower's thirty-first floor speaking to a Secret Service agent stationed at the elevator.

At Thielken, the agent took in impeccable fashion, right out of *Gentleman's Quarterly*, he thought. "Yes, we've been expecting you." The agent knew Jack Crimm because as Thielken's AA, he'd been tasked to ensure all of President Temple's accommodations were top drawer. Thielken, as the Green Globe Award recipient, saw himself as the President's self-appointed host in his fair city, and took the job seriously.

Followed by another Secret Service agent, the two men toured the eight rooms, concentrating on hospitality arrangements. First, the parlor room reception, then the dining room, service for twelve. There would be a light dinner with friends—with deep pockets—before the ceremonies began.

"After dinner," the AA explained to Thielken, "the rest of the guests will leave fifteen minutes early. Temple has asked that you stay over." The AA watched his boss smile at that. "A little chat, then back down the elevator to the ballroom."

"Excellent, Jack. No hitches. Excellent."

Above the ceiling, as elevator cabling labored to take the two informative guests to the garage level, the black matte figure moved to better position himself.

Teal Coro gave thanks to the dulling amber sun descending over the distant Pacific haze. He sat in the grassy brown

San Rafael Hills overlooking the Los Angeles basin, the downtown Westin Bonaventure towers but six miles to the south.

Ryan Voight had given him the trip's itinerary: From Washington, President Temple would fly into Point Mugu Naval Air Station aboard Air Force One. From there he would board a presidential helicopter and proceed the sixty miles north to a landing site just south of the Los Angeles downtown district. From there, it was a ten minute motorcade to the Bonaventure. The question was when and where during the one-day trip would the White Shadow strike.

Though the Secret Service and the local police would be out in force, Coro knew the display would be of no consequence. This assassin was very much like himself, like his people. From the early seventeenth century, the white man also came in force, trying to conquer the Apache. Though never numerous, the Apache avoided pitched battles if possible, preferring stealth, but when cornered fought to the death. As guerrilla fighters they were without peers; unlike the Plains tribes, they could not be starved into submission by extermination of the bison or any other animal. Such was the temper of Teal Coro's ancestors.

He was raised Coyote Shadow, trained to become an Apache scout, and to a lessor extent in the ways of the shaman. As a boy he had earned the respect of tribal elders. For his skills in tracking and approaching wild game seemed almost magic, slipping up close enough to almost touch the unaware animal. It was this scout training he would depend upon as he closed in on his enemy. But that would not be enough come the time for battle, for Coyote Shadow's senses warned of his foe's supernatural abilities. For this he would need his primal mind.

Through his shaman training Coyote Shadow learned of the primal self, the ability to release the animal, the more instinctual self within. It was through the animal that man's present was connected to his distant ancestors, to a time when there was no separation between man and animal. It was the ancient part of his being. Beyond the action of a body controlled by mind, Coyote Shadow learned of a superior action controlled by the primal mind. There were times critical, when his body had to be at peak strength, when the normal interaction between body and mind was too slow. These were the times for the animal within. Once he'd learned to control this direct link between the two, his reaction time decreased, his strength, agility, and endurance transcended normal capability. It was power long forgotten by modern man but implicit in nature, nonetheless.

Then there was the personal level. The violent death of his wife and child at the hands of this Japanese man called White Shadow. To the *yakuza*, it was simply a warning to the FBI to never again interfere in matters Japanese. To Coyote Shadow though, a blow so devastating, that for a time it severed communication with his spiritual world, with the Creator. That break was long behind him now. This evening he felt his heart pure as he readied himself to kill his dark enemy.

As Coyote Shadow sat thinking, an owl landed a few feet away. It's hoot called to him demanding attention. The owl looked directly at him, yellow light glistening from its large black eyes. A chill ran up Coyote Shadow's spine. He saw that the yellow glint could not come from the sun setting in the west. Taking the reflective angle, he turned looking down at the city. And there it was. The sun's rays caught by one of the five glass towers reflected northward upon the owl and himself. The Westin Bonaventure.

To an Apache, the owl was an omen from the Creator, a powerful answer, and maybe a warning. The answer: White Shadow would be found in the Bonaventure towers. The warning: An owl behaving strangely, like this one perched so close, often bespoke of death. Coyote Shadow's thoughts at the time of the owl's arrival had been a blur filled with his enemy and of his own preparation. It disturbed him, for without a lucid image, it left unclear which of the two men would soon join one with death.

John Westin came out of the Sunnyvale funeral home where he'd just paid his respects. He knew more people there than he'd expected. Not only Joan, now a widow, and the kids, but colleagues from Paxton International came out in force.

Craig MacIsaac's casket lay unopened. The little bit he did catch indicated it was a brutal murder. A bizarre murder, the initials "AK" cut into the pupil of his left eye, while he was still alive, the coroner had determined. *Who'd ever want to kill Craig MacIsaac, especially in such a gruesome way?*

As he approached the rental car, he still felt his lungs down deep caught in a relentless grip pushing up into his throat. He couldn't help wondering if somehow it was his fault. Craig not being able to reach him. Beth. *Who's behind this shit?*

"You be John Westin?" It was an Hispanic, cold hooded eyes, shaved head, and tattoos under his left eye. He had a black friend blocking any attempt at escape. Then they came out, each had nine millimeter semiautomatics. "Hands high. Car's over here."

Bolt holes? John saw none, not with two nervous barrels trained point blank. At the tan Ford sedan, door open, the black man moved behind John, directing him in. The kid raised his pistol above John's lowered head, then came down—

"FBI! I wanna see hands. Now!" came a rather serious voice from the right. The two punks spun to see two Smith and Wesson ten millimeter revolvers pointed at their faces. The sound of metallic action as hammers pulled back announced even more credence. Four hands slowly reached for the black sky.

The two agents separated the two gunmen, got their weapons on the ground, lectured them each, took their car keys, then let them go. As the two punks turned the corner at full gait, Westin asked, "Why d'ya let 'em go?"

"Not my chob, man," said one, in obvious reference to his assailants.

"Watching you is," said the other. "That is, until you're on that plane. Roll out in one hour."

Being assigned as Westin's "guardian angle" was a necessity, Shuji Okada understood. But more importantly, it was his ability to make contacts like this one today, he knew, was why his boss, DDI Marshall Douglas, considered him the CIA's most important asset in Japan. Indeed, over the ten years stationed in Japan as a blind agent, he'd established quite a network.

Opposite the low lacquer black table, the other man in the room sat legs crossed on the floor. This was his highest contact within Takara's Misawa Group's organization. They were in a small *ryokan*—a traditional Japanese Inn—outside of Nagoya.

"If there were such a LIST, how do you know about it?" the lithe, fortyish, man asked. He had a smallish head and crafty eyes. In his presence, and especially after a deal was done, Okada always felt a little outsmarted.

"I have been hired to acquire it. I know nothing more than that. My client is prepared to pay handsomely."

The man opposite Okada now worried about the LIST's safety. There was only the original, and it was in the New Misawa Building, tucked away in Takara's office safe. He would have it moved to a safer place immediately.

"Tell your client I'm afraid such a LIST does not exist."

"Moondoggie, how's the arm?" Bloodhound hailed feigning a slap across the healing gunshot wound. He'd asked Moondog to join the SEAL's traditional Thursday night hijinks at McP's. The place was packed, Bloodhound and Moondog stood near the side fireplace.

Moondog ducked playfully, like a boxer, then greeted, "*¿Qúe pasó*, dude?"

"Haven't seen much of you lately," Bloodhound probed.

"Yeah, Man. Nursin' the arm, you know. Takin' time to see the folks, a few friends too."

After a couple of beers, one of the small round tables came available. The two SEAL snipers sat. Bloodhound began, "Ain't that Name Droppin' thing somethin'? Think we outta recruit him?" Moondog's eyes twitched. *Got 'em!* Holy shit.

"Yeah, man. Dude's doing society a service," Moondog came back easily, then pulled on the beer.

Bloodhound leaned in and lowered his voice, "So, Chucho Muñoz, you pick up another handle between here and SCARAB?"

Moondog looked back puzzlement turning to recognition. Bloodhound continued, "*Señor* Name Dropper. Pleased to have made your acquaintance." Moondog dropped his eyes, staring silently at his beer napkin, green four-leafed clovers around a Saint Patty's theme. He wondered if his luck just ran out. Then he pointed to his favorite inscribed fireplace tile and asked Bloodhound to read it.

May the saddest day of your future be no worse than the happiest days of your past.

"Reversin' that logic, Bloody, I got some pretty happy days comin'."

"Talk to me, Chucho."

Moondog emptied his glass. Two more arrived. "Bloody, you probably don't remember. Hell, it was just a two-inch column on page twelve. You met my brother once, the New Year's party at my place?" Bloodhound nodded. "Well, last May he was drivin' his cab somewhere in L.A. At a light, this gang shit steps up and blows him away. Got his fare, too." For nothin'. Chucho lowered his head. "For fuckin' nothin', man." More beer.

"Shit, Moonie." Moondog shook his head, enough. Finally Bloodhound summed, "So you're now a one man vigilante."

"Somethin' like that, I guess."

"They gonna get your ass, you know. How many you get, six, seven?" Moondog held up nine fingers. "Shit, Man, an eye for an eye and an eye and a…Time to quit, Man. You get caught and it reflects on the Teams. You get that! Besides, you're the best shooter—well, night shooter,—" Bloodhound grinned, "SEAL's got. What we gonna do with you in prison? Christ, Chucho, just let it go."

Moondog stayed quiet for a minute or so, then said, "Team look bad?"

"Goddamn right, asshole."

Moondog lowered his head, pondering that one for a minute more, then said, "Okay. Enough killin'." Raising his head, Moondog fixed his eyes in an awkward exchange, then acknowledged the man who bothered to care, "Thanks, Bloody." Bloodhound grinned, then extended his hand, clasping tight—

Beep, beep, beep. His and other beepers were tripping off like crickets into the now silenced room. "We need you out there, Moonie. Gotta get that arm fixed," Bloodhound said, then bolted out the door behind the others.

CHAPTER 31

RUBBER DUCKS

Incirlik air base, outside Adena, Turkey
12:00 Noon Saturday (Local)

"Why does every goddamned thing depend on a guide?" Bloodhound muttered. The "guide" was an Israeli agent working inside Iran, a man who knew the territory, its people, and had the ability to acquire things. Things like information, things like the army truck they would use tonight.

"Israelis, too," chimed Don Millikan, nicknamed Milkman. Milkman, a medium-built man with jet black hair, possessed a heavy beard against pale skin which always looked as if in need of a blade. "They got a bunker mentality," he continued. "Things go to hell and they're gone. Just like our Navy and their precious boats." It was the typical pre-mission jitters. SEALs had supreme confidence in themselves, but none whatsoever in anyone else. They respected SAYERET MAT'KAL's capabilities, but still inbred, they didn't trust them.

The third man in this conversation was Mitch Miller, a six-foot five-inch troglodyte who could lift and carry anything, and would walk through a wall if pointed in the right direction. This was his second platoon, and though he spoke little and seemed to think even less, his sheer value as a pack mule was indispensable. Tonight Miller would carry an M-60 machine gun with fifteen-hundred rounds of linked ammunition. His water, E and E kit, and other equipment all combined to give him a total load of over one hundred and forty pounds. Miller's passage through BUD/S was a study in determination. BUD/S consisted of large quantities of running, swimming, push-ups, pull-ups, sit-ups, and the dreaded obstacle course. His massive body worked to defeat him and he persevered only with immense difficulty. No matter how hard the instructors tried to wash him out, they were met with a grimaced red-face of determination. When they tied his wrists and ankles and shoved him in the pool with his classmates during the "drownproofing" exercise, Miller simply stretched the nylon lines, freeing himself. All the BUD/S instructor could say was, "Now why didn't I think of that?" It was in the shower, where Miller got his nickname, "Tripod."

"It's a simple mission, in and out," Tripod offered.

"Simple! It's fuckin' lame, that's what it is," snapped Milkman, disgusted. Milkman, like the others, knew of the stuffed cat in Creed's rucksack, but not its purpose; if Milkman had, he'd gone ballistic.

"Milk's right," broke in Lieutenant Don Creed. "But they've got a hell of a ticket, chauffeur to Tajrish. Beats anything else I can think of. Remember fellas, it was their mission before it was ours. So we do our job, watch our assess, and make the best of it."

"And besides," Chief added confidently, "For us, if there's anything that's 'bread and butter' it's a rubber duck. Tonight we show the Jew boys what men can do."

Another six men sat huddled at the opposite end of the huge metal hut. Creed suspected those soldiers were having exactly the same kind of conversation.

Colonel Zvi Eitan had a five man squad, plus Rosen, a man

from MOSSAD. This intelligence officer, Eitan could have done without, on two counts: First, he had no previous field experience with the man. But more importantly, even though the operational decisions were his, the mission decisions were MOSSAD's. This arrangement had worked in the past, but still, he didn't like it.

It was Saturday, noon, local. The two platoons were in "isolation," a sort of quarantine, in a large hut at Incirlik air base outside Adena, Turkey. For the past seven hours they'd planned and fine tuned the mission sequencing. Now a long six hours remained before they'd move out.

The platoon built the "duck" inside the hut. They couldn't take the risk of someone wondering what they were doing with rubber boats at a Turkish air base. They brought the covered materials in through the large sliding door: pallet, boats, engines and fuel, the huge cargo parachute, netting, and a full complement of combat gear.

Getting American C-141s over the Caspian Sea obviously required a ruse. The ruse dropped into their lap a month ago. Just like Somalia, the United Nations pressured the United States government to provide food relief to the famine developing in the drought-stricken region around Turkmenistan, on the eastern side of the Caspian Sea. The U.S. held out, not particularly anxious to repeat the Somalian quagmire, at least until an additional and pressing reason arose. That afternoon the C-141s began arriving. Ten of them, from the air base at Rhein-Main outside Frankfort.

The plan involved two of the American relief planes on their first relief sortie. They were to inadvertently stray from the route and descend over the Caspian Sea. Creed and his men would perform a "rubber duck," parachuting two Zodiacs and the men into the water from fifteen hundred feet. From the second plane, the Israelis would follow in kind, meeting up with the SEALs at an isolated point on the Caspian's southern shore. Then meeting the Israeli guide, they'd simply drive to Tajrish. The Israelis, some of whom spoke fluent Farsi, provided knowledge of local customs, culture, and geography.

Creed believed in preparation, but also held lady luck in high esteem. More than once in his career, she'd smiled on his ragged ass. This mission didn't feel right, and at that moment he felt he would need her more that ever before. *You always feel this way*, he tried to tell himself. He didn't like working a joint op either, but had to admit he'd already learned a lot from this very impressive SAYERET MAK'KAL. And no wonder, he knew, Israelis—in one name or another—have been at war with their adversaries for thousands of years.

Then he thought of the hostages, nine total now. Some of them missing for over three months. No telling what kind of shape they'd find them in. If it were him locked up in that compound, he knew, he couldn't ask for anything more: TEAM Three coming over the hill: Chief, Bloodhound, Phil, Johnny, Swede, Tripod, and the Milkman. Couldn't ask for anything more, *or could he?*

An October wind finally blew in over the Caspian Sea, its shores just sixty miles to the north of Tajrish. The wind's compression as it ascended toward the high Iranian desert made for a welcome cooler day at the compound. It was Saturday afternoon as Beth, Sanborne, Jamil Velayati, and Dr. Dech were escorted across the compound grounds back to the Ward Number Two barracks. It donned on Beth that it was exactly a week ago, and exactly this same time, three o'clock, when before they had vacated the lab just so some VIP could have a private visit.

Minutes ago, back in the lab, Jamil wanted to tell her something. Something he'd just heard Shafii say, something about the coming visitor, something important.

Just then, another plane from the south came in low just east of the compound. It had been that way ever since the northern front came through last night...except this one with the high tail configuration wasn't military. She studied the tail insignia: Misawa. *I wonder if.* Then in the western sun she saw that she could read its tail number. She did.

Back in the barracks, same routine, windows covered, no

one allowed access to an outside view. Beth and Jamil settled in on their adjacent cots. Dr. Dech was in the head.

"Jamil, what is it?"

Jamil scanned the room weary of uninvited ears. "I know who is coming. And it's not good." Beth leaned in closer. "A representative of Misawa Group. A deal's been made. He's here to pick up the boxes, a complete set of STAIRCASE materials and samples. All work we've done to date."

Beth ran her fingers through her hair, worried. "So that's why we organized, copied, and collated all that crap."

"Doesn't look good for us, Beth. The representative seems well connected. He's having dinner with Hakim, himself, then flying out tonight."

"Think they just hired out the work?"

"If they did…" Jamil's words trailed off, shaking his head slowly, contemplating his tenuous mortality.

The plane's huge cargo ramp opened up into the early night sky. The interior lights were blacked out, making the faint glow of the western horizon was almost visible. All else was black.

Earlier, with the first eight C-141s just airborne, the two last planes took off heading east toward the Caspian Sea. The SEALs readied in number nine, the Israelis in number ten.

During the flight, they donned parachutes and "tigered" their faces with camouflage paint. Chief double-checked the ducks and everyone's parachutes. Creed went over the plan looking for flaws. Bloodhound coached Tripod and Johnny on Iranian uniforms, showing them the photographs they'd all seen before. Phil sharpened his knife on a small whetstone, pausing occasionally to test it by shaving his arm. Milk and Swede dozed.

Phil Richards was a salty First Class Petty Officer who'd washed out of helicopter training, then put in for BUD/S. That was twelve years ago. Phil had the look of a quintessential frogman: stocky and muscular, with a deeply tanned hide and sun-streaked brown hair. He'd done deployments with seven other platoons. Even though he was a top SEAL operator with a cool analytical mind, everyone knew Phil would never advance to Chief Petty Officer. Johnny, Alex Johnson, the squad's primary communications specialist, brought an AN/PRC-104 HF radio with KY-65 secure voice encryption gear. With nondescript brown hair, eyes, and washed out features, Johnny was the youngest of the squad. Swede, Olie Johnsen, typified a big Swedish boxer, somewhere in the light heavy-weight class. Swede's specially was demolitions.

At drop minus one minute, the crew chief unlocked the duck's pallet. At thirty seconds, two crew members came aft, snapped their safety tethers into the bulkhead, and placed their hands on the duck, ready to push. They rolled it slightly aft. In the howling roar of engines and wind, the crew chief yelled "GO!" In seconds the duck was gone, followed immediately by eight men, practically on top of one another.

For Bloodhound, it was instantly quiet. The plane's roar faded out and the only noise heard was that of the wind rushing passed his ears. The smell of salt quickly overtook aviation fuel exhaust. He looked up to check his canopy, but it was too dark to see; neither could he tell how fast he was falling. He'd never had a malfunction, but as always, he felt tension tightening in his stomach.

Despite their small size, they were heavily armed, each man carrying close to a hundred pounds of equipment. Tripod and Milk had the main firepower with the M-60's, Creed and Swede both had M-203 40mm grenade launchers attached to their M-16 carbines. For the quiet assault, the rest carried MP5 SD2 silenced submachine guns, with Phil also carrying a stockless, sawed-off shotgun in his backpack. They all had grenades, and Chief carried two Claymore anti-personnel mines both with 30-second fuses and electrical firing systems. Swede, with a penchant for blowing things up, was sure to be carrying at least a pound and a half of C-4, probably several yards of detcord, and a few extra grenades of his own. Creed never asked Swede where he obtained his extra ordnance, and Swede never volunteered.

Bloodhound heard someone ahead and below him belch,

then laughter. Still another hooted like an owl. All doubts disappeared, he was in formation. He quickly undid his belly strap and unhooked his reserve parachute, swinging it out of the way. He unbuckled his chest strap and put his hands on the quick-releases attached to his leg straps. They were all that held him into his canopy now.

The duck landed with a loud splash. It was the only thing lighted, rigged with red chemlights on both sides. Then Bloodhound heard splashes all around. He stiffened for the water's shock. When he hit, he released his leg straps and slipped down and out of his parachute harness. He surfaced and pulled hard on one of the risers to deflate the canopy. He swam carefully around the canopy, avoiding the mess of lines, then ensured it was sinking. He could hear splashing to his left. He spotted the dim red chemlights, now his directional beacon.

One by one, the squad members arrived at the ducks. Phil pulled himself up on top, and cut away the cargo parachute harness, then the netting. He shoved the top boat off into the water, then began removing the corrugated "honeycomb" cardboard that padded the motor of the lower boat. Swede went to work on the other boat.

In fifteen minutes, Creed had a "fix" from his GPS receiver. Everyone checked and loaded their weapons. The coxswains indicated ready. After one more sweep of the horizon with his binoculars, Creed finally ordered the coxswains to proceed. With a few cranks, both Mars motors purged sea water and roared to life. The two boats headed south toward the shores of the Republic of Iran, a state that didn't play by the rules. At this point, the last thing on Creed's mind was rules.

They'd been dropped thirty miles north of Iran's Caspian coast. Allowing for a stiff, cool breeze blowing out of the north, Creed figured the pilots missed the planned drop point by seven hundred yards—very satisfactory. The GPS told Creed they were making fifteen knots, which would get them to the beach in two hours, by 2100. Provided everything went right, that left them approximately one hour to reach Tajrish. Good timeline, so far.

Three miles off the beach, Creed brought the boats to a stop for a navigation check. He pulled out his chart, identified landmarks ashore, did a GPS check, then called for fifteen knots.

Ten minutes later his coxswains killed the engines. With his night-vision scope, Creed scanned the dark beach eight hundred and fifty yards away. Behind the coastal towns of Now Shahr to their left and Shahsavar to their right, the squad could see the Elburz mountain range silhouetted against the blue-black sky. The sea lapped quietly on the shore, and the only noise was that of an occasional truck on the coastal road running east-west just behind the beach.

The swimmer scouts, Chief and Phil, pulled on their fins, stared hard at the coastline, then slipped into the black water heading for the target beach. Their jobs: reconnoiter the beach and if clear, signal Creed to commit the boats to a landing.

Thirty minutes later, Chief, crouched on the deserted beach, pulled his strobe from a pocket, checked the infrared cover, then pointed it to sea and lit it off. He heard the capacitor charge and fire three times, then covered the lens with his hand. He waited several seconds, then repeated the signal.

Creed saw it the first time through his night-vision scope, then opened his other eye to ensure it wasn't a visible red light. There were three men in each boat now, only Tripod in one boat and Milk in the other kept their weapons trained on the beach. Creed scanned the sea behind him and to each flank, then signaled the others to paddle slowly ashore.

As soon as bottoms scrapped sand, Tripod and Milkman jumped from the bows of their boats. Tripod took the left flank, Milk the right. The two moved silently ashore just twenty-five yards before dropping to the sand and aiming their weapons at unseen enemies. Bloodhound was awash in the odors of a new country: cooking fires, garbage dumps, car exhaust, rotting fish remains, and his own sweat.

Phil and Chief went to the boats and helped bring them ashore. Awkward and weighing over four hundred pounds, the squad carried each to deep sand, ensuring not to let them drag, lest telltale marks in the sand announce their clandestine arrival.

Four men dug while four stood watch, and when the shallow grave was deep enough, Chief and Johnny slid in the boats, then unscrewed the plugs releasing pressured air. Phil took the motors off the transoms, wrapped them, then set them in the hole enveloped by the collapsed boats. Within minutes the squad was firmly ashore. With no quick exit.

Within a small clump of bushes, Bloodhound had a sniper watch observing access to the beach below. He watched SAYERET MAT'KAL bring in their zodiac, check with Creed, then transform themselves suited from a wet environment to a dry one. To the SEAL, the Israelis seemed very noisy. The more equipment they stowed or broke out, the noisier they got. "What a cluster fuck," he mumbled.

"I beg your pardon." Bloodhound snapped around, his rifle's barrel too long...the intruder too close! Iranian! Bloodhound then went for his knife. "Hold it," whispered the Iranian lieutenant, swinging the fat silencer of an Uzi submachine gun more into Bloodhound's view. "I have already taken one life tonight. Do not make me take another. I'm with SAYERET MAT'KAL," said the soldier grinning, his hot breath right in Bloodhound's face. "Your guide, I think you SEALs call it."

All of the now six Israelis wore Iranian military uniforms. The "Iranian lieutenant" guide had acquired an Iranian Army truck. A "corporal" and a "private" rode in the truck's cab, while the rest of the teams rode in back. Creed and his squad sat nearest the truck's cab on wooden benches that ran along both sides of the bed. Bloodhound was crestfallen that he had been watched the entire time on the beach. The "Iranian lieutenant" on the opposite bench, grinned at him again. Bloodhound swore to himself that would never ever happen again. The "Israeli soldiers" at the rear kept a vigilant, though casual-looking, watch rearward as the driver pulled out onto the road and swung a wide U-turn heading east toward Now Shahr, where they would turn south toward Tehran.

Forty minutes later: "Tajrish," the "lieutenant" announced, pointing through the dusty windshield. From the vantage, they could see the airfield, and a small fenced in compound adjacent on its far south side. The driver swung off the highway onto an intersecting dirt road that took them between old, low buildings. The truck rocked and bounced violently as they worked their way to the town's eastern edge. Then the truck suddenly stopped.

"This is the ancient village of Tajrish," said the Israeli "guide" to the Americans, sounding more like a tour guide than a military man. "Tehran is but thirty kilometers to the south. You will be careful, or bring the Army down on our heads." A major Iranian Army base, the SEALs knew, as well as the greater part of Iran's Air Force and air defenses, lay on the outskirts of Tehran. "We'll park within those trees. Upon your signal, my men will secure the two towers on the far east side. Your men have the west-side towers. You sure you can override the electronic security measures?"

"Just wait for the signal," Creed said, testing his throat mike again. What doubts Creed had about this flea-bitten scheme, he had over the last hours successfully suppressed. Again, they began to surface. If Fritz didn't do his tricks, then plan B was to go in as quietly as they could until all hell broke loose. Then it was frogman balls, and Jewish bagels, or something.

Creed managed a slight smile at that. The compound spread out before them. The tall fences, topped with razor wire, stood in dark silhouette against the brightly lit buildings. There was a guard tower at each of the four corners, and the small hut that stood outside the only gate was well sandbagged, a machine gun on its roof. Just inside the gate, was the helipad, a Hind-D sat quiet and ominous. Creed wondered what that meant, it wasn't on this morning's recon photos.

Behind the huge helicopter was the lab, somewhat isolated from the other three buildings. The long building to the rear, he knew was the barracks: Iranian soldiers on the left, American hostages on the right. The building in front of the hostage's barracks was an old brig, his intelligence briefing informed. But it was the larger building this side of both the brig and barracks, that interested him now; that housed the compound's electronic security control.

Creed moved to position his men: Bloodhound had the northwest tower, Chief the southwest tower. Tripod, between the two snipers, trained his big M-60 on the sandbagged hut outside the only entry gate. The others melded into shadowed crevices around the west and south sides. It was 2240. It was time.

Private Massoud Biryan manned Northwest Tower # 1. He had an acceptable vantage of the west side approach to the perimeter; just acceptable because of the several erosions cut away by last spring's sometimes torrential rains. On the perimeter's north side began the backside of the Iranian military's air base, with a small civilian airport adjacent to its eastern side. His view within the compound, the best of the four towers, included the entry gate and helicopter straight below, and each of the four interior buildings.

At the moment Private Biryan thought about the rumor and what the daytime guard had said. It seemed that today's visitors were a couple of Japs. Loaded their Gulfstream 4 with half the lab, then left for dinner with President Abu Hakim, himself. And the rumor: Their ultra-secret project was being terminated. In the cool night air, Biryan wondered where he'd be stationed next.

Creed had moved to a shadowed position to the left of Tripod. Alone, he pulled Fritz out of his rucksack, depress her activation button, and watched as the five-hour battery kicked her to life. The cat looked around taking in her environment, then indulged in a long satisfying stretch. *Here it goes*, prayed Creed hoping Fritz wouldn't need all her lives tonight. "Fritz," Creed whispered. The cat meowed, displaying casual attentiveness. "Fritz. Zee-tirf." The cat meowed again. "Cattitude," Creed said, specifying the codeword for a pre-instructed sequence of commands. After one more meow, he concluded with a "go," by now feeling pretty stupid.

No! Creed couldn't believe it. Fritz scampered back away from the compound. He managed to keep his eye on the stupid shit, tracking it to, then up the nearest tree. *Goddamn stupid cat. Fuck, whose idea was this, anyway? Westin's the one got the CIA interested in this shit for brains idea. I'll kill the fuckin' sonofabitch with my bare hands! And if anybody finds out about this, I'll kill the fuckin' astronaut again! What a shitass idea.*

After a minute elapsed, Creed began to realize Fritz had chosen a branch from which to observe the compound. *Recon?* he wondered. Could the little four-legged shit be reconnoitering the compound, verifying what it'd been told: the layout; security measures; and personnel, stationed or otherwise? After a couple of minutes, Creed watched the beast come down, then saunter, unnoticed, up to and through a small vertical gap at the compound's closed gate. 2250 local.

The late dinner was over. Hakim led his two guest into a smaller adjoining room, a comfortable place in which to seal the days work. The small parlor room was bathed in pastels: dusty rose-colored walls, ivory ceiling, and a complimenting burgundy-red Persian carpet. Hakim motioned Shimizu to a Duncan Phyfe settee, he and General Rashid each took chairs. Silver service arrived placed before them upon the solid block of pinkish marble, its side carved in fourteenth century arabesque patterns.

Shimizu didn't much like Iran and couldn't wait to leave for Japan. He objected to the ever-present pungent smell in the buildings, the food, the people. Also, it struck him that Iran was more of a police state than a religious state. He counted four muslim-robed guards at the moment.

For Hakim and Rashid the servant filled demitasse with thick black Turkish coffee. General Rashid watched as the Japanese fox took tea. Yet it wasn't Shimizu that Rashid thought about at the moment; nor was it the deal these two men just consummated. It was the American that troubled his mind. Tonight, even more so. *Why?*

Shimizu sipped at the bitter orange liquid, trying not to wince. He knew his host would have dropped several cubes of sugar to counterbalance the acrid assault, but his pallet found that even more disgusting. Fortunately, the small bland biscuit supplied saved the diplomatic moment. Shimizu spoke in English, "It is a fair arrangement, President Hakim." It wasn't, Shimizu judged, but Takara had said at any cost. In addition to the exorbitant sum, Misawa would design a Jewish-trait-targeted STAIRCASE to be delivered before the year's end.

Hakim dismissed the entree with a wave of fingers. Shimizu continued, "Our two countries have always been friends, even during American hostilities. Very shortly Japan expects to take a permanent seat on the U.N.'s Security Council. Takara-san wishes you to understand that Japan, in this new capacity, will be able to help your government as never before."

Hakim set down the fragile-looking cup, fixing a hard stare on this man whose face resembled a fox. That was the effect Shimizu wanted. He wanted to keep Allah's will in check, to keep this filthy religious barbarian from getting too drunk in exercising power with Japan.

Shimizu continued, "Should the U.N. endeavor to dictate to the sovereign Republic of Iran, as it did to Iraq in 1991, Japan with its veto can prevent economic sanctions, or worse military action against Iran."

"Tell Takara-san his offer is accepted in the spirit given. Allah is indeed great." Shimizu bowed in respect. "I understand you leave for Japan tonight. Please stay as my guest if more convenient." Shimizu looked down sucking air through teeth, expressing difficulty. That struck General Rashid's senses. *What was it?*

"I am grateful for your kindness, President Hakim, but I must keep to my schedule."

"What is your flight plan?" Rashid asked knowing the answer, but seeking *something*.

"Over the Indian Ocean, refueling in Singapore, then on to Tokyo. Just under twelve hours, total," he said, again sucking air through teeth. "Very difficult, but still I must leave tonight."

That's it, the general's mind finally clicked. The tape supplied by the American. Its English narrator had a habit of sucking air before describing the more difficult aspects of NIQE chip manufacturing. *Japanese?*

"Shimizu-san, do you know of an American called John Westin?" Hakim's head snapped glowering at his general's indiscretion.

The Japanese seemed surprised by the obliqueness of the question, then answered, "Yes I do. How do you know this man?" Hakim stiffened bolt straight.

"He claims to possess an advanced computer technology, called NIQE."

"This is Japanese technology. The Americans understand it, but do not possess it. Anyone who tells you otherwise is lying."

The knowledge engineers "taught" Fritz about sensation: seeing, hearing, smelling, tactile, and how to sense infra-red heat and electromagnetic radiation.

Coming "alive," Fritz had surveyed her physical world applying the "sense of the common" she'd acquired from the knowledge engineers and the five months of her learning existence. The physical surroundings and its behavior all seemed in place, normal in this new-found environment. She did a recognition check on the human: face (even though blackened), physique, profiled movement, and voice. All matched a Don Creed, aka "Lieutenant Creed," aka "El Tee," aka "DC." Her NIQE-based mind related Creed with Dr. Slaughter and Sean McCullough, aka "Chief." All of whom, she'd been taught to take instructions.

Fritz now worked on the "Cattitude" codeword. Cattitude was a complex sequence of tasks with wide latitude as to how she accomplished them. Always, if at all possible, any obstacle preventing a task's execution would be removed or circumvented. Where impossible situations existed, she'd determine a strategy in which the highest percentage of priority tasks could be accomplished, then begin their execution.

From the tree she'd already compared the current situation with learned expectations from her holographic database. The knowledge engineers, with their reconnaissance photographs had it ninety-five percent correct. Difference: the presence of a helicopter on the pad, and two additional guards bunkered below eye level near the craft.

Now as she approached the gate, she made herself aware of her senses, actuators, database—all responding normally.

At the gate, Fritz calculated a three-inch gap between its closure and the post. Seeing the guard looking outward, she deftly slipped through unseen.

She passed by the conventional mine field corridor between the outer fence and the inner fence defining the compound's interior space. To the right was the building housing the compound's security control. Now to get there. She didn't have to worry about laser-beam trips—too high. But the knowledge engineers did say she'd have to traverse an electronically controlled mine field—sensitivity unknown. She assumed all fields activated. Iranian movement within the compound grounds was coordinated with the security control's selective area deactivation, lest deadly accidents occur.

Besides being new, the two men near the helicopter in the low bunker had a clear line of sight through the door window at Security Control. She decided to neutralize them first. She moved cautiously to the left toward them, amplifying sensor feedback from infrared and electromagnetic flux. The electromagnetics registered the buried network of control wires. Infra-red would sense temperature differentials.

There! A circular edge, cooler than the surrounding ground. Metal. She worked her way full circle to ascertain its size, then continued, stalking. She encountered only two more mines before reaching the hidden bunker. She ignored the sleeping soldier and approached the other man. She purred. Without a word, the soldier smiled, then coaxed her to him. Coyly, she approached his outstretched arms, allowing herself to be scooped up. With infrared sensors, she located a thick surface vein in his forearm, then with extended hypodermic claws injected deadly strychnos toxifera directly into the vein.

The soldier thought nothing of it, the slight hint of nails. Suddenly his eyelids, his face felt numb. His head felt heavy, listing. *Cannot swallow!* His mind panicked, but his body refused to react, his pulse dropping dramatically. His diaphragm, lungs. *No breath!* In seconds, death was sure. Preliminary results from an autopsy would put cause of death due to respiratory failure. Attending to the sleeping soldier, the second man would never again know consciousness.

Moving on toward the Security Control Building, she encountered five more mines before reaching the steps. Easy cat-work, she allowed. She sat on the top step squarely on her haunches, then with paw raised, scratched at the door.

Private Biryan in Tower One, looked down across the compound's interior, then down at the Hind-D and the two new men bunkered near it. Earlier, he'd noticed one was asleep, but as long as the other remained alert, he had no problem with it. But now both men seemed asleep. He hiked his right leg up, the ribbed bottom of his boot always good for a wedged-in pebble or three. *This will stir them awake*, Biryan figured, arcing the first pebble downward.

When the door to Security Control finally opened, Fritz saw black boots, then looked up seeing a uniformed man looking outward.

"Meow." The soldier looked down at a black and white short hair, tail wagging slowly.

"What have we here?" the corporal said in Farsi. Fritz hopped from the step into the dim room bathed in green phosphorescence. *Two men.* She approached a small side table, hesitated, then leaped upward as if suspending gravity. *Panel similarity to (Westin's) description: eighty percent.*

The corporal closed the door, walked over and picked her up, stroking the black fur of her back. "Do you like cats?" he asked the civilian technician in English.

"Dogs. German shepherds," came the man in German-accented English.

The corporal liked needling this arrogant sonofabitch. "You know, Hans, the reason why dogs make such good pets is because they're too dumb to be offended." Fritz liked the corporal. Too bad he had to die.

"Yes," the German contractor replied, "but cats have a certain cynicism for the world, and disdain for the humans in it." The Iranian corporal started to object, the German cut him off, "And that goes double for their owners." Even if it were true, Fritz did not like this man at all. "No animals allowed in here. Get rid of it."

Fritz extended his hypodermic claws inserting one into a vein in the corporal's wrist. As the Iranian flinched, Fritz jumped onto the back of the German's neck. Claws extended, she found her mark, the left side carotid artery. Within ten seconds, both the cat lover and hater were dead.

It had been twelve minutes since Creed last saw the stealth cat. A little long but no cause for alarm. Yet there was concern, the northeast tower guard. The guard seemed to be tossing something to the ground below. *At Fritz?* What would she be doing over there? Creed activated his throat mike, "Tow One, Eyes. You see what I see?" Bloodhound returned two clicks, affirmative. "Tow One, Eyes. Ready yourself. May pop your target early."

Two clicks. Bloodhound saw it too. He could handle it with the silenced MP5 SD2, its being accurate to a hundred meters. But still, the sniper wished for his trusty McMillan 7.62 M86 sniper rifle.

Fritz lost no time getting to work. Using her paws, she flipped to "off" the bank of toggle switches under the label "Laser." She did the same for each of the mine field areas, microphones, and others. The closed-circuit TV camera/monitor system she would shut off ten seconds after she gave the "completion" signal. At the far upper right was the "Gate Control" switch. She maneuvered herself over to flip its toggle switch—

Steps! The door. A soldier. The soldier yelled in Farsi, approaching the German. Seeing him dead, he went for the emergency alarm.

"Screech!" Fritz lunged, claws extended, landing on the man's right forearm. His reflexes were like lightning, spinning, scraping Fritz away with a powerful blow from his left hand. Fritz went flying, hitting her shoulder against the corner of a file cabinet. She fell to the floor an instant before her assailant's head thundered down, bouncing, pinning her left shoulder.

The last pebble hit a helmet. Nothing. Tower One guard Private Biryan pondered what to do. He didn't want to get them in trouble, but still… Finally, he picked up the telephone receiver, then punched the direct line to Security Control.

Fritz flinched at the ringing. Couldn't do anything about that. But she had to free herself. Using the file cabinet for leverage, she frantically pushed hard at the large head. Nothing. The more the telephone rang, she knew instinctively, the more additional task she would have to complete. Using her free paw again, she rocked the soldier's head. It pivoted, then more, then…free! The phone no longer rang.

Biryan took his binoculars and focused them on the building housing Security Control. Through its door window, he could see a figure…slumped over a chair! *What now?* Inform the commander. He reached for the button opening a direct line.

Creed didn't like what he saw. Not one bit. Seeing the Tower One guard hang up without speaking meant trouble. Real soon. "Tow One, Eyes. Clear to fire on your target." Two clicks. "All other units stand by." Two seconds later Creed's trained ear heard the metallic action of the silenced MP5. With his binoculars on Tower One, he watched the sentry's chest punctuate backward, then slump downward onto the tower floor. *Nice shootin', Blood. Fifty yards with a silenced MP5.* "All units, Eyes. Report anything unusual." In a pre-arranged sequence, all members reported quiet. Creed responded, "All units, Eyes. All hold positions."

Fritz had a servo malfunction in her left shoulder. She could move but not with the same freedom, not as efficiently, not as quietly. With difficulty, she made her way to the chair and back atop the control console. She reached with the right paw and flipped the switch to "open."

The signal. I'll be damned. Creed saw the startled guard stand as motors labored to slide the gate open. "All units, Eyes. Engage. Repeat. Engage." He checked his watch: 2310.

CHAPTER 32
THE PROVERBIAL FAN

Tehran, Iran—10:50 P.M. Saturday (Local)

Shortly after Shimizu's revelation, Hakim bid the Misawa representative a safe trip and provided vehicle transportation to his private jet. Hakim had not wanted his new benefactors to see difficulty, difficulty he now addressed.

"How did you suspect, Mohammed?" Hakim growled as he paced the soft-hued, antique-appointed room.

General Rashid ignored the question, preoccupied. Using a nearby telephone, the general summoned his aide. Ten seconds later he gave orders: call the Tajrish Biological Warfare compound's security commander, tell him to act as if an attack is imminent, redouble security, and report any unusual activity or occurrences directly to me.

"You told me the compound was impenetrable," Hakim continued irritably.

"I know, Abu. The compound is secure. But now, we know Westin is CIA. And the CIA has many resources. He secured an audience with you, did he not?" Hakim bristled, swearing this John Westin would die. "This time Allah has provided a sign," Rashid continued, "and I have taken it seriously."

Without unsilenced sniper rifles, each of the other three tower guards had two silenced weapons unleashed upon him. From outside the south perimeter fence, an Israeli covered the door guard posted where the hostages were thought to be kept. The SEAL's MP5s and SAYERET MAT'KAL's Uzis all found their marks, quiet and deadly sure. Simultaneously, Bloodhound silently took out the gate sentry, all the time wishing he had a real sniper rifle.

After receiving confirmations, Creed cleared Eitan to bring his men around to the front, then sent Bloodhound and Swede in to check for occupants in the nearby Soviet Hind-D, bristling with weapons. Eitan's men, quick and stealthy, assembled in less than two minutes. After receiving a clear signal from Bloodhound, Creed gave the signal.

Each team had its primary objective: SEALs the hostages, SAYERET MAT'KAL the destruction of the "toxic agent" lab. Passing the helicopter, both teams fanned out into a wedge formation. All eyes checked windows, doorways, and roof-tops for movement. Groups split per plan: SEALs set up defensive positions with the M-60s, the rest proceeding to the barracks in the converted hospital ward.

SAYERET MAT'KAL cleared the administrative build-ing empty, then set up a Farsi-speaking lieutenant in the small Security Control facility. That completed, the others and the MOSSAD man entered the lab.

The first order of business for the SEAL's was to clear the military barracks in the ward's north end. Then see after the hostages reported to occupy the adjacent south end.

At the barracks, Creed had a stacked formation set up at the door, then gave the signal. Phil kicked in the barracks' wooden door and rolled in a flash-bang. At detonation, Creed and Johnny swept in and "cleaned" the bunk-filled room with their muzzles. Every man-shaped object got two rounds in its

center of mass. Through muzzle smoke, Creed yelled "Clear!"
Phil stayed in making deadly rounds for insurance.

Simultaneously, Swede kicked in the hostages' door.
Bloodhound was in first, followed by Chief and Swede. One
Iranian soldier seated inside. Blood had a three shot burst
across his chest before the man's mind had time to assimilate
the threat. Four hostages lay on cots, eyes wide open. Chief
and Swede continued muzzle sweeping the room clear.

Bloodhound spoke the first words: "Gotta move boys and
girls." No movement. "Okay, I'm Petty Officer Richard
Bedlund. I'm with the United States Navy. I'm here to escort
you to safety. No time to waste."

Reluctantly, they got to their feet, hands in the air. "Put your
hands down. Get some field clothes on. Grab only what you need.
Don't wanna miss the bus." Bloodhound had no idea.

"Where the others?" Chief asked.

"Dead," was the only reply.

"You sure you know what you're doing?" Dr. Dech
protested.

"Don't listen to the bastard." It was Beth.

So that's Westin's woman, Chief thought, admiring more
than her grit. "Yes ma'am." Chief decided to keep an eye on
the man whose black hair and goatee gave an appearance of
the Beelzebub, himself.

In the lab, receiving Creed's clear signal, Colonel Eitan
called in their borrowed Iranian Army truck. His men then
went about setting incendiary charges while MOSSAD's
Rosen inspected boxes. Eitan thought it strange that most of
the shelves were stripped. Everything seemed boxed up, like
the operation was about to move, and soon.

Eitan approached the MOSSAD man, bent over a box,
rifling its contents. "Charges are just about ready. Clear the
area."

"Not until we get these boxes out, Colonel. Have your men
take these three first. I need two more minutes." It was an
order, pushing a gray area of command: between operational
and mission.

"You'll put us behind the time line," Eitan protested.

Rosen snapped, "Colonel, you have your orders. I suggest you obey them now." Eitan started to have the cocky bastard bodily removed, then thought the better of it. That's when he heard the report.

Tripod had opened up on a truckload of Iranian Army regulars stopped at the open front gate. Their seeing the gate guard missing, Tripod heard the barking of orders, weapons readied, and a least a platoon emerge, advancing to the main gate. Tripod, on the ground near the gate, let them as far as the inner fence, then let loose, cutting the two lead men literally in half. Thirty caliber rounds shredded men and truck, which began to burn.

Fifteen seconds later, when the thirty caliber report was but an echo, Creed heard it first. The low wail of a siren coming from the north, from the adjacent air base. They had five minutes, max, he figured. He was wrong. More truck lights came into view heading for the front gate. There was something else.

The Israelis! He watched the MOSSAD man step from the lab and give orders to SAYERET MAT'KAL personnel. There seemed to be some hesitance, before the men picked up boxes…carrying them to the Hind-D! Creed started for the lab when thuds of mortar rounds rumbled the dusty ground in front of him. He, Phil and Johnny hit the deck. Another mortar hit the administrative building showering debris over them.

Rosen went back in just as the explosion thudded behind him. Eitan and one of his men knelt close to the door making final preparation for charge detonation. "Colonel, we must go now," came the icy voice.

"Just thirty seconds. Are the Americans ready?"

Outside they heard more mortar hits. "I order you now. Forget the charges, Colonel." Another round hit just outside the lab door, knocking Rosen atop Colonel Eitan.

"Damn," Eitan shouted, his ears ringing. He'd lost the fuse igniter in the tussle.

"No time," Rosen yelled, grabbing Eitan's Iranian uniform.

I order you to leave now, Colonel. Israel's mission objectives are met." A mortar hit the east wall, rocking the building.

Through the smoke, Eitan stared into the MOSSAD man's cold bloodless eyes, then, turned to his man, "Corporal, MOSSAD orders us to abandon the charges." The two SAYERET MAT'KAL men followed Rosen to the now revving helicopter.

At the helicopter, Eitan grabbed Rosen, "Where are the Americans?"

"No time," came the reply as the MOSSAD man forcibly freed himself from the Colonel's grip, climbed in, ordering the Israeli pilot to takeoff. Eitan's entire professional life as a soldier seemed to distill down to this one quiet moment. The integrity, the honor, the respect he had for his men, for any man wearing his country's uniform, putting himself in harm's way, trusting his life to the man next to him. The only two options his mind entertained at the moment were to either shoot the MOSSAD bastard, or close the door. With his Uzi in hand, Colonel Zvi Eitan lunged away from the huge, thrashing Hind-D, toward the entry gate ready to take on the Iranian advance.

Creed loaded and fired his M-203 as fast as he could, explosions thudding outside the compound. Tripod was still by the main gate, firing long bursts from his machine gun at a barely seen enemy. Phil, on one knee, heaved hand grenades over the double fence, dropping back to his stomach before impact.

Creed heard the increased pitched whine of a helicopter's engines. He looked up through the smoke to see the last of the SAYERET MAT'KAL Team climbing into the tensing Hind-D's belly. He wanted to have Milk level his M-60 on the huge ugly beast, and bring the coward sonofabitches down in a ball of flame. He watched still disbelieving as a cloud of dirt swirled over his men. *Sonofabitchin' Jew bastards. You'll pay for this!* More mortars rained from the streaked night sky. They hit their mark, a volley slamming Creed to the ground, blood emerging from both ears. And the Israelis were gone.

• • •

General Rashid's driver neared his passenger's apartment on the northern outskirts of Tehran. Rashid was thinking what audacity John Westin had to walk right into the lion's den, and get out without a scratch. What was this ex-astronaut up to, he wondered. Was really working for the British, CIA, or what? Maybe he came to confirm STAIRCASE's location before a military strike, a war? Iran was on precarious ground here, possessing American hostages. Until STAIRCASE all hostages were held by Iranian-sponsored third parties on foreign soil. If he knew of their presence, the American president seemed the sort to exact punishment. But Westin saw only the lab, not the personnel. Best to kill the hostages anyway, he thought. Shame about the woman, but still, the sooner the better.

Making the last turn, the car's secure telephone buzzed. "Yes." He listened to an excited lieutenant attached to Tajrish's lab security group: Heavy automatic gunfire at or near the lab compound. A platoon sent immediately upon Rashid's orders had not reported back. Reinforcements nearing the compound. It was 2320.

Rashid then made several calls. He informed president Hakim of the Tajrish news and possible American attack against Iran, itself. The president would wait in the underground shelter until further word. Next, he alerted Air Defense, followed by a general alert to all forces. His last call was to his aide at the Military Command Center, to whom he briefly explained the situation, then ordered a general staff meeting in fifteen minutes.

Chief watched Creed go down.

"Fuck this shit," cried Dr. Dech, "I'm staying right here."

"Suit yourself," popped Bloodhound, watching the man run back into the ward barracks. Then he saw it, center compound. Chief kneeling, holding the El Tee's bloodied head. Bloodhound signaled Swede, then they herded the three remaining hostages toward the lieutenant where he lay.

An Armored Personnel Carrier advanced toward the front gate. Its turret gunner laid down 12.7 mm rounds in wide sweeps, clearing the way for an advance. Tripod was exposed to the elevated machine gunner making an easy target. As the rounds neared the SEAL, the SAYERET MAT'KAL colonel ran toward the Security Control building firing his Uzi distracting the oncoming menace. It wasn't enough. A tracer round exploded his chest a stride before reaching the building's cover. The distraction gave Tripod time enough get his head up; he leveled the big '60 and cut the turret gunner's head to meat, then retreated for better cover.

Iranian mortarmen had zeroed in. A rain of mortar rounds pummeled the ground around them, decimating the barracks they'd just left. The loud crack of the explosions knocked Beth to the ground, sickening her stomach. She looked back to see the building ablaze. Then Dech. He stepped out engulfed in flames, his arms outreached as if disbelieving his fate. She lay prone staring at the gruesome sight. She felt nothing. Chief caught a glimpse of the burning Dech and the infernal behind him; the scene brought up images of the devil himself, basking in his element.

Swede reached Chief and the fallen lieutenant. His hand was bleeding—shrapnel. Then the night fell quiet. Chief lifted Creed's bloodied head. The two men stared at each other trying to read the other's thoughts through camouflage paint.

"Put down your weapons." The words pierced the darkness. At first the amplified voice came in English, then in Hebrew. It brought Chief to the reality of command. Over his throat mike, he asked for a situation assessment.

"Chief, Tripod here. Estimate a battalion-sized unit of infantry and light armor, most set up among the buildings on the western fringe. An APC's near the gate. Another's circling behind you. So where'd the fuckin' Jew boys go?"

Chief understood odds. There was nothing better than Team Three for stealth, infiltration, and demolition. But a squad against a battalion. *Custer he ain't.* "Cease fire! Cease fire! Cease fire!" Chief ordered over sporadic gunfire. He felt sick hearing himself say the words. His men felt even sicker. "I said lay down your weapons. That's an order. Now!"

"Fuck that," yelled Swede. "I ain't givin' up to a bunch of goddamned ragheads."

From behind, Chief grabbed the man by the collar. "From now on, Swedie, it's *Iranians,*" he said. "Put your fuckin' hands up real careful now." One by one, each man dropped his weapon to the ground, raised his hands toward black sky, and made themselves visible. Occasional rifle fire still blurted out in the darkness, then stopped.

"Lie down," Chief said. "Real slow." They dropped to their knees, then down to the ground, hands clapsed behind their necks.

Cautiously, behind armored personnel carriers, Iranian squads emerged from their firing positions, approached the compound, then on in toward the prone Americans. The SEALs and hostages were immediately surrounded, gun barrels in their backs. Officers from behind shouted unintelligible orders.

From a third personnel carrier, the Iranian battalion commander emerged. He was a leather-skinned man who moved in a cloud of cigarette smoke, deep wrinkles worn into the corners of his mouth. He gestured menacingly as he spoke to the Americans. "Where did they take the helicopter? Who is in charge? Speak!" Chief figured Creed's eardrums were blown out, so he answered saying only that he was in command.

"I don't think so." The commander spotted Creed, ears bleeding. Walked over, then kicked him over. Creed instinctively grabbed the boot, twisting, taking the man to the ground.

Crack! Creed flinched once, a reddening hole dead center of the heart. A soldier stepped up and kicked the body off his commander's leg.

"You sona—"

For the outburst, Tripod got another boot to the side of his head. "Get off it, everyone," Chief yelled, trying to block out what he'd just seen. "Just do as they say."

The SEALs and hostages were led the smallest building,

the old brig, which miraculously escaped mortar damage. Chief noted light armor everywhere, soldiers too: inside and outside the perimeter fence, atop buildings, and back in the guard towers. *Fuckin' Israelis. Colonel Zvi Eitan, if it's the last fuckin' thing I ever do.*

Once, in the old brig, they were stripped of all their gear and weapons, tied and blindfolded. The SEALs and hostages were separated into the six rancid cells. Two guards sat just eight feet away, AK-47s trained on their new guests. Two more sat in the outside office area, and two more stood post outside the open door.

It was midnight when General Rashid reached the Military Command Center. He grabbed a cup of caffeine-packed coffee, then proceeded to the sophisticated war room. Only half of the general staff had made it in. He expected that. His Air Defense general was present. That would do for now.

"Anything on radar?" The answer was negative. Not a massive attack. Yet. Anything new from Tajrish? Just then, an aide punched a button silencing the harsh tone, then announced, "Sir. The battalion commander at Tajrish."

Rashid listened to the report, the terrorist's capture, causalities, and the escaping helicopter. Hearing that, Rashid cracked his baton across the console top before him. As the room silenced, Rashid turned to the man in charge of Iranian air defense, "General, a Hind-D was stolen from Tajrish just minutes ago, last seen heading due west. Use all available resources. Locate the craft and shoot it down!"

Back to the telephone, Rashid gave the waiting Tajrish commander his orders, "Hold your position. As soon as possible tonight, I will be there to personally interrogate the commandos. Do not interrogate before then." If there was one thing in which Mohammed Rashid prided himself, it was the art of extracting information.

CHAPTER 33
ATTACHMENTS

Los Angeles—12:30 P.M. Saturday (local)
Atsugi Naval Air Facility, Japan—07:30 A.M. Sunday (local)
Tajrish—00:00 Midnight Sunday (local)

The assassin, crouched silently in the dark, was an exquisite product of centuries. Centuries, over which Japanese refinement turned the business of death into an art. The pinnacle of the art form was called *ninjutsu.*.

The origins of *ninjutsu*, itself, were not military or combative, but spiritual. *Ninjutsu* developed as a highly illegal counter culture to the ruling samurai elite, and for this reason alone, the origins of the art were shrouded by centuries of mystery, concealment, and deliberate confusion of history. The *samurai* had his code of honor, known as *bushido*, the *ninja* practicing *ninjutsu* had none.

Particularly noxious to the establishment of the day was the notion that a person could become his own priest. The teachers of *ninjutsu* knew that culture was unnatural, causing one to lose flexibility and naturalness as they emerged from childhood. The highly structured culture of feudal Japan—and more so in modern Japan—suppressed natural responses, and it was for this reason that such independence of being was so despised and feared.

They were accused of being in league with dark powers able to summon spirits to aid in the realization of their dark intentions. The teachers of *ninjutsu* did little to dispel such myth and indeed fostered unconventional methods of infiltration and assassination.

The *ninjutsu* teacher taught the assassin to work in the dark, to avoid overtly powerful and active means of accomplishing their ends, choosing instead to follow a philosophy of quiet and subtle action unseen in the darkness. He preserved the natural order as much as possible, choosing suggestion rather than force, deception rather than confrontation.

They taught him of extended form of energies, a sixth sense, *haragei*. Being *haragei* adept allowed him to see where the eye could not, to hear what the ear could not. The result was a sphere of perception reaching beyond normal limits, beyond the physical realm.

The core of *ninjutsu* lay in the dropping of attachments to the ultimately unimportant aspects of existence. Even fear was accepted for he had also released his attachment to fear. Throughout his life, he had repeatedly exposed himself to danger, even death. His walking a fine line between life and death allowed personal power and spiritual knowledge to arise. It allowed him to attune with the natural forces within the universe and to channel these forces in achieving his ends.

And in achieving his ends, he had sworn, nothing would stop him. Seven hours now.

Commander Stan Tanner stood on the tarmac watching the big C-141 roll to a stop at Atsugi Naval Air Facility this Sunday morning. Only a half-hour late: 0730. The ground crew moved with motivated precision chocking the wheels as the aft ramp descended.

Not twenty yards away sat an A-6 Intruder. Tanner knew the pilot, the son of the Atsugi NAF base commander. The kid was attached to a squadron aboard the *U.S.S Independence* now four hundred miles out at sea making her way toward Tokyo Bay. From the *Independence*, the pilot had hopped in for his mother's surprise birthday party held last night. If they had a chance, Tanner wanted to show John some of the latest B/N upgrades before the bird returned this afternoon.

For Westin and Coleman, it had been a long flight, refueling at Hickum in Hawaii, then again at Elmendorf, Alaska. Tanner watched Westin and Coleman emerge stretching. Then as he mentally predicted, John hesitated, looking over the menacing A-6E Intruder medium-attack aircraft, its wings folded up. It made Tanner wondered again why John ever left this man's Navy. He welcomed the two stateside men to Japan with a traditional cold beer, put them in a Chrysler K-car, then wheeled them off to the administration building.

In Tanner's office, they met Shuji Okada, their "guide," Westin's chaperon while in Japan. The CIA man kept in the background as the three others caught up on buddies, doings, and work. No one mentioned John's Iranian vacation. Coleman commented on Tanner's double-clutch coffee, noting egg-shells in the drip filter.

An hour later, with schedules coordinated, Tanner bid the three men a good trip. First stop, Misawa Group's CEO, Kenji Takara. This being Sunday, Takara had requested the meeting be held in his retreat, an hour and a half south on the coast.

They began their incarceration in shocked silence at midnight, well over two hours ago. Instead of a brig, the place looked more like an old western jail: an entry office area and back room cellblock complete with vertical steel-bars. Except for an occasional chatter from the two guards seated in the walkway before them, the six cells remained stone silent.

Chief had allowed himself no time to morn the lieutenant's death. Instead he sat quietly in his cell thinking about the situation and his men. He knew the primary threat to a SEAL's fitness was chemical: the alternating periods of intense boredom and violent stress wreaked deadly havoc on a frogman's nervous and endocrine systems. Exhaustion comes not from muscles flexed but from senses focused and threats perceived. At the moment, Chief knew, tension was at the max.

Even though blindfolded, Chief knew the woman was in the cell next to his—he'd heard her cough. He worked his way close and whispered her name, and got a response.

"Anything I should know?"

"Don't trust Dr. Dech. He's collaborated with them."

"He's dead. Anything else?"

"Yes, right...Japs were here. I think they took STAIR-CASE." Chief assumed STAIRCASE to be the stuff they'd been sent to destroy. "A General Rashid oversees security. Tough. If you've got a move to make, make it fast." Chief had already figured that one out.

Other hushed conversations began between blindfolded cell mates. One of the guards rose and raked the steel bars with the butt of his rifle, shouting in Farsi. When he had silence, he returned to his chair mumbling something derisive about Americans, then spat a large flem-wad. It hit Chief's cell bars, slipping, clinging.

A half-hour later Chief still lacked a plan. He began to think of Creed. The best SEAL platoon commander he'd ever trained. In spite of the pressure the "blackshoes" upstairs put on him, he always put mission integrity and the safety of his men first. *The safety of his men...*

Chief jumped. The two guards laughed uproariously. They'd noticed a black and white short-haired cat trot passed them slipping in between the bars. Chief reached down feeling fur. Fritz!

CHAPTER 34

MUSTACHES

Los Angeles—3:30 P.M. Saturday (local)
Atsugi Naval Air Facility—10:30 A.M. Sunday (local)
Tajrish—03:00 A.M. Sunday (local)

Chief sat blindfolded, his hand on pure "cattitude." His mind raced. What in the fuck can this cat do? Take instructions, that's what. Lethal instructions. And he knew Fritz's codeword too, being backup to Creed. Chief formulated his instructions, then mentally rehearsed how to say Fritz backwards.

Chief picked up the cat, she sounded louder than just a purr. He whispered her name, and got a meow in response. Cuddled up close to him, he whispered, "Zee-tirf." After another meow, he whispered his instructions. The guards thought this private conversation funny.

Fritz eased out of Chief's lap, then with a slight limp, sauntered through the bars stopping next to one of the seated guards. She sat on her haunches preening, her tongue licking her short fur just behind the neck. The guard picked her up.

"What's going on in here?" barked a third guard coming down the hall, pistol drawn. He'd heard the laughter. "Give me that cat!"

Fritz had to work fast, for she knew she was fifteen minutes beyond her rated battery life. Allowing the arriving third guard to pick her up, she left her hypodermic mark in the first guard's right forearm. She repeated the procedure into the third guard's receiving forearm. Then she saw the second guard turning to the first guard, surprised to see the man's face seized with panic. Fritz hopped onto the alarmed guard's shoulder, extending claws into the man's neck, then leaped to clear falling bodies.

Chief saw it all in his mind. Hearing the third body hit the floor, he informed, "Okay, everyone. Guards are out. Anyone near free of his bonds."

"Wait a minute, Chief." It was Tripod. Tripod, the one SEAL who could barely swim, but with the strength of hydraulic press. "There," Tripod announced with relief. The plastic cuffs had stretched thinner under the pressure, cutting into his wrist, yet finally the coupling piece broke. He removed his blindfold, then rubbing his bloody wrist, he looked out at the three bodies, and said, "What the fuck happened?"

"Long story," Chief answered. "Right now, give us a hand." Tripod removed blindfolds from those he could reach, then asked, "What now?"

"Tripod, where's Milkman?" Chief asked, his blindfold still on.

"Next cell, got his blindfold off."

"Milk, can you pick these locks?" Chief asked

"Sure, if I had tools, and hands."

Chief thought about that then ordered, "Tripod, do what it takes, break Milk's cuffs."

"Might hurt."

"Just do it," Chief snapped, wanting to yell. "Okay. Tools. What do see out there that the cat could get to the cells?" The question drew silence. "I'm not fucking around here. We got two minutes before we see another guard."

"Two rifles and a gun," said Beth. "They're the only loose items in the room. No keys visible on the bodies."

"Can't pick a fucking lock with a gun," grimaced Milkman under Tripod's stress.

"Best we got," Chief muttered. "Fritz," he beckoned cheerfully, as if the cat were real. Using the codeword, he instructed Fritz to push the pistol toward the cells. The others stood amazed as the black and white cat backed up to the weapon, then kicked with both hind legs. The pistol skidded just beyond Bloodhound's long reach. Fritz's movements were slowing, as this time she put her "Hitler" nose against the trigger guard, nudging forward, slowly…then stopped, dead still.

"The fucker quit! Just quit."

Chief should of known: batteries. Creed had powered her up around 2240, now out of juice, he figured. "Somebody get the pistol, goddamnit! And what kind is it?" A .45 caliber. Bloodhound removed his shirt, tore a long strip making a loop at its end. As he fished, Chief gave instructions, "Strip the piece, use the slide stop pin, the firing pin, the extractor, whatever. You got tools, just find the right ones. Bloody?"

Bloodhound's fifth try barely caught the hammer. The pistol wanted to rotate, instead of drag. In frustration, Bloodhound gave a sharp snap on the noose. The .45 flopped over. Bloodhound again stretched his long arms, fingers touching…

Rashid checked his watch: 0310. He rode in a Soviet Tupelov HIP-C helicopter, now ten minutes away from the Tajrish compound. There were no other incursions reported since Tajrish. A feeble attempt to rescue hostages, Rashid decided, not an all out attack.

The escaping Hind-D had disappeared from the radar net. That meant one thing. Whether by design, strategy or luck, the craft was on the ground, still in Iranian territory. A massive search was currently underway.

Bloodhound managed to drag it in, then passed it over two

cells to Milkman. Phil, in the same cell disassembled the M1911 Colt .45 semiautomatic pistol. Through the bars, Milkman's hands worked the lock, starting with the slide pin stop. Feverishly, he tried other Allen wrench-like parts…"Bingo." Now knowing the nature of the lock and working from outside the cells, the other five would be easy. Phil took a knife from a dead guard, and handed it to Tripod. Tripod cut Phil's plastic cuffs. Phil took the knife to free the others.

Suddenly, a fourth guard appeared, just as surprised as Phil. But Phil made the first move, bolting as the Iranian fumbled for his pistol. Phil came in with a solid kick to the crotch, then sidestepped, left hand grabbing nose, eyes, anything. Right hand drawing the blade across the cocked neck. Two seconds.

Another two minutes and all were free. Chief ordered four of the men to strip and don the fallen Iranian soldier's uniforms. It was then, he noticed the stretcher laid over one of the far cell cots; Colonel Eitan's unconscious body lay still, yet breathing. Chief wanted to spit.

Chief and Swede took the Kalashnikovs and knives, then proceeded slowly down the walkway out into the entry room. There were no guards, both now back in the cellblock dead. The outside door was open. Immediately, he heard the sound of an approaching helicopter, then spotted the back of one Iranian uniform. Chief knew that for brief seconds, all attention would be diverted to the hovering craft.

He laid down his AK-47, drew the Iranian knife, then signaled Phil to back him up. Acknowledged, he went to the door, saw a second sentry's back, but did not hesitate. He repeated Phil's neck procedure on the nearest sentry, then stepped quickly to the turning second man. The man had pivoted in the wrong direction, which allowed Chief to step in and plunge the blade deep within the man's kidney. Seeing the second sentry down, Phil pulled in the first, Chief the other.

Chief reacted instinctively, "Phil, Milk. Out here, grab their weapons, look soldierly." Chief looked at the larger of the two fresh bodies, then ordered, "Tripod, take this one, strip and get dressed. We got three minutes, max."

"That's probably General Rashid," Beth warned.

Chief surveyed what was left of their equipment strewn about the dusty room; their captors had taken the liberty to inspect, some of it looted for souvenirs. The MP-5s and ammunition were still there, they could use those. Swede's rucksack was still in tact, *just maybe*.

The Tupelov HIP-C hovered, then settled onto the concrete helipad. Four handpicked guards emerged into the swirling damp night air, weapons at the ready. Rashid stepped out, baton under arm, greeting the base battalion commander.

"Any change since out last communication," the General queried.

"The compound remains quiet," the leathered-faced commander reported, "We have six commandos under guard in the brig; one, wearing an Iranian Army uniform, is severely wounded. One commando killed. Identities unknown. The barracks were destroyed in the attack killing an American scientist. The three others are locked with the commandos."

"And the lab?"

"Charges set, but not wired. Demolition experts have been called to dismantle."

Rashid expressed his satisfaction and wished to see the prisoners at once.

"Helicopter's down, six men coming this way," Milkman informed as he stood "sentry duty" outside the brig's door, "I smell brass."

"Just get 'em through that door, Milk. Phil, you got that?" Aye was the reply. Suddenly, Chief realized Phil was the wrong man on the post. If Phil gets it, nobody leaves. Too late now.

As the general and his entourage approached the brig, the two SEAL sentries came to attention—whatever that was in the Iranian army. Rashid passed through thinking something was out of place. Donning on him, Rashid reached for his sidearm. Too late. With the sixth man in, the two inside "brig guards" swung their Kalashnikovs around training them on the surprised officers and their guard. Bloodhound ordered the soldiers to the floor; that also brought out the remaining SEALs and hostages. Tripod and Johnny collected weapons, then stripped all six down to their skivvies.

Chief looked at the general, then decided, "Blood, you're promoted to general. Be quick about it." Blood removed his Iranian uniform, donning Rashid's, including his short baton. "Johnny, take the commander's hat, and secure the prisoners." Johnny found more plastic handcuffs and bound the hands and feet of the six prone soldiers. He and Tripod carried each hogtied soldier back to the cells.

Ever since General Rashid hesitated, Chief tried to figure why. *Something about our faces.* That's it! Mustaches. "Blood, get some paint out a rucksack, give everybody a black mustache." Chief handed Swede a rucksack, "This one's yours. We may need it. Find the cat, stuff it in there too."

Chief huddled his team near the brig door so Phil and Milkman could hear. "Okay everyone, this is the plan. SEALs in Iranian uniforms will escort myself and the three civilians to the lab. There, we'll evaluate and act if appropriate. From the lab, we go to the helicopter. Phil, think you can drive us outta here?"

"Been years, Chief. But still, easier than the Hind," Phil affirmed from outside.

"Okay, we got everything in three rucksacks, including the MP-5s. Swede, you got yours. Two of you grab the others. Carry 'em cradled, like fire logs—like evidence. Ready. General Bloodhound, you and Commander Johnny are first out; you'll lead the way to the lab. Civilians and me fall in next. For the flanks: Swede takes the right, Tripod the left. Phil and Milkman, outside, bring up the rear."

"What about the Israeli colonel?" piped Tripod.

"Leave 'em," Chief came back, bitter.

"But Chie—"

"I don't wanna hear it. Everybody ready?"

"They can make him talk," Beth said. "Identify all of you."

Not if he's dead, he can't, Chief's mind reasoned. Chief

looked each person in the eye, then made his decision.

Out of the brig, "General" Bloodhound turned left, baton under arm, leading ten people through the shadowed valley of death. He tried not to fix on the APC and the man in its gun bucket, just twenty yards away. *Halfway now...*

They reached the lab. "Commander" Johnny opened its door for the "General." All filed in behind. Jamil and Sanborne set Eitan's stretcher down. Inside the empty lab, they found a hole in its east wall from a mortar round. The door closed, Chief asked, "Swede, you do anything with this? In say, sixty seconds? Blood, Milk, check fuses and PETN for breaks, damage."

Swede and Chief looked it over and agreed. Always the pack rat, Swede pulled a fuse igniter from his rucksack. Chief helped him wire it up. Two minutes later, Swede pulled the fuse igniter. At the sight of telltale smoke, the procession exited heading for the Tupelov HIP-C, camouflage-painted in desert browns and golds. It was well lighted here. This would be the tricky part, thought Chief.

Chief watched faces begin to puzzle as the "general" and "commander" strode by; a corporal left heading toward the brig. Phil stepped around to the helicopter's left door, the pilot seated winding up his engine's RPMs. With head down, 'General' Bloodhound boarded through the helicopter's right door, followed by the others, Tripod manhandling Eitan onto its vibrating deck.

The pilot began objecting to something. Phil opened his door and put a nine millimeter round into the man's spleen; The thumping rotors muffled the report, aimed low enough to avoid immediate notice.

Over the noise, Chief asked the Farsi-speaking civilian what the pilot had said. Amil said that he protested the weight. Too many people. Chief leaned forward informing Phil, whose sketchy experience concurred. Milkman, in the copilot's seat, unbuckled the fallen pilot. Phil tossed the body out onto the concrete, then buckled himself in. With surrounding soldiers beginning to stir, Milkman looked back toward the brig. It was Rashid, shouting, running half-clothed. "Hit it hard, Phil," Milkman shouted, gesturing low with his thumb.

The cockpit was fairly standard, Phil assessed, but still some things were different. The last time he'd flown a helicopter was when he washed out of helicopter pilot training, some thirteen years ago. And of course, with this Soviet craft, he didn't have the slightest feel for its controls, its performance, nuances. With a foot on each pedal, right hand on the cyclic poked upright between his knees, Phil's left hand pulled up more on the collective. The gawky beast lurched skyward, then hesitated jerkily. Phil finally figured out the foot pedal control, then pulled on the cyclic, banking hard, heading north. He figured over the fence and north—toward the air base—was fastest way to put distance between them and the Iranian soldiers below.

Rashid shouted orders at the soldier in the APC. The machine-gunner rotated the turret, found his target silhouetted against the radiated lights of the adjacent base, then let loose with a slow staccato blaze. Every fifth 12.7 mm round was a tracer, aiding the gunner to the fleeing craft.

"Haul ass, man," Milkman yelled, "Tracers arcing our way."

It sounded like a ricochet, then the world started to spin. "We've been hit," yelled Phil, struggling with the pedal controls, "Tail's been hit. Gotta put her down, fast!"

Chief leaned forward. He saw the military base in front, a small civilian airport to the right. "Put it in there," Chief shouted, pointing to the right. Getting a better vantage, Chief directed Phil to put down behind the limousine parked next to a clean white Lear jet.

Phil struggled with the pedals, juggling cyclic, collective, and throttle, each affecting the other. As they came down, Milkman and Chief observed three suited men, illuminated by the limo's headlights, their backs to the helicopter's arrival. Two were pulling back a portable passenger access ramp, as the jet's engines gradually spun up. It was a rough touchdown with minimal control in the yaw axis, but Phil managed it, now chopping power, right door already open.

In spite of the hunger and fatigue, the SEALs were out in

a heartbeat—pure adrenaline—with MP-5s leveled. Chief and Milkman took the three businessmen, surprised in the limousine's blinding headlights. One reacted reaching. At the sight of the Uzi, both Chief and Milkman flipped to full auto and cut the three men down. "And just what do we have here?" Chief said aloud to himself.

Everyone heard the jet's engines responded to increases in throttle. The limo secure, Bloodhound and Johnny pushed the access ramp back to the Lear's fuselage, then bounded up. The increase in engine whine made communication impossible through the closed passenger door. Bloodhound motioned to Tripod.

Tripod had grabbed an AK-47 from the rear of the helicopter. He came around to the front of the plane now beginning to roll. Seeing the large man fire a long burst in front of the cockpit's window, a stunned pilot jerked the plane to a stop.

Staying clear of the jet's engines on the tail, Chief went to the plane's rear access door and pulled the emergency handle. As the door swung down, making its own steps, Bloodhound and Johnny scrambled in, quickly sizing up targets in the plane's dim interior. Johnny ran forward to the cockpit, turned training his barrel on the cabin's occupants. A blue suit reached inside his suit coat, then thought the better of it. Bloodhound, who'd covered Johnny's back, then stepped forward, taking over the cabin. Johnny then turned, pulled open the flight deck door, sticking his MP-5's muzzle hard into the pilot's neck. Chief appeared at the rear with Amil, who gave instructions in Farsi: "Do not move and you will not be hurt."

Satisfied, Chief stepped outside, motioned the access ramp pushed away, then waved the rest in. Phil paused to look at the helicopter's rear vertical rotor blades, a half-dozen chewed up. As each SEAL entered the cabin, he assessed the situation and picked a man to point his weapon at. Tripod brought up the rear with Eitan's limp body draped across his broad shoulder.

Except for two serious-looking men in western business

suits, all other wore robes; of those, all but a teenager of eighteen or so wore a turban. It was a plush setup, Chief thought: taupe leather seats, polished mahogany tables, plush carpet throughout.

"You are not Iranian soldiers," came a man at a table. Amil translated.

"And you're not Mexican. Who the Hell are you?" replied Chief.

Silence. Chief sensed they were deferring to the older man with the permanent scowl etched on his dark face. His dress was nothing less than royal: purple satin robe accented in black velvet. He'd let it ride for now, then handled logistics.

"We will not harm you," Chief began. "We accept your offer to loan us your aircraft, and promise to return it. We also promise not to harm you, your government willing."

"Then let us go," the teenager demanded in French-accented English. That received a scolding glare from the patriarch.

"If any of you is armed, surrender your weapon now," Chief ordered, then fixed on what had to be the bodyguards. "Slowly."

One of the blue-suited men reached into a shoulder holster and produced a Glock 9mm pistol, placing it gently on the table. Milkman rammed his rifle into the second man's spine, yielding another Glock. Swede scooped up the two block-shaped weapons.

Chief moved up front and gave the pilot his orders: take off and head west. The small airfield being uncontrolled, the white Lear Jet taxied to the runway and took off without permission. It was 0350.

Seven minutes earlier, General Rashid alerted the Military Command Center of a second stolen helicopter headed for the Tajrish civilian air field. After the call, Rashid quickly grabbed suitable clothes, then sought to understand exactly what the Americans had done.

"The lab! What did they take?" No one knew. "What

else?" Nothing. The angry general stomped out heading for the lab with strides hard to match, his immediate subordinates in tow.

Once inside, he smelled smoke. Investigation found a burning fuse close to a "T" joint. Rashid turned to run. Too late, the PETN ignited, and at over seventeen thousand miles an hour, it traveled down two thirty-foot lengths, reaching three pounds of C4 nestled amongst six fragmentation grenades. In milliseconds, the lab was splinters and flames.

Later, the Tajrish battalion commander would be shot for incompetence; General Rashid would be recognized, posthumously, as a state hero, for his initial alert from the president's palace, for his bravery, for his later alert which brought forth witnesses, witnesses who within minutes led the Iranian Military Command to a white Lear jet, headed due west.

The private jet appeared immediately on the air traffic control radars in Tehran. Two minutes later, two fighters from the Tehran Air Force base scrambled vectored on an intercept course.

Aboard Air Force One, President Temple tried to concentrate on the memos before him. He sat at his "V"-shaped oak desk in his specially built private office. Not very large, the office provided an uncluttered somewhat cozy hideaway from the hubbub throughout the rest of the craft. It was quiet here, thick creme-colored carpet made a tasteful contrast with the oyster-grey sound absorbing wall panels. In thirty minutes, Air Force One would touch down at Point Mugu Naval Air Station, sixty miles south of Los Angeles.

Temple looked at his watch again. An eleven-and-a-half-hour time differential calculated out to be three-fifty the next Sunday morning Iran time. The SEAL and Israeli teams, with hostages, were due at the Caspian Sea trawler two hours ago, he knew. The rendezvous missed, and no one knew where they were. With this kink, he now wished he'd blown off the G2 affair and rode herd back in the White House Situation Room.

The only intelligence Marshall Douglas had so far was not

necessarily good. There was a high level of military aircraft activity west of Tehran. Appeared to be a search pattern, CIA analyst conjectured. *It was times like these...*

Westin admired the thickly wooded mountainous area in which they now found themselves. On the flight out Westin had fallen short of the mark trying to explain to Coleman, the concept of Japanese "face." As they headed deeper into mountains, Westin listened to Okada's attempt fall even shorter.

"So Colonel Coleman, it is very Japanese. The accident we saw that Westin-san refers to, where the responsible man left the scene, was simply a matter of his wishing to save face."

"But it's against the law," Coleman protested.

"In Japan, understood rules, not laws, govern its society's behavior. This is different from America where laws are suppose to govern behavior."

"Supposed?" came Coleman's question.

Negotiating the winding road, Okada collected his thoughts, then offered, "Laws in America seem to have little meaning. That is because America has legislated so many laws that people find they can not obey them all, some being completely absurd. From an Eastern point of view, the Japanese can not understand why a concerned government would wish to make criminals of most of its citizens."

"Like the fifty-five mile per hour speed limit?" Westin offered.

"Precisely. Did you ever wonder why America has ten times more laws than Japan? It's because America has one thousand times more lawyers. Lawyers making laws people cannot live with. Then more lawyers representing those people breaking the laws they can't live with. Like those ticketed exceeding the fifty-five mile an hour speed limit. In a perverse way, it is all very logical."

"For lawyers," Westin grumped. Westin hated lawyers.

"What's the worst that can happen to someone who causes a Japanese to lose face?" John asked.

"In extreme cases, revenge." Making a last right turn,

Okada announced, "We are here." They parked and ascended the wide steps of the massive temple-like structure. Concerning "face," Coleman still had no idea what Okada was talking about.

This was a courtesy visit. As usual, things down the line always went smoother, Westin knew, if he took the time to stroke the head cheese. Trouble was, for John, that this head cheese happened to be Takara. Takara suspected Kojima died by his hand. But could Takara prove it? John couldn't see how, but still…

The three men were greeted by two rather serious-looking men in loose-fitting martial arts-like garb. The two "kung fu" gentleman led them to the back of the massive rectangular house. They entered a room with smooth-cut wooden beams running laterally across its ceiling. From the center beam, a large iron pot tied to a rope hung low over a hibachi stove inset into a highly polished wood floor. The rest of the room was fairly bare, save the closed *shoji* screen obscuring the outside view of the valley.

Coleman felt it a split second before John. The back of a thick hand crashing down upon the back of his neck. John passed out. Coleman would wish he had also. Okada acknowledged the precision of the feat, then exited the room, hearing the black man groan amid more blows meted out by the two experts.

Okada entered the spacious east sitting room seeing Takara's stout body facing its enclave; he stood resolute before two swords resting in the okidai's holding slots, against a walled background of bright blood red and white silk— Japan's flag, the rising sun.

In meditation, Takara could feel his *kobun*'s presence. Kojima did not deserve to die, especially at the hands of an American. America, destroying his own family, his Nagasaki home, and now his *kobun*. Takara's hands reached for the top *katana*, his two thick hands grasping the sword's handle and sheath. He pulled to expose ten centimeters studying the matchless edge flashing bluish hues, the curve of its back uniting grace with utmost strength. The *jihada* and *hamon*—

blade and temper patterns—possessed Japan's spirits. And today the spirits cried out for revenge, for death.

Takara snapped the exposed blade back into its sheath, replaced the *katana*, then picked up the disfigured tin soldier clenching it tight. Okada watched the stalwart man close his eyes as if in prayer. Finished, Takara turned. "Okada-san, Shimizu-san has told me much about you. Please join me for lunch. Later, our American guests should be in a better mood to talk."

CHAPTER 35

FACE VALUE

Los Angeles—4:40 P.M. Saturday (local)
Kanagawa Prefecture, Japan—11:40 A.M. Sunday (local)
Tajrish—04:10 A.M. Sunday (local)

As the Lear jet passed eight thousand feet, two Mig-21's swung in behind it, immediately closing to within meters. The copilot spotted the flight leader's plane as it inched dangerously close. The helmeted pilot gave a thumb's down motion as the radio crackled: "Crescent two-seven, this is Tehran Control. You are ordered to turn immediately to zero-nine-five for approach into Mehrabad."

"Uh-uh," Chief warned the pilot.

"They will shoot us down!"

"I'll shoot you if you turn."

"You are crazy!" Now that's the spirit, Chief thought.

"Climb to twenty thousand, then level off and turn south."

"Where are we going?"

"I'll point, you drive."

"Crescent two-seven, Crescent two-seven, this is Tehran Control. If you do not turn immediately to zero-nine-five and descend to flight level seven-zero, you will be shot down. You have thirty seconds to comply."

"Don't answer," said Chief.

"But they will—" Chief flicked the MP5's safety switch to "off."

"Crescent two-seven, you have ten seconds to comply."

Chief looked out the plane's right side and saw the Mig fighters break hard right opening distance between themselves and the little Lear. One of the MIG-21s fell back a quarter mile behind. "Five seconds," the radio announced.

The pilot nervously looked at his watch, counting down. "Gimme the mike." Chief yanked the headset from the pilot's balding crown, then depressed the talk button on the console, "Tehran Control, this is Crescent two-seven. Before you fire, I suggest you find out who we got aboard this plane. It might change your mind." *Good question. Who the fuck are these people?*

"Crescent two-seven, Tehran Control. Stand by."

Outside, Chief spied the two fighters inching back up to their starboard side. "Set your heading for Kuwait City." At eighteen thousand feet, the white jet and its two escorts raced to meet the breaking daylight.

Chief motioned with his gun barrel for the copilot to abandon his seat, and head back to the cabin. Upon request, Phil came forward, then lowered himself behind the right-side yoke and felt the tension drain from his legs and lower back. Phil glanced down at the instruments before him and scanned the altitude, heading, airspeed, and artificial horizon. Was he supposed to understand this shit? He shifted his gaze to the fighters outside the glass, then wished he'd brought a parachute.

In the plane's main cabin, the rest of the squad settled themselves as comfortably as they could. There was a long couch along the starboard side, facing the table and seats to port where the patriarch and the others sat. From an oblique chest wound, Eitan lay unconscious center aisle toward the rear, Tripod's dressing having minimal effect on the profuse bleeding. Swede raided the kitchenette's cabinets for food, passing it out. Team Three ate like it was their last meal.

At just over two hundred and fifty miles per hour, the remaining trip would take ninety minutes. Fighting fatigue, no one relaxed.

CIA Headquarters, Langley: They were in a forth floor room the size of a large living room. A conference table dominated the room's well-lit center. Overhead light dimmed noticeably toward the room's walls. Covering two walls were backlit status boards, charts, and maps. CNN dribbled silently within a bank of television and computer monitors on the third wall.

Amidst telephones and coffee cups, Jordan Barr and most of his TALON'S GRIP Covert Action Staff were seated around the table. The mood reflected a curious mix of tension and despondency. Most eyes seemed blankly glued to a large back projected computerized map of Iran and its neighbors.

"*Coral Sea* AWACS reports picking up voice transmission between Tehran's Mehrabad Tower Control and a Crescent two-seven. Hard copy of the transmission coming in now. AWACS thinks it's a hijack." The room went to a complete hush.

Barr took the hard copy reading its contents. "Heading?"

"Two-ten. Straight line for Kuwait City."

"Nancy, inform our Kuwait station to expect visitors. Give them the password, and have them coordinate with local authorities. Ted, get Admiral Marino on the Pentagon Sit Room line. I'll speak to him myself."

Seventy minutes had elapsed, Phil noted, since he'd taken the cockpit, still pretending to check instruments and the pilot's actions. Thirty minutes ago, their escort jets flared off in a dull roar, only to be replaced by two more. They'd heard nothing more from Tehran Control.

Brown patterns of the Iranian landscape peeked up at them through occasional breaks in the low, wispy clouds. An image came to Chief: the entire country of Iran scurrying around like excited ants reacting to Team Three's big obtrusive foot. The image faded to anger and blame as the picture of Lieutenant Don Creed flooded his mind, the Israelis abandoning the Team in their cowardly escape. "Persian Gulf coming up," the pilot's voice crashed in, jolting Chief from introspection back into reality.

Chief indulged an inward smile watching the two fighters peel off twelve miles beyond the beach north of Ganaveh. He leaned his head back and stared long at the cockpit's overhead. Finally, he turned to the open door behind him and announced into the cabin: "Ladies and Gentlemen, we are now over the Persian Gulf."

The trip's remaining eighty miles over the waters of the Gulf were occupied with preparations for arriving in Kuwait. On another chart, Phil found the frequency for Kuwait Control and dialed it into the plane's radio. Then he thought of what to say into his headset mike, "Kuwait Control, Kuwait Control, Crescent two-seven requests approach to runway two-niner."

"Roger, Crescent two-seven, standby." The voice was cold and bare, like all international controllers. "Crescent two-seven, descend to level one-zero-zero and hold."

"Roger, descending to level one-zero-zero." Phil glanced at the pilot to his left and nodded. "Take her down."

As they reached ten thousand feet, the radio crackled again. "Crescent two-seven, Kuwait Control, turn left to two-five-zero, descend to flight level eight-zero and hold. Speaker, please identify."

How to do this, Phil pondered, then said, "Deuce and a half." It was the password onto the Caspian fishing boat had things gone right.

Phil began to worry. Kuwait Control should have passed them over to Kuwait Approach by now.

Chief came forward, followed by Beth. She grabbed his arm firmly, then whispered in his ear, "We got to warn someone. Nobody knows the Japanese have STAIRCASE. It's critical."

"Ma'am, it's gonna have to keep 'till we get on the ground."

"*If* we get on the ground," cautioned Phil.

"Crescent two-seven, do you copy?"

"Roger," Phil replied.

"Uh, descend to flight level five-zero. Contact Kuwait Approach on two-six-seven point seven."

"Roger that!"

John became aware of stinging cold. For some irrational reason, his mind wanted to deal with the sensation before attempting to open his eyes. He tried to raise his hands. They didn't move. His face felt strange, contorted. Cold, wet, like—

Water! Hitting his face…waking. Where was he? John opened his eyes to slits, looked left, then right. A blurry image. Coleman's black face began to focus, now looking back at him. The Marine's face was bruised and swollen all over. No cuts. John's mind finally took in Coleman's situation: from tied hands above him, Coleman hung suspended like a carcass of beef. The rope securing his hands looped around an exposed crossbeam at the ceiling above. Rope at the ankles secured his powerful legs.

John, tied to the same crossbeam, saw that they were in the same room, his recognizing the iron pot hung low over the floor-inset hibachi. Beyond the hanging pot, Westin saw the two "kung fu" characters standing at the entry door. He started to speak, then felt the pain, like maybe a broken rib. Coleman had said nothing.

Then John saw two more figures approach the room. Takara came into view, then Okada. *Okada's CIA, he'll help*, his mind tried to clutch, but his senses already knew.

The black man was of no consequence to Takara. It was Westin from which he wanted answers. Answers before he killed them both. He didn't have much time so began directly, "What has the CIA sent you here to learn, Westin-san?"

"What?" The response earned him a chop to his left kidney.

"Answer the question, Westin-san."

"You can beat the livin' shit out of me, but I don't know what you're talking about." John braced himself for another blow that never came.

"We'll come back to that," Takara said finally, deciding to

test for truth on a more personal subject. "What happened between you and Kojima-san?"

Takara seemed to have plenty of reason to suspect, John knew; and presently it was a good bet that either lying or telling the truth would yield the same outcome. John told the story just as it happened: his lunchtime visit to Kojima's home, the attack, his near defeat. He told of his creating the appearance of *suppuku* by inserting the *katana* into the knife wound he, himself, had inflicted. Indeed, Takara had checked, forensic analysis did seem to corroborate Westin's story.

When finished, John said, "Now let me ask a question." Takara said nothing. "Why did Kojima-san want to kill me?"

Takara, having heard what he felt was the truth about his *kobun*'s death, decided to answer in kind. Takara, to the best of his ability, answered the question with little satisfaction to John. Takara then philosophized, "Ironic, isn't it. You kill Kojima forty-eight years to the day after your father raped his mother, forever disgracing the Kojima family and its ancestors."

"Now wait a min—"

Whop! It was a bamboo stick, wielded by a "kung fu" guard again aimed across John's kidney.

"Wait a minute, you say. Yes, I have a minute, Westin-san." Takara pulled the tin soldier from his pocket, rubbing its disfigured face. "Tell me about STAIRCASE." Shimizu, in-route, had fifteen minutes ago called. Takara now knew of the interesting bit of conversation with President Hakim and his General Rashid. Coleman watched John flinch at that one.

Shit, John, Coleman wondered, *Who else you tell about STAIRCASE?* Coleman also knew they both were dead men; his speaking up now wouldn't change that.

Takara too saw John's reaction. Yet, at that moment Takara saw only an American: He saw the unspeakable crimes wrought upon Japan; he saw the tragic loss and sacrifice wrought upon his own life. His voice grew cold, arrogant, "The person who destroys my home, destroys my family, destroys my *kobun*, now has the ability to destroy the entire Japanese race." With fist clenched white, Takara spoke with finality, "It is time for balance."

"Balance or revenge," John challenged.

"What is the difference? Restoring honor to Japan's ancestors is the ultimate outcome. Avenging the loss of face of Kojima and his ancestors, of my family and ancestors, of a nation humiliated by the American *gaijin*."

How do you counter ghosts? John's mind struggled. The man lives in the past and fights for ghost. *Where the hell is Superman?*

"Excuse me Takara-san," interrupted one of the "kung fu" men, "A special Misawa courier is here and says he must deliver to you personally." Takara left.

It was Shimizu's courier delivering the LIST to Takara's retreat for safe keeping. Takara returned with a stiff leather pouch holding it up for display, managing a trace of a smile.

From it, Takara produced a sheet of paper. "Do you know why these names appear on this paper? It is because these esteemed people serve two masters. Something quite impossible in Japan. These are people at the highest levels of your American government, people who now do as *Banto* wishes. Yes, Westin-san, *Banto* Society does indeed exist. And soon it will have ultimate control over your government." Coleman's mind raced.

"As for Kojima-san," Takara said, reaching over, then plucking a hair from Westin's head, "this should compensate nicely." Takara pulled a ziploc bag from his pocket, then placed the follicle within its keep. Westin had yet to grasp the full meaning of that.

"You'll be stopped, Takara," Coleman threatened.

"You forget. This is Japan. No one can touch me here. *Sayonara*, Westin-san." As Takara and Okada turned to leave, Takara addressed the two "kung fu" men in English, ensuring the two Americans heard, "Kill them both."

Then Takara motioned one of the "kung fu" men to accompany him and Okada to the front door. There, he handed the man the leather pouch giving more instructions.

CHAPTER 36
CRESCENTS

Los Angeles—4:45 P.M. Saturday (local)
Kanagawa Prefecture, Japan—11:45 A.M. Sunday (local)
Kuwait City—04:15 A.M. Sunday (local)

John hung like a carcass, watching the remaining "kung fu" henchman at the room's door; the man, his back to them, was straining to listen in on Takara's instructions to the other "kung fu" thug. A half-minute later, John heard the distant front door close. Takara and Okada were gone, headed for Tsukuba, forty miles north of Tokyo. Strangely, John began to feel movement. The house. He looked over at Coleman.

Coleman had his legs folded backward, his body swaying backward, then legs straight reversing direction, like on a swing. As his forward motion began reaching the suspended hibachi pot, he veered his legs to miss it. The crossbeam began to give under the Marine's solid two hundred pound momentum. Finally, the beam issued an audible groan. The henchman turned.

Just as Coleman finished a forward downswing, he kicked

the suspended iron pot with two size twelves. It was an even true thrust, the timing perfect, the hanging iron pot transformed into a hurling pendulum. The turning henchman's nose met the oncoming mass, bursting a thunderclap in his now unconscious head.

The guard fell silently to the floor. "Swing, goddamnit," Coleman said in hushed urgency. "The beam." Synchronizing, John starting kicking, knowing what Coleman wanted.

That's not all Coleman wanted. The LIST was in the house. But not for long, not if he could help it. John harbored similar thoughts, but first things first. *Crack!*

It gave way. Coleman hit the floor stiffly, the beam having broken just above him. His hands were still tied and attached to the long rope. John was still suspended, though now a little lower. Coleman searched the "kung fu" man's body. He found three *shuriken*—throwing stars—tucked under his cloth belt. He used an edge to free Westin and his hands, then gave him the stars.

"Come on. We gotta get that LIST," said Coleman, turning for the door.

"But your hands."

"No time. Let's go."

Surprise, they both knew, was their only advantage. As quietly as possible, the two men canvassed the large house as fast as they could. In the east sitting room, Westin grabbed a *katana* displayed before a draped Japanese flag. They went through the large house together, with Coleman dropping behind unable to keep up with the more agile Westin. John saw him first! In Takara's study, closing a concealed wall safe.

John lunged for the Japanese, *katana* in hand. Startled, the man reached for his belt, then hesitated. John bolted leaping a chair closing in on his target, beginning his swing. The Japanese calculated, deftly stepping to the side; he expertly readied his left hand for the assault, while with the other hand, grasped to close the safe's door.

John's swing came in toward the head, then reflexed. Knowing he'd just increased the chances of his coming up short on this exchange, he shifted the *katana*'s advancing path. The Japanese stepped in toward John's advancing body, bare wrist rising catching John in the throat. The shock sent a starburst throughout John's collapsing body. But not before he jammed the thin sword into the shadowed crescent of the closing safe.

The Japanese knelt over John's sprawled body, going for a death blow to the head, then heard another noise. He looked up in time to see a rope descending before his face, tightening around his neck. He managed to thrust up both hands in time to catch it with fingers. Coleman cinched it in tight, tighter. The man struggled with his leg, anything, as his face turned purple, eyes bulged. Then with superhuman strength of *his* ancestors, Coleman broke the man's neck with shearing strength. Two minutes later, Coleman released his grip.

Westin pulled himself up to sit on Takara's office chair. Coleman caught his breath, then removed the sword, retrieving the leather pouch. Through Coleman's puffy face, John saw a shit-eating smile.

Handing the pouch to Westin, the Marine turned his wrist, then said, "Think I could trouble you?" John also managed a smile, freed Coleman's bonds, then said, "Shit, Coleman. Last time I'm ever traveling with you."

"Saved your candy ass. Now let's move it." Stealing a Toyota Land Cruiser in the driveway, they did.

"Yes. But I understand L.A.'s crime is down twelve percent," President Temple goaded the city's mayor, member of the opposition party. Including Temple, there were twelve in all, a few friends and local dignitaries invited up to Temple's suite for a light dinner before the Green Globe ceremonies. Increased Secret Service personnel were noticeably present. Most of the guest enjoyed before-dinner drinks and conversation in the suite's breathtaking Parlor Room. Like the bristling mayor, most were circled around the President.

"Even so, Mr. President, blatant lawlessness will not be tolerated in Los Angeles. Not while I'm mayor."

"Thought that'd get a rise out of you, Walter," Temple

quipped. "Makes me feel safer here already." It was good hearted banter, of course, banter masking what really gripped Temple's mind at the present. All he knew about TALON'S GRIP was that the mission plan had somehow gone sour. The Teams had hijacked a plane and would land at Kuwait City shortly. He expected mild flak on that one. And what about the hostages? He wouldn't get word on that until they landed.

In the adjoining Library, Glenn Thielken had a somewhat hesitant Senator Bill Connery cornered at the far end of the richly paneled room. Two ferns flanked a square glass table where the two men now sat, their backs to a magnificent floor-to-ceiling thirty-first story south view.

Connery was on Thielken's agenda because the man was the chairman of the Senate's Committee on Environment and Public Works, Subcommittee on Nuclear Regulation. Thielken supported Connery's last re-election race to the tune of one hundred thousand dollars.

Connery sat leaning over, hands clasped, elbows resting on knees, talking as if to the carpet. "It's the politics, Glenn. You just don't fuck over your peer senators without due process."

"Fuck Nevada. They've got one of the smallest delegations in Washington. It's gonna happen anyway. Everyone knows it. Just approve Yucca Mountain and let me get started."

"But the test. Not all—"

"That's just what the radical environmentalists want. You know it, I know it. Yucca Mountain has been tested up the ass. The data's solid, Bill. Let's get on with it, and we don't need to wait until your re-election comes up.

Connery saw that one was coming. "Okay, Glenn. I'll see what I can do." Both men stood. Thielken sealed the deal with a firm handshake and a hand on the senator's opposite arm.

"Pardon me, gentlemen," came the Navy steward, "Dinner in five minutes."

"Three? I was told to expect nine," said the unshaven man

from the CIA's Kuwait station. A half hour ago, Ross Sigloh fumbled at the clock radio's five-thirty alarm: time for his early morning run, even on Sundays. No sooner did Sigloh silence the thing than the telephone rang.

"So was I," replied Chief, "Ragheads'd killed five of the poor bastards long before we got there, they said. One, a Dr. Death the woman calls him, decided to stay; died in the firefight."

The Lear jet sat behind two white vans on the tarmac just off a taxiway, and well out from the airport terminal building. An ambulance had just left with Eitan, alive, but with so much blood loss, barely. Most of the SEALs sat resting in the vans; Tripod stood with Chief. Four men from the station's Technical Services team secured the aircraft. One man from the TS team descended the jet's starboard ramp. Chief noticed his serious face approaching as he answered the next question.

"And the Israelis?"

"Fuckin' sonofa—"

"Ross, think you better get over here," came the technical.

Sigloh looked at the white Lear glistening amber in the early morning sun, then asked, "Who are those people?"

"Somebody the Iranian Air Force wouldn't shoot down's all I know. Got two bodyguards too—the blue suits. Should be okay though," Chief grinned wryly, "I thanked them for the ride."

After the two CIA men left for the Lear's ramp, Tripod spoke up, "Chief, couldn't tell you before, but Colonel Eitan—"

"Jew bastard. Wait 'till I—"

"Chief. Chief!" Tripod broke, "Eitan wasn't left behind. I was there near the front gate with the .60. It's like he *wouldn't* go. Stayed to give me cover. Stood his ground too, when the raggies advanced. Saw an APC, .50 cal cut 'em down." Chief looked at Tripod, not wanting to believe it. "Yah, the other Jew bastards left us high and dry. But not Eitan, saved my ass."

"Okay," dismissed Chief. "Get in the van."

As Chief, himself, turned for the vans, he saw Beth Storey coming his way. Might as well say it now, his mind shifted, for he probably wouldn't see her again.

"Chief, we—"

"Me first," he interrupted, "Got somethin' I wanna say." Beth put her hands on her hips, returning an exasperated look. "You didn't hear this from me, okay? Your friend, John Westin, put his ass out there for you. Yep, way out. Found who had this STAIRCASE and last week talked his way into that compound back there. Zeroed in, we took it from there. Good guy you got there, ma'am. Just wanted to say that."

Beth wasn't sure what to do with that, then asked, "Then John knows about STAIRCASE?"

"Suspect he does."

"I've got to talk to John, now. About the Japanese."

"Then I suggest you talk to that man over there." Chief pointed to the unshaven man now descending the jet's starboard stairs.

CHAPTER 37
THORNGILL

Los Angeles—7:10 P.M. Saturday (local)
Atsugi Naval Air Facility—2:10 P.M. Sunday (local)
Kuwait City—06:40 A.M. Sunday (local)

Forty minutes later Beth Storey sat in Ross Sigloh's office at the American Embassy in Kuwait City. All Sigloh knew about STAIRCASE was that it was important enough to justify a special op by joint American-Israeli teams, into of all places, the outskirts of Tehran. That was enough to get his attention, Beth Storey's urgency was enough to get his cooperation.

She was a hostage and had crucial information she insisted on getting to one man, a John Westin working a special project per personal request of the President himself. It was 6:40 A.M. Kuwait time: that meant 10:10 P.M. Langley time.

Sigloh hung up the receiver. After three calls, he had a name and number. Lieutenant Colonel Judd Coleman. Coleman and John Westin were scheduled to arrive Atsugi Naval Air Facility at 0700 local, over seven hours ago.

In Japan right now, Sigloh figured, it would be early Sunday afternoon. Sigloh punched in the numbers he's copied down, a Commander Stan Tanner picked up. After the query, Sigloh heard the Navy man say, John Westin? Yeah, he'd just walked into Tanner's office, but Tanner wasn't sure this was such a good time to talk to him. Sigloh pressed, briefly explaining the situation, then handed the receiver to Beth.

She took the instrument, her heart racing. It took her a moment to compose. Her words were racing too, explaining the visit by Misawa Group and their taking all STAIRCASE records and work to date. She described the large corporate aircraft and recited the tail number. John wanted to know when the Misawa plane had left. She repeated what Amil had heard: dinner with President Hakim, then leave for Japan; ten, ten-thirty last night, she guessed. The conversation closing, she felt the tension in the pause, especially aware of others present in both rooms, then said:

"And John…my middle name is Thorngill. Just wanted to say that," *was how Chief had put it to her*. She hesitated, then handed the receiver back to the still unshaven CIA man.

Five thousand miles eastward, Westin pushed the lighted button, replaced the receiver, then smiled broadly. The pain it induced in his bruised face seemed strangely delectable.

Tanner and Coleman exchanged looks. With affection, Tanner cleared his throat, then both men watched John's puffy face turn even more serious than before. John looked at his watch: two-fifteen.

"Now let me get this straight," Tanner said trying to summarize the story he'd just heard before Beth's call. "Last month, the goons that tried to get you belonged to none other than Kenji Takara, CEO of the two hundred billion dollar Misawa Group. And two hours ago, Takara tried to kill the both of you. And the CIA's Shuji Okada works for Takara too?"

"There's more," Westin said turning to Coleman, "Judd, Takara's got STAIRCASE. He'll have it soon."

"Aw shit," Coleman groaned.

"What's staircase?"

No time to be pleading security, Coleman judged. He gave Tanner's question a brief answer describing its deadly racist potential.

"And if there ever were a nation of racists," Tanner affirmed, "it's Japan. Christ."

"John," Coleman asked, "You said, *soon*. What does soon mean?"

"Westin recounted Beth's message, then asked Tanner if he could locate the plane and its destination.

Tanner obliged, first calling a friend in Japan's equivalent of the U.S.'s FAA. The tail number belonged to a Gulfstream 4 registered to Misawa Group. Then looking at a map, the route was obvious: From Tehran, south to the Indian Ocean and east, then north well off the coast of China. Its four thousand mile range required one stop. Singapore best fit the scenario. After two more calls, Tanner verified Singapore and had the flight plan.

"Tsukuba. The Misawa Complex, their private airport there. ETA: 1500 local."

"Forty minutes," John almost yelled, "We can stop it!"

"How?"

"Shoot the fucker down. They reach Tsukuba, and it's a done deal. Once it goes underground in Japan, nobody finds it. And you think Peal Harbor was a bitch." John was almost out of his seat.

"We can't do that," Tanner countered too quickly.

"Why?" John asked, finally up, pacing.

Tanner wanted to say, *Because we don't do things that way*. But that sounded too bureaucratic, too fuckin' stupid. "Because the Wing Commander's not here, and sure as hell, the Base Commander would never authorize the flight over Japanese territory, not without proper permission from the chain." Westin grimaced. "John, things are touchy around here. You, of all people, should know that."

John sat down, leaned forward, head bowed, running fingers through his matted hair...*Hair*. "Shit! Judd, remember

Takara taking a lock of my hair saying something like, 'As for Kojima, this should compensate nicely.'?"

Coleman got it at once. "Holy shit."

"What. What?" Tanner said, sensing the situation thickening.

Coleman answered, "Using STAIRCASE, Takara plans to kill John, his son, grandson, and any other heir John ever dreamed of having."

"This guy is—"

"One mean motherfucker, Stan," John finished. "And he controls Japan's political system, the country." John fixed a long sobering look on his old B/N. "Stan, we need a plane."

Tanner sat looking at his old friend thinking of the tight places they as a team had been in and out of. Especially Viet Nam, A-6 or barroom sorties. He stared at an unseen place in his mind watching his life race by, most of it his career with the U.S. Navy. Then asked, "You serious what you said. I mean about John and his family?"

Coleman nodded solemnly, then added, "And the madman won't stop there." Coleman just signed up.

Tanner then looked for the photograph on the far wall. It was of John and him standing next to their old Nam warhorse. That photo was taken around the time Stewart was born. Tanner was Stewart's godfather, John always said. Then an image of Stewart's son, little Jeffery formed in his mind: blue eyes under sunshine hair.

Uh-uh. Then sounding like the Stan Tanner of twenty years ago, Tanner spoke, "What the fuck. John, you up for one more ride. You and me, like old times?"

Ten minutes later, Tanner had Westin and Coleman over to a flight ready room. On the way, they had passed the base commander's son's A-6E Intruder still on the tarmac, being readied. Tanner noted an ordnance crew loading the Intruder's centerline drop tank; he wasn't sure why, but he had to smile all the same. In the ready room, the two men found flight gear that reasonably fit, suited up, then waited watching the flight line.

From Tanner's vantage he could see the "ordies," the load complete, now pulling ordnance pins. "Anytime now," he said. Next, the ground personnel pulled the landing gear pin, then external power. "Okay, Colonel, do your stuff."

Coleman took a deep breath, then walked out onto the flight line reaching the readied warplane just before its boarding ladders were pulled down. He approach the Senior Chief, displaying his National Security Council aide's identification card. Over the whine of idled engines, Coleman explained that a "situation" has arisen and that he needed to give the two A-6 crewman a quick and private brief—two minutes max.

While Coleman climbed the port side boarding ladder, a second flight crew approached the readied A-6 and its ground personnel. Reaching the pilot, Coleman pulled a .45 semiautomatic giving clear, simple instructions: exit the aircraft, leaving all systems as is; if they failed to obey, then upon his signal, the two approaching crewmen would begin killing members of the ground crew, one by one; and after that, he added, he'd kill the pilot, then the B/N. At a moments hesitation, Coleman fired a round across the open cockpit, inches in front of the B/N's helmet.

That did the trick. Coleman descended the ladder keeping his pistol trained on potential threats. While the crew uncoupled and deplaned, Tanner inspected the centerline drop tank, ensuring pins were pulled from the loaded thousand pound bombs. As the new crew boarded and settled in, Coleman keeping his charge bunched tight, waited on Westin's thumbs up signal. When received, Coleman ordered the boarding ladders removed and the area cleared.

Once the canopy locked secure, Tanner told Westin he'd explain the cockpit upgrades later. For now, he advised strongly, just get through the alignment and takeoff checklists, and blast their butts outta here. Which John did, much to the consternation of Tower Control.

CHAPTER 38

STAKES

Los Angeles—7:40 P.M. Saturday (local)
Tsukuba, Japan—2:40 P.M. Sunday (local)

The thundering shock wave, now subsonic, rolls toward Mitsubishi Arms Works, Ohashi Plant. The machine shop, an older timber-framed building, lay centered within the giant Mitsubishi steel and concrete compound. At that moment, Tonoki Takara was feeling proud. He had just received a promotion to group leader of the machinist shop, and wondered how to surprise his wife, Mitsu...Timber blasts!...igniting a deafening roar. Nearby stores of torpedo ordnance explode into a superheated Hell. Tonoki's dilemma is short lived, as Death turns East and moves on...

Takara's mind refocused to his immediate surroundings; as usual, after drifting off into the Nagasaki nightmare, he felt an immense urge to crush something. He was at his Misawa Aerospace complex, seventy kilometers northeast of Tokyo. He left his desk, pacing, hands grasping the disfigured tin soldier. Finally he stopped.

Through his window front, Takara surveyed the huge aircraft bay facility some five stories below. His office sat perched on its perimeter like a box seat at an indoor stadium. Except this stadium was underground. Entirely. At its far end, a huge hydraulic elevator received various aircraft into the massive service bay. Window-fronted offices formed the bay's perimeter walls, Takara's being just below the ground above. On the bottom level, offices became machine shops and the like. Today, in various stages of service and retrofitting, Takara saw three aircraft parked throughout the massive bay.

He had come here to welcome Shimizu and his incredible accomplishment. Possessing a genetic virus and having the will to use it meant Japan need never again fear foreign military force. Coupled with being the world's economic leader, also meant Japan was poised for superpower status. Yet to execute its destiny, Japan needed the political will, Japan needed *Banto* leadership in the House of Councillors.

The stakes couldn't be higher. Takara returned to his desk, tossing today's newspaper into the trash can. The election was exactly seven days from today, and still the polls continued to spell doom for the LDP and especially for its secret *Banto* candidates.

After the White House debacle, *Shiro Kage*—White Shadow—had contacted Shimizu. The assassin ensured his aide that the assignment would be done by eight P.M. Saturday, Los Angeles time. Takara looked at his watch: two-forty. Considering the sixteen hour difference, that meant seven-forty, Los Angeles time. Within minutes, the arrogant United States would find itself in need of a new president, a much more suitable president.

Takara had to smile at that, then reached for a sheet of white bond. He placed the disfigured tin soldier upon the desk, then began listing the major points and concessions for the new President Dhillon S. Reed. They would comprise the core of the new President's speech unveiling a new policy toward Japan based on a "mutual" friendship. Presenting the speech three days before Japan's next Sunday's election would shift public opinion, allowing inadequate time for the opposition to effectively respond. *Banto* candidates would prevail. Japan would prevail.

"You're sure? Okay. Thank you." Dhillon Reed cradled the receiver softly. What's going on? It was the same voice, and it was deadly serious. Holy shit. He had signed on for political assassination, but...

The call came unexpectedly finding him in Chicago mixing business and pleasure. Reed began pacing the hotel suite's sitting room, nervous, analyzing his situation, considering the message's meaning: *President Dhillon Sawyer Reed.*

Ultimately, the thought his mind kept surfacing was, *How did it work?* The swearing in. Does the Supreme Court Chief Justice come to him, or vice versa? Well, he'd find out soon enough. His pacing took him to the closet. He opened the louvered doors slowly, almost reverently, as if receiving the light of grace from beyond. The suits. He stood pondering which one would best express deep grief as well as solid control in the tumultuous hours to come.

The conversation heard three days ago and various snippets since, allowed the assassin to piece together a very detailed picture of the President's itinerary. The group now heading for the elevator aside the building's exterior were scheduled to leave fifteen minutes before his target left. His senses now counted ten leaving. Eleven had arrived.

As the minutes elapsed, he assessed the enemy's position: two Secret Service men in the hall below him, one agent—a woman—at the elevator, and two attached personally to the target. These security personnel presented the greatest threat to his mission, to his escape. His devised a plan hinged around the woman at the perimeter elevator. She would hesitate, he knew, fearing the President's safety in her line of fire. But even with a plan, the assassin invariably expected the unexpected.

Teal Coro was in the Emerald Tower's pitch black crawl

space, the thirty-first floor level below. He'd circumvented hotel security, local police, the Secret Service, and even some of his FBI "colleagues."

During the last eight hours, he'd directed his mind away from his enemy, instead disappearing into a different reality: he'd become his environment, he'd become the wooden cross-braces amongst the ductwork. Throughout his slow stalk, he'd felt White Shadow's presence, now crouched just ten feet away, although he couldn't see in the pitch black. He slowly withdrew his shorter fighting knife, so close…so close to avenging the deaths of his wife and child, so close to killing this unearthly demon, this…

Time was near, the assassin could feel…*feel*. His entire body felt it, *haragei*, his sixth sense giving warning. Like a tightly wound highly elastic spring, he unleashed a *shuriken* over his left shoulder into the dark.

The Apache scout was there. Within ten feet, fighting knife drawn. The throwing star came without warning, at a time of distraction. And it found its mark. Coyote Shadow saw a billion stars burst in his head. He dropped the knife and reached up struggling for consciousness, finding a multi-pointed steel object lodged in his left eye! One point of the sharp carbon-steel had lodged deeply within the thick frontal bone above the eye. The rest of the star angled down across the blinded mass into his high cheekbone. Blood gouted soaking his face, his hand. With all his draining strength, he pulled frantically at the wicked leach. An eternity. Finally, it gave before he did. His eye was but a river of red.

"So, Mr. President," Glenn Thielken wound up his pitch, "you see why, ultimately, relaxing tensions with the Japs is good for American bus—"

The black-clad figure crashed through a ceiling panel, *katana* in his right hand, knife the other. He came falling between the President's entourage and just behind the two other Secret Service agents below. The near agents were at center hall advancing the President's and Thielken's way to the perimeter elevator.

Before touching the floor, he'd already selected his first targets: the two advance agents. The *katana* thrust down upon the farthest of the two, a powerful cut through the collar bone descending into to chest cavity and lungs. He touched the carpet lightly twisting gracefully like a ballet dancer, then buried the knife deeply into the turning second man's kidney, penetrating intestines.

As the agent at the elevator went inside her blazer, producing a machine pistol, a tossed smoke bomb flashed five feet in front of her.

The assassin spun, hurling a *shuriken* at the next most threatening target. It was the agent to the left of the President, now stepping forward to shield his charge, machine pistol leveled. The throwing star found its target, severing the agent's larynx and arterial artery. His gun discharged vainly. And there he was, the target. With lightening reflex, his arm coiled, *shuriken* in hand, the assassin unleashed death—

"Hummph!" His right shoulder caved, buckling his knees. It was the man in Washington, at the Metro station. Since then, he had searched his memory and now knew why this man had come. The assassin sprang like a large cat, regaining his balance, taking in the new threat. He saw a man with no shirt, knife clenched between teeth, and a red headband matching his coagulating left eye. In the other eye, he saw rage.

Temple watched Glenn Thielken go down, a metal star lodged deeply into the base of his skull. Coyote Shadow's impact had thrown off the assassin's last second release. Now Temple felt a fierce grip. The agent bringing up the entourage's rear grabbed him by the waist throwing him to the floor in the direction of the circular building's "doughnut-holed" stairwell.

Coyote Shadow removed the long knife from his teeth, posturing himself against the black-clad figure, compartmentalizing the pounding pain in his head. He watched the assassin begin a spinning back kick, then stop, deftly stepping to the side.

Tat tat tat! came a three-shot burst from the Ingram Model 11 held by the agent at the elevator. Seeing the woman step through the smoke and aim, the assassin had moved to put his assailant between him and the threat. The Apache went down.

The assassin quickly scanned the hall behind him. Seeing his target gone, he tossed another smoke bomb, then squatting low, bolted upward penetrating his original hole in the ceiling...and disappeared.

Tat tat tat...tat tat tat, reported more nine millimeter rounds. With the second man down, the elevator Secret Service agent riddled the ceiling over the hallway. She slapped a new magazine into the Ingram, then cursed her earphones, again. Unable to receive anything beyond the immediate thirty-first floor, and being the last person standing, she checked the downed intruder. Satisfied the man permanently down with a round in his bloodied eye, she ducked into the adjacent bedroom to alert the team by telephone.

From the crawl space, his hiding place for the last three day's, the assassin grabbed the equipment he would now need to execute his alternate escape plan. Emerging through the roof's access door and keeping to the shadows, he surprised and silently killed the two Secret Service agents standing sniper watch. Then swinging rope and hook, he landed the grapple secure atop the taller center tower, just fifty feet away.

With rope secured in hand, the assassin counted seconds as the elevator aside the center tower began its decent. Then he jumped, the timing of his pendulum swing calculated to intersect with the descending carriage. Contact! Like a spider, he glued himself against the sliding raindrop. Inside, a surprised woman screamed. He'd selected the express elevator from the penthouse restaurant. Twenty-five seconds later, the black spider leapt clear of the ground cowling, then spoke into a small cellular telephone.

CHAPTER 39

SELFLESS LOYALTY TO ONE'S LORD

Atsugi NAF, Japan—2:45 P.M. Sunday (local)

"Mister, you want to tell me what an aide to the National Security Advisor is doing on my base abetting in the theft of a military aircraft?" It was the Atsugi base commander, Captain/O-6 Norris Styles. Styles was in this Sunday afternoon to see his son off in the now hijacked A-6E just took off. As soon as the A-6E cleared the runway, Coleman demanded to see the base commander. Now five minutes later, .45 surrendered, he found himself flanked by two Marine guards in Style's rather self-flattering office—plaques and photographs of himself everywhere.

Styles had the look of a lawyer gone gung-ho pretending to be an admiral. He sported a salt-and-pepper flat-top, cautious blue eyes, and a thin, skeptical mouth that, to Coleman, looked as if it were about to spit out a bad peanut.

Considering the captain's question, Coleman's mind sort of wondered the same thing: How *had* he gotten into this mess? Coleman explained his special NSC project working with the Japanese. He explained the beating and narrow escape from Takara's retreat. He didn't get into STAIRCASE or the LIST. *The LIST.* Damn! After their escape, John never gave it back!

"Captain," came the speaker phone, "This is Airman Bensen in Base Ops Control. About that unauthorized A-6E take-off, think you better get up here." Styles fixed a long bitter look at the fatigued man before him, then blasted, "Lieutenant Colonel, right now you're an accomplice to a theft of a U.S. Government warplane. And you have my guarantee, Mister, if this turns to shit, so will you!"

Five minutes later, Captain Styles, Coleman and his Marine escort entered the Base Ops Control tower room. "Yes, Airman?"

"Tokyo ATC and Air SDF want to know what we're up to."

"So would I," snapped the captain.

"November Frank 506 bore a hole to four thousand straight over the bay, then turned northwest flight level six-zero."— six thousand feet.

Styles didn't hesitate. "Call Boci Cho—National Self-Defense Agency Headquarters. Get me General Muromoto, if you can." The Commander of Japan's Air SDF was not available this Sunday afternoon, but his new second in command was. Captain Styles explained the situation—as much as he knew of it.

At the Boci Cho, Admiral Kamikura terminated the line with Captain Styles. John Westin again, his mind grated. The last time he saw the American was aboard the *Yukikaze*. He still bristled as he thought of the day. His being forced to give Westin and that Commander Tanner such sensitive information on his NIQE-base weapons programs. It was Westin, he was sure, that stopped the program, a humiliating act, causing him, causing Japan to loose face. And now this reckless action by the American.

Kamikura mulled his options. Of all people, John Westin, gone berserk, now attacking Japan with a most deadly weapon.

Could anything be more fitting? It was his call, did he dare?

Admiral Kamikura punched in a line to the *Yukikaze* dockside at Japan's naval base at Yokosuka. He informed the captain of his intentions, then gave orders to the HVM-J2 Fire Control Officer: Load the Fire Control Computer with the aircraft descriptors: A-6E Intruder, and November Frank 506's tail number. Finally, he arranged for a real-time radar tracking link-up to the *Yukikaze*. Six minutes after his conversation with Captain Styles, the HVM-J2 and its NIQE mind called SAM, would launch.

Tsukuba (pronounced "scuba") is a city forty miles northeast of the northern fringes of Tokyo. This was John's destination as he took off from Runway 01, a direct route away from the Atsugi base, straight out over Tokyo Bay. But continuing that heading would have taken them east into the congested air traffic around the New Tokyo International Airport at Narita. Well over the bay, he turned to skirt Tokyo proper to the west. Now, still climbing passed five thousand feet into clear blue sky, they passed directly over the Yokohama Bay Bridge.

Driving an A-6 again. It felt strange and familiar at the same time. He was completely encapsulated: His helmet, green visor and oxygen mask encased his head. His entire body sat within layers of protective utility: green flight suit under a G-suit, along with a torso harness and survival vest. The rub of the ill-fitting G-suit and torso harness served as a painful reminder of Takara's hospitality, of his diabolical agenda.

"Unknown rider, unknown rider over Yokohama Bay Bridge, this is Atsugi Approach on guard. You are engaged in an unauthorized flight. You are intruding in restricted air corridors. You are instructed to return to Atsugi at once. Unknown rider. Do you copy?"

It was the radio, the U.S.N.'s Atsugi Naval Air Facility. Both men ignored the warning. As part of the takeoff checklist, Tanner had flipped the IFF to transmit and left it there, allowing their radar blip to show up on all air control radars.

Tanner, once again Westin's B/N—Bomber/Navigator—sat on Westin's right, recessed slightly lower and several inches back. At the moment, he had his face pressed against the black hood projecting from the instrument panel; by shielding extraneous light from the radar scope, the hood kept the loss of phosphor definition to a minimum. With his right foot, Tanner keyed the intercom system, the ICS, and said, "Boy howdy. Target rich today."

Now airborne for seven minutes, John concentrated on the aircraft, its feel, and the instrumentation, a couple of items new to him since he last flew the attack bomber in Nam. After takeoff, Tanner quickly explained the new gadgets, most of which were his to worry about. For John really, the A-6E's left side had changed little since the original A-6A and B versions; the radar repeater was gone, that was about it.

John leveled out at six thousand feet, now scanning the sky and the instrument panel: 390 knots true, 365 indicated, heading 300. He adjusted the bug on the HSI, the rotating compass ring, then allowed himself to relax a little within his new but still strangely familiar environment. Resting his left hand on the throttles—where his ICS button was—he keyed, "Some things never change…still feels sluggish with the load. More power though."

Tanner twiddled the knobs optimizing radar presentation and checked computer readouts, then raised his head glancing at the low urban sprawl. He knew what John meant. The Pratt & Whitney V-52 P8 engines developed eighteen thousand pounds of thrust, plenty enough to rip off the broad, swept wings should the pilot stress it so.

Then came the radio again.

Back at Atsugi Base Ops Approach Control, Coleman looked at it too. Everyone in the room stood glued to the radar scopes. A controller up in the Tower called in too: he'd made visual contact looking out the south-facing windows. A missile signature had appeared five seconds ago. It came from up the road, Japan's Naval base also in Yokosuka. It accelerated over Tokyo Bay, then turned to a northwesterly heading. Speed now 1200 knots. No one in the tower had ever seen anything like it. Coleman had.

Just before the missile appeared on the screens, Styles had ordered the controller to try making contact again, "Unknown rider, unknown rider, this is Atsugi Approach Control on guard. You are engaged in an unauthorized fli—"

While the others watched the radar screens, Coleman took two steps, then grabbed the headset from the speaking controller. "John, Japs got a missile in the air. Less than ten seconds ago. From Yokosuka. No active systems. Repeat. No act—"

Coleman found himself in a headlock, compliments of one of his Marine guards. The action chocked off any further words.

"Goddamnit, Mister! What was that about?"

"Sir, they've done nothing hostile toward Japan, not even a threat. I can't stand here and let the Japanese military shoot down an American plane, kill U.S. Navy personnel. I couldn't do that, sir." He couldn't let that LIST be destroyed either.

"Marine, restrain the prisoner," came Styles' response.

Over Tokyo Bay: The knowledge engineers thought of this NIQE-based surface-to-air missile as a *samurai*. One whose code of ethics, like the feudal warrior, was simple: Selfless loyalty to one's lord. The knowledge engineers "taught" SAM everything he knew. They "taught" *him* about existence, about time and three-dimensional space. They "taught" *him* about the abstract and the physical. The abstract *he* "learned" dealt with models: models of being, of relationships, numbers, quantity, quality, order, causation, events, change and power. The physical domain he "learned" described matter and/or energy, along with its properties and forms, structure, motion, and physics: electromagnetics, mechanics, nuclear, electricity and electronics.

They "taught" SAM about sensation: seeing, hearing, smelling, and how to sense infra-red heat and radar sources; they did not teach *him* about touch, taste, pain, or death. SAM

also "learned" about state of being, his state of being: awareness, attention, and now a "common sense"; *he* "learned" how
to reason, and if necessary, to make assumptions and decisions with incomplete information. They did not "teach" *him*
emotion, but they did "teach" *him* volition: They gave *him* will
and the "desire" to kill.

SAM's ramjet had ignited ramping up to full power; four
seconds into the flight, SAM jettisoned the "kick start" rocket
booster. SAM's "thinking" now tuned into the aerodynamics.
Like keeping one's balance, he felt stability at mach three, all
actuators and sensors functioning well. SAM's NIQE mind
recalled the target's trajectory and last position given to him
by the Fire Control Computer milliseconds before ignition,
and mentally projected the target forward by his elapsed flight
time—4.226 seconds. *He* veers northwest and activates *his*
carbon dioxide laser set to coarse beam for target detection.

Tanner sounded worried. "He saying what I think he's
saying? Like that video tape. Aboard the Yukikaze?" Tanner
keyed, remembering the awesome tactical advantage that the
NIQE-brained missile possessed.

"Uh-huh." John's mind raced.

"Holy shit, John! Means we got seconds at best. And it's
passive. We're blind."

Westin banked hard to the east toward Tokyo proper, then
said, "We got eyeballs, Stanner. Gotta be a smoke trail out
there. Right now, let's get it on the deck." Calling him Stanner,
brought Stan Tanner a momentary reflection: Back in Nam,
John always called him that when things got tight.

Over the Yokohama Bay Bridge: SAM's $NIQE_3$ mind
analyzed the laser reflections. It never occurred to the planners
to load a digital terrain map of greater Tokyo into SAM's
holographic memory. That would prove to be a problem.
Taking the target's last downloaded position, SAM's laser
field of view detected a total of thirty-three airborne solid
surfaces in that sector. SAM switched the laser to fine beam

"painting" their profiles. One second later, with the assistance of his holographic memory, SAM had a positive match on the A-6E's unique curved profile. Tracking the target descending into a mass of ground clutter, SAM throttled his ramjet down to sixty percent power for maneuverability.

West of Tokyo proper: "I make missile at twelve miles. Guessing 3100 knots," Tanner advised. One mile per second.

Westin's mind acknowledged; with its superior speed and sensor complement, SAM obviously had the advantage in any engagement. But even more, SAM's NIQE mind made him the perfect missile pilot, the ultimate *kamikaze*, as Admiral Kamikura had said. It was this trained intellect that consumed John's mind at the moment.

But nobody, or in this case, *no thing*, could keep a total advantage, his mind reasoned. Looking at strengths and weaknesses of the two adversarial systems, John's mind produced the one advantage his human-based system possessed: the ability to act unpredictability. To that end, John's first move was to put SAM into an unfamiliar environment: down and dirty within the cityscape.

"Two o'clock. Nine miles." Closure, 3275 knots. "Estimate intercept in...seven seconds."

John had pedal to the metal screaming 510 knots 250 feet over streets, low buildings, and parking lots. Within Tokyo, Shinjuku, one of several prominent business centers, was comprised of a tight cluster of skyscrapers—a modern day butt rising out over the low-roofed terrain below. John knew what he wanted, the New Tokyo City Hall. It looked as if constructed from an erector set, with its flanking twin towers reaching further out of the building to some eighty stories high. John veered left for the structure.

"City Hall now dead nuts, ETA four seconds," Tanner advised trying to contain his voice, "Missile now at our four o'clock. Intercept in three seconds. Two, one..."

SAMs visual sensors fed the last course change to his

NIQE processor brain. He recalculated an easy intercept. At .103 seconds his visual and infrared began to tell another story. His sixty degree intercept would occur just as the target passed between two obstructions. On this course, he would hit the near one instead of the plane behind it. SAM veered up and to the left. At 3130.89 knots, it would take him approximately fifteen seconds to recover and realign for another run.

"Three points! Missile veering to ten o'clock and high! Time to clean out my flight suit," Tanner said sounding relieved. Same ole John, he reflected, unpredictable as ice in a microwave. They'd threaded the tower goal post, shattered windows now showering down its sides to the streets below.

"It'll come back," Westin came back flatly, "Stay with it, Stanner. Tell me everything." John had the A-6 thundering east toward the Imperial Palace.

Ninety-five kilometers east-northeast: "Tsukuba Misawa Control, this is Gulfstream Serria three-oh-three. Forty-five kilometers east Tsukuba Misawa Control. Requesting a visual approach to a full stop."

"Serria three-oh-three, Tsukuba Misawa Approach Control. Clear for runway one-zero approach." It was the huge Misawa Aerospace's single runway. "Wind from southwest at ten knots."

"Roger Tsukuba Misawa Approach. Please advise Takara-san of our arrival."

"Roger, Serria three-oh-three. Will inform."

Westin came in at five hundred feet just north of the Imperial Palace grounds. SAM had bled off air speed, made his turn and came in aft to the skimming A-6E. John began making a right turn lining up on the Marunouchi district just east of the palace grounds.

"Fucker's got us," Tanner said, his head craning back to the right. "Five miles out. Back to 3100 knots, adjusting his course, but still got us: at our six o'clock, five o'clock. three o'clock." John completed his turn south approaching the Marunouchi District, headquarters of many of the companies belonging to both Misawa and Mitsubishi Groups. He let his altitude drop during the turn...300 feet.

Looking at the radar scope, Tanner gave situational status, "Christ. Looks like a steep gorge down there. Your comin' in too low. Two seconds to intercept."

Westin eased the stick forward, leaving altitude behind them. 175 feet.

Tanner ticked the remaining second, "Shit!" He looked up to the right. "Holy shit." It was the twenty-six story Tokyo Kaijo Building blurring by; they were half-way up—150 feet off the street below. To the left he could see the rooftop of an eight-story building. *Any lower, ace, and we'll hook streetlight number three!*

The knowledge engineers had never shown him anything like this. Flying low, yes. But not the narrow slits for canyons with vertical walls. And the pilot knew this environment, possessing a high proficiency rating, SAM estimated.

When the A-6 made its turn dropping low, SAM anticipated the use of these tall structures as shields. He'd scanned forward for a shorter structure behind which the target could not hide. Given position, direction and speed between him and his quarry, he'd selected an eight-story building forward of his target's projected flight path.

SAM's visual sensor reported the A-6 emerging into view. He calculated 410 knots, accelerating, descending! SAM computed a new intercept. Possible, barely. He increased power to his ramjet and zeroed in. 0.682 seconds.

Behind the Kaijo building, John had pushed the throttles to the max still dropping more altitude. Tanner warned of the wall at the long street's end—the steel and mirror-glassed New Misawa Building. Right now all Westin wanted was shielding on his right side. That meant buildings, the lowest coming up fast being just eight stories—ninety feet.

"There!" Tanner pointed at the exhaust trail approaching one-third mile to the west, vectored to pass just inches over the Mitsubishi Syoji Building. "We're too high!"

At 430 knots, the racing peripheral buildings tunnelled vision even more. Westin fought the distortion pushing the stick farther still, descending. 110 feet…100…90…

"Jeeesus," Tanner bellowed into his oxygen mask. Looking up through the Lexan canopy, he saw—no, felt—the apparition scream by three feet above the canape. Then feeling the plane begin to pitch up and left, he looked forward into the mirrored glass of the New Misawa Building straight ahead.

Time became a whisper as John and the other A-6 closed on each other at 440 knots, eighty feet off the deck. The mirrored building before him reflected more than a closing A-6. It reflected his son and young grandson, Jeffery; it reflected himself who now would stop at nothing to destroy that Misawa plane, to destroy STAIRCASE.

Pulling hard left, he pitched the wings vertical trying to gain clearance between the airframe and the building. The A-6 rocked the eastern side of the building, again shattering mirrored windows with thundering exhaust. *Bad luck for someone*, his mind ticked, but still not relaxing.

Leveled out again, Tanner got another fix. "Fat lady's still singing. It's at our ten o'clock, turning in back toward us." John fought for a little altitude, then banked hard right heading south. One more chance?

SAM finally learned: No intercept angles. Come in dead aft giving the pilot nowhere to hide. He didn't have the fuel for another miss. This time he would be sure and deadly. SAM recomputed an aft intercept: 10.552 seconds. The angle was small already since coming out of the corridor, the A-6 had veered to the same heading, then turned south.

"By the bay, see the tall building with a hole in it?" John directed over the ICS. John pointed to the award-winning architecture of the forty-story Kaisha Building, designed in the shape of a tall rectangular doughnut with a slim thirty story rectangular hole in its middle. "The building beyond. Whatdaya got on IR?"

"Two tall buildings. The one behind and to the side has a lot IR coming off its western side—mirrors, sun's reflection, I think. Missile's still on us." Closure, 2620 knots. Seven seconds to intercept.

"Good," John said already half-way to the building. "Hang on." He knew the NIQE processor would have learned by now, learned too much. He had one last hairbrained maneuver to show it. He lined up the A-6E twenty degrees off the doughnut hole's center axis, that put SAM on the same heading. He didn't want SAM seeing him pop out the other side—*or smashing into the internal façade either.*

"Two seconds to intersect." John banked a quick left twenty degrees, straightened to thread the needle coming up fast, faster. Aligning. High center axis. Nothing but building filled their view, and hole before them. Finally, aligned. John jerked the stick, rolling the wings vertical with a jolt. The rotating fifty-three foot wingspan rolled to within inches of building's face...Cleared.

Straining in his harness, Tanner counted down. " Contact."

Screaming out of the hole, John veered right, then pulled the throttles full back, cutting thrust to idle engines, risking a flame out. The word still echoed, *Contact.*

But there was none. John slammed throttles forward to full Military Rated Thrust, glanced to his left, while fighting to keep the iron bird out of the bay below.

It worked. As SAM emerged from the hole, his visual sensor reported two symmetrical A-6 images. Infrared indicated massive heat around the left A-6, minimal heat to the right. SAM veered left bare milliseconds before the kill. Microseconds before intercept, SAM realized the anomaly: visual sensors reported the A-6's image rippling, rippling in the reflective windows. A decoy. Instantly, he gimbaled fins one and three to max. Too late. Before crashing into the building's far corner, SAM had one last NIQE thought.

CHAPTER 40

LONG DISTANCE

Los Angeles—7:56 P.M. Saturday (local)
Over Tokyo, Japan—2:56 P.M. Sunday (local)

"Goddamnit! What is that man up to?" When above the ground clutter of the radar screens, Captain Styles and the others had just watched the A-6 dodge a bullet. It was impressive, but now phones began ringing: Why is an American warplane strafing Tokyo, shooting missiles into buildings? At least the buildings were empty, Styles figured, this being Sunday.

Coleman snapped to attention, ramrod straight, then boomed, "Sir, request permission to call President Temple." That got a double-take, just what Coleman wanted. "It's imperative he get certain information. Information, as you can see, sir, the Japanese do not want out of their hands."

"What kind of information?"

"Career limiting information," Coleman paused looking Styles dead in the eye, "Sir." The next one to speak, Coleman knew, would lose. It took sixty eternal seconds.

"I don't think so, Mister."

"You stay clean either way. It'll take two calls. I'll take the heat."

Styles paused boring hard into Coleman implacable brown eyes, then spoke to Coleman's guard. "Petty Officer, two calls, then put him back under restraint."

With cufflinks removed, Coleman said, "First call's to that A-6 out there." The captain glowered, then grudgingly, nodded to the responsible controller. Coleman slipped on a headset, then asked the controller if the conversation would be recorded. Getting an affirmative, Coleman began, "November Frank 506. This is Lieutenant Colonel J. T. Coleman at Atsugi Base Ops Control. Do you copy? Over."

Recognizing Coleman's voice, Westin responded, "Thanks good buddy for the heads up."

"John, got to make this quick. You never gave back the LIST. I need the names. Pull it out and read them off, now."

John understood. A crash and burn wouldn't leave much of a LIST to read. He set a course northeast, then reached inside his flightsuit. Found and opened, John scanned...*Holy Shit!* Key businessmen, Senators...a Cabinet member...and *Jesus H*.! Each name included a title and international telephone number. John handed the LIST to Tanner with instructions, "Kill IFF, then read the names to Coleman. Nothing else, just names. Make it fast."

Standard emergency procedure always called for getting the President to safety. Usually that meant far away from the scene as quickly as possible, especially after an assassination attempt. Temple exited the garage elevator surrounded by a human wall of agents. This floor of the hotel's parking garage had been cordoned "off limits" to the public; even so, men with guns drawn were everywhere.

Temple found himself stuffed into a limousine along with an aide. With a "clear" signal from the street, Secret Service special agent in charge Bob Upton jumped in the front seat and directed all motorcade vehicles to stomp on it. As soon as the screeching limo exited the underground garage, the secure telephone buzzed.

It was the chairman of the Joint Chiefs. He was in the Pentagon tending to TALON'S GRIP. The general had yet to hear of this latest assassination attempt, and Temple chose for the moment to let it ride for now. Earlier, interrupting the light dinner, the general had briefed him on the good and bad news from the mission: the SEALs and three hostages were out, approaching Kuwait; the bad news had been that the SEAL Team's leader was killed in action, and five helpless hostages had earlier been executed outright. The Israeli team leader had been shot, but was still alive; the rest escaped in a separate helicopter—no word. The dinner time brief indicated no word on STAIRCASE.

Now the general on the line had an update, more good news, bad news: the Israeli team escaping in a borrowed helicopter took a missile just short of the Turkish border. NATO observers witnessed the fireball. No survivors, they assured.

All indications were that the lab and STAIRCASE were destroyed; but one of the hostages, the general had learned, appeared to have some information on that. She wasn't in the SEAL debrief though; left with the local CIA man shortly after arrival. "Anything else?"

Temple listened, hearing about the tiff stirred up by the SEALs. Seems they "borrowed" a plane with Iran's highest Islamic leader aboard, none other than Ayatollah Rashani; they were in route to Switzerland, taking his son to school. Temple assured the general that he could well handle that one, then thanked him and his team for a job well done.

Temple turned to his aide and gave instructions, "Make sure Prime Minister Maklef receives my deepest regrets." Temple observed their limo entering a freeway ramp and felt now maybe Upton had time to give him an update. "Bob, how bad?"

SAC Upton turned to speak. "Not good, Sir. Nelson and

Timms are dead, and James wounded. The attacker's location is currently unknown. The second man, the one without a shirt, we don't know who he is."

"Sir," the aide broke, holding the secure line, "Lieutenant Colonel Coleman in Japan. Urgent."

CHAPTER 41

Forty-Eight Years

Los Angeles—7:58 P.M. Saturday (local)
Tsukuba, Japan—2:58 P.M. Sunday (local)

"Gentlemen," came the Gulfstream's pilot, "Please buckle up. We should be on the ground in three minutes."

Shimizu moved from the crushed velour couch to a leather seat, then buckled up. *Three minutes*, echoed within his mind. Four hours ago he had contacted Takara. Takara had found General Rashid's surprising comments most interesting. *Your star is rising*, Shimizu indulged. Discovering Westin's Iranian connection, and of course successfully negotiating the STAIRCASE deal, securing it aboard this aircraft cinched it. Takara seemed most pleased.

Shimizu now thought he understood the importance of STAIRCASE. The stakes were indeed higher than he'd ever dreamed. For Japan's possessing STAIRCASE would now allow it to stand equally with the United States. And with Japan's superior development in NIQE-based weapons technology, Japan could assert herself again. In his gut, he knew Takara would not hesitate. Japan would not hesitate.

The missile attack had cost them precious minutes they did not have. Still, as far as missions go, it didn't look too difficult: Fly to Tsukuba and circle waiting for their Misawa Gulfstream 4 to arrive on landing approach. Since the A-6 had no cannon, they'd let it to land then drop ordnance.

With the IFF switched off, their presence from air traffic controller screens had disappeared. Now Tanner flipped the ALR-67 radar switch from transmit to standby. The terrain picture disappeared from his hooded scope. From now on, he would depend on visual and his FLIR, the forward-looking infrared system being totally passive, emitting nothing.

Preflight planning and approach plates would have made this cake, Tanner thought. He'd grabbed a couple of aerial photographs fished out of a bottom drawer back at the office. That, and a set of quick coordinates pulled off a chart, were all the navigation aids he had. He keyed in the target coordinates into the computer, then arranged the photos on his kneeboard trying to compare them with the scene sliding by below at 360 knots. One mile every ten seconds.

Tanner found the rail line heading northeast, wishing he had access to local TACAN navigation aid frequencies. Now to identify the towns punctuating its path. He thought that last town was Toride where another railway headed north, farther he matched a spur to the southeast with the photograph. "Got a fix," Tanner said on the ICS, "I think. To verify, John, let's keep this heading down the tracks. We should find Lake Kasumigaura ten miles up. There'll be a fair sized town on its western shore. If I'm right, at the town, you'll come to 270."

One minute and thirty seconds later Tanner saw the lobster claw-shaped lake approaching, along with the town of Tsuchiura. "Bingo. Come to 270 in five seconds. John made the turn west. "Tsukuba, ten miles this heading." Tanner was looking for Tsukuba now, seeing only a few heat-producing IR returns: a power plant and a few factories stood out of the mostly wooded landscape below.

John scanned the sky and the instrument panel. His mind drifted to Takara, the lock of hair, and what the bitter man had said, *This should compensate nicely*. John thought of his son, Stewart, and his grandson, little Jeffery...and then his father. What had Takara said about his father?: *"Ironic isn't it. You kill Kojima forty-eight years to the day after your father raped his mother."* John's mind cringed at that, then something clicked *to the day* he and Kojima...What day? August third. But dad's service record said he had the accident on...August first. Before the rape! "Damn!" he said into the oxygen mask, then, inexplicably, he thought of Beth.

Strangely, he no longer felt anger. He was as calm inside as he had ever been, more so inside a cockpit. There was no room for emotion now, only the mission and its singular objective.

"Tsukuba in ten seconds. The Misawa complex and air field should be out on its northwest edge." Flying at five thousand feet, John made the necessary adjustments. "There, on the taxiway! And it's got a high tail configuration. Can't make out the tail number, though."

John "unloaded" the A-6 exchanging altitude for air speed. They came in hot at a thousand feet. "Got it," Tanner yelped. On the approach, Tanner had locked the computer reticle on the infrared scope to the heat source emanating from the jet's twin rear engines. When John visually confirmed the tail number, Tanner knew he had them. "Infrared's got a lock. Ready for a run."

The infrared images were from a sensor mounted on a turret on the bottom of the aircraft's nose, immediately in front of the nose-gear door. Now, with the help of the inertial, the computer would keep the cursors on the target, and slaved to the cursors, the infrared would continue to track. Tanner did a final track with the laser range-designator, checked the information the computer received as valid, then stepped the system into attack.

"Roger attack mode." Westin began a fifteen mile sweep lining up for the run.

• • •

The Gulfstream seemed dwarfed on the gigantic elevator platform. Remote cameras on the surface showed the plane in position. After receiving a "clear" signal from ground personnel, the elevator operator engaged the hydraulics beginning the platform's descent.

Informed of their approach, Takara came down from his office to personally welcome Shimizu and take delivery of his precious consignment. As he stood watching the aircraft descend, he looked at his watch, then wondered if President John Adam Temple was now history.

Westin lined up the A-6E at two thousand feet coming in from the northeast now four miles out. Tanner struggled with the slew stick trying to keep the computer cursors precisely on the infrared target, a reading decreasing in magnitude. Again, he turned up the magnification. "Something's wrong here. Losing picture. It's there, but—"

"Go for last known position. Then we'll assess another run."

The laser in the nose turret gave the computer precise range and angular information which showed up on the Analog Display Indicator immediately in front of John. Coming in at 360 knots true, his job now was to center his steering commands on the ADI. In the blink of a eye one mile out, Westin saw the problem. A huge square hole in front of a small hanger. It was closing now.

Bomb release.

Takara almost wished the American, John Westin, were here to see this.

Overhead doors sliding to meet each other, narrowed the slit of daylight angling onto the bay floor where Takara now stood. The descending aircraft neared the bottom fifth story, its starboard access door already open. Takara watched Shimizu step out, his face characteristically Japanese in its stern expression. But the pride was there, Takara could tell.

But not for long. The computer released four 1000 SnakeEye Retarded bombs from the centerline drop tank at the precise time required for its trajectory to intersect on the physical point represented by the target blip chosen by Tanner's cursor placement. That point turned out to be eighteen inches off center of the elevator's now closing overhead doors.

All well within the combined margin of error as three of the four SnakeEyes screamed through the waning open slot.

One hit the fuselage of a Boeing 707 parked behind where Takara stood. The concussion rocked the enclosed bay, shattering every window, slamming aircraft, equipment, and people against floors and walls. Like a wind-torn shingle, Takara's body catapulted toward the Gulfstream, landing and rolling under the descended hydraulic platform. Simultaneously, with two more hits, jet fuel and hydraulic fluid reservoirs ignited, feeding an enormous fireball ballooning to fill every corner of the bay. Combined, the fiery explosion thundered upward heaving the above ground skyward, leaving a fifteen acre hole and few survivors.

With the infrared still slaved to the cursors, the nose turret continued to gimbal attempting to track the designated target. Tanner watched the picture on the infrared display glow super-white as the A-6 passed over the target.

"Think we wore out our welcome, John."

"Whatcha got on the radar?"

Tanner flipped the ALR-67 radar switch from standby to transmit. "Holy motherfuckin' shit."

CHAPTER 42

ALONGSIDE YOUR ADVERSARY

Los Angeles—8:05 P.M. Saturday (local)
Tsukuba, Japan—3:05 P.M. Sunday (local)

"Where?" asked Westin.

"Eight from the south, twenty miles. Four northwest, twenty miles. Two west, forty miles. Expect the reception's in our honor."

"Kill the radar." They were being tracked on a southwest heading. As soon as Tanner hit "Standby," Westin took her down into a valley, banked hard right setting a course for the only unoccupied point on the compass. East. "So Stanner, if a dog's front legs are going forty miles an hour, how fast are the back legs going?"

"Haulin' ass," came the B/N's reply. For these two men, the joke was a ritual, bleeding off tension, putting mortality in perspective. "Estimate feet wet in three minutes." Pacific Ocean. Then what?

Hauling ass was what Westin was doing: treetops at 514

indicated. Treetops quickly gave way to choppy water. Westin eased her down fifty feet above Lake Kasmuigaura, then up and over the peninsula. "Feet wet. Where we goin'?"

"Beats the shit outta me. You're the navigator," John tossed out, now climbing off the deck to lessen their rapid fuel consumption. "Turn it on, Stanner. Long enough to see what we got."

Tanner acknowledged, then reported, "Bogies on our tail, ten miles aft and closing."

Must be Japanese Air SDF F-16s, John figured. Fighters against an attack-bomber. Well, *no regrets—*

"Twelve miles, for what it's worth," Tanner advised as they passed Japan's extended territorial boundary. "Wait a minute—"

"November Frank 506. This is Devil 2 from the *USS Independence*. How do you read?"

"We copy, Devil Two," John replied flatly, not sure what to make of this.

"November Frank 506, we are ten miles out at your two o'clock. Proceed course one-one-zero to our location. *Independence* will guide you in on from there on 363.2 frequency. Me and the boys'll stick around and apologize to your host for you two leaving so soon. Seems you got friends in high places, buddy. You require any other assistance?"

"Devil Two, *Independence* sounds just fine. Thanks guys," John acknowledge with relief. But on another level, the word *independence* resonated awkwardly in his mind. Indeed, it no longer sounded "just fine." Especially now as an alluring image of Elizabeth Thorngill Storey worked its way into his anxious mind.

The first tie was much too bright. In front of the gilded-edged mirror, Dhillon Reed worked the second one. Striving for the perfect knot, he again cinched the silk snugly to the collar. *Perfect.* Maroon and gray strips against a crisp white shirt and the dark charcoal suit. *President Dhillon S. Reed* couldn't hide the satisfying smile now taking his face.

Yet, the knock at the door caught him by surprise. It was

almost ten-thirty, Chicago time. Must be his Secret Service detail come to give him the tragic news. He removed his suit coat draping it carefully over the back of a chair, then opened the door *to his future*.

"Sorry to disturb you, Sir." Reed looked at four very serious men flanked by his two Secret Service men. "My name is Clarance Taggat, head of the FBI's Chicago Field Office. These men are special agents. May we come in?"

Of course. He hadn't thought about increased security. Reed invited them in. Immediately, two of the men moved through the four-room suite.

"What's going on here?" Reed demanded.

"Uh, Sir, via executive order from President Temple, FBI Director Kendall has instructed me to detain you and others pending a formal warrant due within the hour."

Blood drained from Reed's wooden face. Then composing himself nicely, he asked, "Did I hear you correctly?" Reed challenged.

"Sir, those are my orders," Taggat replied, wishing the Vice President were in someone else's town right now.

"On what basis, Mr. Taggat? What is the charge?"

"As I was told by the director, Sir, the initial charge will be under 18 US Code 871, threatening the life of the President of the United States."

"What!"

"Sir, there's been an attempt on the President's life—"

"Oh my God."

"And, he has reason to believe you were involved."

"Dhillon! What's going on?"

The FBI man responded, "Sorry to disturb you, Mrs. Thielken, but I've been instructed to inform you that under 18 US Code 871..."

Outside the Bonaventure, under the shadows of illuminated palm trees, the assassin had silently approached the last cab in a long waiting line, stabbed its driver, then proceeded to the 110 Freeway south. His Washington contact had provided two items critical for his a back-up plan: first the Secret Service's emergency plan, and second, an assistant.

It was the assistant he called just two minutes ago. He'd timed it perfectly for just ahead he could see flashing lights everywhere—the fleeing motorcade heading for the President's helicopter's staging site.

Passing Firestone Boulevard. *Any time now.*

"Calling agent-in-charge, Upton. This is Helo One, just above you," came a more than concerned voice over the radio. Secret Service special agent Bob Upton, sitting in the front seat of the President's limousine, acknowledged. Upton was nervous. This had been agent Jim Rhode's assignment—until four days ago. Rhodes was dead, but in some twisted way Upton now resented him for it. Upton didn't know the nuances of this trip's security plan, and in his heart of hearts, he knew he was no Jim Rhodes. "Sir," the L.A.P.D. officer came back, "Accident ahead. South-bound traffic's beginning to back up."

What to do now? And quickly. Upton pulled out his folded map, studied the marked routes, knowing he had seconds to make a decision. He depressed the microphone's transmit button, and gave orders, "Okay. Take Imperial, proceed south on Western Avenue until 110 clears, then guide us to the next entrance ramp resuming the planned route. Keep me informed."

"Copy that. Will advise all L.A.P.D. detailed."

The assassin's cellular phone rang, he listened, broke the connection, then speeding up, took the nearer Century Boulevard exit. Reaching Western Avenue, he ran the red light, hooking a hard left. Barreling down Western, the stolen taxi ran another red light almost clipping a beat-up station wagon—someone's "mobile" home.

The plan was simple: ram the President's limousine, the middle one. Then do what it took to see his target dead. Even if he, himself, must die. For such was the way of *ninjutsu* teaching: far better for a warrior to die with honor, than to live with dishonor—failure.

Three blocks ahead, he saw the first motorcycles pulling over to a stop to block southbound traffic. The President's limo would be a hundred meters behind, he knew; he slowed a little timing his impact. He hadn't look in his rear view mirror.

What?...in the street! People! Ten or more, just milling around. He braked and swerved angling a path with the fewest bodies...skidding...broadside into a parked car. Miraculously, he'd hit no one from the scattering crowd. He looked ahead. Just a block and a half! He saw the first of three limousines appear, slowing to make its left south on Western. He restarted the cab's engine, stomping the accelerator.

Crash! It came from behind. A car smashed into the driver's side door at an angle, buckling metal twelve inches inward toward the steering wheel. Pinned between the cars, the assassin kicked out the cab's windshield, grabbed his *katana*, then leaped to the hood.

Coyote Shadow jumped out of his car's door flung open. He'd submerged his head in a fountain, before stopping a motorist commandeering his car. Two of the spikes of the four-pointed metal star had anchored into bone, above and below the eye, bridging the eye itself. He'd pulled his red headband tight over the rent eyebrow suppressing its bleeding. Now he had vision, albeit limited vision between swollen tissue and irritation. He'd lost his fighting knife in the confusion. As for the bullet from the female Secret Service agent, it had grazed his temple, temporarily rendering him unconscious. Now, what pain his wounds generated, he accepted, allowing it to pass through and out his body.

It was back at the hotel, while on the hallway floor, that Grandfather's voice returned to speak to him. He'd been in the crawl space above the thirty-first floor for eight hours, stalking the assassin. During those hours, he'd directed his mind away from his enemy's powerful senses...until the end. It was then that his thoughts had surfaced, thoughts of his wife, child, and revenge. That's when it happened, the assassin feeling his presence. Now, he knew what the owl's presence meant. And the meaning of his Grandfather's distant words, "Pains from your past work alongside your adversary."

That was behind him now as Coyote Shadow looked at his adversary standing on the taxi cab's hood. For the only thing Coyote Shadow possessed at this moment was the present. He had no past. Had no future. Had nothing to lose. And there was nothing more dangerous on the planet than a man with nothing to lose.

The assassin flicked a poison-coated *shuriken*. Coyote Shadow focused an eternity onto its flight directed at his throat. The feint seemed so casual as spinning death sailed within an inch of his neck. Two more. Like comets glistening in the street's light, they headed for his chest. Coyote Shadow pivoted his body allowing one to buzz by, and deflected the second with his long knife's blade. Then the night turned nova bright, from the flash-bang tossed by the black-clad figure.

The assassin turned looking for another car, anything to get at the escaping President. *Haragei*. He spun around to find the Indian on the hood of the parked car he'd skidded into. For an eternity, eyes fixed like locked swords, unyielding. Yet, strangely, each man acknowledged their common ground. The Japanese bowed slightly, then withdrew the *katana* holding it one handed, high like a batter; in his left hand angled outward across his chest, he held a short blade. Coyote Shadow tightened his headband, then drew his bowie knife gripping it in ice-pick fashion.

In the moment, the assassin—*Shiro Kage*—glanced up the street and beyond. The last of the presidential motorcade had just passed; patrolmen now sped away, their blocking duties complete. He turned back to the man responsible for that, then seethed, "American, you have chosen a violent death."

The assassin instinctively deferred to the most basic of *ninjitsu* training from the *Go Rin No Sho* and its four hundred years of refinement. He now accepted death and thought only of cutting his enemy. Using *Chinese Monkey's Body*, elbows and *katana* close to the body, he moved in quickly.

The night crushed in on itself as things mortal stepped back. Blades clashed, muscles tensed, strengths measured, all while feet tested the support beneath.

With *katana* and long knife locked, the assassin's free short blade blurred upward toward the Indian's under-jaw. Coyote slammed down on the approaching blade's hilt, catching it with the leading edge of his forearm. Instinctively, Coyote's free hand seized the deflected wrist, forcing its grasped blade inward toward the black form's own solar plexus. Gritting his teeth, the assassin growled, pressing his strength, finally stopping death's determined advance.

For an instant in time, veins ribboned throughout severe bodies, as muscles flexed in perfect opposition. Hot breath and sweat. Strain and guttural language assaulted the still night, each man reaching deep for power, power only a master could know.

With awesome strength in his arms, using the *katana*'s square hilt against the opposing knife's, the black form lifted his enemy off his feet, hurling him off the car's hood. Like a hawk, the powerful black form leapt after his fallen prey.

Coyote reacted to the moving shadow cast from above: dropping flat to the ground, he reversed momentum rolling back toward the car's grill. The assassin soared overhead, tucked and rolled one revolution, then sprung like a cat, *katana* at Lower attitude. Simultaneously, Coyote bolted toward the spinning apparition, seeking to crowd in on the *katana*'s reach. His knife crashed against fine Japanese steel, a powerful thrust up to the hilt forced the blade to the side; simultaneously, his other hand found the other forearm, gripping it fiercely.

Even though the assassin's sword was effective in all situations, his foe continued to diminish its advantage by moving close in—a counter-intuitive strategy. The assassin repulsed the Indian with the *air-sea change*, breaking the deadlock, achieving distance, regaining his *katana*'s advantage. Sizing:

Enough: Without raising his sword, the assassin deftly avoided the Indian's next strike, a move designed to show an expert's contempt for his untrained attacker. In the exchange, Coyote caught a glint of his enemy's eye, flat portals devoid of emotion yet laughing at him derisively. It was then, he realized that until this moment this ancient form simply toyed with him, measuring.

The assassin whirled away, deftly positioning the streetlight's glare, temporarily washing out his foe's vision. The assassin now defined the battle, and just as importantly, the battlefield. He moved to embrace the darkness—*Shinobi iri*. Coyote saw the moving shadow, yet didn't.

From behind, a blade laterally sliced the thick night air. Coyote Shadow instantly collapsed his body, rolling over. Drawing up his legs, timing. With both feet, he exploded a kick upward at the unseen enemy. He found a solid mass, heard a grunt, then pain seared through both his calfs. The assassin's reaction with the short blade was instantaneous. He'd chosen to exchange a blow to his sternum for a chance to slash his enemy's lower legs. Two crimson ribbons now caught the light arcing like fireworks cascading earthward.

Immediately Coyote sprung to his feet, testing his legs. Then came the blow, unhumanly fast. He was flung back staggering, as if by an explosion. The *katana* again. Coming down.

Coyote stepped aside, watching honed steel descend centimeters from his face. He kicked an exposed knee, then parried the short blade aimed at his now extended leg. Both Titans went down into a blinding struggle.

Across the asphalt, they twisted like entwined rattlesnakes, hissing, blades glistening in the artificial street light. The assassin broke the deadlock, only to receive a blow on the side of his head. With his own body laying on his *katana*, the assassin's short blade now arced. The Indian instinctively raised his knife, though unsure of the point of attack; his vision seemed more blurred. Coyote's knife made contact with steel, then discontinuing the parry, he twisted its blade, and raked hard. He found tendons, cleanly severed across the Japanese's left wrist; the short blade fell from extending fingers.

The man-shaped figure leapt away to a crouched position, *katana* in right hand, the other streaming red. Then it became a blur, driving in again, then…gone.

Coyote raised up on one knee, the blow came to the back of his head, from powerful coiled feet. His ears reverberated with the slow snap of a splintering tree, his own neck. Then again. He was totally unprepared for the violent onslaught. The knife in his hand seemed to weigh as much as the ingot which had borne it. *Where was he?*

The next blow hit him just as he staggered crouched to his feet. He heard a sickening crack within his body, and sensed a partial loss of control of his left arm. Collarbone. It was like a dream, no human could be so powerful, so relentless.

With all his strength, Coyote Shadow leapt to his feet. He did not want this unworldly figure to see injury, weakness, fatigue.

Then they were close, very close, Coyote had his first good look into the assassin's eyes. It was but an instant, but in that instant, he peered into a window, a window to the ancient past. His concentration wavered. Almost contemptuously, the Japanese flicked at Coyote's knife with his own weapon, leaving no time to react. The killing machine slashed the retreating cheek, hot blood flowed crimson.

Coyote saw the Japanese's lips move. He vaguely understood the power being evoked: hypnotic, invisible action (*saiminjutsu*). Yet understanding and resisting were two different things. His arms felt enormously heavy, appendages made from lead. He jerked his head as a strike almost slipped through.

Lips still moving, exploding with power, the onslaught was merciless. Viciousness from a dark past. His black pupils enlarged, darkening the night. Coyote managed to repulse the sentient tempest, yet backing up giving ground.

He staggered back against the car. *How had he gotten here, so turned around?* He scrambled up onto its flat hood. Again, the ungodly thing was there, the attack more ferocious.

He seemed not able to feel his legs, he fell. His fingers were numb, his grip faltering. He saw the raised *katana* glisten against the streetlight beyond.

The assassin slashed again. Across Coyote Shadow's chest, blood sparkled the night. His blood. He watched as the Katana raised high now came down for the final blow. Agony filled him and it seemed as if he could not breathe…

…*could not breathe*…and then his mind found itself in the airless confines of the superheated sweatlodge. From the orange-red rocks amid the blackness, he watched the shimmering spirit scout appear, then transform before him…into a large, powerful, yellowish-gray beast. Wildcat. Coyote Shadow looked deep into the exquisite animal's large amber eyes, their vertical brown slits revealing. Himself, a primal self. The animal's spirit moved toward him, eyes closer, melding with his, becoming one. Him moving within the untamed beast, the untamed beast within him…

In a blur, Coyote's torso bucked. With superhuman power and ferocity, he lunged up at his foe and the descending sword. His fingers arched like claws dug into the crouched form's throat, ripping at skin, the larynx. The assassin lost balance and the power behind his downward thrust, then grabbed for his exploding throat.

Blood spurted wet, covering them both. The assassin threw himself back, now standing stunned. He saw the amber eyes of an enraged animal, slits to an eternity. On the car's hood, he saw not a man, lunging; but a powerful cat gone rabid, horrifically screaming with forearms extended, claws of death.

Wild, cornered, the animal attacked ferociously with violence beyond comprehension. His strength appalling, even to the assassin. The assassin felt engulfed by a frenzied assault not borne of this civilized world, intensity over thought, crashing his senses, threatening orientation. Under the frantic onslaught, he fell back against the windshield, *katana* poised.

He slashed laterally at the airborne beast. Fresh blood. It kept coming…for the throat. Its two hands clawing, grabbing both forearms, like vices, bursting veins, crushing cartilage. The *katana* fell from his paralyzed hand. Teeth punctured the left side of the struggling black figure's neck, like steel pincers, finding the carotid artery, savagely biting, severing the blue life line. Thick ink-black liquid fountained, like a severed fuel line whose pump continued to labor.

The assassin let out a guttural sound, resonating millions of years into a primordial past. He fought like a demon, finally twisting himself on top. Blood gouted everywhere, it smelled of salt and copper. He managed to free his right hand, then lunged three-fingers—*shime waza*—into the throat of the savage beast.

The animal screamed, struggling wildly, the black form's power undiminished. Slippery blood was everywhere, preventing a solid grasp on the death grip now strangling air.

The two forms thundered, twisted, clawed. Finally, the Indian found himself atop the black monster, its fingers still ripping at his throat. Then with both hands he lurched fingers into the two holes of the matte-black hood. Finding the inhuman eyes, he dug deeper, pinching, seizing hold from the inside skull. The vice-grip lifted the struggling head, then with powerful blows, smashed it against the car hood, again, again…and again. Until strangling fingers released their hold. Falling limp.

Continuing to pin his prey with superhuman strength, the animal with the brown-slitted amber eyes raised its head over the kill. He watched the ink-black fountain turn to a slow stream, life draining from a primordial body. He watched for an eternity.

The brown slits in the wildcat's eyes began to widen, fading the amber, until the link with the primal mind passed to another dimension. Coyote Shadow's heart pounded as the surging thoughts of defeat finally passed.

He reached down and pulled the black-matte hood from the assassin's face. He watched dark eyes glower against a face turned ashen, life taking leave. He watched blood gurgle in a mouth unable to speak. And finally he understood the question forming in the assassins eyes now veiling with death. The answer echoed a universe, which in that instant of time, seem much more than benign.

"Apache."

Then with the blade of his knife, reaching down, Coyote Shadow took his first scalp.

"What the fuck, man," came a voice from a car just arrived. The Apache turned to watch a young man emerge, strutting with purpose through the now gathering crowd. Two of his pals were trying to keep up with the anger in his stride. He carried an AK-47.

A bloodied Teal Coro slid off a fully restored cherried-out '64 Chevy Impala, hearing a tirade of filth directed at him. Coro looked up to see a face in some respects more menacing than the assassin's he just killed. Hispanic. Head shaved, two tear drops tattooed under his left eye. The AK now leveled directly at him.

"Fuckin' sonofabitch! Christ, the bomber!" El Cid screamed, then put the assault weapon two inches from Coro's face. There were ten of them now, dressed alike, all carrying guns.

"You dead, motherfucker," El Cid lowered his voice, flipping the safety to off, raising the barrel pressing it between the Apache's eyes. Denied the satisfaction of seeing fear, he squeezed—

Crack!

Teal Coro watched the angry face blur red, the rest of the assemblage scattering into the night. Yet, he did not see the man who just saved his life. Did not see the hot .308 brass casing laid down. Did not see the lettering etched on its side:

El Cid.

POSTSCRIPT

They were in Beth's home snuggled up on the couch, the radio played out a light-rock background.

"You know," John said, "STAIRCASE got ripped while being transported to a government lab in L.A. Coleman said the White House flipped out, started calling it Pandora's Briefcase. You think when the gods loaded up Pandora's box, they ever had the likes of STAIRCASE in mind?"

"It should be destroyed," Beth said, absently pulling at a button on his shirt.

"And that's exactly what the President intends to do, or so says Coleman." John slipped his hand behind her shirt tail feeling the smooth warmth.

"Thank you, Pandora," said Beth adjusting her folded position for comfort.

"Huh?"

"The myth. All you male chauvinist pigs ever mention is her unleashing humankind's evils. Pandora did a good thing too. In her horror at what she'd done, she immediately closed the box's lid, but too late. Except at the bottom of the box, there remained one good thing—Hope." Beth turned to look at him, saying, "It makes me hopeful that President Temple would even think about destroying STAIRCASE, much less actually doing it."

John scooped her up into his arms, heading for the bedroom, then said, "Elizabeth Thorngill Pandora. Has a nice ring to it. Don't you think?"

Feeling the blood rush to her face, she pounded his chest playfully. Leaving the room, neither heard nor cared about the radio's top-of-the-hour news now beginning:

Last night, an earthquake centered 70 miles northwest of Las Vegas rocked communities as far as Redlands, California. USGS Seismologist at the National Earthquake Information Center, Golden, Colorado, reported a shock measuring 6.9 on the Richter Scale registered at 8:25 P.M. PST. In spite of its magnitude, little damage was reported throughout this relatively sparse area.

However, the epicenter occurred directly under a ridge called Yucca Mountain, located in the southwest corner of the Nevada Test Site. Yucca Mountain is the proposed repository for the nation's nuclear wastes. The quake brought a fast reaction from some of the nation's leading environmentalists, now expressing alarm. A DOE spokesman admitted that this development would initiate a serious second look at the site and the DOE's current plans.